MW00848511

Famous Last Words

CONTENTS

FAMOUS LAST WORDS

C.W. FARNSWORTH

CHAPTER ONE

CONOR

I ce is *not* a forgiving surface.

A truth I learned when I put on my first pair of hockey skates at age five. Knowledge that has been affirmed hundreds—maybe thousands—of times over the past seventeen years.

Knowing it'll hurt doesn't make hitting the frozen sheet that feels as firm as cement any less painful. It might explain why I love skating so much, though.

Forgiving isn't an adjective anyone would use to describe me, either.

I grab my stick and pull myself up, the blades of my skates sliding under me effortlessly. Skating is second nature. Easier than walking.

The sharpened metal glides across the polished ice effortlessly.

I suck in a deep breath of chilled air, doing my best not to let Robby Sampson know that hit pretty much leveled me out. I'm going to have to scour the freezer for some peas tonight.

"If you manage to limp over to Gaffney's, I'll buy the first round," Hunter Morgan says as he stops a few feet away, purposefully spraying white shavings this way that arc across the center line and coat me from helmet to skate.

I yank my right hand free from the glove so I can flip my best friend off, then shake the front of my practice jersey to clear the snow away. "I'm fine. Never felt better. Ice can't damage iron." I lift my arm and flex my bicep for emphasis.

If you've got it, flaunt it, right? I've never gotten any complaints.

Hunter snorts at the obnoxious move, unimpressed. "Save the lame lines for the ladies, Hart. I'm the one who's going to be stuck listening to you groan about that bruise for the next few days."

"I don't groan," I grumble.

"Need me to grab you a walker, *captain*, or can you make it back to the bench all by yourself?"

"Dick," I mutter as I skate toward the boards.

Hunter laughs. He heard me. Good.

I take a seat on the bench and squirt some Gatorade into my mouth, wincing as my side throbs with what I'm sure will turn into a nasty bruise. The third line gets into position for the continuous in-zone drill we're running. I watch as one of the sophomore wingers, Cole Smith, enters offside.

Wait for it…

Seconds later, "Smith!" is bellowed across the ice.

Cole receives a lecture from Coach Keller that—if I had to guess—involved lots of colorful vocabulary and at least one reference to skills learned back in the PeeWee days, then play resumes.

Two more shifts, and my line is back on the ice.

I skate between my linemates toward the blue line. The throbbing pain in my ribs fades as I inhale deeply, cold air filling my lungs. The signature scent of sweat and ice and rubber and Zamboni fuel found only in a hockey rink has always been like that for me.

A salve.

A relief.

An escape.

On the ice, I'm untouchable.

Metaphorically speaking. Hockey isn't known for being a non-contact sport.

Dean Zimmerman, the assistant coach, drops the puck between me and Aidan Phillips. Aidan earned his spot in the center of the second line. He's always quick to react to the face-off and fight for possession.

I'm faster.

The second the puck hits the ice, I'm in motion. I swipe the black circle into the sweet spot on my stick and take off toward Willis, who's trying to cover every inch of the goal he can with his six-three frame.

I could send the puck straight past him. I've made plenty of shots from farther away. Willis is favoring the left side because I'm veering that way. I doubt he'll have a chance to correct if I shoot right. I've got a seventy-five percent—hell, eighty if I go top shelf—chance of this puck going in.

It'll earn me a lecture from Coach Keller on teamwork. Not the first; most definitely not the last.

Holt University's men's ice hockey team has plenty of problems.

My ability to score goals isn't one of them.

That's what convinces me to slow, circle, and send the puck over to Hunter rather than take the shot myself. Hunter glances between me and Louis Jamison, trying to decide who to pass it to next. One of us hasn't landed a single shot between the irons all practice, and that person is not me.

But it's called *practice* for a reason.

Hunter comes to the same conclusion. He passes to Louis, who manages a slapshot that almost makes it past Willis. Our goalie snags it out of mid-air at the last second, tossing it out of his glove and against the scuffed boards with a harmless bounce.

A shrill whistle pierces the cold air.

"That's a wrap, boys. Hit the showers."

That's all he says. Unless one of us is running a play incorrectly or late to practice, Coach Keller is a man of few words. Rumor on campus is he had higher aspirations than coaching season after season of spotty records under a perennial rain cloud. Literally. Sunny days are a rare occurrence in Somerville, Washington, where Holt University is located.

"Do you think Coach will crack a smile if we win Friday?" Hunter asks as we step off the ice and stomp along the rubber mats that lead to the locker room.

"He looked passably amused before we lost in overtime during playoffs last year," Aidan calls from behind us. "What day was that, Sampson?"

"March tenth," Robby answers as we step inside the locker room and start stripping off our sweaty gear. Sampson has an uncanny ability to recall dates no one else would think twice about. He'd make a good detective.

I knew the answer too, but not because I have a good memory.

Aidan shrugs as he unlaces his skates. "I'm shit at math. Seven months ago? That's a long time to scowl. He'd better perk up a little if we beat Rockford on Friday. I can't remember the last time some part of my body didn't hurt, and the season hasn't even *started* yet."

"You and Hart should form a support group," Hunter suggests, smirking. "I can already hear him complaining about his ribs for the next few days. Thanks a fuck ton for that, Sampson."

Robby shrugs. "He was gonna score otherwise."

"Hart is our only hope of a championship. Be careful with him," Aidan instructs.

I roll my eyes before heading for the showers.

Despite the lackluster water pressure, the warm spray feels like liquid heaven against my sore muscles. It's not just the hit from Robby earlier. I've spent the same seven months Coach has been humorless putting my body through the ringer. Daily runs. Extra weight sessions. Endless laps around the rink. I'm in the best shape of my life. I've dedicated my entire hockey career to always being the fastest guy on the ice, so that's saying something.

Unlike Coach Keller, *my* higher hopes are still in the mix. Professional hockey teams don't sign players from schools like Holt on the off chance they might stumble upon the next Wayne Gretzky amidst mediocrity. If I want a shot, I need to make noise. Noise scouts can't tune out. Noise of the jaw-dropping stats, outstanding season, national championship sort.

I'm good.

The problem is hockey is a team sport. And as great as the guys in the locker room are, none of them could have played at a school with a better hockey program than Holt's. I could have, and the fact that I'm not is one of many things I'm bitter about. Along with the untimely—to say the least—summer skills camp concussion that made me miss the combine and the draft two years ago. Getting signed as an undrafted free agent is my only hope of playing professionally now.

I soap my hair and watch as the white suds disappear down the drain, then shut off the water and grab a threadbare towel. Holt spared expenses when it came to their athletic facilities. I pull on a matching pair of *Holt Hockey* sweats when I return to my locker—pretty much all I wear—and ruffle the ratty towel through my short hair as I wait for Hunter to get his stuff together.

My car is in the shop, so it's either rely on him to get around or walk in the rain.

"Gaffney's?" Hunter asks as he pulls on his own *Holt Hockey* sweatshirt.

"Yeah, sure." All that's waiting for me at our shared house is a bag of peas and a pile of homework.

"Gaffney's, Sampson?"

"Hell yeah, I'm there," Robby replies.

"Me, too," Aidan adds.

"How about you, Williams?" Hunter asks Jack Williams as he exits the showers.

"Can't, man. Study group tonight."

Hunter and I exchange looks, and it's a miracle neither of us burst out laughing. Jack is the sort of preppy people pleaser I picture playing golf, not hockey. He's a decent defender but an outlier on the team. Unlike the rest of us, he seems to have higher aspirations for his college years than getting drunk and screwing around. And playing hockey, of course.

Word of our post-practice plans spreads rapidly among the rest of the guys. Hunter finishes getting dressed and we head out into the light sprinkle that's falling from the sky. Holt's athletic complex consists of three buildings: the ice arena, the basketball gym and weight rooms, and then the pool that also has a couple of rooms with generic exercise equipment like treadmills and ellipticals.

Unlike larger and more sport-centric schools, Holt doesn't grant any preferential treatment to its student athletes over the rest of the school or the surrounding town. We have to schedule our ice time around the Somerville Sharks—a local youth hockey team—and open ice-skating sessions for the general public two nights a week. Time in the weight room is a tense negotiation between us and the basketball team.

The only upside is that the University's apathy toward its athletes is shared by most of the student body. We're fighting for time and space against other sports teams and elementary schoolers. Few other Holt students make the long, often wet walk to the sports complex on the fringe of campus to work out on any sort of regular basis.

Or drive here. The parking lot is mostly empty as we approach Hunter's green SUV. Aidan heads for the shiny, red truck that's the source of endless teasing from the rest of us. It's a shade similar to a fire engine. Against the muted, gray backdrop of a Washington fall on the cusp of winter, it stands out. Aidan isn't one to blend in, so I guess it fits him. And his vehicle is functioning, which is more than can be said about my car.

The trip to Gaffney's only takes five minutes. We're already on the periphery of campus closest to downtown Somerville. It's a straight shot down the unoriginally named Main Street to the small collection of buildings that serve as the town hub. What could be described as a mall contains a few box stores and a supermarket chain, followed by the town's library, post office, and elementary school. Just past it is where Holt students spend the bulk of their time off-campus. There are a couple of coffee shops, an Italian restaurant, a bookstore, a popular doughnut place, and then Gaffney's is at the far end of the block.

Hunter parks in the lot located alongside the outdoor patio that doesn't get much use. Drinking a cold beer with a hot girl is a much less enjoyable experience in the rain, I've found.

Aidan's assault to the eyes slides into the next available spot a few minutes later. We loiter in the parking lot to wait for what turns into most of the team. There's a blatant shortage of options for entertainment in the evenings, especially on a weeknight. Also, despite—or maybe because of—the significant amount of time we spend together, we're a close-knit group. Hanging out off the ice isn't a rare occurrence.

Half the guys here aren't twenty-one yet, but it won't matter. Hockey players are rarely short or skinny. Few of the guys on the team look underage. We're also within walking distance of Holt's campus and the nearby neighborhoods where most upperclassmen live. The most dangerous drunk decision you could make would be to walk south rather than north, toward the Sound's icy, dark depths.

We head inside as a boisterous, freshly showered group. Team morale is high headed into the season. It's nice to see, as captain, but I care most about how it'll translate into Friday's final score.

Gaffney's has a casual feel that's natural, not curated. It's scuffed floors and old country songs and trivia nights.

The bar is busy when we enter, most of the patrons other Holt students.

Tuesdays mean wings and pints are offered at half price, an easy sell for broke students dismayed the week is only half over. Usually I'd be one of them, but Friday's game has me second-guessing a wish that time will speed by.

Seven months of preparation for one hour on the ice.

It's the first game of my final college season. There will be more of them. Thirty-four, to be exact. But Friday is my chance to finally put plans into motion.

There is no such thing as a second first impression. An explosive start before other storylines eat up the limited coverage college hockey receives is my best shot at drawing the attention I desperately need to.

"Hey, Harlow."

I'm distracted from stressing about Friday's game by Aidan's greeting as we pass by one of the occupied high-top tables. Several of the other guys I'm with repeat it, cheerfully acknowledging the redhead that I walk past without a word. If I wasn't exhausted and distracted, it wouldn't have taken me this long to spot her.

I might act like she doesn't exist, but I always notice her.

Harlow Hayes and I share history.

It's not the sort we wrote ourselves.

That makes it complicated. Messy. Conflicting.

It was one thing freshman year, when I would, at most, catch a glimpse of her distinctive hair in the dining hall or out on the quad. Our paths didn't cross.

Holt isn't a huge school, but it's big enough to avoid someone if you're motivated enough. We both were. Are.

Sophomore year Harlow dated Jack Williams, my most responsible teammate. They broke up after a couple of months, but their brief fling somehow resulted in a camaraderie between her and half the hockey team strong enough that they refuse to follow my lead and ignore her.

When it comes to most things, they'll follow me over a cliff.

But when it comes to someone who made the team chocolate chip cookies *once*? Laughed at a couple of their more amusing jokes? They could care less what I think.

She also happens to be the hottest girl on campus, which is probably a factor in the guys' friendliness and is absolutely on brand with my shitty luck.

Hunter shoots me a bemused look when he plops down in the chair beside me at the table I chose. He says nothing, but I know it baffles him—puzzles the whole team, actually—why I refuse to talk to Harlow.

I have a short temper on the ice. I'm usually the first to drop gloves when an opponent starts chirping. Nine times out of ten,

I'll take the shot instead of passing. My penalty minutes are the highest on the team. Off the ice, I tend to be an easy-going guy. I party and drink and hook up, just like the rest of the guys. One random girl inciting my unwavering wrath doesn't make much sense.

Even more confusing is Harlow's behavior.

I've seen her laugh and joke around other people. But she matches my perpetual rudeness. Whenever I'm around, Harlow has been just as insistent about ignoring me as I'm set on pretending she's invisible.

Our cold war is frosty on both fronts, which the guys notice, even if they don't get why.

Explaining would require sharing parts of my past I don't discuss. Painful truths I'm sick of letting define me and resolved to stop letting do so as soon as I left the small town I grew up in. No girl is going to change that.

"Way to take off, Hart," Aidan says as he takes the chair across from me. "Do you want the stands to be empty this season?"

"I'd rather win than play in front of a crowd."

"Well, I'm hoping there will be a *crowd* watching us *win*."

I grunt, aiming my attention at the television affixed to the wall behind the bar. Football is on. Highlights from Sunday night that I'd rather focus on than engage in any conversation involving Harlow.

"I don't get it," Aidan pushes. "What's your problem with her?"

Beneath the table, my hands clench into fists.

"He's mad Williams got there first," Hunter says.

There's murmured agreement amongst the guys.

I don't know any details—because I avoid the topic of her at all costs—but I do know Jack did not take the break-up with

Harlow well. I don't think he's dated anyone since. No guy on the team wants to break bro code by getting involved with Harlow, and that probably means I should stop making Vineyard Vines sale jokes at Jack's expense, because it's absolutely a best-case scenario for me.

A waitress comes over to take our orders. She's a perky blonde who's served me before. Stacey, I remember, thanks to the nametag jauntily affixed to her T-shirt. Conveniently drawing attention to her cleavage.

"Hey, boys," she greets, surveying the table. Her brown eyes light up when they land on me. I wink at her, and she blushes.

I grab the laminated menu to look over as Stacey takes Aidan's order. I get a burger and beer every time, but it's either scan the other options or listen to Robby deliberate whether he should get wings or pizza. So I stare at the words spelling out Gaffney's limited offerings until they blur.

I glance up. Instead of watching the sports highlights playing on the flatscreen or checking out Stacey's C-cups, I turn my head to the left. Fix my gaze on the table I passed when the rest of the guys paused.

She's not looking this way.

Harlow's attention is on the girl sitting next to her, who's waving her hands around as she tells some story.

They're with a group of other people, but I don't register a single detail about anyone else at the table. I allow myself to study Harlow Hayes—the girl I've never talked to and never will.

She's hot. Gorgeous. Stunning.

Whatever.

Hatred doesn't make me anywhere near as immune to her looks as I'd love to be. She's a Canadian export far more appealing to look at than lumber or maple syrup or anything else that's crossed the border.

11

Red hair.

High cheekbones.

Pouty mouth.

But… *What's my problem with her?*

She's guilty by association.

CHAPTER TWO

HARLOW

M ist hangs in heavy curtains along the craggy coastline, the gauzy drapes preventing a perfect view of the water. I shiver as I climb out of my car, immediately mourning the loss of heat. I tug the sides of my yellow raincoat closer together in an attempt to block out the chill sneaking beneath the thin layer of coated polyester. Then grab the coffee cup out of the cupholder, savoring the warmth soaking through the paper cup.

Fall in Washington usually contains a handful of sunny days.

Today is not one of them.

Salty air coats my hair and little exposed skin. The breeze swirling is rich with the ripe scent of fish and the bitter bite of winter approaching.

No one stops me or asks me what I'm doing here as I walk along the rocky shore and down the gangway. Everyone is too fixated on their own list of tasks to worry about me wandering around. After three years of loitering, everyone's stopped paying any attention to the lone woman hanging around at all.

Well, *almost* everyone.

"Ah, you made it!" A broad smile transforms Samuel

Prescott's weathered features as I near the end of the dock. The corners of his eyes crinkle, forming lines that droop down into the creases around his mouth. "What a sight for tired eyes."

"Me, or the coffee?" I tease.

Sam chuckles. "Caffeine's no replacement for good company."

"I won't tell the crew," I say, handing him the cup before I swing one leg over the side of the boat. "I did get you hazelnut today, though."

"You spoil me," Sam says, sniffing the small opening in the lid.

"I always stop anyway. And it's the least I can do for you letting me tag along."

Sam waves away my appreciation, just like I knew he would. "No trouble at all." He takes a sip of coffee. "Brent just called. He and the boys are running a bit late. Timmy's off fixing a net. We might get off behind schedule this morning."

"I'm ready whenever." An incoming wave rocks the entire boat. My grip on the side tightens.

"I know so." Sam chuckles. "That exam you were worrying about last week go all right?"

"It did," I reply. "At least, I think it did. I won't get the grade for a few more days."

"I'm sure you did well." Sam offers me a reassuring smile. "You work hard. When I was in school, me and the guys I hung around with didn't take tests too seriously."

"That's true of plenty of people at Holt," I tell him.

One person in particular comes to mind, but I don't say so. I don't ever mention him. And Sam is a hockey fan.

"Net's good to go." Timmy appears. He tosses a ball of rope mesh into the open back of the boat, then climbs aboard. "Morning, Harlow."

"Morning, Timmy," I reply. I take careful steps toward the bow where my milk crate sits waiting.

Brent, his brother Jerry, and his two sons arrive a few minutes later, all four greeting me with friendly grins. They climb aboard and move around the boat like performers doing a well-choreographed dance, the routine of tasks a familiar ritual. Each piece of gear gets checked. Ropes are untied and knotted before we slip away from the dock. Nets are spread out in preparation for being dropped into the sea.

I yawn as we move farther away from the shore, hoping the caffeine I downed earlier will kick in soon. Cold, salty air blows straight into my face, pulling strands out from my ponytail.

Churning water becomes the only scenery as we chug deeper into the Sound. Lingering mist paints the fading coastline like a watercolor painting, smeared and cloudy.

A couple of hours pass.

I stare out at the water for every minute of them, never looking away from the choppy, gray surface of the sea as my eyes strain to look through the veil that never fully lifts. I mark each spot where we stop on the spreadsheet on my phone with a black X to note the lack of any sightings.

"Apologies to the cetologist on board," Sam bellows as we cruise back into the marina. "Fish were biting. Orcas were nowhere to be found."

"Hopefully next week," I say, trying to mask my disappointment with a smile.

I slip my phone into my pocket and slide my numb fingers beneath my thighs in an attempt to warm them up. Gloves would have been a good idea.

Witnessing whales in the wild is a privilege, never a forgone conclusion. Living in the Pacific Northwest, I'm luckier than most aspiring marine biologists. I've lost count of how many times I've witnessed the majesty in person, but it never becomes any less spectacular. Holt's location is one of the main reasons I chose to come to school here.

We tie up to the dock. Sam's crew begins to unload the boxes filled with ice and today's catches.

"Thanks, Sam. See you all next week!" I say as I step off the rocking boat and back onto the sturdy dock.

Most of the slips are still empty. Sam is nearing retirement age, meaning his trips are shorter than most making a living in the seafood industry. It serves my purposes perfectly. I love being out on the water, but not so much that I want to spend all day stuck on a boat.

The men call farewells after me as I head for the gravel parking area. It's not quite as chilly as it was earlier, but the air temperature hasn't risen by much. It's a relief to climb into my car and start blasting the heat. I'm eager to get home and take a hot shower.

My phone rings as I'm pulling out of the marina's parking lot. I smile when I see Landon Garrison's name flash across the car's display.

"Hey," I answer.

"Why do you sound so awake? It's barely eight," my best friend grumbles.

"I went for a swim," I lie. "I'm on my way back home now."

For some reason, I've never told anyone about my weekly trips out onto the Sound in Sam's fishing boat. I'm not really sure why. Anyone who knows me well is aware of my obsession with the ocean. That my dream is to make a career of studying the species who live in it.

My time on the boat is different. It's separate from academics, not a school assignment or a research project. I'll take notes on my phone of the pods we encounter. Their numbers, whether they've been tagged. But that's just for me.

Being out on the water is freeing. It's always been my happy place where fears and frustrations can't touch me. Keeping my early morning outings to myself is my way of protecting that, somehow.

And I *do* go swimming most mornings, so it doesn't feel like a real lie. Just a small stretch of the truth.

"Wow. Swimming before eight on a Saturday. You must have had a crazy Friday night, huh?" Landon asks.

"Absolutely wild." I match his sarcasm. "Eve and I had a James Bond marathon."

"Since when do you watch anything besides nature documentaries and old sitcoms?"

"Eve chose. She has a thing for Daniel Craig. I mean, who doesn't?"

"No one is immediately coming to mind," Landon replies.

I snort. "What are *you* doing up this early, rockstar?"

"Studio time. I was shocked, but not many people want the eight a.m. on a Saturday slot."

"And you convinced the rest of the guys to show up?"

Landon takes his music very seriously. I've always gotten the impression his bandmates are in it for the free beer most of their gigs provide and the dream of one day having groupies.

"I think so? Adam will probably be late, but he promised he'll show."

"Are you guys recording new stuff?"

"No. That would require having new stuff *to* record."

"Ah, right."

"Dad has started back in on the Plan B talks again." Landon sighs. "Not even waiting until I'm a senior."

"Just write a song that will win you a Grammy," I suggest.

"Then you can hold up a shiny gramophone every time he says anything about a back-up plan. Tell him to talk to the Grammy."

"Oh, *perfect*. Why didn't I think of that?"

I laugh at his heavy sarcasm. "He wants you to succeed, Landon."

"Yeah, I know. And it's not like I don't know music is a hard industry to break into." He exhales loudly, then falls silent. "Did you see the email?"

I hit the blinker a little harder than necessary as I turn onto my street. "Yeah."

"Did they ask you about it ahead of time?"

"No."

"I'm sorry, Harlie." Landon only breaks out my childhood nickname when he's trying to annoy me or is worried I'm more upset about something than I'm letting on.

"It's fine. They don't need my permission. And it's a really nice idea. It'll just be…tough to get through."

"Because it's being run in memory of your parents or because it's a marathon?"

"Both."

"Well, if it makes you feel any better, I'll definitely have a worse time than you. Not to mention my parents. I'm going to need to hire a personal trainer. I refuse to finish after them. Dad still goes for jogs all the time. Once a jock, always a jock." He scoffs.

"You guys don't have to run the full marathon. You can run the half. Or you don't have to run at all."

"Of course we're all going to run it. They're raising money by the mile. Besides, that's what family does."

A lump forms in my throat as I experience a swell of appreciation toward the people who took me in after my parents' passing.

Made me feel like I still have a home, not just a place to crash during Holt's breaks.

After twenty years of friendship, Landon can sense I'm overwhelmed, even through the phone.

"Mom and Dad are talking about visiting Holt soon," he tells me. "Mom said you sounded stressed last time you talked to her."

"Senior year of college is stressful," I tell him. "You'll find that out next year."

Landon is nine months younger than me, so we've always been a year apart in school.

"Can't wait," he deadpans.

"They don't have to come here," I say. "Thanksgiving isn't that far away."

"They want to visit you, Harlow."

"I know, but…"

"They shouldn't be unable to visit you just because of *him*."

I'm silent. The dysfunction that could be the plot for a semi-successful television drama is a minefield I do my best to avoid. I'm surprised Landon is bringing Conor up. He rarely does, unless there's an opportunity to make a caustic comment. Landon is the friendliest, most relaxed person you'll ever meet.

Until the topic of his half-brother is broached.

"Are you having another movie marathon tonight?" Landon asks after the silence has dragged for a few beats, not even bothering to act like it wasn't a blatant attempt to change the subject.

"No. Eve wants to go to a basketball game."

"Really?"

Landon has met my best friend and roommate Eve before. Her many eclectic interests include interior decorating and embroidery. Not sports.

"Yeah. She came up with this list of things to do before the end of college during our Bond-a-thon last night. *Go to a sporting event* made the cut."

I don't share some of the other tasks that made the twenty-item list. Eve talks a big game, but I'm guessing—hoping—most of them will fall by the wayside.

"And you decided on basketball?"

"Are there other winter sports?" I ask innocently.

"Harlow…"

"I never even see him, Landon."

It's the second lie I've told my best friend this morning. I saw Conor Hart at Gaffney's four nights ago. He ignored me, and I acted like he wasn't sucking up all the attention and oxygen in the bar by simply existing.

"Good."

I stop in front of my house and turn off the car. "I'd better go, Land. I just got home, and I stink like chlorine."

Make that three lies. Although I do smell.

"'Kay. I'll talk to you soon. You can always come to Brighton. Mom and Dad could visit us both."

"Yeah, that would be fun," I reply, despite knowing I probably won't. I love Holt's sprawling campus and living in sleepy Somerville. Aside from seeing Landon, Brighton University holds no allure to me. "Good luck recording."

Landon snorts. "Yeah, thanks. Talk to you later."

The call disconnects as he hangs up.

I remain sitting in my parked car, staring at the light blue exterior of the little house I share with Eve. I pushed the email I saw early this morning to the back of my mind. My conversation with Landon brought it right back to the forefront.

The tiny town on the west coast of Canada where I grew up hosts an annual marathon every summer. This year, it's being run in honor of my parents to raise money in hopes of saving others from the same sad fate. I suppose they decided four years was enough time to commemorate. It's a thoughtful, considerate gesture I should be and *am* appreciative of.

It's also a reminder of a night I like to pretend never happened.

I'm not in any form of denial that my parents are gone.

Their deaths are a reality I face.

How one stranger's decision to get behind the wheel drunk forever altered my life.

How things you take for granted—like having parents—can vanish in the same short stretch of time it takes to blink an eye.

How unfair life can be.

Just because I accept it doesn't mean I want to be reminded of it.

I climb out of my car and head up the front walk to the duplex I share with Eve. Aside from Landon, who's known me practically since birth, she's my closest friend. I've done a terrible job of keeping in touch with the people I grew up with. Just like the upcoming marathon, they're a painful reminder of the past. I'd rather remember the good times with my parents. Not the sympathetic looks for the final year of secondary school. The grief group I attended sporadically.

It's going to make for an awkward homecoming if I follow through on my plan to move back to the town I grew up in after graduation.

I unlock the front door and enter the small mudroom. Eve and I were lucky to snag this place for senior year. Houses close to campus and downtown move fast, and they're usually hogged by sports teams. Two-bedroom places like this one are rare finds.

The kitchen is empty when I walk inside. I'm not surprised Eve is still asleep. Spilled popcorn is spread across the countertop from our movie night. I sweep the kernels into the trash before heading down the hall to my bedroom.

I'm very tempted to take a scalding hot shower. But my apprehension about the marathon isn't just because of the painful memories it'll drag up. I swim regularly, but running? That hasn't happened in a while. I doubt I've run forty-two point two kilometers in my entire life, let alone in one day.

When I was a kid, the marathon was always a casual event. There are no medals or prize money offered at the finish line. It's a fundraiser for charity.

It's still a *long* distance.

Landon was kidding about hiring a personal trainer—I think —but I might need to seriously consider it.

I sigh as I swap my yellow raincoat for a sports bra and fleece pullover, deciding I'll jog downtown and back. Start somewhere. Swimming has always been my preferred form of exercise, an extension of my obsession with the ocean. I don't know anyone who runs regularly for fun or for fitness. Masochists.

There's still no sign of activity in the neighborhood as I head outside into the damp, chilly air and start to jog.

It's not terrible. At first.

The pounding of my sneakers on the asphalt is rhythmic. Air gushes in and out of my lungs easily.

I don't know if this is the runner's high people talk about, but I'm feeling pretty damn good.

So good that I extend my original distance and run all the way down Main Street to the edge of Holt's campus before turning back on to Spring Street.

All of a sudden, running isn't quite so effortless.

It feels like the percentage of oxygen in the air has plummeted. Hitting the hard cement feels more jolting than relaxing. My calves cramp, protesting each step.

Almost there. Almost there. Almost there, I chant internally as I force myself to keep jogging and not slow to a walk.

I don't know how far I've run, and I don't want to.

I don't want to know how abysmal an athletic achievement this is. Just like I wish I could lie to myself about how far I have to run still.

Six blocks.

One block later I pass Mr. Goodman, who lives across the street from me and Eve. He's out walking his dog. I wave at him, hoping I look better than I feel.

He doesn't call an ambulance, so I must.

Five blocks to go. Four. Three. Two.

I can see my car.

The front walk.

The front door.

I collapse on the lawn, not caring the grass is wet. It feels good, actually.

I pant and heave and stare up at the cloudy sky until I can breathe normally again.

My legs are not thrilled about more movement, but I can't lie here all day. I stand on shaky limbs and head for the front door. My entrance is a ruckus. I toss my sneakers and topple the umbrella stand as I yank my fleece off, then stumble into the living room that transitions into the kitchen.

Eve is standing at the kitchen island, eating a banana.

"What the hell happened to you?"

"I went for a run," I wheeze.

"*Why?*" she asks, looking aghast.

Excellent question.

"I'm running a marathon in the summer."

"Why?" Eve repeats.

I shrug. "It seemed like a good life goal. Character building, you know?"

She raises both eyebrows and takes another bite of banana. It shouldn't be a persuasive expression, but it works on me.

"It's being run back home. In memory of my parents." I head for the fridge and grab the water pitcher to fill a glass. "The money is going to an organization that works to keep drunk drivers off the road."

I take a sip of water and glance her way. Eve's studying me.

"It's fine. I'm fine," I assure her.

Eve is the only person at Holt who I've confided in about my parents. That they're dead and how they died. I've let all my other friends here believe the care packages the Garrisons send are from my parents, not my mother's best friend and her husband. It's just…easier.

"Do you need someone to train with you? Because I totally will."

I smile at her, hoping it conveys my appreciation.

Coming from Eve, that's a generous offer. She goes for long walks so she can listen to her favorite podcasts, but I know her preferred maximum speed is just that: a walk.

"I wouldn't make you do that. I went by myself today, and it was fine." I leave out the fact I'm not sure I'll be able to move tomorrow. "I'm going to shower."

Twenty minutes under a steaming stream of hot water helps wash away the traumatic memories of this morning's exercise. I put on my comfiest pair of sweats and make myself a smoothie before snuggling on the couch with my laptop.

Eve has settled at the kitchen table to work on her latest art piece.

It's a typical Saturday.

I lounge on the sofa, alternating between studying and

watching old episodes of *Arrested Development*. I only move when my stomach starts grumbling, hobbling into the kitchen for some snacks.

Eve's pencils scratch in the background the whole time as she sketches.

They don't stop moving until it's necessary to turn the lights in the living room on. Well, *I* don't turn them on. Eve does. I was content to keep lying in the semi-dark watching television. I squint at her.

"It's time to go! The basketball game starts in twenty minutes."

I rub my eyes and groan. "I thought you forgot."

Eve makes a sound of disbelief, then points to the bulletin board hanging to the right of the stove. The senior year bucket list she scribbled last night is prominently displayed beside our small collection of takeout menus.

I sigh and roll off the couch.

"Ten minutes!" Eve calls after me as I head down the hall to my room.

I'm tempted to wear my sweats but resist the urge. I feel gross after lying around in them all day, and I'm guessing we'll go out after the game.

I pull on my favorite pair of dark skinny jeans and a gray *Holt University* hoodie. My hair is a mess from drying while I was sprawled on the couch, so I pull it back in a loose bun I hope looks more intentional than lazy. A swipe of mascara, and I'm ready.

Eve is already waiting for me by the front door. She's changed out of the leggings she was wearing into corduroys and a pink sweater. Most of her wardrobe consists of articles of clothing I could never pull off, but on Eve, they work.

"Ready?" She beams at me.

My expression is less enthusiastic. "Yeah, let's go."

"I'll drive." Eve spins her keys around one finger as I tie the laces on my sneakers and pull on a coat.

"Who knew you'd get this excited about sports?" I ask as we head outside.

"Mary said the games are super fun."

"Mary likes basketball?"

Eve gives me a sly look. "Mary likes Clayton Thomas."

I laugh. "Oh. Got it."

I know next to nothing about basketball. I know Clayton is a popular figure on campus. Unlike the other well-known athlete—people call him *Hartbreaker*, which is a stupid nickname but also catchy—Clayton is also a decent guy. We had a humanities class together last spring.

"I think Mary's hoping you'll introduce her," Eve tells me.

"And the plot thickens," I drawl as I climb into her car.

Eve shoots me a sheepish look. "I've heard about Clayton for weeks in our painting class, okay? I told Mary I'd try to strike up a conversation with him. But I'm not on a first-name basis with all the sports teams the way you are."

"That's a massive exaggeration."

"The *entire* hockey team stopped to talk to you when we were at Gaffney's on Tuesday."

Not the whole team.

Conor strode past me without a word, and I wish I hadn't noticed. Although a petty, vindictive part of me was glad he didn't look pleased about his teammates talking to me.

"That's just because of Jack," I say. "You know that."

I don't entirely regret dating Jack Williams sophomore year, but if I could go back and change it, I would. I had no idea he was on the team until he mentioned it on our first date. I'd made a point to steer clear of any Holt hockey players until then. They were easy to spot, always wearing some item of clothing with the *Holt Hockey* logo. Jack dressed like he was headed to a country club.

When I learned Jack was on the team, I decided not to let Conor influence my life. That stubborn stance drew my relationship with Jack out longer than I meant to let it last; something I feel guilty about every time I see him.

"Jack wasn't even there," Eve points out. "Just say hi to Clayton when we see him and if Mary and I happen to be with you, then you can introduce her."

"When we see him? You know the team doesn't come over and make chitchat with the spectators at halftime, right?"

"People talk plenty at the party after, though."

I'm very glad I changed. "Uh-huh. And when were you planning to fill me in on the whole itinerary for tonight?"

"If you'd tried to leave the house in your sweatpants."

I roll my eyes as Eve parks outside the sports building that houses the basketball gym.

Mary hurries over to us as soon as we enter the lobby. She's an art major like Eve. Unlike Eve, she's petite, blonde, and quiet. I'm surprised to learn Clayton Thomas is her type. He may not be a jerk, but he has plenty of other stereotypical jock tendencies. I don't think I've seen him with the same girl more than once. He also spent plenty of our shared humanities class hitting on me.

"Hey, Mary," I greet.

"Hi, Harlow," she replies, giving me a shy smile.

"Harlow is on board with the plan," Eve announces, winking at Mary.

"I really don't know Clayton all that well," I tell Mary. "But I'd be happy to introduce you."

She blushes. "Thanks."

The three of us head inside the gym, which smells like sweat and stale popcorn. Turnout is lackluster, the bleachers mostly empty.

I'm not shocked. Holt leaves a lot to be desired when it comes to school spirit. If a student likes sports, they're usually playing on a team instead of sitting in the stands.

"Not much of a crowd, huh?" Eve reads my thoughts.

"No. But you should have seen the hockey game last night," Mary tells us. "Completely insane. It seemed like the whole school was there."

"Since when do you go to the hockey games?" Eve asks.

Mary giggles. "Darcy and Teegan wanted to see Hartbreaker play."

I barely resist rolling my eyes. Of course.

"Did Holt win?" Eve wonders.

I could tell her the answer, but I don't. Maybe it's the Canadian in me—or that my dad was a big fan—but hockey is the one sport I have any interest in following. I read the recap of the game on my phone last night while Eve was making popcorn.

"Yeah," Mary replies. "Conor scored both goals."

"Damn. We should have gone to the game last night." Eve looks to me. "And you should have gone for Conor Hart instead of Jack Williams. Conor is *way* hotter." Eve's attention jumps back to Mary before I respond. Probably for the best. "She and Jack had a thing sophomore year, remember?" she asks Mary.

"Oh, yeah. Wasn't…"

I tune out Eve and Mary's discussion of my dating history.

I might have confided in Eve about my own past, but I've never told anyone about the tangled web that connects me and Conor Hart.

We have no trouble finding seats, and then it's just a matter of waiting for the game to start. Mary and Eve chat about an art assignment while I scan the bleachers for familiar faces. Of the fifty or so people here, I'd say I know a quarter of them by name. One girl I had Advanced Biology with last fall waves at me.

The game begins without much build-up. One minute the players aren't on the court, the next they're shooting warm-up shots. Some go in, but most miss.

I start to get the sense this will be a long game.

Sure enough, it drags.

With ten minutes left, Holt is down by twenty points.

"I'm going to the bathroom," I tell Eve and Mary, then stand and skirt the edge of the court, heading out the first door I encounter.

Once I'm alone in the hallway, I release a long breath. It's a relief to be away from lackluster clapping and the scent of burned popcorn. Someone at the concession stand must have fallen asleep on the job.

I look to the left. Then to the right. Both directions look identical.

The pool is in one of the other two athletic buildings. I've haven't been in this part of Holt's sports complex more than a couple of times. Both were for orientation events held in the gym I just left.

I opt to go right.

There isn't a single door along the length of the linoleum hallway. I round the corner and stop dead.

I'm outside the entrance to a room filled with exercise equipment.

The lights are on.

The door is open.

And Conor Hart is lying on one of the black, narrow benches people use to pump weights. Doing exactly that.

I'm frozen in place as I watch him lift and lower the bar.

Ironic, considering it feels like my body temperature has risen by a couple hundred degrees.

I don't consider myself to be a shallow person. I judge people based on how they treat others. The things they say. The way they act. I've never been dazzled by good looks or clout.

Conor has both in spades. His attractiveness is a pretty illusion—skin-deep—and I haven't forgotten that.

There's just a *lot* of that skin on display. And it's a view I drink in like I've been lost in the desert and am in desperate need of hydration.

He's shirtless, wearing nothing except a pair of black mesh shorts that ride low on his waist. *Low*. The carved V between his hips is fully visible. So is the trail of dark hair that disappears into the elastic waistband of his shorts. His abs clench and contract as he lifts a bar with a lot of heavy-looking weights on each end.

My gaze wanders down his sculpted torso to the muscular thighs straddling each side of the bench that doesn't look sturdy enough to support someone in that sort of shape lifting that much weight.

Holy shit.

I swallow rapidly a couple of times. My fingernails dig into my palms. I have no idea how long I've been standing here, staring at him. Checking him out, if I'm being honest.

Clayton Thomas is objectively as good-looking as Conor Hart is. He has golden hair instead of dark. Sweetness instead of swagger. Friendliness instead of derision.

I've spent the past hour watching Clayton sprint around and sweat. Had a front-row seat to his muscles and masculinity. Nothing. Nada. No effect.

I was so bored I made up a trip to the bathroom.

But watching Conor lift weights? I could stand here forever and not have my fill of this view. I rarely let myself look at him, and it seems to have had the unsettling effect of me not wanting to look away now that I have.

Metal clangs as he sets the bar back in its holder. Conor sits up, the muscles of his back rippling as he leans down and grabs the water bottle by his sneaker.

I don't realize he's standing and turning until it's too late to react. I'm already frozen, but a fresh wave of heat washes over me when our eyes connect.

There's a dizzying rush of horror and embarrassment.

Panic, about what he'll say or do.

I've never given much thought to what Conor Hart thinks of me. But I'm uncomfortably aware I look like a stalker right now, standing here in an empty hallway watching him work out.

I wait, for a biting barb or a crude innuendo.

Nothing. Conor just stares at me, holding me hostage with his intense gaze. He looks as focused as he did lifting weights, except now that singular attention is aimed at *me*. It's the most thrilling and terrifying sensation I've ever experienced. Like seeing a five-thousand-kilogram whale breach a hundred yards away.

I have no clue what to say. And it doesn't seem like Conor is going to speak.

So I turn and walk away, resisting the urge to glance back to see if he's still looking. Fighting the urge to run and forcing my steps to stay a normal speed until I'm around the corner.

I don't bother trying to find the bathroom. I head straight back into the gym. There are only a few minutes left in the game that I barely register a second of. According to the scoreboard, Holt ends up losing by twenty-eight points.

As soon as the game ends, Eve suggests heading to Gaffney's. I agree quickly. Maybe a cold beer will bleach the sight of a shirt-less Conor from my brain. Wash away the mortification.

The bar is packed, which is no surprise. I don't think I've ever been to Gaffney's and *not* seen it crowded. There's something to be said for limited options, but the relaxed, friendly feel of the place would probably ensure its popularity even if there were lots of other choices in town.

We can't find a table, so we end up leaning against the bar to order and eat before walking to the house that is hosting the basketball crowd tonight. Along with anyone else who happens to wander in. That's one of my favorite things about Holt. There's no sign of the cemented social hierarchy present at so many other schools. The few times I've visited Brighton it was obvious the artsier crowd Landon is part of is separate from any sports teams. Here, they mingle freely.

Attendance at the post-game party far surpasses the crowd at the game itself. We have to push our way through the front hall and into the stuffy living room.

I spot Clayton standing in the corner with a teammate and nod in his direction. "Let's go say hi," I tell Mary and Eve.

Mary blanches. "Uh, no, that's okay. He's talking to someone already. I don't want to interrupt."

I glance at Eve, who shrugs.

"He won't care," I say. "Come on."

Mary shoots Eve a panicked look.

"It's okay. Harlow knows what she's doing," Eve assures her.

I snort as I head toward Clayton. He catches my eye as I approach. Clayton claps his teammate on the back before stepping around him and walking this way. If it wasn't so conspicuous, I'd send Eve and Mary a *told you so* look.

"Hey, Harlow!" Clayton greets me enthusiastically, even pulling me into a quick hug.

"Hey, Clayton. Nice game." I smile at him, and he grins back.

"Were you at the same one I was playing in?" he asks dryly.

My smile shifts into a smirk. "Yeah. Condolences. Tough loss."

Clayton shrugs, retaining his good humor. "You win some, you lose most. Right?"

I laugh. "Sure." Mary and Eve reach us. "These are my friends. Eve and Mary." I nod to each of them as I make the introductions.

"Hey, ladies." Clayton flashes them both a charming smile. "I'm Clayton."

"Hi," Mary manages. Her cheeks are pink. Eve is looking back and forth between the two of them, grinning. Subtle, she is not.

"I was just heading to the kitchen. You girls want drinks?" Clayton asks.

"Sure," Mary replies.

"I'm going to run to the bathroom. I'll meet you guys in the kitchen," I say, winking at my two companions and then heading for what I think is the dining room.

This time I *do* have to go to the bathroom. If I can find one.

I push through the crowded dining room and emerge into a back hallway that looks promising.

"Hey, Harlow."

I glance to the left, at Aidan Phillips leaning against the wall.

My steps pause.

"Hey, Aidan," I respond, smiling as my stomach sinks. I had no idea the hockey team would be here. And they tend to move as a group. Aidan's presence means Jack is probably here. Means Mr. I Work Out Shirtless is possibly here. "How are you?"

"We won last night, so pretty awesome." He grins widely.

My smile stays in place. "Yeah, I heard. Congrats."

"Thanks." Aidan takes a sip from the cup he's holding. "Hey, I was driving on Spring Street earlier. Was that you out jogging?"

"Uh, yeah, it was."

He tilts his head. "Thought so. You a big runner?"

I snort. "No, not really." I'm surprised—pleased—it wasn't obvious I was close to collapsing on the sidewalk.

"Trying something new?"

"Sort of. I'm running a marathon in the summer."

Aidan's eyes widen. "No shit?"

I nod. "Shit."

"Wow. What's your training plan like?"

"My training plan?" I echo. He nods. "Uh, run a lot, I guess?"

Aidan laughs. "Freestyle. I like it. You know who you should talk to…" His eyes leave mine, looking at something—someone—behind me. He grins. "Hart!"

Immediate hot flash, knowing he's near.

I *refuse* to glance down the hallway and find out how close.

I know Aidan is aware of the fact Conor avoids me like an infectious disease. I've always gotten the sense he's a shit stirrer. But he's a decent guy and a loyal friend, which tells me he has no idea why Conor ignores me.

The only reason I'm not panicking right now is that I know Conor won't come over here. Not toward me. Avoiding each other seems to be the one—and only—way in which we're on the exact same page.

Except…he *does* come over.

I smell his cologne or soap first, the scent of pine and salt making me want to inhale deeply.

And to *flee*. Too bad Conor wasn't standing behind me when I was running earlier. My time would have been a lot better.

"What?" The word is a terse snap.

He's in a bad mood. Shocking.

Aidan seems unbothered by Conor's moodiness. Probably due to extended exposure.

CHAPTER THREE

CONOR

The puck finds the back of the net, and I'm immediately mobbed. Three games into the season, and we're undefeated. Despite the hockey team's lackluster performance on the ice in past seasons, our stands are usually packed.

We may not always win, but we're damn entertaining to watch lose.

At least, that's what the girls who come up to me after games we lost say.

"That's what I'm fucking talking about!" Hunter shouts in my ear as his stick hits my back. Robby claps me on the helmet with his glove.

The guys on the bench are all standing, banging their sticks against the boards. I swoop down the line, knocking gloves.

Scoring goals is expected of me, but it doesn't make delivering on the points any less satisfying. I'm good at hockey, but even the greatest players have off days. So far, my senior season has been a consistent stretch of the best games of my college career. The timing couldn't be better.

There are thirty seconds left in the game, but we don't stop pressing.

Our opponent tonight, Burham University, hasn't even been able to pull their goalie. We're up by two goals. I feel good, and so do the rest of the guys.

The third period got off to a shaky start. I passed to Phillips instead of Powers, and Jeff was wide open. We got called on a sloppy penalty and almost gave up a power play goal. Small mistakes like those can get in your head, gnaw away at collective confidence. But we pulled it together. We're holding it together.

The energy in the arena hums like a live wire: raw and exposed.

Twenty-five seconds.

I pass to Hunter. He passes to Robby. Robby passes back to me.

Fifteen seconds.

The poor guy assigned to defend me grimaces. He lunges, but I'm anticipating it. I send the puck along the boards, behind the goal, and onto Aidan's waiting stick.

Five seconds.

Satisfaction creeps up my spine and spreads, chasing away the nerves. The fear that three wins was a fluke.

Four straight sounds more dominant.

Sounds like noise. Like momentum. Like *hope*.

The buzzer blares and the whole team mobs me. Despite the trials and disappointments in my hockey career, I don't think I could be surrounded by a more supportive group of guys right now. So maybe some shit works out the way it's meant to.

Aidan is celebrating like we just won the championship itself, and the packed stands seem on board with that level of enthusiasm. Screams and shouts reverberate off the high ceilings of Holt's hockey arena, decorated by one solitary banner from decades ago. If I have my way, there will be a brand-new, brightly colored one hanging from the rafters in a matter of months.

The euphoria carries into the locker room. I'm tempted to tell the guys to cool it, that we've got a long way to go, but I don't. It's easy to get caught up in only celebrating the bigger victories in life. But smaller ones are worth appreciating too. The next joyful moment is never guaranteed.

"Nice work, boys," Coach Keller compliments before heading into the small office that juts off the far side of our locker room. He pairs the words with a meager smile that causes us all to burst into applause.

The office door slams shut in response.

I laugh before heading to the showers.

Hunter, Aidan, and I decide to hit up our favorite Mexican place after we've changed for a post-game fuel up. It's a hole-in-the-wall spot a couple of towns over from Somerville that we discovered sophomore year. There's no line when we arrive, and I don't waste any time before ordering two burritos. I just burned about a thousand calories.

Hunter has a thing about anyone eating food in his car and I'm too hungry to wait until we get to the party, so I take a seat in one of the rickety wooden chairs and dig in. The tortilla is still steaming, barely containing the rice, beans, veggies, and seasoned meat filling it. I finish the first burrito in about four bites and start in on the second at the same time Aidan takes a seat across from me.

"Thanks for waiting, Hart," he tells me sarcastically before digging into his tacos. I'm too busy inhaling my second burrito to reply.

I'm finished eating before Hunter has even taken his seat, so I get up and order some chips and guacamole.

"Damn, that was good," Aidan states, leaning back in his seat once he's finished eating. The wooden folding chair creaks beneath his tall frame. "Now, I just need a few beers."

"I'm not cleaning up your puke again," I tell him.

Aidan rolls his eyes. "That happened freshman year. *Once*. But I'm not planning to sleep at the house tonight, anyway."

Hunter and I exchange an amused glance. Neither of us is celibate by any stretch, but Aidan sees more ass than a public restroom's toilet seat. Based on his drunken rambling the same night as the puke incident, I have my suspicions he's trying to forget someone. Despite some of the debauchery I've seen them engage in, Aidan and Hunter are two of the most decent guys I've met. But we don't discuss our pasts. A plan I'm fully on board with, for obvious reasons.

"Rebecca?" Hunter asks.

"No, that's over," Aidan replies.

"How come?"

Aidan shrugs. "I'm just over it."

I snort.

"Don't pretend like you didn't ask me to borrow a condom last weekend, Hart."

"What, you wanted it back?" Hunter laughs, glancing between the two of us. "I didn't say a thing, Phillips. As long as it doesn't affect hockey, you can fuck the whole state for all I care."

My aversion to commitment is well known on the team. When it comes to women, at least. I have no issues dedicating elsewhere. Even if I hadn't grown up with constant reminders of how a supposedly monogamous relationship can backfire, I doubt I'd be enthused about the idea of dating. When girls throw themselves at you on a regular basis, limiting your options doesn't seem like the smartest move.

"Is Sarah coming tonight?" Hunter asks me.

"How the hell should I know?" I dunk a chip in guacamole.

Truthfully, if I bothered to read my unopened texts, I could tell him most, if not all, of the people who will be in attendance tonight.

"The Hartbreaker strikes again," Aidan comments.

He got wind of the fact some girls on campus re-appropriated my last name at the start of the semester and has brought the stupid respelling up at least once a week since.

I know some guys who string girls along, worried they won't get any if they don't act like there's a chance they'll be in it for the long haul. I'm the exact opposite. I won't hook up with a girl if she's acting like she wants anything serious.

I've seen the destruction lies about intentions leaves behind, and I want no part in it.

"Conor the Hart-less," Hunter adds.

I ball up my burrito wrappers and roll my eyes. "Are you two finished so we can leave?"

"Yeah, let's go."

———

Most of the hockey team is already in attendance when we arrive at the sophomore house. Sports teams tend to live together based on class year. Almost a third of the team this year are seniors, so Aidan, Hunter, and I got our own place. Tonight, the five sophomores are hosting. Their house is across the street from ours and close to downtown, meaning there will be a big influx once Gaffney's stops serving. Our parties draw a large crowd regardless of their location, though.

I wander through the living room, stopping to talk with a few of the guys and rehashing parts of the game. Despite his small smile, I know Coach will have plenty of criticism to dish out at practice tomorrow morning. For now, I soak in the sweet sensation of victory along with the rest of the guys.

None of them are as serious about playing as I am. I'm a one-man wrecking ball headed for a championship trophy.

They all knew I would be. Know this season is it for me.

Knowing something and watching it take place are two different things, I guess.

Tonight, I felt my energy coursing through the rest of the team for the first time this season. Maybe some of them had doubts about whether we could pull it off. But I'm no longer the only guy on the team with trophy-shaped stars in my eyes.

It both eases the pressure and enhances it. A group goal is more achievable than a singular one. If the rest of the team is working just as hard, that takes some of the burden off of me to perform. But if we lose, I won't just be letting myself down.

I eventually head toward the kitchen to grab a soda. I don't drink any alcohol during the season. A few hours of loose inhibitions aren't worth the headache or the sluggish skating the following morning. It's never resulted in fantastic decision-making skills, either. The one time I didn't remember to tell a girl it was just sex *before* the sex was after too many Heinekens sophomore year. I don't think she appreciated the reminder mid-hook-up.

Sarah Clark approaches me as soon as I enter the kitchen.

"Hey, Conor." She flashes me a bright smile that makes her dimples pop.

"Hey," I reply, grinning back.

Sarah has always taken the just-sex line like a champ, and it's the main reason she's the closest thing I have to a regular hook-up. I'm mostly certain she wants nothing more from me. I'm completely certain I've made the fact *I* want nothing more clear to her.

I open the fridge and grab a can of soda out.

"Want anything?" I ask Sarah.

Contrary to what Harlow Hayes thinks, I can be a gentleman. I'm not a total ass. I do have a tendency to display some ass-ish traits around her, though. Something Aidan chewed me out for after the basketball party last weekend.

My life would be easier if she'd chosen a different college. Or better yet, remained in another country.

"Nah, I'm good. I just did a couple of shots," Sarah tells me.

"Hunter?" I ask.

She laughs. "Yup."

I roll my eyes. Hunter has a bizarre obsession with Jell-O, and it has resulted in every party the hockey team has ever thrown featuring alcohol encased in jiggly gelatin.

I see no appeal. Just another reason to stay sober.

More of my teammates wander into the kitchen, including Hunter, who starts making the rounds with his tray of wiggling cups. Some of the basketball guys approach, trailed by their own fangirls. I'm talking to Clayton Thomas when I catch a flash of red out of the corner of my eye and stiffen.

I'm distracted by a warm body rubbing up against me. "Conor, you played *so* well," Emily Orens gushes.

"Thanks, babe," I reply, then take a sip of soda.

Clayton grins. Hunter rolls his eyes from his spot next to me. I want to roll *my* eyes right back at him.

Like Hunter can judge. His pickup lines are terrible. Just tonight, I've heard him use *Here I am. What are your other two wishes?* and *I seem to have lost my phone number. Can I have yours?*

I've never put effort into picking up a girl. They've been flinging themselves at me since middle school.

43

But I'm not paying any attention to the girl doing so right now.

To any girl—except one.

Harlow is standing in the corner of the kitchen, and my eyes keep flickering over there.

I can't focus on anything else. Not Emily rubbing up against me, not Hunter trying to talk me into downing one of his disgusting shots, not Sarah nodding toward the stairs, not any of the people coming over to congratulate me on the win.

Harlow talks to a blonde girl, then to Cole Smith, and then she's all alone.

Fuck it.

I shake Emily's hand off my forearm and approach Harlow's spot by the stove. She's looking at her phone, but not in the way one does when they're bored and have nothing better to be doing.

Twin lines of concentration are furrowed between her eyebrows as she scrolls through something on the screen. Maybe she's looking at one of the fifty-seven training apps designed for novice runners to learn how to increase their mileage. One guess on how I know that. Eight minutes of my life I'll never get back.

"Why'd you ask me?"

Harlow startles.

A rap song is blaring from the speakers in the living room, but it's the sound of *my* voice that has her jumping. She almost drops her phone, makes a desperate grab for it, then bangs her elbow on the edge of the marble countertop.

I almost apologize when she winces, but don't.

She looks me up and down, and I think there's a flicker of heat in her expression. But this is *Harlow Hayes*, so I'm probably misreading things. She did stare at me in the gym for a lot longer than necessary, though. Stupid as it sounds, second-guessing a girl's attraction is a novel concept to me.

"Aidan." Harlow shrugs like that's a complete answer.

As if I don't know why Phillips called me over when he was talking to her last weekend. As if she isn't aware my teammates have no clue what my issue with her is or how deep the resentment runs.

"I play hockey. I'm not a runner."

Things she knows.

Things I didn't need to say.

Another small shrug. "You're athletic."

Harlow manages to make the simple statement sound like an insult. I'm surprised she's bothering to respond to me at all. Equally shocked when I choose to keep the conversation going.

"So are the other guys on the team. You're *buddies* with most of them." I make how I feel about that friendliness clear in my voice.

Harlow rolls her eyes. Ones I'm just noticing are green. "I wouldn't ask any of them."

"But you asked me?"

"*Obviously* I asked you, or you wouldn't be over here badgering me about it."

She crosses her arms, drawing my attention to her chest. Unlike most of the half-dressed girls here, she's wearing a cotton T-shirt that barely shows any cleavage. Unfortunately, the top still looks good on her. *Really* good. I'd never hook up with her, but it's an unfortunate reminder…she's hot as hell.

"Something on my shirt, Hart?"

Busted.

Harlow has more sass than I was expecting.

It should be a turn-off. It's not.

"What? You're allowed to check me out but I can't return the favor, Hayes?"

She doesn't deny it, which I'm annoyingly pleased about.

"I was looking for the bathroom," she tells me.

"It's down the hall on the left."

"No, not here—" Red creeps across her cheeks as she abruptly stops talking.

"*Oh*. You were referring to the *other* time you checked me out."

She bites her bottom lip. More red spreads. But she meets my gaze defiantly, eyes the color of pines bearing into mine.

This is when I should walk away. Take Emily or Sarah upstairs. Maybe even down one of Hunter's disgusting shots, just to wash away the weirdness of this encounter. Do *something* to shake this strange compulsion to remain exactly where I am.

Harlow sighs. "Look, Aidan saw me out running that morning. He was asking about my training. He called you over. I knew you'd say no. You did. End of the story."

She's eager to end this conversation, that much is obvious. Waiting for me to walk away. I wonder if it's because she's aware other people in the kitchen are glancing over at us. Our private feud is only common knowledge among the hockey team, but people pay attention to who I talk to.

I move on to the other part of her request that's been bothering me. "Why the hell would you sign up for a marathon, anyway? Especially if you've never run before?"

She keeps looking at me but says nothing. I'm being appraised—judged—for this moment and for many others. It's uncomfortable.

I don't leave, though. I wait.

Finally, she answers.

"It doesn't matter why I'm doing it." Harlow grabs a green can of ginger ale off the counter. We're probably the only two sober people at this party. She taps it against the soda I'm holding.

"Congrats on the win, Hart. If you'd passed to Powers at the start of the third, it would have been 5-2."

She smiles mockingly, then walks away and leaves me standing here.

And I suddenly know with absolute certainty that wasn't the last conversation I'll have with Harlow Hayes.

Just the first.

CHAPTER FOUR

HARLOW

Persistent poking wakes me. I toss one arm over my eyes, certain I'm imagining it. I'm alone in my own bed. Who the hell would be poking me?

"Harlow. *Harlow*!"

I shift my arm away and reluctantly open my eyes.

Eve is perched on the side of my bed. Her dark hair is a mess and her glasses are askew.

"What's wrong?" I mumble the words, my eyes already half-closing.

"Wake up." Another jab in the ribs.

I mutter something unintelligible, hoping she'll just give up.

"Harlow!"

"Is the house on fire? There better be some emergency—"

"*Conor Hart* is here."

That gets my attention. I open my eyes all the way and focus on her. "What?"

"Conor Hart. The hot hockey player. He's here. At our front door. Right now."

"What?" I repeat, flabbergasted. "*Why* is he here?"

"I don't know!" Eve flaps her hands around. "I opened the door thinking it was the doughnuts I ordered, and there he was looking ten times more delicious!"

I rub a palm across my forehead. *Eve.* "You ordered doughnuts?"

"I tried to, last night. I thought they were finally getting around to it."

"That makes no sense. Holey Moley doesn't even deliver."

"Who cares, Harlow? I was asleep, and I didn't see you dragging your ass out of bed to answer the door. The point is—the hottest guy I've ever seen in real life is at our front door. Get up!"

I refocus, although I am craving a doughnut now. "You didn't ask what he's doing here?"

"Of course I asked! He said he wants to talk to you."

What the fuck?

I woke up in an alternate universe. It's the only explanation.

Approaching me at the party last night was strange enough. Coming to my house is incomprehensible. I try to think of a single reason why Conor might be here and come up totally blank. "Tell him I'm not here."

"Harlow."

Eve gives me a *look*. For all her brash proclamations, she's a moral epicenter; the type of person who doesn't approve of hiding from conflict. Or from a hot guy. In this particular instance, I'm also positive she wants to eavesdrop.

What she doesn't understand—what I can't tell her—is that me avoiding Conor is for the greater good.

Talking with him last night was not only unexpected. It was also exciting. There's a dangerous thrill that comes along with the forbidden, I guess. Or maybe that's how every girl feels while talking to him. Eve definitely looks dazzled, which I'll be teasing her about once this morning is nothing but a distant, outlandish memory.

"Eve." I match her tone.

She sighs, then stands. "Fine. I'll tell him you must have snuck out the window in the middle of the night to meet your forbidden lover."

"Sounds great." I flop back down on the mattress and pull my pillow over my face.

She won't. I hope. Then remind myself I don't care what Conor thinks.

My bedroom door shuts. I peek around my pillow to check the time on my phone. 7:05. I'm *almost* impressed Conor is up this early. He was still at the party when I left last night. Maybe he hasn't gone to bed yet.

I roll back over, but I can't fall asleep.

Curiosity burns away exhaustion.

What was he doing here?

Our conversation last night rattled me, if I'm being honest.

It wasn't finally deciding that his eyes are more gray than blue.

Or him standing a lot closer for a lot longer than I was expecting. Long enough for me to accept what I've been aware of since I caught my first glimpse of him freshman year—I'm attracted to Conor.

Or the way everyone stared at us.

It was that *he* approached *me*. That the hostility wasn't there. He wasn't friendly, but he wasn't outright rude, either. One conversation, and I'm worried I get the fascination with Conor Hart I thought I was totally immune to.

I can't fall back asleep, so I roll out from underneath the warm sheets. I yank on a one-piece bathing suit and cover it with a pair of sweatpants and a fleece.

Eve's door is closed when I walk past it. Clearly, she was able to go back to sleep. I resist the strong urge to knock and ask her what Conor said when she sent him away. But I *do* resist it, because it's Conor Hart. I've always seen the physical appeal, but unlike the girls who fall for his charm and cocky smirk, I know what's beneath the stormy surface.

Know the carefree indifference masks uglier inclinations.

Know the fury that makes him such a force on the ice has repeatedly hurt people I care about.

I use the bathroom, make my usual smoothie, and snag my car keys from the bowl by the door. It's raining—no surprise there. My black rain boots make an unpleasant squelching sound as I walk to my car.

I don't bother pulling my hood up for the short trip. My hair is about to get soaked, anyway.

There are only two other cars in the parking lot when I arrive at the sports complex. It's 7:40 a.m. on a Sunday. Not shocking at all.

I walk through the drizzle to the front entrance of the building. A swipe of my student ID card, and I'm inside the lobby. I veer to the right, into the women's locker room.

I shed my clothes and stuff them inside a locker. Grab my goggles, then enter the pool area. There's not a single person in here.

I pass the *No Lifeguard. Swim at your own risk.* sign and walk the length of the pool to the blocks.

Getting into the water is always the worst part. The air in here is humid and warm but I know the pool won't be. I snap my goggles into place and climb up onto the plastic platform. I lean forward and grip the front, then fling myself off of it and into the pool.

Cool water coats every centimeter of my body. I start kicking, propelling myself through the chlorinated liquid. The initial shock fades as I fall into familiar, rhythmic motion. I do four laps of each stroke, then switch. Freestyle. Backstroke. Butterfly. Breaststroke. Repeat.

I love swimming.

Love the way sounds are muffled.

Love the feel of my arms and legs churning through the water.

Love the weightlessness of gliding along.

Too bad there's no option to swim a marathon.

I pause at the end of the lane. The large clock hanging behind the now-occupied lifeguard chair tells me it's past nine. I climb out of the pool. Water sluices off my body, dripping back into the cement rectangle containing hundreds of gallons of it. My mind is blissfully blank, my muscles beginning to tingle with lactic acid.

"Have a good day, Jerry." I wave to the middle-aged man who lifeguards here in the mornings as I head into the locker room.

"Bye, Harlow," he calls after me.

The locker room is still empty. I grab a towel to dry off, then pull my sweatpants and fleece back on. Toss the damp towel in the hamper and make my way over to the door that leads back to the entrance of the athletic center.

I step into the lobby and collide with Conor Hart.

I'm staring at generic gray fleece, but I know it's him, even before I glance up. Along with his eye color, I've memorized Conor's scent. It's far more appealing than the chlorinated air I've been inhaling for the past hour plus.

I almost fall on my ass in my haste to put some distance between us.

Conor's alone, which I think is a first. Whenever I see him on campus, he's surrounded by people. Friends. Teammates. Fangirls.

We stare at each other for a few uncomfortable seconds.

I'm uncomfortable, at least. I can't tell what he's thinking.

I clear my throat. "Are you lost, Hart? This is the pool. The *frozen* water is next door."

His lips quirk. My entire body reacts to the tiny movement. "I didn't know you swim."

All of a sudden, I'm *very* aware of my appearance. Wet hair. Circles around my eyes from my goggles' suction. No makeup. Clothes only Eve sees me in. Plus, I reek of chlorine.

"The first time you said more than *no* in my presence was last night. So you not knowing my daily exercise routine isn't really all that surprising."

His nod is slow, his lips turning up a tiny bit more.

"Daily, huh?"

"It means every day," I inform him.

"Yeah, thanks. It would have taken me a couple of minutes to look up that definition on my phone."

I scoff, then move to walk past him. Whatever *this* is, it's dangerous. The same hum of awareness I experienced talking to him last night is back. And it scares me, honestly. I've never felt it before, around anyone else.

Conor blocks me, stepping to his left as I move to my right. "Your friend's a shitty liar."

"I have no idea what you're talking about," I tell him loftily.

"Oh, yeah? So, you were...where when I stopped by this morning?"

My mind goes blank. "I forget."

He grins, and my lungs stop working.

I've never seen Conor Hart wear anything but a scowl on his annoyingly attractive face. Amusement transforms already striking features, softening the sharp slash of his brows and the tight clench of his jaw.

"I didn't want to talk to you. And I *thought* that'd be a plan you would be on board with."

Our road of resentment is a two-way street.

Conor seems to have turned onto a one-way without warning me.

"Were you at the game last night?" he asks.

"No. I'm not one of your *puck bunnies*, Conor."

He smirks. "How'd you know about me fucking up that pass to Powers, then?"

"I heard someone at the party talking about it."

For a few uncomfortable, thrilling seconds, he studies me. Then shakes his head. "Nah, I don't believe you."

"I have better things to do with my time than go to your hockey games, okay?"

Conor tilts his head, not looking the least bit offended. "Is it because of Williams?"

"It's because of *you*." I glance around the lobby, confirming we're still alone. "And you know exactly why."

I'm expecting the reminder to fracture this bizarre conversation.

Conor looks unfazed. Unbothered.

I exhale. "I read the game recap, okay? My dad was a hockey fan. I guess I maybe like it a little bit."

I was expecting him to look smug about that admission. Instead, *now* he looks bothered.

Because...*he knows*, I realize. I forgot that Conor Hart is the one person on this campus besides Eve who knows about my parents.

I look away, feeling even more awkward.

"Was your dad a Canucks fan?"

I swallow before nodding. "Diehard."

"Did he take you to games?"

I can't believe this is happening. That I'm casually talking to *Conor Hart* about a topic I don't discuss with anyone.

"We went once. Have you ever been to a pro game?"

For some reason I can't comprehend, I keep the conversation going. Actually, I know the exact reason: I like talking to him. Which is both shocking and concerning.

"With *my dad?*" There's a new, mocking edge to his voice. I flinch, and Conor notices. "No, I've never been to one."

"You should go."

"Planning on it. But I'll be playing, not watching." He takes a step closer. I fight the urge to put more distance between us. "Aren't you going to ask why I stopped by your place this morning?"

"No. But I'd like to know how you knew where I live. Little stalker-y, Hartbreaker."

Unfortunately for my oxygen levels, the second grin he flashes is just as arresting as the first one was.

Conor rubs the back of his neck with one hand, looking almost…embarrassed.

"You heard about that, huh?"

"The whole campus heard about that."

There's a buzzing sound. Conor pulls his phone out of his pocket, glances at it, then does a double take. "Fuck. I'm going to be late for practice."

Based on his surprised tone, we've been talking for longer than I realized.

He holds his phone out to me, open to a new contact. Messages keep showing up at the top of the screen.

> HUNTER: Where the fuck are you?

> ROBBY: Everything okay???

AIDAN: HART!

AIDAN: Are you quitting the team? Because I could use a vacation.

I glance from the screen to him. "I'm not giving you my number."

"I need you to text me your class schedule. Between my classes and hockey, I don't have a lot of free time."

"What the hell are you talking about, Conor?"

He exhales like he's exhausted. "I'll do it, okay? I'll train you for the marathon."

I fight through the shock and manage to say, "I'm good."

"You found someone else?" His tone is a challenge.

"You turned down helping me. Rather rudely."

Conor rolls his eyes. "All I said was *no*."

"It wasn't what you said. It was how you said it."

"Couldn't have come as much of a surprise. You're…. you." I purse my lips in response. "Come on, you can't honestly tell me it hasn't affected your perception of me."

"Nope, it *definitely* has," I tell him.

"Then why ask me?"

"I told you!" I reply. "Aidan."

"Bullshit. Why did you really?"

"Maybe I wanted to see if you're a better person than I thought," I snap.

"Well, I'm not."

I study Conor—*really* study him. Owning up to shortcomings is a hell of a lot harder than denying them. A self-awareness I didn't think Conor had. It sparks a flicker of curiosity.

"Glad we're on the same page." I move to walk past him, again.

He stops me, again.

"Jesus Christ," Conor mutters. "Look, I know I've been kind of an ass before, okay?"

Another shock.

Although I snort at the "kind of."

"Just let me make sure you've got some idea of what you're doing. Especially now that I know you're kinda athletic," he continues, nodding toward the pool entrance. "Even if it's swimming."

"What's wrong with swimming?"

"It doesn't get much sports coverage. That should tell you all you need to know."

"Last I checked, Division III hockey doesn't get much coverage either," I tell him.

A muscle in Conor's sharp jawline jumps. Bullseye on a sore spot. When I've puzzled the enigma that is Conor Hart—which up until now was an infrequent occurrence—one of the main questions is the mystery of him being one of my classmates.

He had other—better—options than Holt University. Options that would have made his plan to play hockey professionally after graduation a much easier goal to achieve.

"It will this year," Conor says. Determination drips from the words, reflected in the features of his face that have turned stoic and unamused again.

I shrug. "We'll see, won't we?"

Inadvertently, I've implied I'll be following the rest of his season. That checking the recap of his last game was not a one-time thing.

"Yeah. *We* will." He caught it. Oblivious isn't an adjective that can be used to describe Conor. "I'll be at the running track at four p.m. tomorrow. Your move, Hayes."

———

When I get home, Eve is eating a bowl of cereal in the kitchen. She wrinkles her nose when I pass by to grab water out of the fridge.

"You were at the pool?"

"Yup." Eve's mother is a hairdresser, and both she and Eve are horrified by the fact I dunk mine in chlorine on a regular basis.

"You're using the shampoo I got you, right?"

"Yes." I pour water into a glass and drain it. "It smells funky, though."

"Put on extra perfume before our double date tonight, then."

"Shit. That's tonight?"

Eve doesn't answer. She just points at the calendar, where *Double Date* is written in bold letters on today's date. It's the only event that made it onto the calendar this month, further emphasizing its importance.

"Why are we going out on a Sunday night, again?"

Eve shrugs. "Ben chose the night. He'll be here with David at eight."

I sigh. Eve has been dating Ben Fletcher since freshman year. They met at one of those school-sponsored first week events I didn't think people actually went to, let alone found love at. Ben is nice enough, and he adores Eve, which is all I want for her. Unfortunately, he seems to have an endless supply of friends who are "amazing guys" and are "looking for the right girl."

Spoiler alert: I haven't been the right girl so far. For any of them. All of Ben's friends are smart, nice, and, for lack of a kinder word, boring.

Tonight's outing is the third double date in as many weeks. The final set-up, I've decided.

It's not like I can't find dates on my own. I'm going out with a guy in my aquatic resources class next week. But Eve is on a mission to make our senior year the best one yet—hence the bucket list and how I ended up at a hockey party last night—and so far I've indulged her.

"Fine. I'm going to shower and get some work done." My plan was to put all of my assignments off until later, but that was before I was reminded about our evening plans.

"You should watch a classic movie, too," Eve tells me.

"A classic movie? Why?"

"David's a film major. The first thing he asked me when I met him was what my favorite movie is. You need better material than *Legally Blonde*."

"But that *is* my favorite movie," I insist. I'm dressing up as Elle Woods for Halloween on Thursday.

"I doubt David has heard of it. He prefers dramas to comedies."

That bodes poorly for our compatibility, but I don't say so.

I promised Eve I would make an effort tonight, and I will.

It takes me until it's time to get ready to finish my homework, so I don't watch a classic film. I scan an article listing the best films of all time for some conversation material while I do my makeup. I haven't seen a single movie that's mentioned.

Eve is always chatty, but Ben is a man of few words. His friends tend to be the quiet, serious type as well.

Within minutes of meeting David, I know it will be a long night. He's nice. Cute. He's taller than me, and at five eight that's not always a given with guys. Unfortunately, none of David's height accommodates a sense of humor.

I drive the four of us to Gaffney's. David spends the short trip detailing French film angles and their technical brilliance. I kind of want to hum *Proud to be an American*, even though technically, I'm not. Singing *O Canada* wouldn't send the same message, though.

Eve gives me a glum, sheepish look when we climb out of the car. Despite her advice earlier, I'm sure she realized the first time she met David that he and I are not headed for a happily ever after. Hope springs eternal in Eve's world, though. I'm more of a pessimist. Comes with the territory after having your world toppled.

Half the hockey team is leaving Gaffney's as we enter.

"Hey, Harlow," Aidan greets.

"Hey," I reply.

My gaze roves over the guys he is with, annoyed to realize I'm not randomly glancing around.

I'm searching for *him*.

Conor is standing by the long table the rest of them must have just left, talking to a blonde waitress. She laughs at something he says and strokes his arm. He grins down at her, and something ugly twists in my stomach.

I look away, straight into Jack's searching gaze. He glances at David next to me.

Jack. The hockey player I *should* feel some emotion at the sight of.

"HARTBREAKER!" Hunter calls. Loudly.

Pretty much everyone in Gaffney's was already looking this way, but that takes care of the few who weren't paying attention to the hockey team.

Several of the guys behind Aidan exchange grins.

"He's gonna be pissed," Aidan tells Hunter.

"Then he shouldn't have been late for practice. I'm not going to be able to walk tomorrow."

Aidan nods, then glances over his shoulder. "Get her number so we can go!" he shouts.

Laughter rumbles among the players. David and Ben are staring at them like they're another species.

"Hart drove," Hunter tells me.

I nod, glancing at the empty hostess stand and wishing Eve hadn't made a reservation so we could just seat ourselves.

Conor heads this way. With the blonde waitress right behind him. Her name is Stacey, according to the nametag attached to her blouse. She's blonde and petite with big boobs, and I wonder if that's his type. I've heard plenty of comments about Conor being the campus heartbreaker—ergo the nickname—and I've seen lots of girls circling him, but I've never actually witnessed him flirt or seen him pay attention to anyone in particular.

"Sorry for the wait," Stacey says. "Do you guys have a reservation?"

"Yeah, we do." Eve steps forward.

"Hey, Hayes."

I lose track of everything except him, my eyes leaping to meet Conor's gray ones.

"Hi, Hart."

There's visible shock on his teammates' faces that Conor acknowledged me. It's almost funny, seeing their stunned reactions. Aidan's mouth is half-open.

Conor must notice their response too because I catch a glimmer of amusement in his expression before he looks next to me. There's no reaction as he spots David and Ben. Then, "Hey, Eve."

That's all he says before heading for the door. His teammates immediately follow, like a row of baby ducks following a parent. Aidan grins at me as he passes by. Jack offers a tiny wave.

And then they're gone.

"You know Conor Hart?" Ben asks Eve.

"No," she answers.

I forgot to ask Eve about what exactly Conor said to her earlier. And I'm surprised he took the time to ask her name, let alone remember it. I figured he was one of those guys who had identifiable traits—*brown hair, plays tennis*—in his phone instead of girls' actual names.

Ben's eyebrows furrow. "How did he know your name?"

"He's probably secretly in love with me."

Ben sighs. "Eve…"

"Your table is right this way," Stacey says. Her expression is neutral, no reaction to the conversation about Conor.

I wonder how well they know each other. Remind myself *I don't care*, and resent how often I've had to do that today.

Stacey leads us over to a four-person table in the far corner.

Another waitress named Amy takes our drink order. Everyone except me orders beers. I opt for water. Eve offered to stay sober tonight, but I'm happy being the designated driver.

"So…" I search for possible topics. "What are you guys dressing up as for Halloween?"

Ben glances at Eve. "Whatever Eve tells me to wear," he states.

Eve shoots him a proud smile, then looks to me. "I think I'm settled on Adam and Eve. I ordered the leaves earlier."

"Cute," I say, then glance at David. "What about you, David?"

"A director. Hitchcock, probably."

"Was he French?" I ask innocently.

Eve kicks me under the table.

David takes my question seriously. "He was British, actually. I'm sure you've seen his films. *Notorious*? *Lifeboat*? *The Birds*?"

I shake my head. "Nope, not ringing any bells."

David looks stunned. "There's a theater in Mayfair that shows his movies. We should go sometime."

"Maybe," I say.

"Who are you being for Halloween?" he asks.

I smile. "Elle Woods."

Blank expression.

"From *Legally Blonde*?"

David shakes his head slowly. "I've never heard of it."

Across the table, Eve sighs.

Probably thinking the same thing I decided earlier: *This is going to be a long night.*

CHAPTER FIVE

CONOR

"What are you doing?" Hunter asks as he walks into the kitchen, glancing over my shoulder and squinting at the screen of my laptop. "You don't even have class today."

"I know," I reply. Any senior who has a Monday class is either an overachiever or slacked so much up until now, they didn't have a choice. "Just doing some research."

"On distance running? Why?"

Hunter heads toward the fridge, pulling out a carton of orange juice.

I sigh and shut my laptop.

Aidan has a big mouth. Hunter will hear about it eventually.

"Because Harlow Hayes asked me to train her for a marathon."

Hunter coughs mid-swallow. "What? And you *agreed*?"

He's incredulous, and I don't blame him one bit. If I understood how it happened myself, I might try to explain it to him. I didn't intend to agree to train her. I just felt guilty and decided to apologize for shooting her half-assed request down. Somehow that resulted in me browsing marathon training forums this morning.

"Yeah. Phillips chewed me out about being nicer to her."

True. But I didn't just agree to help her. I ended up being the one practically begging her to let me, and I'm still trying to figure out how the fuck *that* happened.

She gave me an out. Multiple of them, actually.

"Is that why you said hi to her last night?" Hunter asks.

"I guess."

For the first time, ignoring her felt wrong. It was a relief, actually, not having to pretend like I wasn't aware we were in the same place.

"I run already," I say. "It's good cross-training. Who cares if she jogs alongside me a few times?"

Hunter's eyebrows rise. "So, what? You just mysteriously got over your weird issue with her?"

No. "I don't know what you're talking about."

"Uh-huh. Do you have a thing for her?"

"What? No, of course not."

"*No, of course not?* You've *seen* her, right?"

"So she's hot. Whatever. I don't want Williams's sloppy seconds."

I feel guilty as soon as the words leave my mouth, and they're ineffective anyway.

Hunter appears unconvinced. "Speaking of Williams, are you going to tell him about this? He looked like his dog died when we saw her out on a date last night."

"There's nothing to tell. I'll make sure she knows how to avoid getting shin splints and that will be that."

"If you say so." Hunter still looks doubtful. "This is *the* season, Hart. Are you seriously willing to risk your shot at the pros for a chick you claim to have no interest in?"

He's right. I know he's right.

But I still say, "I'm not risking shit."

Technically, Harlow didn't even agree to show up later. But I'm betting she will. She may not want to, the same way I don't know if I really want her to.

But she's curious about me, the same way I am about her.

Despite what I just told Hunter, I know that's dangerous.

———

I avoid meeting Hunter's worried gaze when I leave the house a few hours later.

Half the team is over at our place hanging out before our evening skate. None of them ask where I'm going but Robby smirks as I head for the front door, letting me know where he *thinks* I'm off to.

"Don't be late, Hart!" Aidan calls after me. "I'm not doing suicides for you again."

I was late to hockey practice for the first time—ever—yesterday. When I was a little kid, I'd have my mom drop me off a half hour early to make sure I was the first one on the ice. I've shown up on time hungover. With the flu. In a snowstorm.

One conversation with Harlow Hayes, and I forgot there were twenty-seven guys and one extremely pissed-off coach waiting on me. I've gotten a lot of shit from the team about it, but it would be ten times worse if they knew there was a girl involved in my tardiness. Distractions don't win championships.

I jog through the drizzle to my SUV. The engine roars to life, as it very well should after the three hundred dollars I just dropped getting it fixed. I know nothing about repairing cars. Learning how to change the oil or put on a spare tire sounds like the type of thing you do with your dad in the driveway.

Maybe that's why I don't know how to do either.

The drive to the football stadium only takes a few minutes.

Rain-splattered glass blurs the landscape into gray, brown, and green. I park right next to the bleachers. There are still a couple of weeks left in the football season, but the stadium looks as though it's been abandoned for years.

Probably because the football team is neither successful nor entertaining. The crowds that swarm our home games are notably absent. At least, that's what I've been told. I've never been to one myself. Never seen the appeal of sitting on hard metal and watching a bunch of guys spend minutes lining up for mere seconds of action.

My disdain for football might be colored by the fact that the athletic half of my DNA came from a former wide receiver.

If holding grudges were a sport, I'd be better at it than hockey.

I climb out of my car and into rain that's suddenly falling faster. I'm wearing the same sweatpants and jacket I pulled on early this morning. They're soaked within minutes, so I don't bother walking under the bleachers' cover. I lean against the chain-link fence that surrounds the running track and wait.

Harlow shows up five minutes later, parking in the spot next to my car.

She doesn't get out right away, and I wonder if she's considering leaving.

She stays.

Harlow climbs out of her car in the ugliest jacket I've ever seen. It's *bright* yellow—a stop-and-stare shade that burns my eyes. Paired with her vivid hair, she stands out against the muted landscape of brick buildings, bare trees, and grass.

Her hood remains down as she walks toward me, appearing unbothered by the rain saturating her red hair and dripping down her face.

"How was it?" I ask when she reaches me.

"Huh?" She looks confused.

I barely manage to tamp down the smirk that desperately wants to form. "The ugly raincoat competition you just came from. Did you win?"

She flips me off, but I catch a lip twitch.

"Is this your Halloween costume? The McDonalds logo?"

"You hate the coat. I get it. And no, I'm dressing up as Elle Woods."

"But you're not blonde," I tell her.

"So…"

"It's literally *in* the title. *Legally* Blonde."

Harlow stares at me. "You have *not* seen *Legally Blonde*."

I nod. "Sure, I have."

She crosses her arms. "Prove it."

"Okay." I think for a minute. "This is the dance they do in the hair salon, right? The bend and clap or whatever?"

I pull off a pretty flawless rendition of it, if I do say so myself. I even remember it's a snap, not a clap.

Harlow stands frozen for a few seconds. Then she doubles over and bursts out laughing. It continues for a *while*. She has to clutch her stomach. Wipe tears from her eyes.

It's at my expense. But I'd do that stupid shimmy all over again, just to watch her laugh like that.

"I *can't believe* you did that. That you've seen it. You play *hockey*."

I arch one eyebrow. "Way to stereotype. I can't watch a comedy if I play hockey?"

"No, I just…" Harlow shakes her head. "Never mind." She mutters something under her breath. All I catch is some mention of cooking.

"My mom loves that movie."

I don't know why I say it—why I share that—but I do.

Then I head for the gate that leads onto the running track. I open it and gesture for Harlow to walk through first.

She doesn't; she remains in place.

Our silent stand-off lasts for thirty seconds before she walks through the opening onto the track. She wasn't anticipating any gentlemanly behavior from me, clearly.

I normally thrive on being the cocky player people expect.

Surprising Harlow Hayes might be my new favorite hobby. Watching her green eyes try to figure me out. Making it difficult for them to do so.

Once we're on the track, I switch to business mode. "Okay, I did some research. You should start with six to twelve weeks of base training. Begin by running three or four times a week. You should start with only a couple of miles, then slowly start adding mileage. Goal will be to get up to five or six miles by the end of base training. Build slowly, and it's about hitting the distance, not speed. If you need to alternate running and walking, then do that."

Harlow nods. She's listening carefully, and it feels different than when I coach my teammates through a drill or tell them to add on more reps. I'm conscious of every word I'm saying.

"Once you're through base training, then you begin adding mileage. One longer run a week, plus several shorter ones. By then, you should start upping your diet and doing rest days. Cutting back on swimming. But we can figure all that out later. For now, consistency is key. And stretching, so you don't injure yourself. Leg swings are popular, lateral and front-to-back. Like this." I demonstrate both. "I usually do walking lunges. And butt kicks. You can also—"

Harlow suddenly smirks.

"What?"

"Nothing. I just never thought I'd hear you say the words *butt kicks* to me. It was kind of funny. Keep going."

I say the first thought that pops into my head. "If you're laughing at *butt kicks*, you must be a real riot in bed."

She snorts. "Stop saying *butt kicks*. And yeah, it's gotten awkward a couple of times."

I blink at her. I was expecting her to get offended or tell me it's none of my business. Not *agree*.

"Awkward how?"

"How do you think?" Harlow raises one eyebrow. "Killed the mood. You know." She holds a finger straight out, then drops it.

Now I'm the one snorting.

I've never discussed sex with a girl while we're both fully dressed with no intention of *having* sex. Never had a girlfriend or a girl who was a friend.

It's entertaining. Or maybe that's just Harlow.

"Your turn," she says.

"My turn for what?"

"To tell me something embarrassing about you."

I raise both eyebrows. "How was that embarrassing? That you're a boner killer?"

"Yeah. *Exactly that*, Conor." She rolls her eyes.

"If you were laughing, they were doing something wrong. Not you."

It wouldn't happen with me. Thankfully, that's a thought I keep to myself.

Sex with Harlow will not be happening. I'm not even sure if she's interested. I shouldn't be interested. She's Williams's ex. Landon's best friend.

Most importantly, she *distracts* me.

My phone buzzes with the timer I set earlier, and I'm shocked.

That means it's already been thirty minutes since she got here. We've done nothing.

"I've only got ten minutes before I have to leave for practice," I tell her. "Do fifteen of these." I show her a knee hug. "Then we'll jog a few laps."

Harlow nods. She lifts her leg and pulls it into her chest, drawing my attention to her bottoms for the first time. I was so distracted by her ugly raincoat I didn't notice the black, tight leggings she's wearing.

"Hold your knee for a few seconds," I say, tearing my gaze away from her ass.

Those guys are idiots. Even if she kept the awful raincoat on, I could easily get hard.

But those are the exact opposite of the thoughts I'm supposed to be having, so I force myself to focus on her form.

Harlow finishes stretching, then we set off at an easy jog.

Neither of us says anything. There's just the sound of the rain and the pounding of our feet against rubber.

"Are you really not going to tell me something embarrassing?" she asks me after two laps.

"Hayes, I didn't ask to know about your sex life. You're seriously asking about mine?"

"Let me guess. You don't have an embarrassing story. Models magically fall into your bed, and you pound them into the headboard."

"Jesus, Hayes." I laugh, continually surprised by the stuff coming out of her mouth. It's a flattering perception, I guess. "Of course I have stories."

"Great. Go."

I glance over to make sure she's still good with this pace. We don't have long, so I'm running about the average speed I usually do. She's keeping up. There's a tiny kernel of pride, like I have anything to do with it.

"Freshman year, this girl was giving me a blowjob. She hadn't had anything to drink, but I guess she had a gag reflex. Threw up all over my dick and the carpet. My roommate was pissed. Our dorm room smelled like vomit for a couple of weeks."

"That's disgusting, not embarrassing."

I exhale. "Aidan called me Puke Dick for the rest of the semester."

"I still don't feel bad for you."

"Okay, fine. In high school, I was hooking up with this girl in the backseat of my mom's car and I got a nosebleed. She was traumatized and I had to explain to my mom why there was blood all over the seats back there."

"What did you tell your mom?"

"The truth. That I had a girl back there."

"And she was cool with that?"

"No. She grounded me for a month. But that was mostly because I lied and told her I was going to a friend's house."

"Okay, that's worse," Harlow says. "But still not that bad."

"Well, I'm out. Other than that, it's been all models and broken headboards."

She laughs, and I want to savor the sound.

"What did the guys say?" I ask.

Immediately, her laughter stops. "It doesn't matter."

"Come on, I gave you details."

"Fine. One guy started talking about my body like I wasn't even there. Like sorta describing it? He had a lot to say about my boobs, and I started laughing. He was super embarrassed and never talked to me again. The other was right..." She exhales. "Right after my parents died. He knew about it, obviously, and I think he thought I needed more help getting in the mood or something? He started talking like he was narrating a porno, and again... I lost it. He apologized for five minutes." She pauses. "I've never had a serious boyfriend. The longest I've dated a guy was Jack, and that wasn't...the feelings weren't there for me. He was such a gentleman and I didn't know how to..." She exhales. "I can't believe I'm telling you this."

"I asked."

Harlow is silent for a minute. I was going to keep track of how many laps we've run, but I lost count a while ago.

"So, your plan is to play professionally after graduation?" she asks.

"Yeah."

"Why?"

No one's ever asked me that. *"Why?"*

"Yeah. Why do you want to play hockey professionally?"

"Money, fame, women, glory?" Harlow says nothing. It forces an honest answer out. "Life is simpler on the ice. Stuff that I'm worried about—upset about—well, it can't follow me out there. I'll chase that feeling as far as I can."

She still seems unsatisfied by my response.

"You don't have anything that makes you feel that way?" I ask.

"No, I do." She doesn't elaborate.

"You're moving back to Canada?"

She gives me a questioning look as I mention her future plans. I guess Harlow has forgotten I know just as much about her as she thinks she knows about me.

I shrug in response to her silent question. "People in Clare-mont gossip."

"Oh. Right." We're getting uncomfortably close to the shared history between us. Closer than I ever thought we might get together. "Yeah, probably. That was always the plan. Come here for university and then go back."

"It was?"

"Yeah. Kinda flipped the rebellious teenager stereotype. I wanted to be just like my mom, and she always raved about her time here. It's how she met Allison. They were in the same dorm freshman year."

"Oh."

She did it.

She mentioned them. Just Allison, but still.

Weirdly, I'm more occupied by another piece of her past falling into place. I assumed she resented ending up at Holt for college, not that it was her first choice.

"I also liked the location."

I look around at the scenery. Past the sad, empty bleachers, the grass is a vibrant green. The sky is gray, which makes the orange and red leaves pop.

"Yeah, it's nice, I guess." Not as nice as white ice and boards.

Harlow follows my gaze. "I meant the Sound. I'm a marine biology major. I like being this close to the ocean."

"So you're a swimmer who likes water, huh?"

She glances at me, eyebrow raised. There's a strange jolt when our eyes connect, and I tell myself my heart rate is only accelerating because I'm exercising. "You're a hockey player who likes ice, huh?"

My phone buzzes in my pocket again.

My steps slow as we approach the gate where we entered the track, and Harlow's do too.

I pull my phone out and silence the alarm. Keep staring at the screen, pretending I took my trainer role more seriously than losing track of time talking to her. "Seven thirty mile. Not bad. You could aim for four and a half hours as your target time."

"My target time?"

Harlow reaches up to collect the red strands that have escaped from her ponytail. I force my eyes away from the strip of stomach the motion reveals.

"Yeah. Your goal time to finish in."

"My only goal is to cross the finish line, Hart."

"And you're running a marathon...why?"

She looks away. "It's stupid. Bucket list shit."

"Bucket list shit?" I echo. "If you want to start running, why not aim for like, a 5K?"

"I didn't think I'd need to explain the concept of competitiveness to Holt's all-time leading scorer in hockey."

I don't take the bait. Don't jump on the compliment she just offered up on a silver platter. I don't let myself wonder what her knowing my stats means, either.

"Fine." I'm annoyed with myself for being annoyed she won't tell me the real reason why. "I've gotta get to practice. See you."

"Conor."

I pause, three steps away. "What?"

The rain eased off while we were running. Now it's picking up once more, soaking my damp clothes all over again.

"Was this...it?"

I glance back at her. There's no sign of the teasing smile or the vulnerability on display when we were running together. She looks serious.

"Do you want it to be?" I ask.

"I should." Harlow steps closer. Holds out a hand. "Give me your phone."

Silently, I unlock it, then pass it to her.

She types something quickly, then returns it to me.

I glance down at a phone number. Hers, I'm assuming.

"I know you're busy. But if you have time to meet again and want to text me..." She bites her bottom lip. "I'll show up."

"Okay. Bye." That's all I say. I need to get my ass to practice —now.

I spin and hurry away.

Leaving her standing on the track in the rain.

CHAPTER SIX

HARLOW

I tap my pen against my notebook. Marine Evolutionary Biology is my favorite course.

Most lectures, I can't scribble down what the professor is saying fast enough.

During today's, I'm barely listening. I'm distracted.

I have been ever since Conor walked away from me three days ago.

I shouldn't have gone to meet him at the track. I knew it before I arrived at the football stadium, and I'm just as certain of it now.

But I did.

And it was nothing like I expected.

The fascination that appeared after our first conversation in the kitchen was nothing compared to my intrigue after talking with him while running on the track.

Conor Hart confuses me.

I know what type of guy he is.

I've heard the stories swirling around campus about the fights on the ice. Seen the girls hanging all over him. He's a cocky player in both senses of the word, and he acts like it.

He's also…more.

Funny. Intuitive. A good listener.

I formed my opinion of Conor Hart a while ago—long before I saw him, much less talked to him. It was amplified when the Garrisons took me in after my parents died. When I witnessed the kindness Conor seemed to lack up close and every day.

I never considered choosing sides. I was just…on theirs.

I also never considered anything from Conor's perspective. I've seen the anger on Landon's face when he talks about his half-brother. The hurt on Hugh's whenever the topic of his older son comes up.

But I've never thought about what it must have been like for Conor to grow up without a dad.

For your father to have a separate family.

Class ends, and I've taken less than a page of notes. I huff an annoyed breath as I pack up my belongings, pushing them into my backpack and then heading out into the hallway.

I debate my destination for a few minutes once I'm outside. All around me hoods are being raised, but I don't bother to lift mine. It's misting out, but the damp air feels refreshing after the stuffy, dry classroom I just spent an hour in.

Rather than head home, I walk toward the library. I have a microbe lab analysis due tomorrow, and I know it'll take me twice as long to complete on the couch in sweats as it will here. And tonight is my date with the guy in my aquatic resources class, so I need to get this done as quickly as possible.

I stop at the water fountain just inside the main doors to fill up my bottle. I'm holding it under the stream and staring out at the sea of tables, trying to decide where to sit, when a male voice speaks behind me.

"Hi, Harlow."

I turn to see Hunter Morgan standing behind me, holding his own water bottle.

"Oh, hey," I reply, in what I hope is a casual manner.

Hunter makes me nervous.

Not because he's ever been anything but nice—because he hasn't—but because I know he's Conor's best friend. I'm confident Conor has shared nothing about his family life—the fractured half, at least—with his friends here. Hunter has always looked just as confused by his behavior toward me as all the other guys. That doesn't mean he's not privy to plenty of other parts of Conor's life, though, which he confirms with his next question.

"How was your Monday?"

I take my time capping my water bottle. "It was fine."

"Hart can be a real drill sergeant. And I'm not sure whatever marathon training forum he found was legit."

"It wasn't that bad." I hobbled around all day Tuesday, but that was due to a stupid urge to impress Conor, not because he set too rapid a pace or ran for too long. I forced myself to jog downtown and back yesterday and I was still able to dance at the Halloween party last night, so maybe something is working.

"Huh." Hunter is eyeing me like he wants to ask more questions, but something is stopping him.

"I've got a lab report to finish. See you around, Hunter."

He nods and smiles.

I find an empty table and spend the next two hours finishing my lab analysis, then head for the main parking lot where I left my car this morning.

I know where I'm going, but I lie to myself about it. Mostly to combat the nerves and excitement fighting for real estate in my stomach.

There aren't many cars outside the sports center, but the black

SUV Conor drove to the track is one of them. I hope the many available parking spots means hockey practice is over. The last thing I want is the whole team watching while I talk to their captain.

Cold air laced with the smell of stale sweat greets me when I step inside Holt's hockey arena for the first time. It should be gross but somehow isn't. I inhale deeply as I walk along the rubber mats covering the floor.

There's only one figure out on the ice. I walk up to the boards that surround the rink to look through the clear plastic. Shove my hands into my jacket pockets as I watch him.

I could count on a couple of fingers the number of times I've been skating. I prefer my water in liquid form. Watching Conor skate is the first time I've experienced any appreciation for its frozen state.

He glides across the ice like a bird of prey in flight. Wild, controlled strength eats up the entire length of the rink in the blink of an eye. He barely leans, and he's turned, flying along the opposite side of the ice.

Conor makes skating look effortless. Easy. Graceful.

My two times on the ice left me with the distinct impression it is anything but.

I can hear the scrape of metal blades against the ice, but that's the only indication he's exerting himself at all. He flies around and around the rink in rapid circles.

Sometimes he shoots one of the pucks into the goal.

Sometimes he turns it into a blur of black, weaving and spinning around invisible opponents.

Sometimes he abandons it on the ice and rests his stick on his shoulders.

Suddenly, Conor stops, sending a white spray across the ice

right by the bench. Pulls off his helmet and runs a hand through his hair. Glances down toward me.

I swallow, realizing he knows I'm here. Walk down toward where he's standing, fiddling nervously with the zipper of my jacket.

His eyes look more blue than gray against the light background. The unblemished ice and bright lights.

"You're really good," I blurt.

"Thanks." There's no sign of a smirk. The word is matter of fact.

I glance around the rink. "So…this is it, huh?"

"Yup."

He hasn't texted me.

And nothing in his expression says he's pleased about me showing up here.

Maybe this was always Conor's intention, to streak across my life like a comet and then disappear just as fast. Technically, he helped me, just like he said he would. Except he kept using the word *we* when we were at the running track, and I relied upon that. I might not need his help, but I want it.

"I just, um, I wanted to say thank you for Monday. I'm not sure if I ever said it, so, thanks…"

"Don't mention it," he says.

I'm not sure if he means that literally or more as a *you're welcome*.

"Okay, then. See you—"

"Do you skate?"

I raise a questioning eyebrow. Conor says nothing else, just waits for me to answer. "Not well."

A door in the boards creaks open. "Come on."

I glance between the gleaming white surface and my black rain boots. "What, now?"

"Yeah. Come here."

Conor takes his glove off and holds a hand out. I pull my hand out of my pocket and reach for it as I step from the mats onto the ice, forcing myself not to react when our palms connect. His fingers are calloused and warm, wrapping around mine securely.

Heat races up my arm and spreads through my entire body. I imagine his hands running *over* my entire body. I'm positive I wouldn't laugh. Couldn't, no matter what came out of his mouth. He's…consuming. His proximity wraps around me like a warm blanket, insulating me from the chill emanating off the ice.

I look around, pulling in deep breaths of cold air that burn my lungs.

Conor guides me to the center of the ice, towering over me in his skates. He matches my slow pace, my tentative steps and his slow strokes drawing us closer and closer to the middle.

He drops my hand once we're there.

I shove my hand back into my pocket and then look around. The ice is polished to a flawless gleam that resembles glass, stark red and blue lines the only interruption. There are a few spots where the lights reflect the marks Conor's blades left on the ice. Bleachers stretch all around the rink. They must accommodate a few hundred people when they're full. It must get *loud* in here, instead of church quiet.

"Wow," I say.

Conor leans on his stick, his gaze focused on the goal at the opposite end. Then his eyes flick up. I follow their motion, focusing on the worn banner hanging from the high ceiling. The only decoration among the beams.

"Only one championship."

"For now, yeah," he tells me.

I shake my head, smiling.

I used to find Conor's confidence irritating. But now, I'm a little in awe of it. I've never felt that sure about anything. I know I want to work as a cetologist, but I also know it's a hard field to make a living in. Grants and funding can be hard to come by. The money my parents left me is a safety net, but I'm reluctant to rely on it completely. There's a good possibility I'll have to settle for something else and use my degree as a hobby.

"Can I ask you something?"

"You just did."

I roll my eyes. "Why did you choose Holt?"

Conor glances over, a new tension appearing on his face.

"You're really good. You could have played at a school with an arena that fit *thousands* of people. That's won *dozens* of championships. And I know it's not because you don't think you could have, so…"

It's a question I have no right to ask him. But if this is the last time we talk—and that's the vibe I'm getting from this conversation—it's something I've always wondered ever since I found out we were attending the same college.

He doesn't answer right away. Maybe he won't.

"I wanted to stay close to my mom," Conor eventually says. "Holt was my best option in state."

I do a poor job of hiding my surprise at his response. I thought selfish was a synonym for his name. Thought his list of priorities was just the word *hockey*, bolded and underlined.

"What about Brighton?" I ask. It's the biggest school in the state. And Brighton University boasts competitive athletics, including a Division I hockey program. "Couldn't you have gone there?"

Conor nods. "Yup. Got a full ride."

I don't voice the question, but I know it's scrawled across my face.

He looks away. At the old banner again. "You know Hugh went there?"

"Yeah, I know." Shock ripples through me. I can't believe he mentioned his biological father.

"Well, I promised myself a long time ago that I'd make different choices than he did."

"Is that why you didn't play football?"

"No. I just always preferred hockey."

"What would you have done if he'd played hockey?" I ask.

Conor doesn't answer right away. "I don't know," he finally admits. "Guess I'd have to decide if I love the game more than I hate him."

"What if not going to Brighton cost you your shot at going pro?" I ask.

I'm treading on thin ice—literally—with these questions. But I'm desperate to know more. To hear more, from his perspective.

Is he selfish or stubborn? Neither? Both?

"Then I don't get to play pro. At least I'll have my damn pride."

I've never had any doubts about how Conor feels about the Garrison family. The resentment has been obvious every time he's looked away from me. Walked in the opposite direction. My last name isn't even Garrison, and I've felt the chill of his contempt.

"Hugh ate the pumpkin pie I burned last Thanksgiving," I whisper. "No one else would even try it."

Hugh Garrison has done a lot more for me than just eat an overcooked dessert. For some reason, it was the first thing that popped into my head. And in this moment, looking at Conor's flinty expression, it's the best defense I can come up with for the man who's become a second father to me.

"My mom was working a double shift at the hospital on Thanksgiving," Conor states.

Does that mean he spent the holiday alone? He sure didn't spend it with us.

"People make mistakes."

His eyes flash like blue steel. "Have you ever done the math between my birthday and Landon's?" It's more of a demand than a question.

"I don't know your birthday."

It's a cop out, and we both know it.

"He's a year younger than us. Eleven months younger than me."

"I had…an idea," I admit.

I might not know the exact date of Conor's birthday, but I know Landon's. Know the two of them are just a year apart in school. Know when Hugh says *Conor has good reasons* every time an invitation gets shot down, he's not just saying it; he means it.

And those good reasons were a lot easier to ignore back when I thought Conor Hart was just an obnoxious hockey player.

"Passing the puck when you should shoot it is a *mistake*. That…he…it fucked up my whole life. My mom's whole life."

"He's tried to make amends."

"By inviting me to spend time with his new family? Visit the house that's five times the size of what my mom can afford?" Conor snorts. "Some things can't be forgiven. Can't be fixed."

I swallow, hearing the certainty in his words.

Maybe he's right. If the drunk driver who killed my parents had survived the accident, I don't think I could have forgiven her decision to get behind the wheel.

I've known Hugh Garrison for most of my life. He's been nothing but kind and loving toward me. But the more time I spend in Conor's presence, the more I find myself facing the unwelcome reality that the man who has stepped up as a father figure for me didn't do the same for one of his biological children.

"Hey! Conor!"

I glance toward the voice. A little kid, probably around eight or nine, is standing in the open door that leads off the ice. Waving this way and beaming at the guy beside me.

The annoyance dissipates from Conor's expression as he waves back at the kid. "Hey, Cody."

"Friend of yours?" I ask.

Conor glances at me. "I help out with the PeeWee practice on Fridays. It's why I'm still here."

"Oh," is all I can think to say.

It's humbling, realizing just how completely wrong I was about him.

"Cody shows up early, but the rest of them will be here soon."

"Right." I start shuffling across the ice toward the door, Conor skating silently beside me.

"Are we doing the same zone entry drill this week?" Cody pays no attention to me as I step off the ice, his focus entirely on Conor.

"Up to Coach Cassidy," Conor says.

"Could you ask him about it? Please? I've been practicing all week."

"Yeah, I'll ask him." Conor's eyes flicker to me, and I realize I'm staring.

"I'm, uh, I should go," I say.

Cody glances at me. "Who are you? Another coach?"

"Uh, no. I'm…"

"Harlow's headed out," Conor says. "You're stuck with me. Come on. You should get changed and I need to get the cones out."

"Okay," Cody agrees easily, totally forgetting about me once again. I can see the hero worship on his face as he gazes up at Conor. It's a purer form of the admiration I've seen aimed at Conor many times before.

Conor glances at me. "See you, Hayes."

"Bye," I say.

I was hoping he'd use my first name again. I'm searching my mind for a time he's said it to me before, and I'm not sure he has. Because it's still affecting me, many seconds later.

Conor and Cody head past the bench, toward what must be the entrance to the locker rooms.

And I have to force myself to turn and walk away.

CHAPTER SEVEN

HARLOW

"Didn't you say your date is at 7:30?" is the first thing Eve asks as soon as I walk through the front door.

I glance at the clock, realize it's 7:20, and swear.

Time moves differently when I'm with Conor Hart. An anomaly the scientist in me has no good explanation for.

"What are you wearing?" Eve asks, following me as I rush down the hallway.

I drop my backpack on the floor and toss my coat on the unmade bed.

"I don't know."

"Where the hell were you?"

"Library," I lie. "I lost track of time."

"Wear this sweater." Eve pulls a black one out of my closet and tosses it on the bed. "I'll find some jeans."

I strip out of my sweatshirt and yank on the sweater, then sit down at my desk to put some makeup on.

"I had a weird encounter with a hockey player earlier," Eve tells me as she digs through my dresser.

My hand stalls mid–mascara swipe. "Oh?"

"Some guy named Hunter said hi to me. Should I be expecting him at our front door next?"

I roll my eyes. "No."

"Did you ever find out why Conor was here?"

I'm surprised it's taken her this long to ask.

"Uh, yeah. He heard I was running a marathon and had some tips."

All true, just a heavily edited version.

"That's…nice, I guess."

"Yeah." I finish up my makeup and then stand.

There's a knock on the door.

Eve tosses a pair of jeans at me. "I feel like you live here and I'm your doorwoman."

I laugh as I finish changing and grab my down coat, glancing over my appearance in the full-length mirror.

Slowly, my smile fades.

I was *excited* about this date. Unlike with Eve's set-ups, I have a lot in common with Eric. He's sat next to me in class for two months. He's cute and funny and nice.

Exactly my type…I thought.

The problem is I can't get the one guy I was certain *wasn't* my type out of my head.

I push thoughts of Conor far, *far* away and head down the hall. Eve is loitering in the kitchen, doing a terrible job of acting like she's not waiting around to witness this.

Eric is standing in the small entryway. He smiles as soon as he sees me. "Hi, Harlow. Wow…" He looks me over, his gaze approving. "Wow, you look really nice."

"So do you," I say, smiling back. "You met Eve?"

"Yup," he confirms. "She did a great job opening the door."

I hear a muffled laugh from the kitchen. She's definitely listening.

"Great. You ready to go?"

"Sure am," he says.

"Bye, Eve," I call.

"Bye, kids. Have fun!"

The air outside is chilly, but not as damp as it was earlier. I snuggle into the warmth of my coat as we walk to Eric's car.

"So…I couldn't decide where to take you and made reservations at three different places," Eric tells me, giving me a sheepish smile. "Do you want me to tell you the options and you can pick one?"

God, he's *so* nice.

"Sure."

"Okay. Italian, Mexican, or Japanese?"

"Mexican," I decide. I could seriously go for some tacos right now.

"Excellent choice."

He opens the car door for me. I scan the inside of his sedan while he's walking around to the driver's side. It's clean and smells like mint.

Eric is easy to talk to. On the drive to the restaurant, we discuss an upcoming exam in our shared class, debate which professors we want on our thesis committees in the spring, and discuss potential employment prospects. I tell him about the Canadian government's specialized whale conservation program that is my dream job after graduation.

"I didn't know you're Canadian," he says.

"Uh, yeah. My dad was born in a small town in Ireland and my mom grew up in Cincinnati. He was stationed here for work for a few years, and he met my mom when she was a student at Holt. They ended up in Canada for my dad's job."

"What does he do?"

I don't correct his use of the present tense. "Nautical engineering."

"Wow. Smart runs in the family, huh?"

"Yeah, I guess. What about your dad? What does he do?"

"He works in construction. Has a small company in Oregon he started himself. I help out there in the summers."

"So you can build a house?"

"Part of it," he replies modestly as he pulls into a small parking lot.

I glance around, not recognizing any of the scenery. "Where are we?"

"Loughton," he replies, which is a town two over from Somerville. "There's not a ton to do here, but there's one Mexican restaurant that's amazing."

"Sounds good," I say, climbing out of the car. It feels even colder now after sitting in the heat, and I'm glad I wore my warmest coat.

I've driven through Loughton before, but this is my first time stopping. Eric was right; there's not much to see. The downtown section is even more limited than Somerville's.

I follow Eric past a dentist's office and inside a building I would have missed if I'd been walking along the sidewalk myself. We walk down a short alley, and then we're inside an explosion of color. Brightly colored flags and twinkling lights decorate the walls. Cheerful music pours out of the speakers.

The interior of the restaurant is tiny. The far side is mostly taken up by a serving counter, and the rest of the floor is filled by a few small tables and folding chairs. One table is occupied by another young couple, but the only other people in here are employees.

My stomach grumbles, grateful we won't have to wait to be served.

"I usually get the chicken burrito," Eric tells me. "But I've never had anything here that wasn't good."

I nod as I scan the menu.

I end up ordering fish tacos. The food is prepared right in front of us, and we grab one of the two open tables.

"Wow, this *is* really good," I state as soon as I've swallowed my first bite. The tortilla is warm, the fish is fresh, and there's a tangy sauce covering the slaw that is one of the best things I've ever tasted.

Eric grins. "Told you."

"Did you do anything for Halloween last night?" I ask.

"Yeah. I went to a party a buddy of mine hosted. How about you?"

"Same thing, pretty much. One of Eve's friends was hosting and it was mostly art majors. *Lots* of very impressive costumes."

He laughs. "What were you?"

"Elle Woods."

I wait, weirdly disappointed when his response is "Who's that?"

"Movie character. She's in *Legally Blonde*."

"Oh, that's cool."

It's an improvement from David's reaction, at least.

"So are you…"

The rest of what Eric is saying gets lost in the sudden *whooshing* sound filling my ears. It feels like I'm standing in a wind tunnel, watching Aidan Phillips walk into the restaurant. Conor is right behind him, talking to Hunter.

Aidan spots me first. Instead of the smile I'm expecting, he glances at Conor.

"Harlow?"

I force my gaze back to Eric. "Sorry. I know a couple of those guys. Got distracted."

Eric glances over his shoulder. I keep my eyes on my food.

"Want to go say hi?"

"No, it's fine." I take another bite.

I should have picked Italian or Japanese. I don't know what the odds of running into Conor here are, but they must be minuscule.

When I glance up again, the guys are all ordering at the counter.

I continue eating my tacos, trying to focus on what Eric is saying but mostly straining to listen to what Conor and his friends are saying. I can't make much out over the music playing, just the low hum of their voices.

And then they take their food and leave without a single acknowledgment.

I stare at the closed door, confused.

Hurt.

It feels like the last few weeks never happened, like time has rewinded to before Aidan asked me about my training plan. Except, back then *he* would have said hi to me, at least. But Conor ignored me at every opportunity, like he did just now.

I make myself focus on Eric, hoping he didn't notice my distraction.

We finish our food, then sit and talk for a while before heading back outside. It's raining now, of course, and we hurry back to the parking lot where Eric left his car.

"Are you warm enough?" Eric asks once we're inside his sedan, fiddling with the dial that controls the heat.

"Yeah, I'm good," I reply.

"We could get some doughnuts?" Eric suggests. "Or go to Gaffney's?"

"I was up pretty late last night. Mind just dropping me off?"

"Yeah, of course."

The easy conversation from the car ride to the restaurant is glaringly absent as Eric drives me home. He turns on some music about five minutes in, rescuing us from total silence.

I chew on the inside of my cheek, debating what to say to him. I don't have a single good explanation for why I don't want to go out with him again, except for the truth.

I have feelings for someone else.

A very unfortunate someone else.

You can't choose who you have chemistry with. I found the passion that's been absent with every guy I've dated, and I wish I hadn't. Caring *sucks*. If I'd walked in a restaurant and seen Conor eating with another girl, I wouldn't have an appetite anymore. He didn't seem to care I was there with Eric.

Eric stops in front of my house, shifting into neutral. I watch him do it, avoiding meeting his eyes for as long as possible.

"That was fun," he says.

I nod. It was.

But it felt like grabbing a bite with a friend. Not a date.

I pull in a deep breath. "If we hang out again, maybe it should just be as friends?"

His smile is wry. "Right."

"You're a really great guy. I just…I don't think I'm in a great place to start something right now."

"I get it. We're good, Harlow."

Eric doesn't sound upset, but I can't read his full expression that well in the dim car. If he is more bothered than he's letting on, I figure me sitting here isn't going to help. There's not really anything else left to say.

I tell him "Thanks for dinner" and then climb out into the cold, watching his taillights until they disappear down the street.

My thumb rubs against the ragged metal edge of my house key as I walk up the path to the front door. Halfway there I veer right, toward the driveway where my car sits.

Eve's is missing. She's probably over at Ben's place.

It's wasteful, to drive the few blocks to the neighborhood where a lot of the athletes live. But it's dark and cold out and I want to get there before I have the chance to think through this rash decision.

I park on the street and climb out quickly. It's still raining but I wouldn't be shocked if it switches to snow soon. It feels plenty cold out for it.

This is the first time I've been to his house. I've avoided most parties thrown by the hockey team. The only one I've attended was held across the street, where the sophomore players live.

I press the doorbell and then shove my hands back into my pockets, bouncing on my toes in an attempt to stay warm.

It swings open a few seconds later. Conor is standing there, wearing the same outfit as he was at the Mexican restaurant and a surprised expression. "What are you doing here?"

"Can I come in?"

I don't wait for an answer, just step forward so he has the choice to accommodate me or have our bodies collide.

He moves.

I glance around the front hall. His house is bigger than mine. And cleaner than I'd expect, considering three hockey players live here.

The slam of the door closing interrupts my perusal.

I follow Conor into the kitchen. There's a wooden table with an open laptop and a plate that has the remnants of a burrito on it. No sign of anyone else.

"Where are Hunter and Aidan?" I ask.

Conor walks over to the kitchen table, closing his laptop. "They went out. I didn't feel like it."

He takes the final bite of his food, then carries the plate over to the sink. Rinses it and places it in the dishwasher, then heads for the fridge and pulls a sports drink out.

"You're here…alone?"

"Yeah." He caps the plastic bottle, then turns to face me. "How was your date?"

Absolutely nothing on his face gives me an indication of whether he cares what the answer will be.

"Great."

He nods. "You've got quite the roster of guys rotating, huh?"

"Don't be an asshole," I snap.

"What are you doing here, Harlow?" The question is quiet and serious.

"I wanted to know if we're back to ignoring each other. If we are, fine. I just need to know so I can plan accordingly the next time you show up somewhere."

"You wanted me to crash your date? It looked like you were having fun."

"It didn't seem like you even noticed I was there."

Conor studies me. "I'm…confused."

"Forget it." I shake my head. I'm confused too. Confused why I'm here. Confused why I care so much when it comes to anything involving him. "Delete my number, okay? I won't bother you anymore. Good luck with hockey. Maybe I'll make it to a game."

He sets the Gatorade down and strides toward me. "Wait, hold up. I'll still help you with training, when I can. I jog most mornings anyway."

"That's not necessary. I'll just walk the marathon if I have to."

Conor shakes his head. "What is it with you and this damn marathon? Just drop out of it, Harlow."

"I *can't*."

"*Why?*"

"Because it's being run in my hometown in memory of my parents."

Conor exhales. "Why didn't you just tell me that?"

"I'm sick of people feeling sorry for me. I didn't want your help because I'm an orphan and you pitied me."

"That wouldn't be why I helped you."

"Well, up until you came over to me in that kitchen, I didn't think you'd help me with anything for any reason."

"You don't think that now?" he asks.

I shake my head. "No."

His nod is slow. "Let me look at my schedule for this week, okay? We've got a dryland session tomorrow afternoon but I could probably—"

"No. I mean it. Thank you, but I've got it from here."

Conor runs a hand through his hair, ruffling the dark strands. His shirt lifts an inch, flashing me a very distracting view. "What the hell, Hayes? You show up here mad I'm not training you and now—"

"That's not why I was mad. I was mad because you ignored me earlier, and I thought we were past all that."

"You were out with another guy! You wanted me to interrogate him or something?"

"No, I wanted you to say 'Hi, Harlow,' and keep walking."

His exhale is exasperated. "Fine. The next time I see you out with him, I'll say 'Hi, Harlow,' and keep walking. Okay?"

"I'm not going out with him again."

"Why not?"

"I'm just not. I'll see you later."

I turn to head back into the hall—to leave—but Conor's reflexes are way faster than mine. He grabs my arm, holding me in place.

"I want to help you, Harlow. And it's not pity, but especially now that I know…" He swallows. "Let me help you train. Please."

"It's a bad idea."

Conor is still holding my arm, which I don't think he's aware of but I certainly am. I can feel his touch, even through the layers of down. "What's a bad idea?"

"Us spending time together."

"Why? Because of the Garrisons?"

I shake my head, although it's certainly a complication. Landon would lose his shit if he knew I was standing in Conor Hart's kitchen right now.

"Then what?"

"Because…" *I like you. I like you more than I've ever liked a guy, and that's terrifying.* "Because I want to have sex with you."

Once it's out, I can't take it back. And I'm not sure if it's better or worse than admitting my crush.

Conor's shocked reaction is *almost* worth the mortifying realization I said that to him.

His eyes widen and his eyebrows fly upward. "Are you drunk?"

I sigh. "Unfortunately not. Maybe when I get home. I think Eve has a bottle of vodka in the freezer."

I pull my arm away and take a step back.

"I don't do girlfriends," Conor says.

I nod. "You don't have to explain—"

"I'm not. I'm clarifying. You're good with just sex?"

I stare at him, feeling my heart rate start to pick up. It almost sounds like he's…considering it?

"I'm good with just sex."

He kisses me.

It's like downing a shot of espresso. Jumping into a cold pool.

A shock to my system I'm not sure I'll ever recover from.

And I know, as Conor kisses me with a skill that's literally stealing my breath, that this is a *really* bad idea.

Turns out, some bad ideas feel really good.

CHAPTER EIGHT

CONOR

I have no idea how I ended up here.

I resolved to stay far away from Harlow Hayes. And it wasn't just a *Yeah, I should probably do that*. More of a firm *Definitely do that.*

I was within a minute of being late to Monday's practice after meeting her at the running track. I'm in the thick of midterms—I had two exams this week and have a ten-page paper due on Tuesday. The team is still undefeated and I'm determined to keep it that way.

A hot redhead is not a distraction I need.

But somehow, she's currently straddling my erection and pulling her top off.

Harlow flings it away so it joins my joggers and her jacket on the floor. The bra she's wearing is flimsy and lacy, doing more to display her boobs than to cover them. I can see the dusky circle surrounding her nipple.

And, yeah, there's no way this isn't going to happen. We're far past the point of no return.

I'm going to fuck the one girl I told myself I would never so much as talk to.

She's my half-brother's best friend.

The girl my father sees as a daughter and knows better than me, his biological child.

Right now, as she's pressed up against me, I can't see her like that. The lace of her bra rubs against my chest, and there's none of the repulsion my body is supposed to produce. Stopped producing the first time I talked to her. There's just lust and heat and hunger. I'm *painfully* aroused.

I'm not the only one.

Harlow is kissing me like she needs me more than oxygen. Like she's desperate for me. It doesn't feel like a third kiss or a fourth kiss or however many times it's been. We made out in the kitchen for a while before coming up here. Even then, there was no awkwardness or unfamiliarity.

Her lips move to my neck and her tongue comes into play, and *holy shit*, am I having trouble thinking straight right now.

Harlow slips her fingers beneath the hem of my Henley and ghosts them along the strip of skin just above the waist-band of my boxer briefs. She swivels her hips, the denim of her jeans a rough scrape I can feel through the cotton I'm wearing. Her tits bounce with every movement, slowly driving me insane.

I reach behind her and unsnap her bra, finally getting my first look at her bare breasts. She shivers as I slide my hands over her ribs to cup them. Moans, when I suck her left nipple into my mouth and then release it with a wet *pop*.

Harlow groans my name, grinding her pussy against me even harder. At this rate, there's a chance I'll come before she's even naked.

"Off," she says, tugging at my shirt.

I pull away to yank it off and toss the balled cotton away.

I've caught glimpses of interest on her face. This is the first time I'm seeing the blatant attraction she just admitted to.

"Goddamnit," she mutters, her hungry gaze roaming over my chest and then down to my abs.

I chuckle, then kiss her. She's so responsive—so eager. We both groan as her boobs brush against my chest. Her nails scrape my shoulders and down my chest, the slight sting of pain driving my desire higher. Driving it to the point it's a legitimate concern that I might come in my boxer briefs instead of the wet heat she's torturing me with.

I grab her hips and flip her off of me, my patience wearing down to nothing. Harlow smirks, her hair a red wave spread across my navy sheets. I unbutton and unzip her jeans, tugging the denim down until all she's wearing is a sheer thong that matches her bra. It's hot, until I remember she was on a date earlier and probably wore it for him.

The hot pulse of annoyance is unfamiliar.

She's not mine, I remind myself. She can date or hook up with whoever she wants.

Her thong is wet, when I pull it off. Then Harlow is totally naked beneath me, and I just…stare.

Looking at her body makes me feel like a kid in a candy shop. There's too much I want to touch. To taste.

I never thought I'd get to see her like this.

"What, you've never seen a naked girl before?" Harlow teases.

Her voice is light. Unaffected. But I catch the thread of uncertainty.

I can tell she's nervous. I turned on a lamp when we came upstairs, so I can see the subtle definition of goose bumps on her skin. Can see the fluttering of the pulse in the hollow of her throat.

"I've never seen *you* naked before, no."

My eyes can't decide where to look. And my dick is so hard that it's worked its way out of the waistband of my boxer briefs. That's where Harlow's gaze is focused. I catch the bob of her throat as she swallows.

Her hand moves from her hair, sliding down her body and straight toward her exposed cunt.

"Should I just take care of things myself—"

She moans, back arching as I beat her there and push one finger inside of her. She's totally soaked, dripping onto my hand.

"This what you wanted, Hayes?"

Another moan, her breath hitching as I add a second finger, stretching her a little. *Fuck*, she's tight. Her legs are spread wide, offering an obscene view of her bare pussy.

"Guess I'll never know if you're a real redhead, huh?"

Harlow rolls her eyes. "Get some original lines, Hart. I've heard that one before."

Based on our talk at the track, I assumed that she wasn't a virgin. But it bothers me in a way I've never experienced before, hearing her mention other guys seeing her like this while she's naked in front of me.

Competitiveness that's only ever appeared on the ice sparks to life. Like hell is she going to find anything else to *compare* me to.

"That guy you were with earlier? Did you let him touch you like this?"

Anger sparks in her green eyes. "None of your fucking business."

"Did he get you this wet? Or is this all for me, Hayes?"

I'm barely aware of the shit spilling out of my mouth. I'm so turned on it's ridiculous. And I'm…jealous. I finally identify the ugliness. I've experienced it before, but never because a girl was involved.

"Fuck you," she spits.

I grin. "You're going to. You can hate me all you want, but you want my cock, don't you?"

I pull my fingers out and crawl over her, lining our bodies up so that she's humping my dick instead. She soaks my boxer briefs immediately. Then, in a move I'm not expecting, she hooks her feet into the elastic waistband and tugs them down. Not all the way, just enough for them to be ineffective.

Nothing has felt better than the tip of my cock slipping into tight, wet heat. I've never let it get this far with a girl without putting on a condom. It's torture, pulling out when all I want to do is thrust deeper.

I get rid of my boxer briefs and reach over to my bedside table, fumbling with the handle of the drawer as I yank it open. Feel around until I find the box of condoms. I sit back, tearing the foil wrapper open with my teeth and rolling it on as fast as physically possible. My balls are drawn up tight and throbbing, desperate for release.

And then I'm over her, pressed against her entrance with no intention of pulling out this time.

But I *pause*, when I never have before.

Everything that's happened between us—the connection we didn't choose and all the unexpected interactions since—disappears. There's just this moment, suspended in time. I told myself it wouldn't matter when we were downstairs. I was stunned at first, then rationalized that sex with Harlow wouldn't be any different than with another girl.

I was wrong.

All the anger is gone from Harlow's expression. She studies mine, her teeth sinking into her bottom lip and chasing away the pink.

"You sure?" My voice is low, my entire body tensed with restraint.

"I'm sure."

"Say it, then. Tell me how badly you want my cock."

I'm lined up to enter her perfectly, but I don't. Not yet. I rub the tip of my penis along her soaked slit, focused on every shift of her face. Her chest heaves and her hands clench into fists. Her mouth stays shut, defiant.

I swore this would never happen between us. I'm guessing Harlow was sure of the same. And if we're going to do this, I need her to acknowledge that. Assure me that this isn't a moment of insanity. That she wants it badly enough it's inevitable.

I push into her an inch, then pull out. Harlow swears, lifting her hips as she tries to keep me inside of her.

Anticipation buzzes in the air between us, the same electricity I experience just before stepping onto the ice.

"Tell me, Hayes. Tell me how badly you want me to fill this pretty pussy. How much you need to get fucked."

I need her to fold *now*, before I do. I'm hard enough to hammer nails with my dick.

"Isn't your ego big enough?"

"*Say it*, Harlow." I slap her clit with my dick, and her moan is the sexiest sound I've ever heard.

It echoes in my head as she spreads her legs as wide as possible. "I want your cock, Conor. More than I've ever wanted anything. So badly I'm having trouble breathing. Is that what you—"

Harlow cries out when I push into her. She's wet enough the first few inches are easy. Then, I hit resistance. I groan at the feel of her squeezing me, slick and hot and tight as a fist. Feeling her spread around me, struggling to accommodate my size.

"Still breathing?" I ask.

"If you *force* me to talk dirty to you, you can't make fun of me for it."

I rock forward another inch. She's so tight and I'm way too worked up.

"You're in, right?"

I grit my teeth as ribbons of heat race up my spine. "Nope."

My hand moves to just above where I'm entering her, stimulating her clit. She convulses around me, relaxing enough for me to press into her the final few inches.

"Too much. Way, way too much."

She squirms beneath me as I slide all the way in for the first time, her pussy pulsing in protest.

"You're taking me, Hayes. *Fuck*, look at you taking me so well."

I pull out, grind her pelvis against my dick, and then thrust back inside of her. There's no resistance this time. She's scooting toward me, so I slip in faster and deeper.

"You good?"

Her green eyes are hooded and heated. "So, *so* good."

Any restraint is long gone. I fuck her with rapid, brutal strokes, angling my hips to push into her even deeper, the slap of our skin sliding together the only sound in the room aside from the sounds we're both making. Pounding into her so hard it seems like there will be a permanent indentation left on the mattress.

Harlow moans my name over and over again, wrapping the long legs I've spent hours—pretty much every one I've spent with her—admiring. Trying to trap me in place the same way her pussy is fisting my cock.

I feel it, when she starts to come. She tightens around me even more, which I didn't think was possible. Squeezes me until I can't hold back any longer. Everything fades to black as blinding pleasure hits me hard and fast. It's the sweetest relief. I come with a loud grunt, my cock jerking as I spill into the condom over and over again.

I should feel satisfied right now. I just experienced the best orgasm of my life. But staring down at Harlow—the content smile on her face, the way she's sprawled across my bed like she's too well-fucked to move—all I can think about is how badly I want this to happen all over again.

And out of all the unexpected things that happened tonight—that's the most shocking.

CHAPTER NINE

HARLOW

I had sex with Conor Hart, is my first thought when I wake up.
I had sex with Conor Hart.

I had sex with Conor Hart.

What the *actual fuck* was I thinking? I had sex with Conor Hart.

The hottest sexual encounter of my life—by far—was not supposed to be with him.

I can still feel him between my legs. Hear echoes of his dirty words. Taste him in my mouth. Smell him on my skin.

Landon's half-brother. Hugh's son.

Admitting my attraction to him was only supposed to ever happen in my head. Him overlooking my current home address and agreeing to it was not supposed to happen. But at the very least, sex was supposed to extinguish the heat between us. One of those experiences you overhype in your mind but then the reality falls short.

No such luck.

I glance at the clock on his bedside table. Then at Conor asleep next to me, only moving my neck and keeping the rest of my body completely still so I don't risk waking him up. I have fifteen minutes before I need to leave for the marina. I usually set an alarm but forgot to last night for obvious reasons. I guess my body is trained to wake up early on Saturdays by now. Or maybe it's some self-preservation instinct, to get myself out of this uncomfortable situation.

I've never slept in the same bed as a guy before.

And it's weird, having someone asleep beside me.

But that strangeness is eclipsed by the fact it's *Conor Hart*. He takes up more than half the bed, his presence impossible to ignore.

I had sex with Conor Hart.

No matter how many times I say it in my head, it never sounds normal.

I wanted it. I *told him* I wanted it.

He wasn't supposed to say yes.

His hatred was supposed to be stronger than mine. And his willpower. Every girl on this campus has a crush on him. It's not like I was his one and only option for getting laid last night.

I can make out the shape of his huge cock beneath the thin sheet. A traitorous throb starts pulsing between my thighs, reminding me how he felt inside of me.

All I'm wearing is one of his T-shirts. He offered it to me, and I accepted like some sex-addled idiot. Then, I also said yes when he suggested we watch a movie. Halfway though, his fingers crept under the hem of my—his—shirt, and it somehow happened again.

This is so, *so* bad.

For a whole lot of reasons, but especially that I *still* want it to happen again. Twice wasn't enough.

I'm getting wet just looking at him. All messy hair and muscles, with a peaceful expression I've never seen him wear when awake. He's usually intense and focused, not relaxed. There's a purplish mark on his collarbone and some red scratches on his chest that must be from me.

Another hot flash. Conor is like a space heater, hot in every sense of the word.

I shift an inch to the right, closer to the side of the mattress. I'm not sure at what point I fell asleep, but it wasn't a deliberate choice to spend the night here. I've never navigated a morning after situation and I have no idea how to.

I don't regret last night, but I'm worried he will.

The sooner I get out of this bed, the sooner I can avoid him for the rest of my life. We don't share any of the same classes or the same friends. We can easily go back to living separate lives, just like we did for three plus years. There are only seven months until graduation.

A few more inches, and I'm almost off the mattress. I decide to just grab my clothes off the floor and get dressed in the hall-way. I can leave his shirt…somewhere.

"Sneaking out?"

My heart tries to leap out of my chest as my entire body jolts with surprise. I glance over at him, my pulse racing.

Conor's gray-blue eyes are wide open and staring straight at me. His expression is smooth, no sign of emotion. And his voice is too raspy with sleep for me to detect any tone.

I decide to be honest. "Yes."

There's no reaction to that answer.

Then he sits up, tossing the navy sheet off. "I'll walk you out."

I swallow as soon as his dick is revealed. He's not fully hard, and it's still impressive. I can't believe *that* fit inside me.

"You don't have to do that," I manage to say. Not moving, mesmerized by the sight of his naked body. It's just…a lot. I saw it last night, but I was horny and nervous. The morning light creeping in through the window is a different sort of display.

Conor follows the direction of my gaze. Smirks. And then wraps a hand around his growing erection, stroking himself.

"See something you like, Hayes?"

God, I need a cold shower. Air conditioning. I don't care that it's November. Warmth is creeping across my skin like the lick of a flame, burning away all my inhibitions and any common sense.

He's fully hard now, his cock jutting up toward his abs proudly. The flared tip is flushed purple, leaking pre-cum. My thighs clench together beneath his shirt, the throbbing pulse becoming more persistent.

"Yeah. I'm a fan," I say.

It's not like he doesn't know I'm attracted to him, after last night.

I don't think Conor was expecting me to answer him. There's a flash of surprise, followed by heat. The sheet covering me gets yanked down, leaving me in just his shirt. His eyes darken even more when he sees how tightly my thighs are pressed together.

"Are you sore?" His voice is the consistency of gravel, low and deep.

I manage a "Yes."

It's a good sore. A satisfied sore. A *stretched* sore.

But I won't be able to move for a while without remembering last night.

He's stopped stroking himself, his warm palm landing on my left calf instead. His hand moves higher and higher, forcing my legs to part. I gasp when cool air hits the wetness leaking out of me.

"Holy fuck. You're soaked." There's the thick rasp of lust in Conor's voice. And a note of pride too, knowing he's the reason.

His thumb rubs tiny circles around my pelvic bone, each

sweep creeping closer to the spot where I'm swollen and aching for him.

Then his hand moves away. I whimper. Conor grins, reading the disappointment on my face. Then he's shifting, down, his hands cupping beneath my thighs and spreading them wide. His lips land on the same spot where his thumb just was, and I realize what's happening.

"You don't have to do that."

"Stop saying that, Hayes. I don't do shit I don't want to do."

The first swipe of his tongue is electric. I writhe beneath him, trying to get closer or away, I'm not sure.

It's *too much*, just like when he filled me last night, an undiluted stream of pleasure stimulating everything. Overwhelming everything. My fingers push into his hair, fisting and pulling at the dark strands in an attempt to release some of the pressure rapidly building.

Conor groans around my clit, the vibration reverberating everywhere. His arm slides beneath my hips to bring me closer to his sinful mouth, his tongue tracing my entire slit before slipping inside of me.

I'm boneless, thoughtless. All I'm aware of is him, grinding against his face shamelessly. I've never experienced anything like this before. It's never *been* like this before.

And it's not just the sensation. It's *him*.

His dark head hovering between my open thighs. Knowing it's Conor's teeth grazing my clit, his tongue tasting me. Watching his hips move against the mattress and knowing he'd rather I was taking his dick than riding his face.

He's a *selfish ass* who's prioritizing my pleasure over his.

That realization sends me over the edge. My pussy clenches as I press harder against his talented mouth, using his body to chase release. My hands move to his upper back, probably leaving marks there too.

Conor doesn't seem to mind. His grip tightens on my waist, keeping me in place as his tongue continues moving against sensitized flesh. He doesn't pull away until my inner muscles stop pulsing.

I slump against the mattress, the remnants of pleasure humming throughout my entire body. It feels like I'm sinking into a cloud. Lost in a mindless haze.

Last night was incredible.

I didn't think it could get any better.

So bad, I tell myself. That's knowledge I didn't want to have.

"Show me your tits." It's a demand, more than a request.

I reach down and grab the hem of his shirt, pulling it up to my collarbone. Conor is on his knees now, fisting a painful-looking erection. It seems like my body should have run through all the arousal it's capable of producing by now. But, no. My breathing quickens, watching the muscles in his forearm bunch he strokes himself, getting off to the sight of my naked body. Staring at his hand stroking himself from the base of trimmed hair all the way to the wet tip.

Seconds later, hot ropes of cum spurt from his dick and splatter onto my chest. No guy has ever come on me before. I can only imagine what I look like right now. I can't figure out how me intending to sneak out ended up here—shirt pulled up like I'm flashing him, covered with his semen. Every time I'm around Conor, there's some crazy domino effect. One thing happens and then I'm looking back at a long line of decisions I don't remember making.

Conor grabs a couple of tissues and wipes his cum off me carefully.

"Sorry," he rasps. "Got a little carried away."

My chest tingles in every spot he just wiped, like there's an invisible brand tattooed to my skin.

"I didn't mind. It was hot."

His gaze is intense—too intense.

I look away, right at the clock.

"*Fuck*." My fifteen minutes to spare have turned into being five minutes late. I told Sam I'd be there today, so I'm going to hold the entire crew up.

I scramble out of bed, hunting around for my underwear. Putting them back on feels gross, but I don't have another option. I'll shower once I'm home later.

"What's wrong?" Conor asks.

"I have a…Saturday morning thingy," I say, focusing on the awkward shimmy slash jump I have to do to get these jeans on.

"A *Saturday morning thingy*? What does that mean? Church?"

I snort at that, pulling off his shirt so I can put my bra on. "I think most religious ceremonies are on Sundays, but this sorta is my version of it, I guess."

A pause, then "Swimming?"

"No." I yank my shirt on, grab my jacket, and then turn around to face him. He's put on boxer briefs, which is slightly less distracting. "I—um, I'm going fishing."

"What? *Why?*"

"I like looking out at the ocean," I admit. "It's my ice rink, I guess."

Conor studies me for a second, then asks, "Can I come?"

I'm…stunned. "What? Why?"

He rolls his eyes, walking over to his dresser and opening a drawer. "Okay, never mind. Let me just get dressed, I'll walk you out."

"Is there a bathroom up here I can use?" I ask.

"Yeah, end of the hall. Just…Aidan and Hunter are probably home. Asleep, I mean. But home."

"Got it."

I slip out into the hallway, passing a closed door before I reach a bathroom. It's bigger than mine, the floor a white tile that's surprisingly clean. I pee, wash my hands, and then use the same soap to wash my face. Desperate times. I pat my face dry with the towel on the rack and then head back into the hallway.

Conor is waiting at the top of the stairs, wearing a matching pair of sweats that both have the *Holt Hockey* logo on them. I pull my jacket on as I walk, tired of carrying it around.

"All set?" he asks.

I pull in a deep breath. "If you still want to come, you can."

He studies me. "You sure?"

My face flushes, recalling the last time he asked me that. And my answer is the same. "I'm sure."

"Okay. Just let me grab my phone."

Conor disappears back into his bedroom.

I like that he left it, that he didn't presume I'd change my mind. Unfortunately, the general consensus ever since he approached me in that kitchen is that I like a lot of things about Conor. Too many things.

He's back a few seconds later, and we head downstairs silently.

It snowed overnight. A light dusting of white covers every-thing once we're outside. It's beautiful, glimmering in the muted morning light.

"I'll drive," I say. My car is parked on the street directly in front of his house, obvious for anyone to see. I'm anxious to move it.

"Works for me." Conor yawns.

"You sure you want to come?" I ask.

He—we—didn't get much sleep last night.

"I'm fine," he says.

"It'll be a few hours," I warn.

I'm not sure how to explain to Conor that I'm worried all the lines I drew around him are blurring, and that sharing this piece of myself I've never told anyone else about might erase them more.

"I want to come, Hayes."

"Okay." I head for my car, him right behind me.

―――――

Just as I feared, most of the slips are empty when I pull into the marina's parking lot.

I climb out of the car and rush toward the gangway. Conor keeps up with me easily, shoving his hands into the front pouch of his sweatshirt and looking around with interest as I hurry toward Sam's boat.

"I'm *so* sorry I'm late," I blurt when I reach it. "And I didn't have time to get coffee." I cast Sam an apologetic look.

He's not looking at me. None of the guys are looking at me. They're all focused on Conor.

"This is Conor. Is it okay if he joins us?"

"Of course," Sam replies. "The more the merrier."

I exhale. "Great." Grip the side of the boat and climb aboard.

Conor does the same, managing the move much more effortlessly than I did my first time aboard.

Sam holds a wrinkled hand out to him. "Samuel Prescott."

He's sizing Conor up the way a dad might, and there's a silly squeeze around my heart.

Conor shakes it. "Conor Hart."

Sam's eyes widen. "Huh. Well, how about that? You're having one hell of a season, son."

116

"The whole team is," Conor responds.

"He's being modest," I state, heading for my milk crate. Something I used to think he wasn't capable of.

"Put that together myself, Harlow," Sam says, looking amused.

The rest of the crew introduces themselves to Conor. Brent and his son Levi strike up an immediate conversation with him. Sam has to shout to stop socializing before we actually leave the dock.

Although it's both smaller and older than most of the fishing boats that head out from the marina each morning, the barnacle-covered hull parts the churning, salty water effortlessly. Timmy and Brent move about the deck, tying lines and dropping nets. Conor helps drag the nets out, chatting with Timmy the whole time. Sam steers us along; an easier job today than on most. It's turning into a brilliantly clear day, sunlight dazzling the surface of the sea and illuminating the snowy peaks of the mountains in the distance. It looks like a postcard.

I watch Conor with the crew for a few minutes, then focus back on the water. It usually takes about ten minutes until we're far enough from shore to spot a pod. But I pull my phone out just in case, opening the spreadsheet so I can note any sightings.

"Whatcha doing?"

I startle when I hear his voice right behind me. "Uh, I keep track of the sightings."

"Sightings of what?"

"Orcas. There are a few pods that live around here."

Conor looks at the water. "How often do you see them?"

"It depends on the time of year. Peak season is the summer months, which I'm never here for. But pretty regularly."

He takes the phone out of my hand, squinting at the notes. "Is this for an assignment?"

"No, just for me."

"That's cool." He hands my phone back to me, and our fingers brush. Even now, that he's touched me so much more intimately, my body reacts.

"If you're regretting coming, we're stuck out here for at least another hour."

The length of Sam's trips vary greatly. It depends what mood he's in, what the weather is like. Whether we see any pods.

"You're awfully worried I'll regret this, Hayes. Did the last person who came out with you fall overboard, or something?" he asks. "Should I have signed a waiver?"

I scoff. "No. I've never told anyone I do this, let alone brought them with me."

"Never?"

"I wasn't exactly thinking straight this morning." I try to make a joke, worried he'll read too much into it otherwise.

"Me neither. Hottest sex of my life, Hayes."

I still when he says it. Maybe it's a line. Maybe Conor has said that a lot, to a lot of girls.

But my gut says he hasn't.

I focus on the water, the same way he is. The mist that sometimes shrouds anything farther than a hundred feet is noticeably absent. The only limit to the scenery this morning is my eyesight. I try to focus on looking at everything I can, instead of at him. This has always been a place I can think, where distractions can't reach me.

Conor is *very* distracting.

Sudden motion catches my eye.

"So, what is the—*shit*!"

The curse is practically a shout. It took the black and white body breaching the surface for Conor to spot what I noticed a few seconds ago; three orcas are nearby. One just came up closer than

I was expecting. So close, a few droplets of salty water hit my cheeks.

"Holy…" Conor glances wildly to me, then back at the frothing water that's the only evidence of what just occurred. "That was…wow."

I nod eagerly. "Right?"

I'm thrilled by his reaction. By the awe and excitement on his face.

The ocean itself is a vast, powerful, fathomless force. Witnessing the animals who engineer that strength in streamlined speed is breathtaking. And it feels special, sharing this with him.

"You knew that was going to happen?"

"I saw a few dorsal fins, so I thought there was a chance."

"A little warning would have been nice, Harlow. Holy shit." Conor shakes his head a couple of times, but I notice he's keeping his gaze on the water, like he's reluctant to miss any more activity.

"Are they going to leap up again?" he asks.

"Not that group. They're already headed back around the island. Probably to meet up with the rest of their pod. See?" I point at the tall, black fins cutting through the water like sharp knives.

Conor squints. "Maybe?"

I pull my phone out and mark the sighting on my spreadsheet. This is a spot I've had good luck before. Since it's been a few weeks without any sightings, I'm excited. More for Conor than me, if I'm being honest. I'm happy he got to witness it.

"Not a bad show, eh?" Sam calls from the captain's chair.

I shake my head and grin.

We don't see any more whales, but it ends up being a good morning for fishing. All the boxes on board are filled by the time Sam steers his boat back into the marina.

Timmy jumps out from the hull when we reach the right slip and starts tying us to the metal cleats. Brent begins offloading the day's catch so it can be repacked in fresh ice and shipped off for sale.

"Thanks, Sam," I call out, climbing off the boat and waving. Conor is still talking with Brent. He heads my way a few seconds later, pausing next to Sam when he says something. Conor nods, then continues toward me. The rest of the guys call goodbyes this way as we walk along the shifting dock.

"What did Sam say to you?" I ask.

"He wished me good luck this season."

He's lying. I'm not sure how I know, but I do.

"Oh. That was nice."

"Yeah. He's a good guy." Conor glances at me. "How did you meet him?"

"I'd hang around here freshman year, trying to see orcas from the shore. He took pity on me one day, invited me out on his boat. I've been coming back every Saturday ever since."

He nods as we walk up the gangway and toward my car. The silence isn't uncomfortable. It feels more like we don't have to fill the quiet with unnecessary words.

Watching Conor fold his tall frame into my passenger seat is just as entertaining the second time as it was earlier this morning. I take more time to appreciate it now, since we're not in a rush.

"Shut up," he grumbles, as I make no attempt to hide my grin while he attempts to slide the chair back. It's already as far as it'll go.

"I didn't say anything," I tell him as I shift into reverse.

Just as I've pulled out of the parking lot, I get a call. *Landon Garrison* flashes across the screen display, and I freeze. I know Conor can see it. I feel the sudden tension humming in the air.

At some point, I forgot about the fact I'm best friends with the half-brother Conor doesn't speak to. Doesn't even acknowledge. It somehow became a secondary consideration. An uncomfortable connection I have to be *reminded* of, the way I'm being reminded right now.

I reject the call as fast as I can.

But the damage has already been done.

Now, the silence *is* uncomfortable.

A block from his house, Landon calls me again. Conor huffs an unamused laugh, resting his elbow on the car door and his head against the window. Literally leaning away from me.

I stop in front of Conor's, not sure what to say to him.

He speaks first. "I had fun. Thanks."

"For the fishing trip? Or the sex?"

A muscle in Conor's jaw jumps. "What do you want me to say, Harlow?"

"Not *thanks*."

Landon calls me for a third time, and I'm tempted to throw my phone out the window.

"Better get that," Conor says, opening the door and climbing out. "Seems like someone *really* needs to talk to you. And one of the guys might see you. That's why we took your car, right?"

He shuts the door without giving me a chance to answer, heading toward his house without glancing back once.

I smack the steering wheel with my palm, wince, and keep driving. Once I have my chaotic emotions somewhat under control, I call Landon back.

He answers on the first ring. "Hey."

"Hi."

"I've been trying to call you. Is everything okay?"

"Yeah, sorry. I was driving back home from the pool, and I think there's something wacky going on with my phone service. Your calls kept dropping."

I'm a *terrible* person. An *awful* friend.

"Huh. That is weird. You can hear me okay now?"

"Yup," I chirp. "Clear as a bell. What's up?"

"Well, I was letting you know that we booked a gig near Claremont two weeks from today. It's not a huge venue, but it's legit. Not a birthday party or an open mic. We're the openers."

"That's amazing, Landon! Congrats!"

"Are you free to come home for it? I know it's really close to Thanksgiving, so the timing isn't ideal. But we haven't hung out since August, and I know Mom and Dad would love to see you."

I hesitate, and I hate that I do. Because it's not because I have plans with Eve that weekend or an exam the next day. It's because of Conor, and my fear any progress we've made is being erased.

Landon has been there for me through everything. He's my oldest, closest friend. We grew up together, many of the happiest memories I have with my parents including him and his. He was there for me when I lost my entire immediate family, helping me pack up my life and move it into his parents'. Supporting him should be a no-brainer.

And what did I do this morning? I woke up in bed with his least favorite person on the planet.

I've never asked for details on Landon's relationship with Conor. His cutting comments about his half-brother have some-times made me uncomfortable, because an unbiased observer would probably say that Conor has better reasons to resent Landon. Landon ended up with two happily married parents. Conor didn't. Maybe it's some warped sibling rivalry I can't fully comprehend as an only child.

"Harlow?"

"Yeah, sorry. I was just trying to…think. I thought that maybe I'd promised Eve I'd do something with her, but that's the weekend before. I'll be there."

"Are you sure? If you've already got something going on, don't…"

"I'm sure. I'm excited to see you guys play!"

That's true, at least.

"Okay, great. I'll let Mom and Dad know." He hesitates. "Mom said she hasn't heard from you in a while. Everything okay?"

"Yeah, everything's great. Just been busy."

"Okay. Talk to you soon!"

"Bye, Landon."

I hang up the call, then stare at the outside of my house for a minute. It's not even ten a.m., and I feel like a whole day has passed.

When I walk inside Eve is snuggled up on the couch, eating a bowl of cereal. She scans my outfit—the same one I was wearing last night.

"Date went well?" She smirks.

I huff a laugh, shaking my head as I pull my jacket off. Eating dinner with Eric feels like a lifetime ago. "Uh, no. I mean, it was fine. He was nice. Dinner was nice. Everything was nice. But there was no spark. I think—hope he felt the same way. He took it pretty well when I said we should stick to being friends."

I know what question is coming next.

"If you weren't with Eric, where were you last night?"

I'm too tired—too confused—to lie.

"Having sex with Conor Hart."

Eve's mouth drops open. "Holy shit. Really?"

I nod.

"Oh my God."

I nod again.

"Oh my God," Eve repeats. "How was it?"

"Uh, good."

"You're blushing," she teases.

"Fine, it was really good. *Ridiculously* good. He's better at sex than hockey."

"How big is he?"

I snort. "Big."

Her nod is expected. "Yeah, I totally get that energy from him."

I roll my eyes. "Whatever. I need a shower."

"Does this mean he'll be showing up at our door more often?"

All I can see is his hunched shoulders, walking away.

"No. I think it was a one-time thing." *Two-time. Three-time*, if I count this morning.

"And you're good with that?"

"Of course. I don't *like* the guy."

I'm trying to convince myself, as much as Eve.

She nods, looking like she believes me. "Okay, okay. I was just asking. I mean, he's *Hartbreaker*, right?"

I scoff. "He's not going to break my heart. I need a shower, then some food. Want to go to Holey Moley for donuts?"

"Yeah, sounds good."

I nod, then head for the hallway.

"Oh, wait. One other thing, actually. Mary and I ran into Clayton Thomas last night."

"Okay…"

"I mentioned that you and Mary go bowling every Saturday night."

I raise both eyebrows. "Mary and I *don't* go bowling every Saturday night."

Eve offers me a sheepish smile. "Well…he wants to go with you two next weekend."

"What? Eve!"

"I know, I know. I'm sorry. Mary wasn't saying much and he

asked if you were coming to the party he was having that night and it just kinda snowballed from there. Random stuff started coming out and next thing I knew there was a *plan*."

"So, I'm supposed to, what? Chaperone their date?"

"Or double. At the time, I thought maybe you could bring Eric. Does he like sports?"

"No idea," I say. "It didn't come up."

And even if Eric was some bowling afficionado, I wouldn't drag him into this. It was one thing to go out with him with honorable intentions. But now that I know I'm not interested, I can't stomach doing that.

"Please?" Eve pleads. "Maybe Mary and Clayton are soulmates. And also, if they go out and hit it off, I won't have to hear about it anymore in class."

"Uh-huh. *Super* selfless of you," I state sarcastically. "I am not making any promises," I warn. "But I'll think about it, okay? Mostly how much you'll owe me for this."

Eve beams. "Okay."

I head for the bathroom to take a much-needed shower.

Wishing it will be as easy to remove Conor from my head as it'll be to wash him off my skin.

CHAPTER TEN

CONOR

I'm still half-asleep when I stumble into the weight room. I didn't mean to close my eyes earlier, but I did, and now I'm even drowsier than I was before my three-hour nap. I'm tired and irritated, in a grouchy mood in general.

I join the group of guys huddled around the whiteboard where Coach Zimmerman is scrawling out today's circuit. There are a couple of groans around the room when the guys get a good look at it, then start to lumber toward their assigned stations.

"Hey. You good?" Hunter asks, glancing over from his spot next to me.

"Yeah. Why?"

"You bailed last night—Phillips is pissed you didn't show up at Thomas's party, by the way—and then you were in your room most of the day. That's why."

"I felt a little stuffed up yesterday. Just needed to lie low for twenty-four hours. Rest up a bit."

Hunter looks even more concerned, and I feel like shit for lying to him. I'm not sure how he'd react to knowing I was with Harlow last night after his warnings to stay focused. It's not like

I've been celibate during previous seasons. But I've also never been distracted the way Harlow affects me before.

I recognized that, and that's why last night was never supposed to happen. But it did, and I don't want to talk about it.

"I'm fine," I say, then glance at the whiteboard and head for an open barbell. I cover up another yawn as I load up the end with plates.

If I'd woken up with enough time to spare, I would've stopped for a coffee.

Aidan comes over to me as I'm clamping the collars on each end of the bar. "Hart! Why didn't you show up last night? I texted you five times about Thomas's party."

"I didn't see them," I reply truthfully.

"Man, there's commitment, and then there's crazy. You are rapidly heading toward the second category. Have some fun, all right?"

I'm half-tempted to tell Aidan the truth: that I missed the party because I was busy having the best sex of my life. Just to get him off my back about being too committed to hockey. But Aidan has a huge mouth. If I tell him, the entire team—hell, the entire school—will probably hear about it.

And it feels...cheap, to diminish last night to proof I don't think about hockey all the time.

"I have plenty of fun, Phillips," I reply. "Worry about your points, and let me worry about my social life, okay?"

"Plenty of fun? Good one, Hart."

"This is my shot, Phillips," I remind him.

He's wrong that I'm consumed by nothing but hockey, but he's right that I'm focused on it.

I'm worried some guys on the team have gotten complacent about winning. Easier to do than you'd think, when you're coasting on an undefeated season. When you're expecting to win.

But with each victory, we're creeping closer to the playoffs. Even at the lowest Division level, that means the pressure and the expectations will ratchet up.

I can't be the only one prepared for it to. That's what has happened for the past three seasons.

"Yeah, I know," Aidan replies, losing his smirk. "Second line will be ready. I promise."

"Great." I lie down on the bench and lift the barbell.

I hate lifting weights. I get it's a necessary part of building muscle and know that strength will translate on the ice. But I'd much prefer to be running or out on the ice than lifting and lowering a weighted bar repeatedly. There's nothing to do except study the cracked plaster ceiling of the weight room as I coax my muscles to keep cooperating, even after they begin to tremble.

The entire weight-training circuit takes about an hour, and then we move to the film room to watch some tape on our next opponents.

Calling it a film room is a misnomer. Unlike at schools that are generous with their athletic budgets and have a robust one to begin with, ours is bare bones. Reminiscent of a middle school physical education classroom. Scuffed linoleum, walls that were once painted white but veered gray a long time ago, and metal folding chairs that squeak when you sit in them. There's a whiteboard that lost its ability to be wiped clean. Faded swipes of black and blue marker mar the surface, adding squiggly lines to the video that's being projected up on the screen.

Coach Keller's strategy has always leaned heavily on watching film. I know players—and other coaches—who prefer to work on individual skills than spy on opponents. I suppose there is a mental component to it. Watching a superior team can be demoralizing. But anticipating other players' moves has always been a strength of mine. It's far easier to do that when I have a good sense of their playing style before stepping onto the ice.

Weekend practices can be a crapshoot. Filled with distractions and grumbles. I'm impressed there aren't any mutters or time checks throughout the entire film session. Or when Coach announces that we'll have ice time at eight tonight because of a flu going around that's affecting half the Somerville Sharks.

I'm impressed by the guys' composure. Despite my dedicated pursuit of it, I'm under no illusions a championship is a safe bet. Confidence in my teammates, in not only their skill but also their commitment, will go a long way.

"Hart. Got a minute?" Coach asks as the rest of the guys shuffle out of the darkened room.

"Yeah, sure."

I walk up to where he's fiddling with the projector.

"What's up, Coach?"

"Been getting a few calls about you, Hart."

My heart leaps. "You have?"

"Yup," he confirms. "No such thing as a guarantee in sports, but you're in a good spot. You're leading the charge on one hell of a streak."

I blow out a breath. "What if that streak ends?"

It's a growing fear, exacerbated by each added mark to the W column, appearing every time I suit up for a game. I step onto the ice worried we'll lose, instead of hoping we'll win.

"Then it ends. I'm the damn coach, Hart. My job is to make sure we're the team with more goals at the end of the game. Yours is to be the best center you can be. Don't think I haven't noticed how you've stepped us as captain, this season especially." He points toward the locker room. "Those guys in there? They'd follow you over a damn cliff. I've never seen a more determined team. If it were possible to win a championship by wanting it the most, there would already be a new banner in that arena. You stay focused, keep doing what you're doing, and let me worry about the scoreboard. We're still a way off from losing a game meaning the end of the season. If it happens, we'll work harder to win the next one."

I nod. "Okay. Thanks."

"Get out of here," he tells me. "I'll see you at eight."

"See you later, Coach."

Coach Keller nods before he turns back to shutting off the projector. His phone rings and he pulls it out, saying "Hi, honey" before I have a chance to leave the room. I know nothing about Coach's home life. If he's married or has any kids. He's always been a closed book when it comes to anything not related to hockey. A lot like me, I guess.

I head into the locker room. Most of the guys are already gone, probably rushing to eat dinner or finish homework before our evening skate. Aidan is sitting on the bench tying his sneakers. Hunter and Robby are talking about a paper in one of their shared business classes.

I pull off my sweaty shirt, deciding not to bother showering. I'll just have to take another one later, after our skate.

Aidan glances at me, then does a double take. "*Goddamn*, Hart. Did you lose a wrestling match with a cougar?"

Robby and Hunter both look this way.

I swear—loudly—in my head.

I don't need to look down to know what they're all seeing. I noticed the marks on my chest when I changed before coming here. Pretty sure there are some on my back too.

"I thought you stayed in last night," Hunter says accusingly.

"I did. I just wasn't alone." I pull a clean shirt out of my bag and quickly yank it on.

"I was wondering why there was a car out on the street," Aidan says. "Was it Sarah?"

"Yeah," I reply, then clench my jaw. I didn't mean to give Aidan a name. I'm just trying to escape this conversation as quickly as possible.

"Well, good for you, Hart. See you guys at home." Aidan stands, grabs his bag, and leaves.

Robby is right behind him.

Hunter stays. "You weren't with Sarah Clark last night. I accidentally walked in on her with some other guy at the party. Wanna lie to me a third time?"

I exhale. "I just agreed with Aidan so he'd stop asking questions. None of his business who I sleep with. It's not yours either."

"It was Harlow Hayes, wasn't it?"

I zip my bag up and turn to face him. "What the fuck did I just say, Morgan? Do you have a thing for her, just like Williams and half the team?"

"No, I don't. But that would bother you, if I did, wouldn't it?" Hunter shakes his head and scoffs. "What the hell is with you and this chick? You hate her for years, now you're screwing her?"

"What do you care?" I snap.

"I care about *you*, Conor. I want to buy your jersey and tell every person I meet that my best friend plays hockey professionally. You deserve it. You work harder than anyone I know. And we're so close. *You're* so close. Just wait until the end of the season, if you're going to get involved with her. Don't tell me it isn't affecting you. You were like a zombie today. The whole team noticed. And if you don't care about screwing up your own future, think about them. We're all busting our asses, trying to get you your shot. You wanna tell the guys you were too busy getting laid to focus on winning?"

He walks out without giving me a chance to say anything. Don't know what I would have responded, anyway. Hunter's disappointment is like a heavy weight in the locker room, even once he's gone. He's the most even-keeled, level-headed guy I know. It takes a lot for him to get worked up, to stick his nose into someone else's business.

My phone buzzes in my pocket. I pull it out to see a text from my mom, asking how I am and saying she'll call me before her shift tomorrow. I respond, letting her know that I'm fine and I'll talk to her soon.

Then I stare at my messages. I've never texted Harlow, but I have her number. And I've been considering using it all day, apologizing for how we left things this morning. For walking away.

We're all busting our asses, trying to get you your shot. You wanna tell the guys you were too busy getting laid to focus on winning?

I shove the phone into my pocket and leave the locker room, telling myself it's for the best.

CHAPTER ELEVEN

HARLOW

Five, four, three, two, one.

I count down the strokes in my head, then somersault underwater, pushing away from the rough edge of the pool's wall. Kick until my lungs are screaming for air, breaking the surface and then starting freestyle.

I swim ten more laps before stopping. Glance at the clock, confirming I've been in here for over an hour.

My muscles are sore, shaking with exhaustion as I heave myself out of the pool and head into the locker room. I slept in this morning, exhausted from yesterday, then headed to the library first to get some work done. Ended up spending most of the day there and then came here to swim before leaving campus.

The locker room is empty, so I take a shower. Eve has a major project for her painting class due tomorrow. She told me this morning she'll be home late. I might as well grab some dinner while I'm out. And, according to Eve, the less time I let chlorine sit in my hair, the better.

After I shower and dress in leggings and a cozy sweater, I leave the pool building. Cold air chills my wet hair, making me shiver as I rush toward my car. Yesterday's dusting of snow is already gone, but it feels freezing out.

Once I'm in my car, I deliberate for a few minutes.

I could get food from Gaffney's or stop at the pizza place downtown. I decide to head to the Mexican place Eric took me to on Friday night. The food was amazing, and I'm in the mood for a longer drive. All my schoolwork is done and all that's waiting for me at home is an empty house. I turn up the fan in hopes my hair will dry faster and blast the music.

When I step into the tiny restaurant, I'm immediately greeted by the smell of spices and citrus. I glance around at the cheerful, colorful surroundings. After sitting in the library all day and then swimming, it's kind of a sensory overload.

They're busier than they were on Friday night. All the tables are occupied. Two girls are ordering at the counter. I get into line behind them, scanning the menu. I'm undecided on whether I should get the fish tacos again or try something different.

I'm distracted from deciding by the girl closest to me continually glancing in this direction. I don't recognize her, so I doubt she's looking at me.

"Hayes."

I freeze. Only one person calls me that. Plus, I recognize his voice.

Running into Conor here did not occur to me as a possibility when I decided to grab food. He was just here on Friday night. So was I, I guess.

"Hart," I reply coolly. It's a stark contrast to my body temperature, which has skyrocketed.

"Good weekend?" he asks.

"Nothing memorable."

When I finally glance over at him, the corners of Conor's lips are tipped upward with amusement. Lips that have been on mine.

Lips that have been all over my body. And it was *very* memorable, but it no longer feels acceptable to admit that.

"That's too bad."

"Yup."

The girls ahead of me finish ordering, and it's my turn. I decide on a chicken burrito. Conor orders a beef one.

I'm worried he might try to have more of a conversation while we wait for our food. Disappointed when he doesn't. He just scrolls on his phone, ignoring the two girls whispering about him, until his food is ready. They ran out of chicken, so my order got delayed. He doesn't even look at me as he takes his food and leaves, and I decide that's just fine. He acknowledged me, at least, and at one point that was all I wanted from him.

My number gets called and I go up to the cash register, pulling out my credit card.

"It's been paid for, miss. Have a good night." The woman pushes the paper box with my dinner in it toward me.

I stand, stupefied, until I realize I'm holding up the line.

I thank her and then head for the door. There still aren't any tables available and I'd rather eat on my couch anyway.

Conor's waiting outside.

My steps stutter as soon as I spot him standing by the curb, but I try to hide the reaction. My grip tightens on the box as I approach him slowly, deliberating about what to say.

"Thanks," is what I settle on, nodding toward the food I'm carrying.

A wry smile appears. "Thought you weren't a fan of that word."

I suck in a breath. "I wasn't sure if we were talking about…that."

His nod is slow. "I'm sorry about yesterday morning. I shouldn't have reacted that way."

"It's fine."

"No, it's not. I just…" He exhales. "I knew that you're friends with him. I didn't *know*, though. And it caught me off guard. Does that make any sense?"

"Yeah, it does."

It's easy—too easy—to not think about complications when I'm around Conor. To remember there are *reasons* we avoided each other for the past three years.

"Do you have practice tonight?" I ask.

"No. We usually have Sundays off."

I pull in a deep breath. "I spent all day in the library catching up on homework and Eve has an art thing to do tonight. My plan was to watch television and eat this on this couch. If you're, you know, bored."

"Yeah, okay."

"Yeah?" My heart leaps, and I tell it to calm the fuck down.

He nods. "I'll see you at your place."

———

Conor pulls into the driveway right behind me. He literally followed me here, his headlights twin beacons in the rearview mirror every time I glanced at it.

I grab my dinner and my backpack off the passenger seat and climb out into the cold night air.

"Wasn't sure we'd make it here by morning," Conor teases as he steps out of his SUV.

I roll my eyes. I know I'm a slow driver; plenty of people have told me so before. The only downside to living in Somerville is that driving is often required. I've always found it stressful. And my parents died in a car accident, so there's that.

I unlock the front door, glancing at Conor as we step inside. He looks around curiously.

The living room is messy. I drop my backpack and set down my food, kicking off my rain boots so I can straighten the pillows and fold the blanket on the couch. The pile of Eve's sketching pads gets moved to the table in the corner instead of the coffee table.

"You don't have to do that." Conor has already taken off his shoes and is shrugging out of his *Holt Hockey* jacket.

"That's my line," I say.

He smirks, walking over to the couch with his food and sitting down. "We talking about that?"

"I asked you first."

"I don't want to pretend it didn't happen, if that's what you're asking." He opens the box and starts unwrapping the foil around his burrito.

The smell makes my stomach rumble. I give up on cleaning—it's not like I'm going to pull out the vacuum—and grab my own dinner before sitting down beside him.

I'm careful to leave a foot of space between us.

I'm rarely sure where I stand with Conor. He's hot and cold. Teasing and serious. Understanding and irrational. I get some of his reactions and motivations. Others confuse me. Why did he walk away yesterday but is here tonight? Did he just need time to cool off? Has he thought about me, the way I puzzle over him?

All questions I'm not brave enough to ask.

I hand him the remote, lean back against the cushions with my burrito, and tell him "Your choice."

"I figured we'd be watching *Legally Blonde*."

I snort. "You've already seen it. Allegedly."

"*Allegedly*? Did you forget about the dance routine I performed for you? Because I'll do it again, Hayes."

"Just pick a movie, Hart."

He chooses *Wedding Crashers*, which is better than the super-hero movie we watched on Friday night. I already forgot the name of it.

After finishing my burrito, I grab two ginger seltzers from the fridge, offering him one. He takes it with a "Thanks," and then I sit back down on the couch.

A little bit closer to him this time, which I tell myself isn't deliberate but absolutely is.

I didn't invite him here with any expectation of what might happen. It seemed polite, after he paid for my food and apolo-gized for yesterday. Plus I wanted to spend time with him. No matter what questions get answered or which conclusions I come to about him, Conor intrigues me. He's quicksand, dangerous and impossible to ignore.

Eve texts me a half hour into the movie.

> EVE: All done. But I'm going to spend the night at Ben's. See you tomorrow!

I like the message so she knows I saw it. Then glance at Conor, who's still pretending to watch the movie.

"Eve's spending the night at her boyfriend's," I say, then set my phone back on the coffee table.

I don't want him making any assumptions about who I'm texting. And, yeah, it's a little bit of an invitation.

Conor nods. Then asks, "How long have they been together?"

"Eve and her boyfriend? Uh, a while. They met at one of those Freshman Week events."

Another nod, then he refocuses on the movie.

"Are you actually watching?"

He glances at me. "The movie you told me to put on so we could *watch* it? Yeah."

"Are you interested in other entertainment options?"

His eyes darken as I pull my legs up on the couch. Graze my foot, very deliberately, over the growing bulge in his sweatpants.

Conor slouches back, spreading his thighs so the gray material stretches tighter across his erection. "What are the other entertainment options?"

"You're hard."

"No shit," he tells me, adjusting himself. "We've been alone on a couch together for the past hour."

I'm feeling far from my best, still wearing the leggings I put on after showering in the women's locker room. I dried my hair with my car's vents, and I don't even have lip balm on.

Him reacting to me under these circumstances? I feel sexy.

"Well, I've been waiting for you to make a move for the past hour."

He's the one who walked away. Who never texted.

Conor's jaw works a couple of times. "I didn't come over here to hook up."

"Why did you come over here?"

"I wanted to," he tells me.

I climb into his lap. "What if I want *this*? What if I want your cock again, Conor?"

His groan is low and tortured. And grows louder as I start to move my hips, creating some friction.

"Do you have a condom?" he asks.

"I think Ben—Eve's boyfriend—keeps some in the bathroom. But…he's about a foot shorter than you. So I'm not sure…"

Conor smirks, understanding what I'm saying. In this position, it's impossible to ignore his size. "I'll grab one out of my car. One sec."

He stands, then heads out the front door. I stand too, pulling off all my clothes and then sitting back on the couch. Even with the lights dimmed and the blinds closed, it feels very weird to be sitting in the living room totally naked. This is just sex, though, and I need reminders of that. A quickie on the couch is less intimate than bringing him into my bedroom. At least, that's what I tell myself.

Any weirdness is worth Conor's reaction when he returns.

His expression immediately transforms, the desire obvious on his face as his eyes skim over my naked body. As soon as he reaches the couch he tugs his sweatpants down, tearing open the condom and covering his erection.

My entire body tingles, watching him. My heart rate accelerates and so does my breathing, anticipation spreading through my system. A second, persistent pulse starts between my thighs.

He's unfairly attractive.

Overwhelmingly masculine.

And tonight, he's all mine.

Conor sits on the couch, yanking off his sweatshirt. "Get over here, Harlow."

He didn't even bother pulling his sweatpants all the way down. It seems like he's as impatient and eager as I am, and my body reacts to that the same way it's dazed by his physical appearance.

I settle on his lap, moaning when his huge hands cup my breasts at the same time my pussy brushes his erection. He kisses me, which I'm not expecting, every stroke of his tongue stoking my arousal higher.

Conor's right hand leaves my breast and skates down my stomach, the slight rasp of his callouses sending shivers skittering across my skin. He finds my clit, rubbing it with a skill that has me moaning into his mouth. And then the fat head of his penis is there instead, teasing my entrance. He guides his cock back and forth around my opening, occasionally brushing the bundle of nerves he was just playing with.

I try to sink down, only for him to pull away. I growl, irritated. Sink my teeth into his bottom lip and feel his chest rumble with amusement. And then—finally—there's the delicious stretch I've already become addicted to.

I know he's big. From this angle, he feels *huge*.

At first, getting filled is a relief. And I keep waiting for him to bottom out, but it doesn't happen. I can tell how tight and swollen I am, feel how he's forcibly spreading me open. *Splitting me open*, it feels like.

"Relax, Hayes. You already took me twice, remember?"

"Well, third time is *not* the charm."

Conor's chest vibrates with another laugh. Then he's moving us forward, giving my knees more space to stretch on the couch instead of being crammed against the cushions. His lips move down the sensitive skin of my neck. His tongue traces along my collarbone. And then his thumb is back on my clit, circling right above the spot where he's penetrating me. My body responds, pulsing and then relaxing around him. He slips deeper. And deeper. And then, *finally*, I can feel his balls against my ass.

"Good girl," he tells me.

He leans back, his hands landing on my hips. He tugs me even closer, so our pelvises are completely flush. My clit rubs against his pubic hair, and I whimper.

"Holy fuck. Look at you, Hayes." His tone is admiring, his mysterious eyes stormy with arousal. I look down as I lift my hips, watching him slip out of me. Once only the tip is left, I sink back down. This time, it's a much easier glide.

Conor's jaw is clenched tight, the tendons of his neck raised as he watches his dick disappearing inside of me.

"Little faster?" he suggests.

I huff a laugh. "You try doing some of the work."

I'm not sure I'm athletic enough for this. He's just so…massive.

He moves faster than I'm expecting, lifting me off his lap like I weigh nothing. "Lean over," he tells me.

I do.

Then his hands are back on my hips and he's entering me from behind. I suck in a surprised breath that quickly turns into a moan when he starts to thrust. The pace is punishing and impatient, pounding me so fast I have to fist the couch cushions to keep from falling forward. Not bringing him into my bedroom was a mistake. This feels *plenty* intimate and I'm no longer going to be able to study on this couch.

My orgasm builds quickly, each thrust adding to the pressure.

Heat scorches my skin. I'm so, so close. And then I come with a shout, calling out his name before I collapse forward. He fucks me through my orgasm, then I feel his dick pulse inside of me as he finds his own release.

Conor pulls out of me slowly, grabbing one of the napkins that came with his dinner off the coffee table to wrap the condom in. I roll onto my back, still breathing heavily. Endorphins buzz throughout my body, my muscles loose and relaxed.

My memory of sex with him was nothing like experiencing the real thing again.

He grabs his sweatshirt and yanks it back on. I sit up and grab my own clothes, not wanting to be the only naked one.

"Can I ask you a favor?"

Conor pauses as he's pulling his sweatpants on. "Interesting timing." He smirks. "Sure, go ahead."

I don't think he's going to agree to this even if he did just get laid. But I figure this is the best time to ask. And since Eve mentioned it yesterday, I decided I want to help Mary. I very much doubt she and Clayton are soulmates, but who knows? I never thought Conor Hart would be in my living room right after we just had sex. Crazier things have happened.

"You're friends with Clayton, right?" I ask.

"Thomas? Yeah, I guess so."

"I have a friend, Mary—well, actually she's really more friends with Eve, but—"

"Get to the point, Hayes."

"Will you go out with me on Saturday night?" I blurt. "I mean, not just *us*. With other people. Mary has a crush on Clayton but she's shy and she doesn't want to go out with him on her own. Eve made up this crazy story about how Mary and I go bowling—which we don't—and I guess Clayton agreed to go. I don't want to third wheel with them. And if you're friendly with Clayton, it'll be way less awkward."

"This sounds like a double date." I can't get any read from his tone as I focus on getting dressed myself.

"I know. But it's not. It's a hang out. Or half a date. We would be the non-dating half, obviously."

He says nothing. Then, "Yeah, sure, I'll go."

"Really?" I wasn't sure if he would. Assumed he wouldn't.

Conor nods as he grabs his car keys out of his pocket. He's leaving, and I hate that I'm disappointed. "Yeah. But you have to do a favor for me too."

"Is it…sexual?"

Conor snorts. "No. You have to come to my game on Friday night."

I was already planning to go, but I don't tell him so. I just agree. "Okay."

"Cool. I'll pick you up at eight on Saturday."

"I can drive myself," I offer.

"I don't mind driving. See you then, okay?"

"Okay."

He nods, spins his car keys around one finger, then heads for the door.

I throw away the box from my dinner, straighten up the couch, do some dishes, and then get ready for bed.

My phone buzzes with a text right after I climb under the covers. Then another. And another. They're all from an unknown number. As soon as I read the first message, I know who it is.

CONOR: Good night, Hayes.

CONOR: Thanks for the—never mind.

CONOR: *You're welcome* for the sex.

I smile, biting my bottom lip. He's such a smartass.

HARLOW: Who is this?

CONOR: You seemed to remember my name just fine when you were screaming it an hour ago.

HARLOW: That still doesn't narrow it down much...

CONOR: Try this shit in person, Harlow. I'll make you beg for longer next time.

HARLOW: Next time?

CONOR: Next time.

CHAPTER TWELVE

CONOR

G ame days always feel different. There's a quiet hum in my bloodstream. A special awareness tingling behind every thought. Every molecule and muscle knows what is coming later, primed to perform.

I know what is expected of me.

I don't know how it will end.

There's an added excitement to that. Even if I could choose to know what the scoreboard will read at the end of a game, I wouldn't. There's a thrill to the unexpected. To the challenge. Knowing the undefeated season I've worked so hard for could slip away at any moment. There's no room for complacency.

I'm making noise. Nine games into the season, and we've won every single one of them. There was an article about Holt on *Center Line Commentary* last week, titled "Division III's Dark Horse?"

One article is not enough to get me signed anywhere. But it might be enough to get a few people to dig into my background. To realize there's a good reason why I didn't attend the combine.

Enter the draft. To realize I'll work three times as hard as one of the rookies already under contract with millions of dollar signs in their eyes.

A chip on your shoulder is a much better incentive than a fat check. At least for me.

The alarm on my phone starts blaring. I roll out of twisted sheets and swear when my toe collides with a textbook on the floor. My room needs a thorough cleaning. One I know it probably won't get anytime soon.

I pull on a pair of sweatpants and a shirt and make my way downstairs in search of coffee.

Hunter eyes me when I hobble into the kitchen. The pain in my toe has begun to recede, leaving behind the reminder that skating for an additional hour last night was a massive mistake.

"Jesus, Hart. The other guy look better?" Hunter asks.

I flip him off. "I'm fine. I stayed at the rink a while after practice ended."

Hunter looks worried. "You sure you're fine? Hampton is going to be out for blood tonight. Yours, specifically."

I don't need the reminder.

"I know. I'll be ready," I assure him. Hunter has already brewed coffee, so I fill a generous cup.

"I'm serious, dude," Hunter presses. "Are you all right?"

"Yes," I snap. "Let me worry about the game, okay?"

"Okay." Hunter raises both hands.

I sigh. "Sorry."

"We spend a lot of time together, Hart. I already know you're a grump most of it."

I roll my eyes as I pull a carton of eggs out of the fridge. The scent of frying bacon and scrambled eggs is enough to draw Aidan downstairs. He stumbles into the kitchen in just a pair of boxer briefs.

"Well, isn't this domestic." He nods between me standing at the stove and Hunter pouring a glass of orange juice at the fridge.

"Good thing you're here to ensure it's no longer family-friendly," Hunter comments. "Do you own pants, Phillips?"

"Yup," Aidan replies in a cheerful tone. He's one of those annoying people who wakes up with a smile on his face.

"So you're walking around like that because you think we want to see your beer belly?"

Aidan laughs and pats his abs. "I'm out of clean clothes. I need to do laundry."

Hunter rolls his eyes. "Your smelly ass better be planning to sit in the front of the bus then."

"My game gear is clean," Aidan replies, grabbing some coffee.

I tune out their boring-ass clothes conversation as I eat my breakfast and scroll through my phone. I end up in my messages. I send the whole team a reminder about what time the bus is leaving. Then open the text thread with Harlow. I haven't texted her since Sunday night, when I got back from her place.

I've wanted to, but Northampton is one of our main rivals in the conference. Preparing for tonight's game has meant my schedule is especially hectic. It hasn't just been Coach. Regardless of what he told me, it does feel like keeping the undefeated season going is one of my responsibilities. Hinging on my ability to score goals, my work keeping the guys focused. Me staying focused.

This week I've squeezed in extra practices and watched hours of Northampton's recent games, doing everything I can to ensure we'll win tonight. Maybe part of me is also trying to prove to myself that Harlow isn't a distraction.

I shut off my phone and stick my breakfast dishes in the dishwasher.

"I'm headed to class," I tell my two roommates, who have moved on to debating different brands of laundry detergent. "Do *not* be late, got it?"

"We got the reminder, Captain." Aidan flashes his phone screen at me, displaying my latest message in the group chat.

I roll my eyes before I grab all my stuff and head outside. A light mist is falling from the sky, coating everything in a thin layer of moisture. I toss my backpack and hockey gear into the trunk of my car and drive toward campus.

I only have one class today: an African American literature seminar.

Most of the guys on the hockey team are Business majors. It's well known to be an easy path to a diploma, but I enjoy my classes. I have no idea what I'll do with an English degree if hockey doesn't pan out, however. Hopefully it's something I won't have to figure out.

I'm early; there's no one else in the room besides the professor. Since this is a smaller seminar, it's not held in one of the larger lecture halls on campus. Just an average-sized room overlooking the quad.

"Hi, Conor," Professor Ashland greets as I walk inside.

"Hey, Professor," I reply, slinging my hockey jacket on the back of a chair and dropping my backpack on the floor.

Professor Ashland glances at the door and then back at me. She pulls a stack of papers out of her briefcase. "I was going to wait to return these until the end of the class, but since you're here early…" She grabs one and walks over toward me. The essay I turned in last week has a big red A at the top of the page. "I was very impressed, Conor."

"Thanks, Professor."

"Have you given any thought to your plans after graduation?" she asks me.

"I'm hoping to play hockey professionally," I admit.

It's common knowledge on campus, but I usually avoid saying the words out loud. Doing so seems like a taunt to the universe. *Here's what I want!* A glaring neon sign pointing at what will hurt most to lose.

Professor Ashland nods. "I heard the hockey team is having quite the season. Congratulations."

"Thank you."

"I imagine there's some uncertainty about the path to becoming a professional athlete."

I nod at the understatement. "Yes. Quite a bit."

"You're a very talented writer, Conor. It doesn't hurt to have options. If you're interested in applying to any graduate programs..." The door to the room opens, and Adelaide Jackson walks into the room. I cover my essay with my notebook. "Just think about it," Professor Ashland says.

I nod. "I will. Thanks."

Preparing for a Plan B is smart. I have no idea what my odds of actually getting signed are, but I know they're discouragingly low. There are guys at schools with huge, respected hockey programs who will never make it to the professional level. Holding on to hope that *I* will is probably a wasted effort. But... considering alternatives feels like giving up. Like accepting those shitty odds. And I can't bring myself to do that, no matter how logical it is. Heart over head, I guess.

"Hey, Conor," Adelaide says as she takes the seat beside me.

"Hey," I reply.

Freshman year, I could tell all the girls in English 101 were wary of having a male classmate. They all assumed it was a joke or I wouldn't take it seriously. Now, I'm one of two guys majoring in English in my graduating class. The other, Paul Deering, looks a lot more like the stereotypical literature student:

glasses, button-down shirts, and a thick mop of curly hair. A fitting reminder not to judge a book by its cover.

Class starts with a discussion of the book we're currently reading and ends with Professor Ashland returning everyone else's essays. I head straight for the door. I've got ten minutes to get to the bus on time. After threatening everyone else to not be late, it would look especially bad to show up tardy myself.

Hunter and Aidan are waiting by one of the benches outside the humanities building.

I clutch my chest. "Aw, you two are so sweet to wait for me."

"Told you he'd be a dick about it," Aidan tells Hunter. "We walked to campus and we're bumming a ride to the bus. Hunter is worried you're not in the zone." Those two sentences are directed at me.

"Yeah, remember how I said that, and *then* I said to keep it between us?" Hunter says, scowling at Aidan.

Aidan rolls his eyes. "How's he going to know you're worried if you don't tell him you're worried?"

"I have told him. Just like I told you he wasn't listening to me."

"I can hear you both," I say, heading toward the parking lot. I ignore the looks being cast my way. Nod at the people who call out to me but don't stop to strike up any conversations. I'm not in the mood and the clock is ticking.

"Want to tell me what Morgan is so worried about?" Aidan asks, falling into step beside me. "Or do you want me to get it out of him and then act surprised when you tell me?"

"I have no idea what Morgan's problem is," I tell Aidan, sending a hard look to Hunter. There is only one topic we've butted heads on lately, though, so I'm pretty sure I have an idea.

"Does it have anything to do with Harlow Hayes?" Aidan asks innocently.

Damnit. "Absolutely nothing," I insist.

"I thought you were training her for the marathon? Did you back out of that?"

"No, I didn't back out of it. I've been distracted, preparing for tonight."

Hunter mumbles something. Aidan laughs.

I close my eyes and take a deep breath. "Jesus, you two. Can we focus on a winning a hockey game? You're worried I'm not focused? Seems like that's you two."

Silence. Just feet pounding pavement.

"I think he's ready for the game," Hunter mock whispers to Aidan.

I snort and keep walking.

The rest of the team is already standing around the coach bus that's going to transport us to Hampton University for our game tonight when the three of us arrive at the sports center.

"That's everyone! On the bus, boys!" Coach shouts.

No one moves. They wait until I stash my bag in the cargo compartment.

As soon as I reach the stairs, there's a rush of activity as everyone follows my lead.

I smile. Even as a freshman, I was a leader on the team. Part of it is my stats. On what has historically been a mediocre, dull team, I'm the flashy star who scores goals and steps on the ice with confidence. The leadership role comes naturally to me.

But this year is the first time we've worked as a cohesive unit rather than just pockets of talent. I'm the central component, and there's not a guy on the team who doesn't know it. And I *feel* it. That hum I woke up with is close to reaching the fever pitch that always corresponds with the drop of a puck directly in front of me.

Hunter plops down in the seat beside me. "I didn't tell Phillips to bug you," he tells me. "I've seen you prepping this week. You're in the zone, man."

"Yeah. I am."

"And I'll drop—" He glances across the aisle at Sampson. "I'll drop the other thing. I was just worried, man. I want this for you and…it just seemed like maybe you needed a knock to the head, to get it on straight. But it's your business. I trust your judgment on the ice. I trust it off the ice too."

I pull my headphones out of my bag and plug them into my phone. "Thanks, man," I say.

Coach starts calling roll. I raise my hand when he reaches my name, then start my usual pre-game playlist.

A new message flashes across the screen, right before I turn my phone off.

HARLOW: Good luck, Hart.

————

Fifteen minutes from campus, I decide to reply to Harlow's text. The bus is dark and quiet, most of the guys fast asleep. All of the celebrating faded about an hour ago. Holt is too cheap to spring for hotel rooms for the whole team, so we had to make the three-hour drive back to Holt after beating Hampton University by five goals. I scored two.

It was a dominant performance against what's historically been a better team. Another mark in the win column. Our streak has continued.

I'm exhausted, my entire body battered and bruised. Hampton took a high-sticking double minor penalty for splitting my bottom lip. I prod the cut with my tongue, wincing.

Fuckers.

CONOR: You awake?

She replies instantly.

HARLOW: Congrats.

She checked the score.

A stupid grin forms on my face.

My mom always came to as many of my games as she could. And every time we talk, she asks how the season is going. But she's busy. She can't check scores in the middle of a busy shift at the hospital. So I've never felt like I had a cheering section, anyone who was concerned with just *me* instead of the game's outcome as a whole. I blame that warmth—that appreciation—for my response.

CONOR: Can I come over?

HARLOW: See you soon.

Once we pull into the parking lot of the sports center, I elbow Aidan awake. His mouth is open, and I'm pretty sure he's drooling. I wish Hunter had sat next to me on the way back too, but he ended up in the row behind.

Groans echo around the bus as the lights flicker on.

Coach Keller stands in the very front. "Hell of a game tonight, boys. And because you all worked your asses off today, I'm cancelling practice tomorrow." Loud cheers erupt. Coach has cancelled practice...never. "Back to the usual schedule Thursday," he barks. "We've got a game to win on Friday. Get some sleep."

We file off the bus, shivering as we wait for the driver to open the cargo compartment so we can grab our gear. I can see my breath in the air.

I grab my bag and sling it over one shoulder, waiting for Aidan and Hunter to grab theirs before we all head for my car.

"Do we stop for food?" Aidan yawns.

"Nah, I'm not hungry," Hunter says. "I just want to crash."

"Yeah, all right," Aidan agrees.

I say nothing as I drive toward our house. Pull up along the curb, instead of parking in the driveway. Aidan shoots me a questioning look from his seat on the passenger side.

"I'm going to Harlow's. See you guys tomorrow."

There's a beat of silence.

"Harlow…*Hayes*?" I don't know what Hunter said to Aidan about my distraction, but it couldn't have been much, because Phillips sounds stunned. "You're *sleeping* with her?"

"See you tomorrow," Hunter says, then climbs out of the back. *Bails*, in other words.

"Night, Morgan," I tell him.

"*You* are having sex with *Harlow Hayes*?"

"Yup. Can you get out of my car, Phillips?"

"How is it?"

I glare at him. "Get out!"

"Okay, okay. Jeez. You'd think you'd be in a better mood if you're getting laid. I thought you were having a major dry spell. Have fun, Hart." He smirks, finally climbing out.

Once he shuts the door, I pull away from the curb, making the short drive to Harlow's. I park behind her car, wincing when I climb out of the driver's side.

I walk up the path, knocking on the front door. It opens a few seconds later.

Harlow's in her pajamas, her long hair pulled up in a ponytail.

"Hey." I sound like a chain smoker, my throat raw from shouting on the ice for an hour.

"Hey. Come on in." She steps to the side, letting me into the small entryway and closing the door behind me. "Do you want anything to…" Her voice trails as she gets a look at my face. "Shit."

"It feels better than it looks," I lie.

It feels like I took a stick to the face, which is exactly what happened. At least we got a power play goal out of it.

"Do you want anything to eat? Or drink? I have—"

I shake my head, cutting her off. "I'm good. The bus stopped on the way back from the game."

"You look tired," she says.

"It was a tough game."

"Were you wanting to…"

"Only if you want to. I mean, I always want to. But I also feel like I just got *hit* by a bus. So sleep sounds good too."

"You came here to sleep?"

She sounds surprised. I can't get a read on anything else.

I'm acting like a boyfriend, and she's not my girlfriend. I just…wanted to see her. And it's been less than two days. *Fuck.*

"Yeah, I'll go. See you."

She grabs my hand when I try to turn and tugs me deeper into the house, flipping lights off as we walk. We pass the couch where we hooked up on Sunday night, then Harlow pulls me down the hallway and into the room on the left.

I look around her bedroom curiously. It's more settled than mine. A large bed—a queen size, I'd guess—takes up most of the far wall. Her desk is to the left, piled high with textbooks that have *marine* or *aquatic* in the title. A large wardrobe is on the right, clothes literally spilling out of it.

"Wasn't expecting company," Harlow mumbles, picking up a sweatshirt off the floor.

I smile. "I don't care about the mess, Hayes."

I step out of the sweats I put on after my post-game shower then pull off my sweatshirt, leaving me in just my boxer briefs. A reddish-purple bruise is blooming across my ribs thanks to a couple of the hits I took tonight.

"Jesus, Conor."

"They started playing pretty dirty toward the end, trying to get through to Willis."

"Don't you wear protective equipment?"

"This *is* wearing the protective equipment."

She gnaws on her bottom lip, and I realize…*she's worried.* Aside from my mom, I've never had anyone express concern about my well-being. And I can't believe it's *Harlow Hayes*, who's looking at my bruises with a mixture of alarm and anger, like she's contemplating taking on Northampton's defenders herself. A month ago, I wouldn't have been shocked if she'd tried to shove me in front of a bus.

"Seriously, I'm fine."

She exhales. "Okay. I'll be right back."

I snoop around her room while she's gone. There are a couple of framed photos on her desk. One of her with a beaming couple. Her parents, I realize. They're standing at the edge of a massive cliff, blue sky behind them and vivid green grass in front. The other photo…my jaw clenches. Two kids—probably about nine or ten—sitting on an old porch swing. Harlow's hair is shorter than it is now, pleated into two pigtails. And the guy next to her—I don't see any resemblance. But I know it must be Landon.

It's the same uncomfortable jolt as when he called her in the car on Saturday. I knew they were friends—it's the whole reason I avoided her ever since I heard the girl the Garrisons had basically adopted as a daughter was attending Holt as well. But now that I know Harlow, it's much harder to ignore.

This can only work if I keep them separate, though. If I pretend I don't know anything about her except what she's revealed to me herself.

I flip through her aquatic resources textbook as a distraction. That's what I'm doing when Harlow walks back into her room, holding a bag of frozen blueberries. "This is all I had in the freezer," she tells me. "I keep forgetting to get more fruit for my smoothies."

Something thickens in my throat.

"This is perfect, thanks."

If my lip wasn't split, I'd kiss her.

"What are aquatic resources?" I ask instead.

She glances at the textbook and scrunches up her nose. "Seriously?"

I nod.

"Uh, marine reserves, protection of endangered species, extinction risk, population dynamics. Stuff like that. Most life on Earth lives in the water. There are zooplankton and phytoplankton you can't even see, and then cetaceans that are over a hundred feet long."

Harlow's eyes are alight; her cheeks flushed.

It's the same expression she wore when we went out on the Sound and saw that orca. Maybe the same way I look, when I step on the ice.

"What?" she asks.

I shake my head. "Nothing."

"You think I'm a nerd, huh?"

"No. I think it's cool, that you found something you're so passionate about. Some people never do."

I head for her bed, the dark green comforter thick and invit-

157

ing. This should feel strange, climbing into bed with a girl and having no intention of having sex. Just like being in her room should be weird. But…it's not.

I climb under the covers like I've done it a thousand times before, tucking the frozen blueberries against the bruise on my side. It does help some.

Harlow pulls off her sweatshirt. My blood heats as soon as her boobs appear, perky and perfect. She opens the wardrobe topless, sifting through a few sweaters before pulling out an oversize T-shirt. It's one I have too, the generic class shirt they handed out at orientation. Blue and white, for the school colors.

Her leggings go next, leaving her in black lacy boy shirts. Maybe I should look away, but I can't. It's not like she doesn't know I'm here. She steps into a pair of pink cotton shorts patterned with ice cream cones and then climbs onto the bed, crawling over me carefully and then settling down on the other pillow.

I relax into her mattress, Harlow's warm body on my right and the cold bag of blueberries on my left.

I don't fall asleep right away.

But I pretend to.

Being here isn't odd, but I feel weird that my first instinct was to come see her. Worried what Harlow might read into it—what she should read into it.

I also don't want to keep her awake. I no longer have a weight session first thing, but she might have an early class.

I'm not sure how much time passes before Harlow rolls over to face me. She stills, like she's waiting for a reaction. Like she's making sure I'm still asleep.

When I don't move, she inches closer. Little by little, until she's pressed against my uninjured side.

Her hand rests gently on my chest. And then she lets out a soft, contented sigh.

Finally, I fall asleep.

Snuggling her.

CHAPTER THIRTEEN

HARLOW

The noise hits first. I look around in shock as I step inside Holt's hockey arena for the second time. Rather than silence and the smell of stale sweat, the chilled air is buzzing with anticipation and excitement. Crowds of people mill around, families and older couples from Somerville. And then lots and lots of students.

Eve and Ben look stunned. Eve wanted to join me when she found out I was coming to Conor's home game tonight and Ben decided to tag along too.

"I guess we should find seats?" I suggest, eyeing the packed bleachers dubiously.

They're filled with shirtless guys with painted chests and girls in tight tops holding homemade signs. I read a few signs. It's impossible to miss *Hart* and *15* are featured on most.

I lead the way up the center aisle. The stands close to the ice are all packed. There's a space about halfway up that I aim for. Even managing that requires some jostling of spectators who already snagged seats. We should have arrived earlier, I guess. I figured it would be busier than the basketball game. I wasn't expecting…*this*.

"Wow," Eve states, echoing my thoughts as she takes the seat next to me. Ben sits down on her other side. "I had no idea anyone at Holt had this amount of school spirit."

"Wish we had these many people show up to our film screenings," Ben grumbles. Eve pats his arm consolingly.

"So…which number is your boyfriend?" Eve pretty much shouts the question as her attention turns to me.

The two girls seated directly in front of us both look back.

I glare at my best friend. "He's *not* my boyfriend," I hiss.

"He's slept over at our house *twice* this week. I don't think that's the definition of a *one-night stand*, Harlow."

I have no good response to that.

Eve's right. First Conor came over after his away game on Tuesday. And then last night he stopped by after his film session. We had sex, then fell asleep.

The whole thing felt very relationship-y. But we're *not* in one, which Conor made clear and I haven't lost sight of. We're a series of one-night stands, I guess. The sex is incredible and I like being around him. There's no reason to put a label on it.

Players appear on the ice, and Eve gets distracted. Gray jerseys appear at one end first, then Holt's cobalt blue on the opposite end. Both teams whizz around in rapid circles, passing pucks and sending shots at the hulky body centered between the iron posts of the goal. A few players squat on the ice closer to the circle at the center. The splits and stretches are honestly…sexual. I recall Conor coaching me about butt kicks, and smirk to myself.

I can't find him.

I scan over the jerseys, looking for number fifteen. He's not by the goal or one of the guys stretching.

Finally, I spot him by the bench.

He's leaning across the boards, talking to a gray-haired man who must be the head coach. Their expressions are serious as they alternate speaking.

I'm worried something is seriously wrong when Conor suddenly grins. His coach slaps his shoulder and then he spins, putting his helmet on in one effortless motion as he eats up the end of the ice in rapid strokes.

He stops by the Holt goal, sending a spray of white shavings into the boards. Talks to the goalie, Willis, who pulls his mask up and sprays some water into his mouth, nodding along to whatever Conor is telling him. Both guys laugh, and then Conor joins the line of guys waiting to take shots on goal. One of the blue jerseys stretching gets up and skates toward him. *34* and *Phillips* is on the back of his jersey. Aidan, I realize.

They continue skating circles. Shooting toward goal. About half of the shots go in. I'm not sure if that's good or not. I want Holt to score and I also want Willis to keep pucks out of their goal.

Both of Conor's shots find the back of the net. I know they don't count for anything, but I experience a jolt of pride each time. Like he's mine to be proud of. Which he's *not*, but I let myself pretend. Just for the game.

There are two minutes left on the giant clock above the scoreboard when all the blue jerseys gather by their goal.

"What's going on?" Eve asks me.

"No idea," I reply, looking for Conor.

I find him right by the opening of the goal. His helmet is off again, revealing his intense expression as he runs a hand through his hair. His lips start moving, and I realize why the whole team is gathered around him, leaning on sticks and nodding.

He's talking to them. Leading them.

The gray jerseys at the opposite end are still circling, most of the heads turned toward Holt's end to try and figure out what's going on down there, why they've stopped warming up.

Conor says something, and all of Holt's sticks hit the ice rapidly and repeatedly, like they're clapping for him.

Then they're all skating toward the Holt bench.

Most of the blue jerseys file off the ice. Conor and four other players remain on the ice, plus the hulking shape of their goalie.

This time they gather around the coach Conor was talking to before.

A loud buzzer sounds, indicating the end of warm-up time.

The loudspeaker crackles to life, welcoming everyone to the game and running through emergency procedures. The national anthem plays, only twelve players on the ice. I can't see the back of the Holt players' jerseys as they turn toward the flag, but I don't need to.

I know which one he is.

The confident stance.

The way all the other players keep glancing at him.

I tune out the introductions for the other teams' starting line-up. The rink is the quietest it's been since we arrived.

It grows gradually louder, as Willis is introduced.

The two Holt defensemen.

Then "Robby Sampson!" Applause.

"Aidan Phillips!" More applause.

There's a pause. A deliberate one, it feels like.

"And your captain and leading scorer…CONOR HART!"

My ears are still ringing a minute later from the eruption of noise that follows his introduction.

Eve glances at me but says nothing. Or if she does, I can't hear it.

The players all take their positions on the ice, Conor in the very center of the rink. The referee says something that has him nodding, then there's a flash of black as the puck gets dropped. All the players react immediately, like sprinters responding to a starting gun.

Conor playing hockey is grace and power and poetry in motion. It's even more breathtaking that watching him circle the ice solo was. This time, I can tell how much faster and quicker he is than every other player on the ice. Witness the way he blows past them like they're motionless. Steals the puck like it's easy.

I've always viewed hockey as a brutal, bloody sport. One that appeals to base instincts and bruised knuckles. Filled with pushing and shoving and hate. There is some of that taking place, evidence of how Conor got the bruise that's still stretching across his ribs, but it's also…beautiful.

Precise shots.

Sprays of ice shavings flying.

I don't think about how complicated my feelings toward one particular player have become. I don't think about how Hugh Garrison has never seen his son play hockey. I don't think about how much Landon Garrison would hate that I'm sitting in Holt's rink right now.

I just…watch.

I don't follow all the nuances. Reading game recaps or watching a game with my dad didn't leave me with any vast understanding of what each penalty means or why the refs randomly blow whistles. I can't hear what any of the players are saying when they argue on the ice. I have no way of anticipating what circle they will line up in. No idea why one gray jersey gets sent to the penalty box ten minutes into the game.

But I can appreciate the speed and intensity. It resounds throughout the arena with each rattle of the boards and every roar of the crowd.

I spend all of the game watching Conor. He seems to tower

over all the other guys on the ice. The *15* emblazoned on the back of his jersey in white is a stark contrast to Holt's blue jerseys, the same way each Holt player stands out against the white-gray colored ice.

He flies across the frozen surface effortlessly, hurtling toward the tiny, black circle they're all chasing after. You don't need to have seen a hockey game before to tell that he's on a whole different playing field in comparison to the rest of the players.

Conor barrages the opposing goalie with shot after shot after shot. The rest of Holt's team keeps passing to him, assisting with the single-man assault even as the gray jerseys try to congregate around Conor, knowing who Holt's star player is. They come for Conor over and over again.

Hunter Morgan has never treated me with the same friendliness Aidan does. But I clap and cheer for him after he sends a gray jersey headed for Conor into the boards with a slam that makes *my* teeth rattle.

It happens suddenly.

My ears adjusted to the noisy arena, I guess, because the thunderous roar takes me off guard. So does the loud buzzer and the flash of light at one end of the ice. All of the blue jerseys are suddenly huddled in one spot.

Eve figures out what happened before I do.

"We scored!" she screams.

Under most circumstances, I would tease Eve for her enthusiasm. She spent most of the basketball game we went to discussing art with Mary, despite it being her idea to go to the game in the first place.

But I'm too busy yelling right along with the crowd to judge anyone's reaction. Even Ben seems to have gotten over his irritation about the disconnect between Holt students' appreciation for cinema and hockey. He's clapping and whistling right along with the rest of us.

The loudspeaker crackles to life. "Holt University goal scored by number fifteen, Conor Hart. Assisted by number twenty-two, Hunter Morgan. Time of the goal, thirteen minutes and thirty-two seconds into the second period."

Conor's goal seems to set off a domino effect. Aidan Phillips scores a couple of minutes later. Then a sophomore whose name I don't recognize. Then Conor again.

Holt is ahead by four goals to nothing with only three minutes left on the clock. Fifty-seven seconds tick by, and the other team pulls their goalie. Conor gains possession of the puck and zips down the ice like a blue bullet. I wait for him to shoot it between the pipes, but he doesn't. He passes it across the ice to a player wearing the number seventeen.

I didn't memorize the team roster, so I have no idea who number seventeen is. But whoever he is, he sends the puck right into the net, prompting a fresh roar from the euphoric crowd. Five to nothing. That's still the score when the time expires.

"Oh my God! We won." Eve sounds half-shocked, half-happy. "We actually won!"

"The team is undefeated this season, Eve," I tell her.

She sticks her tongue out at me before turning back to watch all the blue players celebrating on the ice as a line of gray disappears from sight.

I'm only focused on one.

———

"Wow," Eve says, appearing in the opening that leads to the kitchen when I walk into the living room.

"What?" I say, grabbing my down coat off the hook and

pulling it on over my sweater.

"You straightened your hair. Showered. You did the smoky eye you complain takes you twenty minutes. You're wearing your sweater that shows the most cleavage. And…" She sniffs. "You used that fancy perfume your mom's best friend got you."

"So?"

"You *like* him, Harlow. You did not go through this much effort to hang out at a bowling alley."

"It's been a while since I dressed up. I just…felt like it."

"Uh-huh." Based on her tone, Eve is not buying it. Nor should she.

This is the problem with living with someone who knows you well. They know what music you want to listen to and your favorite brand of chocolate. They also know that you only straighten your hair for occasions deemed to have some special significance. To put those in context, I haven't bothered to in months. Not since the party the oceanic research firm I worked at this past summer threw for my final day.

I'm very nervous about tonight. I told Conor it's not a date. He doesn't consider it a date. It's a favor I'm still surprised he agreed to.

But tonight *feels* like a date. I thought there was a better chance of going out with a Hollywood actor than with Conor Hart.

But here I am, waiting for my best friend's half-brother to pick me up. Because he *offered* to for our non-date.

Eve watches me closely as she moves around the kitchen. Probably fixing herself a bowl of popcorn to watch this uncomfortable scene unfold. I plop down on the couch and pull my phone out to avoid her discerning gaze.

The doorbell rings minutes later.

I stand and smooth my sweater. Eve returned from the movie

she went to with Ben about ten minutes ago, so she wasn't home to witness the embarrassing length of time it took to pick out the jeans and sweater I'm currently wearing. The simple outfit is deceptively well thought out. The jeans are my favorite: stretchy yet snug. The sweater I'm wearing is casual but not bulky enough to look careless. Underneath it, I'm wearing a lacy top.

Conor is standing with his hands in his pockets when I open the front door, staring off into space. He glances toward me when the hinges creak. Living in a perpetually damp climate means a lot of rust, I've learned.

He says nothing at first, just looks at me. The old bulb in the porch light is too dim for me to tell much from his expression. But it's more than a cursory glance. Instead of his usual sweatpants, Conor is wearing jeans and a red Henley visible beneath his *Holt Hockey* jacket.

"Hey, Hayes," he greets.

"Hi, Hart," I reply, closing the door behind me.

It's misting out—of course. I pull my hood up, so the fifteen minutes it took me to straighten my hair weren't a total waste.

Conor says nothing else as we walk to his SUV. It's the first time I've ever been in his car. There are a couple of empty water bottles in the cupholders, but the front seat is mostly clean. He's got one of those cheap pine air fresheners you can buy at a gas station hanging from his rearview mirror.

A folded paper falls out of the door pocket and into the footwell when I close the car door. I pick it up as Conor tosses the water bottles into the backseat, my eyes drawn to a large, red A. My eyes widen. I glance up to find Conor's on me.

"What?" he asks.

I turn the paper so he can see what I'm looking at. "Impressive."

Conor shrugs, nonchalant.

I scan the heading. It's for an African American literature class. "You're an English major?"

"Yeah," he confirms.

"I would have guessed business," I admit.

Conor's lips quirk as I call out the stereotypical jock course of study. "I wouldn't have guessed marine biology. Did you see any whales this morning?" he asks.

There's a funny flip in my stomach, realizing he remembered how I spend my Saturday mornings and is bothering to ask about it.

"Not this morning, no. Sam got a good haul in though. He, uh, he said to tell you congrats about the win last night. So, congrats."

"What did *you* think of the game?"

"It was great. You were great. The team played great."

I cringe, after possibly setting a record for using the word *great* in a very short time span.

I didn't text Conor after going to his game last night, and I'm not sure why. I couldn't come up with anything more original to say than *good game.* And it felt like I should say something more meaningful. Since I couldn't come up with anything I sent him nothing.

Part of me thought he might have texted me. But he didn't. I assume he celebrated with the team last night. Maybe with other people too.

"So...great?"

There's a teasing lilt to his lips when I glance over.

"I don't really know how to describe it. It was nothing like I was expecting. It was so loud and exciting and it was...you were one of the guys playing."

"Did I forget to mention I was on the team, or something?"

I huff a laugh. "It was different seeing you play, that's all."

"Different how?"

"I don't know. I cared more about how it ended, I guess."

I'm saying way too much. I don't just care about the score. I was invested…in him.

"I'm glad you came," Conor says.

"Yeah, me too."

We drive in silence for a few minutes.

He speaks first. "You didn't tell me Thomas asked you out."

I glance over at him, not expecting the subject change. "Why would I? And how do *you* know that?"

"It came up."

"Came up with who?" I ask.

"It doesn't matter."

"Then why are you mentioning it?"

"It just would have been nice to know, before I agreed to this," he tells me.

"Why? I thought you were friends with him."

Conor mutters something that sounds like *Not anymore*.

"We had a humanities class together last spring."

"Did you go out with him?" Conor asks.

"No."

"Did you…sleep with him?"

My mouth drops open. "Are you—are you *serious* right now? How the hell is that any of your business?"

"We're going on a double date with him. I'm just trying to figure out how awkward this is going to be."

Conor pulls into the bowling alley's parking lot. I climb out of his car as soon as it's stopped.

"Harlow!"

I keep walking.

"*Harlow*!" Conor grabs my arm, forcing me to spin around. He must have jogged to catch up to me, but he's not even winded. Stupid, in-shape guy.

"What?" I snap.

"I'm sorry, okay? It's none of my business. I just…" He exhales. "I saw Thomas last night and he said some shit about you and it—I'm sorry."

"What sort of shit?"

Conor's jaw works. "Let's just say he's not coming on this outing because he's interested in your friend."

I look away. "Do you think he'll say something to her?"

"No. Thomas doesn't like to rock the boat. He just wanted to make sure *you* were going to the hockey team party later."

"Well, I'm not."

Conor's forehead wrinkles. "What do you mean, you're not?"

"I wasn't invited."

"Wasn't invited—" He laughs. "Harlow, come on. What are you talking about?"

"I didn't know the hockey team was having a party tonight. I figure it was last night, and that's where you were."

"I was with Aidan and Hunter," Conor tells me.

"And Clayton."

"Yeah, he and a bunch of guys showed up for beer and video games later."

"Sounds like a *blast*."

Conor studies me for a few seconds. "I don't know what you're upset about," he finally says.

"Nothing. I-I just thought you might text me last night."

"I was going to. Then the guys showed up and I just… I figured you were busy."

That's flattering, I guess. Because I was *busy* staring at my phone, alternating between wondering what to text him and wishing he'd text me. Pathetic.

"You're invited tonight, all right? This is me, inviting you."

"Hart! Harlow!"

We both turn, watching Clayton approach. He slaps hands with Conor and then hugs me. Conor's hands fist at his sides before he shoves them into his pockets.

The parking lot is dark and chilly, so we head inside to wait for Mary to arrive.

It smells like a concession stand inside, trays of greasy pizza and rotating pretzels to the left as soon as we walk in. The carpet is a swirl of orange and purple. There's a long counter spanning a dozen feet to the right. A middle-aged man is standing at it, looking like he'd love to be elsewhere.

We all give our shoe sizes and he hands the ugly shoes over.

It's been a long time since I've been bowling. Probably at a birthday party when I was little.

Mary shows up a couple of minutes later, blushing bright red as soon as she sees Clayton. I'm relieved when he hugs her, then leads her to the counter to get her shoes.

I glance at the lanes, watching a father help his daughter lift a ball from the rack. My chest squeezes, the way it often does when I see little kids with their parents. *I got seventeen years*, I remind myself. That's more than lots of people get. And a hell of a lot better than nothing.

"Are you any good at bowling?" Conor asks me.

"No," I reply. I keep my eyes on the lanes instead of looking over at him. I'm still unsettled from our conversation earlier, and I have no idea how to act around him as a result.

"Do you think Mary is any good?"

"She's more artistic than athletic."

"Good. Then we'll probably beat Thomas."

"If you want to win, why don't you play *with* him?" I snap.

"Because we're on a fake date, Hayes. And if I play *with* Thomas, I can't *beat* him."

"I thought you two were friends. That's the whole reason I invited you, to make this less awkward. Not *more*."

"Yeah, well, I started feeling a lot less friendly toward Thomas last night."

I finally look at him. "What the hell did he say to you?"

Mary and Clayton join us before Conor can answer. I'm not sure he would have, anyway.

We move to our assigned lane and swap out street shoes for the uncomfortable bowling ones.

"Why couldn't they be cute?" I groan as I pull the left one on. "Or just more comfortable. I feel like my feet are strapped to a wooden board."

Mary smiles sympathetically. The guys ignore me.

I still have no clue what happened between Clayton and Conor last night, but there's definitely some strange, hostile energy humming in the air.

"I'll start off?" Clayton suggests.

"Sure," I say.

Clayton heads toward the ball rack, grabbing a red one off of it and pausing at the top of the lane. Then he flings the ball forward. It starts straight, then veers toward the right. Only one pin gets knocked down before the ball drops out of sight. Clayton grabs another ball, throwing this one with a little more force. This time, he hits two pins.

He turns back toward us with a grimace. "Three out of ten. Not great."

"Sounds like your season record."

I shoot Conor a *Cut it out* look for that comment.

"I'm gonna go grab a beer," Clayton says. "Anyone else want one?"

"No, I'm good," I reply. "Thanks."

"I'll take one," Mary says.

"Hart?"

"Nah, I'm good," Conor replies.

Clayton nods. "I'll be right back. Want to come, Mary?"

She nods eagerly.

"What the hell are you doing?" I hiss at Conor, as soon as they're out of earshot.

"What?"

"You, turning a bowling game into a pissing match. Who cares what the basketball team's record is?"

"Not me," Conor says. "And not many people. I think they're more like two and twelve by now."

"If you're going to be a dick, you should just leave."

"I'm your ride."

"I'll walk home. Or get a ride with Mary."

Conor exhales. "I won't say anything else, okay?"

I don't reply. Because, *pathetically*, I don't want him to leave.

"Do you drink?" he asks suddenly.

"What?"

"Alcohol. Do you drink alcohol?"

"I—what?"

"You turned it down just now, and I realized—I've never seen you drink."

"Yeah, I do. Just not that often."

He nods.

"What about you? Why aren't you drinking?"

"I don't drink during the season," Conor tells me. "And even if I did...I wouldn't tonight."

"Why not?"

"You're probably the last person I ever thought would be promoting drinking and driving, Hayes. If you're in my car, I'll be stone fucking sober."

I look away. I keep forgetting Conor knows my past. And I try not to care, that he wouldn't have anything to drink before driving me, but it's not very successful.

"Want to show me your bowling technique while the competition is off getting wasted?" he asks.

"No."

I glance toward the concession stand, just to make sure that Mary is good. She's beaming, I'm relieved to see. But there's no sign of anyone at the bar, which makes me think this will be an extended delay. We haven't even gotten through one frame yet.

"Fine," I say. "I'll bowl *once* and then you can give me pointers."

I stand and grab a purple ball from the rack.

The pins have all been replaced at the end of the lane from Clayton's turn. I stick my fingers into the three tiny holes and test the weight of the ball.

I line up in the center on the lane, relax my fingers so they'll slip out of the ball, and am about to send it flying toward what I hope will be a strike when a hand curves around my waist. I startle, almost dropping the heavy sphere I'm holding on my foot.

"What are you doing?" I snap at Conor. "I was in the zone."

"You were about to throw a gutter ball," he informs me.

"No, I wasn't! I was perfectly lined up to—"

"Throw a gutter ball," Conor finishes.

I grit my teeth. "Do you boss the hockey team around this much?"

"Yup," Conor replies cheerfully. "Checked our season record lately?"

"The deal was I bowl and *then* you provide commentary."

Conor sighs. "Fine."

He steps back. I let the ball fly…directly into the gutter. When I spin back around, Conor doesn't make any attempt to mask his smug smile. At least he doesn't say *I told you so.*

Instead, he steps forward again, handing me another ball. I'm expecting his hands to touch me this time, but my body reacts like it's a surprise. Goose bumps erupt on my skin as his touch somehow sears through the two layers I'm wearing.

"Turn your hips like this. Drop your shoulder…" Conor makes the adjustments to my body himself, so I tune out the specific instructions. I just listen to the murmur of his deep voice speaking so close to my ear.

His hand lingers on my waist, then slides toward my ass.

I hiss his name. "There are little kids right next to us."

There's a low chuckle.

Next, his thumb is rubbing along the exposed skin between my sweater and jeans. I lean back into him without deciding to, my body responding to the touch that's become familiar. Conor shocks me by kissing the top of my head before stepping away.

"Try it again."

My anger has dissipated, my body missing his. But I refocus, the wooden lane, the people around us, the ugly carpet all rushing back into my awareness.

This time, I knock down eight pins.

A flock of butterflies appears in my stomach when I see Conor's proud expression.

Clayton and Mary return with frothy cups of beer. Mary bowls next.

Just as I predicted to Conor, Mary's bowling isn't all that impressive. She rolls a gutter ball on her first try. I smile when Clayton gets up to help her with her second attempt down the lane. She manages to hit four pins and they celebrate together.

Conor rolls a strike on his first try.

Clayton chugs half his beer.

And despite what I assured Conor, I feel like I'm on a date.

CHAPTER FOURTEEN

CONOR

We won last night. Decimated. Destroyed.

I'm reminded of that when I walk into the living room of the sophomores' house. They're hosting tonight's celebration.

We've proven that this isn't just a lucky streak, that our dominance isn't a fluke. Another win was what everyone expected, but that didn't make it any less satisfying to know that a 5-0 victory is being permanently marked on our season record. Plus Willis earned his first shutout.

People are starting to talk. To take notice. We're coming for the championship, and the teams that normally lead the division are sitting up and sensing the threat. Being watched feels different than being the underdog. Now, we have something to protect along with something to prove.

Right now, I couldn't be less worried about it. I soak up the cheers and bask in congratulations as I fight my way through the crowd of drunk Holt students, knocking fists with the guys and flashing around the confident grin girls seem to lose their minds over.

Last night, we celebrated as a team.

Tonight, it feels like the whole school is here.

When I reach the kitchen, Harlow is still behind me. We were a united team earlier, beating Thomas and Mary easily. Familiar. In sync. I'm not sure how it happened and…I don't hate it.

"No wonder your ego is the size of Washington," she mutters as I open the fridge.

I grin as I grab a ginger ale out of the fridge. It's what she was drinking the last time we were at a party together, and I didn't realize I'd remembered that until right this second.

"Want one?" I ask, holding it out to her.

"Sure. Thanks."

I nod as she takes the can from me, then grab another soda out for myself.

"Do you have any vodka?"

I raise an eyebrow, surprised. Harlow raises one right back.

"Smith!" I call.

Cole appears a few seconds later, holding a cup of beer in one hand. "'Sup, Hart?"

"Do you have any vodka?"

His eyebrows shoot up toward his hairline. "Holy fuck. You're drinking?"

"Not me. It's for Hayes." I nod toward Harlow.

"Hey, Harlow." Cole smiles at her, a dopey grin that pisses me off almost as much as Clayton Thomas telling me he bet the basketball team fifty bucks he'd sleep with Harlow by graduation. He's lucky I only beat his ass at bowling, not literally.

"Hi," she says, then hands the can back to me. "Can you hold this for a sec?"

I don't realize what's happening until the sweater is already over her head, leaving her in a silky tank top that has lace along the hem. I'm staring. Cole is too.

"Smith!" I bark. "Do you have any vodka or not?"

He jumps. "Uh…lemme check with Pierce. He usually keeps the good stuff in his room when we have people over."

"Great."

Cole goes off to check with Andy Pierce.

"I didn't mean to make this some big production," Harlow tells me. "I'm good with just this." She leans forward to take the ginger ale back from me. The neckline of her shirt gapes open a little more, offering a mouth-watering view of her tits.

"It's good for Pierce to learn how to share," I tell her. "He's a puck hog on the ice too."

Harlow snorts, then cracks the can open and takes a long sip. I watch the muscles of her throat contract for a second, then quickly look away. Basically anything she does turns me on, it seems.

And this is a new experience for me. I've never shown up at a party with a girl. Never kept track of someone walking through a crowded living room. We spent the past three hours together on what felt suspiciously like a date. I should be eager to get away from her. I should be wanting to talk to my teammates. Or make out with a random girl. But my motivation to move anywhere is glaringly absent.

"Hart!"

Jake Brennan, a junior defenseman, appears and grabs my shoulder from the right, slinging his arm around me.

"Having a good time, Brennan?" I ask, noticing his glazed eyes and ruddy cheeks. I should scold him for consuming an amount of alcohol that's going to make him sluggish as shit at practice tomorrow.

Jake smirks. "Hell yeah, I am!" He glances past me. "Hey, Harlow."

"Hey." She smiles at him and then takes another sip of soda.

Jesus. Is there a single guy on the team who *doesn't* know her? I struggle to keep the annoyance off my face. I don't get possessive over girls. My teammates acknowledging Harlow Hayes's existence has always bothered me. Now, it's just for an entirely different reason.

"Were you at the game last night? Fucking Hart." Brennan gives me a proud grin. "Calder Trophy winner. I'm calling it now."

Jake lifts his red cup in an enthusiastic *cheers*. The rapid motion causes some of the beer to slosh out of the rim and onto the bottom hem of Harlow's top.

"Fucking hell, Brennan. Nice hands."

Jake is staring at the wet splatters on her shirt. Actually, he might be looking higher. "I'm *so* sorry."

"Don't worry about it," Harlow says, handing me her drink again. "I'll just run to the bathroom. Clean up."

"Sorry again," Jake calls after her. His tone is apologetic. His eyes are focused on her ass.

"Eyes up, Brennan."

Jake shoots me a confused look. "I—Isn't she single?"

No is the first word that pops up in my head, and it scares the shit out of me.

I've never witnessed any of my teammates try to hook up with Harlow, and I always attributed that to her history with Jack. But now I'm realizing it probably has more to do with the way she's avoided the team—avoided me—both before and after they dated. If one of the guys makes a move on her...I'm not sure how I'll react but I know it won't be with a high five.

Pierce walks into the kitchen holding a bottle of vodka, saving me from answering Brennan.

I fill a cup with ice, measure out two ounces of vodka using a clean-looking shot glass I find in a cabinet, and then add a healthy splash of ginger ale from the can Harlow left with me. Andy and Jake watch me, wearing identical, puzzled expressions.

Hunter comes into the kitchen with his disgusting Jell-O cups, distracting the guys and bringing a new wave of activity with him. I field congratulations from a few more guys and then head into the living room to look for Harlow.

Sarah Clark steps in front of me.

I swear under my breath, then stop.

"Hey, Conor."

"Hey." My grip tightens on the cold cup I'm holding. I left my own drink in the kitchen, I'm just realizing.

"You're having quite the winning streak. Wanna go upstairs, and I'll congratulate you?"

She smirks, glances at my dick deliberately, and it doesn't even twitch. I'd be genuinely concerned about my equipment working, except I got half-hard watching Harlow drinking soda ten minutes ago.

"Not tonight," I tell her.

Sarah pouts. "Why not?"

"I'm just not feeling it."

"Well, I bet I could get you in the mood." She comes closer and I quickly step back, conserving the same amount of distance between us.

"I'm here with someone, okay?"

Sarah looks stunned. "You have a *girlfriend*?"

"*No*. She's not my girlfriend. We're just..." *Sleeping together* sounds sleazy. "Hanging out."

"That sounds like you have a girlfriend to me."

Fuck. Maybe she's right. I'm not sure what to call this compulsion to be around Harlow and the way my cock is only interested in her, but it's nothing I've ever experienced until now.

"Have a good night, Sarah."

I keep walking before she can say anything else. There's no sign of Harlow in the living room, so I head into the dining room.

She's here, playing beer pong. She and Robby against Clayton and Aidan. The red cups are empty, no one wanting to drink anything the ball touches after it bounces on the floor that was probably last cleaned a decade ago.

I spot Harlow's friend Mary standing off to the side, smiling as she talks to a few other girls. Clayton's not paying her any attention, his focus all on Harlow as she tosses the ball into a cup in the back row.

I continue walking toward Harlow, nudging her arm with the cup once I reach her. "You forgot this in the kitchen."

She spins toward me, her expression startled. Glances at the cup. "What happened to the can?"

"Pierce parted with some of his precious vodka. I mixed it up for you."

"*You* did?"

At first, I think she's implying I'm incapable of making a cocktail. Then, I realize what she's concerned about. I've never heard about anyone getting slipped anything at a Holt party, but I've heard horror stories about it happening at plenty of other schools.

I lower my voice. "I've had it this whole time. No one else has touched it, I swear."

She nods and takes a sip.

And I realize…she trusts me.

Harlow smiles. "It's good. Thanks."

"Sweet! You bartending, Hart?" Aidan asks. He's grinning this way, looking between me and Harlow, and I shoot him a look that makes it clear his commentary isn't appreciated.

"No," I snap.

Harlow scans my expression, like she's looking for an explanation for my sudden, dark mood.

I don't have one for her. I don't even understand what I'm feeling myself. I'm irritated, and it's for no good reason. The one thing that's always governed my mood—hockey—couldn't be going better at the moment. I should be thrilled, not testy.

"Nice shot," I tell her, then head back out the same way I entered.

I think Aidan might call my name, but I don't turn around.

I wander around the first floor, not sure what to do with myself. I don't feel like talking to anyone. All we have tomorrow is a film session, but I don't really feel like drinking. I'm not interested in hooking up with Sarah or another girl who's not Harlow.

When I reach the back door, I decide to head outside. The small backyard is totally empty, probably because it's a good forty degrees colder out here than it is inside. I lean back against the side of the house and stare up at the dark sky, shoving my hands into my pockets.

I'm not sure how much time passes before the door opens and closes again.

I glance over automatically, my heart literally skipping a beat when I see her.

She came after me.

I don't realize that's what I was hoping for until I'm staring at Harlow, her expression creased with concern as she studies me. "What's wrong?"

"Nothing." I huff a laugh. "I'm in a shitty mood for no reason. Sorry if I was short with you back there. I just needed some air."

She takes a step closer, instead of heading back inside. "Are you mad that I came?"

"What? No. I invited you, remember?"

"Yeah, I do. But back there…it felt the same as it used to. When you'd see me and try to get away as quickly as possible."

"That's not it. I promise."

Her nod is slow, and then she starts gnawing on her lower lip in a very distracting way. "Thanks for the drink."

I glance at her empty hands. "Do you want another one?"

"No, I just downed it for some liquid warmth."

I still have my hockey jacket on. But Harlow's just in her tank top.

I push away from the wall, realizing she must be freezing. "Where's your sweater? Or your jacket?"

"I left my coat in your car. And I looked for my sweater, but I couldn't find it." She makes a face. "Someone probably took it."

I step toward the door. "I'll look for it."

"Wait." She grabs my arm before I can take another step. "Before you send out a sweater search party…tell me why you're upset."

"I told you, nothing."

"Is this about the thing with Clayton?"

"No." I don't know if it's a lie or not. I'm still pissed at him, the same way I'm angry at Brennan's wandering eyes. But it's bigger than that. More about me than either of them.

"I'm not interested in Clayton," Harlow tells me.

"Good. You could do better." And I'm thrilled Thomas is going to lose his dumb bet.

"I'm doing *you*, Hart."

Then she kisses me.

I kiss her back in the way I want to claim her in front of Thomas and every other guy at this school, urgent and confident and loud. If anyone saw this—if I kissed her this way when I handed her the drink earlier—they'd all be able to tell what I'm just admitting to myself: I have serious feelings for this girl.

I'm not just attracted to her.

This isn't just lust or fooling around.

I *care* about Harlow in a way that's completely unfamiliar to me. In a way that terrifies me, because I'm used to being confident in my decisions and I have no clue what I'm doing where she's concerned.

She moans my name, and just like that, my dick is fully erect. I cage her between my body and the house, pushing a knee between her legs. Harlow grinds against my thigh as her hands slip under my shirt. Her hands are freezing, digging into my back, and it spurs a new sense of urgency.

I can't fuck her like this—it's so cold out I can see our breath in the air—and I don't have a condom, but that doesn't mean I can't remind her what it's like between us.

I tug down the thin top she's wearing, which has been slowly driving me insane ever since I first saw her in it, until her left boob is out. "You're not wearing a bra?" I groan.

"It has a built-in," she tells me. Then gasps, when I lean down to circle her nipple with my tongue. "So no straps."

She's rocking against my thigh now, her breathing ragged and uneven.

"Can you come like this?"

"Probably." She blushes.

I'm too impatient. It's a competition in my head, getting her off as quickly as possible. A boost to my ego, seeing how responsive she is to my touch. I pull back just enough to reach the waistband of her jeans, unbuttoning and unzipping and tugging until I can wedge two fingers in between her thighs.

Harlow moans. Her underwear is soaked through, the heat of her pussy scorching against my hand. As soon as my fingers push inside, Harlow tilts her head back, arching into my touch as her eyes hood. I can feel every reaction, her walls clenching around my fingers like she's trying to keep me inside of her.

I've never *not* responded to the sight of her. Never *not* been attracted to her.

But this—her lips swollen from my kisses and her hair messy from my hands and her pussy so wet it's soaking my fingers? It's my new favorite look on her. And it's called *mine*.

And as much as I'd like to just stand here and admire the view, I haven't forgotten where we are. I'm blocking her body with mine, but I still don't want anyone seeing her like this. And Harlow is impatient, squirming against me and trying to force more friction. Her jeans are keeping her thighs together, so she feels even tighter than usual.

I fuck her with my fingers as fast as I can in the limited space, kissing her when I feel her walls start pulsing, using my hand to get her off. Even after all the tremors have stopped, I keep kissing her. She tastes like ginger and vodka and something special that's just Harlow. I only pull away when I feel her shiver against me.

It's way too cold for her to be half-naked out here. I smirk at her surprised expression when I lick my fingers clean. Then pull her jeans back up and right the strap on her shoulder.

She watches me closely. "Now I smell like a brewery *and* sex."

"I happen to know a place across the street with clean clothes…"

"Don't you want to stay? Celebrate with the team?"

I'm honest. "No."

They're all drunk and we spend most of our time together already. I'm only here because it was expected I'd show and I had nothing better to do.

"Do you want to stay?" I ask.

She shakes her head. "I only came because the captain of the team invited me, and it seemed rude not to accept."

I smirk.

"Let me just text Mary, make sure she's good." Harlow pulls her phone out of her pocket and starts typing.

I shrug out of my jacket and drape it around her shoulders.

"Thanks."

"Purely self-interest, Hayes. If you get hypothermia, I can't fuck you."

She hums, a small smile appearing on her face as she types something on her phone.

"Okay. Mary is good. Let's go."

We walk around the house toward the sidewalk.

"We've got another home game next weekend, you know. If you didn't hate this one."

Harlow's silent.

"You don't have to, obviously. I just—"

"No, I'd love to go. I just...I won't be here next weekend."

That's all she says. And I know what the lack of explanation means, even before I ask, "Where are you going?"

"Claremont. Landon has a...gig."

"Oh." We reach the curb before I think of anything else to say. "He's a musician?"

"Yeah. He's in a band."

I know nothing about my half-brother. Likes. Dislikes. Interests. Pet peeves. Hobbies.

"Are they any good?"

"Um. They're a work in progress."

I wonder if Hugh is musical. I don't think so. I wonder if it irks Landon how my interests align more closely to our father than his do.

It irks me.

I glance over at Harlow. She's watching me cautiously, like she's expecting me to stomp off at any moment. React the same way I did when Landon called her.

Does it bother me, that she's going to visit the Garrisons next weekend? Yeah.

Does it change any of my feelings toward her? No.

And since I can tell Harlow's wondering if it does, I reach out and grab her hand, twining our fingers together.

That's how we walk, the whole way back to my house.

CHAPTER FIFTEEN

HARLOW

The dull staccato of crashing cymbals starts off the song. The guitarist, Adam, comes in a few seconds later. Then Landon steps up to the microphone standing in the middle of the stage and starts singing. He has a throaty, deep voice that I've always enjoyed listening to, even if his band's music isn't to my personal taste. I mostly listen to indie folk. I blasted The Head and the Heart for the drive from Somerville to Claremont earlier.

Landon's band—whose current name I can't remember because they're constantly changing it—is more alternative rock. I think. I'm far from a music afficionado. My playlists are mostly songs that come up as suggested based on who I've saved as my favorite artists.

"Aren't they incredible?" Simone shouts.

"Yeah," I yell back at her.

I met Simone twenty minutes ago, when Landon and his bandmates headed backstage before their twenty-minute set. I've gathered she's here because she's hooking up with the shaggy-haired Adam, who has opted for the *starving artist* look for this gig. He's wearing a ripped T-shirt that shows patches of the pale skin covering his lanky frame.

Landon's gig is at a small club one town over from Claremont. It's dark and kind of damp inside, sort of like a basement. A long bar takes up most of one wall, black leather booths lining the rest. Most of the space is open, a few hightop tables scattered close to the stage. The turnout is decent, at least sixty people clustered in here.

I'm sure Landon will be thrilled. This is, by far, the closest his band has come to a professional performance.

The song ends. Simone and I applaud loudly and there's some scattered clapping around the room.

"I'm going to grab something to drink," I tell Simone. "Want anything?"

She doesn't take her eyes off the stage. "I'm good."

I nod and then head for the bar, finding an opening about halfway down. The middle-aged bartender comes over a few minutes later, nodding when I order a sparkling water with lime. He returns with my drink right away, waving away payment when I offer. I thank him, shove a few dollars into the tip jar, and then turn around to head back toward Simone.

There's a guy blocking the way, wearing a flirty smirk. His hair is messy and light brown, and he's wearing a black T-shirt.

"Hey, I'm Macon." Based on the way he says his name, I'm supposed to recognize it.

But I've never seen this guy before in my life.

"Hi…"

He chuckles, tugging at the collar of his shirt. "Oof. I figured this was one place I'd get recognized. I'm the headliner."

Macon nods toward the nearest booth. On the wall above it is a massive poster of his face, with *Macon Gray* written across his forehead in big, block letters.

"Oh. Uh, cool."

"So...not a fan?"

"I've never listened to your music, so I couldn't really say. I'm here to support my best friend." I point toward Landon on stage.

"Ah. They're decent."

I nod.

"Can I buy you a drink, Red?"

I fight the urge to make a face.

I like the look of my red hair. It's a connection to my mom, who had the same shade. A reminder of my heritage. But I hate—absolutely *hate*—being called Red. And I don't get why so many guys do it. If I had dark brown hair, I'm positive he wouldn't have asked *Can I buy you a drink, Brunette?*

"I have one, thanks." I hold up my water as proof.

"Then how about a dance?"

"I have a boyfriend."

The sentence I've never said before in my life spills out naturally. Usually I'd tell a guy *I'm not interested* or *I'm here with friends.* I've never used the boyfriend excuse, not even when I've been dating a guy.

I don't *have* a boyfriend, but it doesn't sound like a lie. Doesn't feel like one either.

I wonder what Conor would do if he was here. He was definitely bothered by whatever Clayton said to him about me, which I'm guessing was some reference to the fact he's been trying to hook up with me for a while. Was that part of some macho competition to be the biggest man on campus? Or was he jealous?

"Of course you do," Macon says. "Could I take him?"

My lips quirk. "He plays hockey."

"Damnit. Well, if that ever changes...look me up. Gonna be a big star one day."

Macon flashes me a grin that makes me think he probably does have some groupies, and then heads toward backstage.

I find Simone easily. She's by far the most enthusiastic audience member, jumping and waving her arms around. I doubt she noticed I was gone for so long.

Landon's band plays another two songs, then head offstage. Simone and I migrate over to the bar to wait for them. It's only a few minutes before the four guys reappear, all holding cold beers.

I suppress a sigh. I was kind of hoping to head straight home after his set. I got up early this morning to swim, had two labs, and then drove to the Garrisons'. I barely had time to dump my stuff before Landon and I left to come here.

"You guys were *ah-mazing*!" Simone trills.

"Really good," I agree, nodding.

"You should bring some friends to our next gig, Harlow," Adam suggests. "We need more fans."

"When is your next gig?" I ask.

"We don't have one," Landon tells me.

"We will," the drummer, Matt, predicts. "I told you my uncle's bar is looking for acts."

"Get us a tryout then," Landon tells him.

We have to move away from the door so some equipment can get rolled through, ending up crammed into one of the open booths so the guys can drink their beers and relax. Rock music blares from the speakers as a couple of guys rearrange the stage. I sip my water, feeling a headache form. It's too loud in here to make much conversation, the guys mostly nodding and grinning at each other. Jubilant after their successful show.

The speakers cut out and there's a bunch of applause before a male voice says, "How's everyone doing tonight?"

More applause. Landon and his bandmates are now looking toward the stage.

"Good, good. I'm Macon Gray. If you're here, you probably already know that. Although…" He chuckles. "You might not. I'd like to dedicate this next song to the redhead who broke my heart earlier by falling for a hockey player and not waiting for me. Brains over brawn, baby."

I almost laugh, until I realize everyone in the booth is staring at me. Landon, the hardest of all.

"What's he talking about?" he asks me.

Guess I'm the only redhead in here.

I roll my eyes. "Nothing. He hit on me at the bar. I told him I wasn't interested."

"Because you're dating a hockey player?"

"I told him athletes are more my type. He drew conclusions, I guess."

My heart beats faster and faster with each lie that I tell.

Landon has no idea I've ever even *spoken* to Conor.

It's the biggest secret I've kept over the course of our twenty-year-long friendship.

I didn't feel like I needed to tell Landon about our talk in the kitchen. Or the run-in at the pool. Or the training at the track. I could even rationalize keeping the sex to myself, it's not like I told him details about that before Conor happened to be the guy in question.

But every time I talk to Conor, text him, kiss him, touch him —all of which I've been doing a lot of lately—I feel guiltier and guiltier. Not that I'm doing it, but that Landon doesn't know. Especially since my feelings toward Conor only seem to be getting stronger, instead of fading the way I assumed—hoped— they would.

"Huh." Landon looks confused, not suspicious.

"Athletes?" Matt, the drummer, shakes his head. "Macon's right. Mistake. They're notorious fuckboys."

"I've heard that about musicians too," I say.

Matt winks at me. "Only successful ones."

Landon punches Matt's arm. Either because of the implication they aren't ones or because he's sort of flirting with me. He might be a year younger than me, but Landon has taken on the protective, big brother role since we were kids.

The guys finish their beers, Landon grabs his guitar, and we head out into the parking lot.

"So, what did you think?" he asks as soon as we start driving.

"I told you; you guys were great."

Landon glances over. "Adam was in the wrong key for half the set."

"Simone didn't notice."

He laughs. "Yeah. At least we have *a* groupie."

"I was there too," I remind him.

"Thanks for coming, Harlie."

I shove away the guilt, focusing on the road. "Of course."

We talk easily for the remainder of the drive, catching up on the past couple of months. With one notable exclusion on my side.

My stomach grumbles as I park my car in the driveway next to the big, brick house. Landon's gig was at seven and it's almost eight now. Allison promised to have dinner waiting when we got home, and I missed her cooking.

"Hungry?" Landon grins.

"Starving," I reply, climbing out of the car and stretching before I follow him up the stone walkway to the front porch.

The door opens before we even reach it, and Allison Garrison steps out. She starts clapping, and Landon's cheeks turn red.

"Mom. Stop it," he grumbles.

"You wouldn't let me come to your show, so this is my way of congratulating you."

Landon rolls his eyes. "How many famous musicians do you think bring their moms along to their shows?"

I can't resist saying, "Taylor Swift. Have you heard of her?"

Allison laughs, pulling me into another hug. "Ah, I missed you, Harlow."

"I missed you too," I say, resting my chin on her shoulder. She's the closest link to my mom I have left. They were best friends for half their lives, meeting as freshmen at Holt.

Allison's arms tighten around me, like maybe she's thinking the same thing.

"The next Bob Dylan is back already?" Hugh Garrison steps out of the kitchen and into the front hallway. He smiles at Landon, then his gaze lands on me.

"Harlow," he greets warmly.

He was at work when I arrived earlier. This is the first time I've seen him since I left for Holt in August. Hugh looks the same as he did then. Tall, with the same brown hair and hazel eyes as his younger son.

"Hey, Hugh," I greet, stepping forward into his open arms.

For the first time, it occurs to me: *I'm hugging Conor Hart's dad.*

He's always been Landon's father in my head. Allison's—my mother's best friend's—husband.

I wonder if Conor has ever hugged his father. I doubt it.

"I just pulled dinner out of the oven. Your timing is perfect," Allison says before heading into the kitchen.

I hang up my coat in the front hall and then follow her. It smells amazing, a tray of roast chicken and vegetables sitting out on the counter next to a green salad. Way better than anything I cook for myself.

Hugh and Allison barrage me with questions about classes and friends as we set the table and sit down to eat. It feels normal.

Comfortable. A routine that's taken place many times before, because it has.

They ask Landon questions about his gig, the pride unmistakable in their tones. Landon could probably decide to pursue a clown career, and they'd support it. And I know he appreciates that. But I can't help but compare it to Conor. I don't think his mom has been to a single game this season. If she has, he hasn't mentioned it.

"You couldn't have worn something nicer to perform in?" Allison is asking, eyeing Landon's outfit critically.

"Seriously, Mom?" Landon glances down at the *Brighton* sweatshirt he's wearing. "What's wrong with this?"

"To start, it's dirty." Allison nods to a stain on the sleeve that looks like coffee.

Landon rolls his eyes, then pulls off his sweatshirt. Underneath, he's wearing a long-sleeved T-shirt he slept in recently, if the number of creases in the cotton are any indication. "Better?"

"Worse," Allison says. "I'll put in a load of laundry after dinner."

I bite my bottom lip to keep from grinning.

"Musicians have better things to do with their time than laundry."

"Just because you want to be a starving artist doesn't mean you need to dress like one," is Allison's response. I wonder what she would have thought of Adam's outfit. At least Landon's shirt is in one piece.

"Is Kelly visiting this weekend?" Hugh asks in an obvious attempt to change the topic.

"No. We're taking a break," Landon replies.

"Oh," Allison says before exchanging a glance with Hugh.

Neither of them look dismayed by the news. I've never liked Landon's girlfriend all that much, either. She spends an unhealthy amount of time complaining. He could do much better, in my opinion.

"What about you, Harlow?" Allison looks to me.

"What about me?" I ask, spearing some salad on my fork.

"Didn't you say you were going out on a double date with Eve and her boyfriend a little while ago?"

"Oh, yeah. That happened."

"How was it?"

"Not great," I say bluntly. "We definitely aren't soulmates."

"What about that guy in one of your classes? Aaron?" Allison isn't deterred. Maybe she feels like she needs to ask the questions my mom isn't here to.

"Eric. We went out too," I admit.

"And?"

I sigh. "He was nice."

"That's promising!"

"Nice is code for *not interested*, Mom," Landon says.

I roll my eyes, acknowledging he has a point. "I don't think we'll go out again," I tell her.

"Well, that's fine," Allison says. "There are plenty of great guys out there."

"Plenty of jerks, you mean." Landon scoffs. "Most of the guys at Brighton are total tools."

"All of your friends seem perfectly nice," Allison replies.

"Well, yeah. They're not *jocks*."

I have a feeling that comment is aimed at me and my alleged *athletes are my type*.

"That's awfully stereotypical, Landon. Your father played sports."

"Yeah, I know." Landon rolls his eyes. "Apple fell far from the tree."

There's an awkward pause I don't think I'm imagining. But

maybe I am. I could count on my fingers the number of times I've heard Conor's name uttered out loud in this house since I've been living here. But he comes up in innocuous idioms like the one Landon just spoke. On Father's Day. Whenever Holt or hockey is mentioned.

He's a shadow in the background.

Subtext in conversations.

I've always had some vague sense of it. I'm painfully aware of it now. Because Conor is no longer a shadow or subtext to me. He's vivid color. Larger than life.

After dinner, a few of Landon's high school friends come over to catch up. We end up lounging around in the den.

Landon's friends are similar to him: sweet, slightly nerdy, and happier spending a night in than out. The decision to watch one of the *Lord of the Rings* movies is met with great enthusiasm—from everyone but me.

I entertain myself by scrolling through social media on my phone.

Suddenly, several of the guys stand up from the couch.

"Movie over?" I ask. Based on Landon's eye roll, the question came out too eager.

"No. Popcorn break," he replies. "Want any?"

"Nah, I'm good. Thanks." I snuggle back into the cushions.

All the guys leave the den except for Steve Essex. "Senior year going well?" he asks me, taking advantage of the extra space on the couch to spread out some.

Steve has always been more outgoing than the rest of Landon's friends. He's the closest person I have to a friend in this town where I hardly know anyone.

The Garrisons would always come to visit my family in Canada. Landon was still in high school when I came to live with them, but I only lived in Claremont for a couple of weeks before moving into Holt's dorms to start my freshman year. This town doesn't feel like home.

"Yeah, pretty good," I reply. "Crazy to believe I'm almost done with college."

"Tell me about it. I can't believe I'm more than halfway done. All the senior guys on the team were messes at our last game." Steve smiles. "Weird to think that'll be me soon."

I recall he plays soccer at a small college in Oregon. An exception to Landon's *my friends aren't jerks because they're not jocks* rule.

"Did you guys have a good season?"

"Not bad. We're Division III though, you know? Not the biggest deal."

"Yeah, Holt is the same way."

Steve glances at the sliding door that leads into the den, then back at me. "Not when it comes to hockey, from what I hear."

I shift uncomfortably. "Yeah. Not for hockey."

"I get why Landon hates him. I do. But I went to high school with Conor too. He had his moments…but he's not a bad guy. Evan Sanford was on the soccer team with me. He was Conor's right winger in the winter. Couldn't say enough good things about the guy. I just…well, it couldn't have been easy for Conor, either, you know?" Steve shrugs. "Nice to see some things working out for him now. I hope he makes it to the pros."

I just stare at him.

My silence unnerves Steve. He glances at the doorway again before leaning forward. "This is just between us, right? You won't…"

"I won't say anything to Landon," I assure him.

Steve lets out a relieved sigh. "Okay. Good."

Loud chatter announces Landon's return, along with the rest of the guys. When it comes to fantasy trilogies, they all have plenty to say. I shake my head when Landon holds the popcorn bowl out to me and keep my eyes fixed on the television screen as the movie resumes.

I'm too distracted to even attempt to immerse myself in the movie. I stare at the screen until the credits roll, then say good night to Landon and his friends and head up to my room.

It's one of several guest rooms in the five-bedroom house. I haven't changed any of the furnishings that were here when I moved in, despite Hugh and Allison encouraging me to make any changes I wanted.

I get ready for bed and then slide between soft flannel sheets, grabbing my phone off the nightstand. I chew on my bottom lip for a good minute before texting him.

HARLOW: Hey.

I wasn't sure if he'd reply. It's a Friday night. But he does immediately.

CONOR: Hey. You made it okay?

HARLOW: Yeah, the drive isn't that long.

HARLOW: ...which you know.

HARLOW: Did Cody decide the drills this week?

I'm surprised when his response is to call me.

"This is easier than texting," Conor says when I answer. "I'm trying to ice my ribs."

"Are you okay?"

"Yeah. Just Sampson being a dick. He claims I was about to score."

"Were you?"

A pause. "Well, yeah."

I laugh.

"And, yes, Cody had lots of requests this week, like always. He also told me I was skating too slow. He's in for a surprise when he gets old enough to play with boarding allowed."

There's a muffled slam on the other end, followed by a faint version of Aidan's voice.

"Do you mind?" Conor rumbles.

"I told you we were leaving at ten. What the fuck, Hart?"

"And I told you I'm not going. Look at this."

There's a rustle.

"Fucking Robby," Aidan grumbles. "Fine, we'll skip Gaffney's. Can we get pizza? I'm hungry. Who are you on the phone with, anyway?"

I hold my breath.

"It's Harlow."

"You mean your girl—"

"*Out*, Phillips! I'll be downstairs in five, okay?"

"Fine. Tell the girl you're fucking and talk to all the time that—"

There's a thud on Conor's end, then silence.

"How much of that did you hear?" His voice is normal again, no longer muffled.

"All of it."

He sighs. "Fucking Phillips. If he wasn't a good winger and a great friend, I'd never talk to him again."

I play with a stray thread on the comforter. "How much did you tell him?"

"Absolutely nothing. He's just the nosiest guy I know and happens to know my hockey schedule. And he made me and Morgan put our class schedules up on the fridge, so anytime either of us go anywhere that's not either hockey or school-related, we get questions. Morgan hardly goes anywhere, so he doesn't really care."

"Maybe you should do the same thing to him. Ask Aidan where he goes all the time so that he realizes it's annoying."

"Tried that." Conor sighs. "He loved it. He's an oversharer anyway." He pauses. "I'm not, Hayes. If that's what you're worried about."

"I wasn't." Although it's nice to know.

"I'd better go. Phillips *will* come back up here."

"Yeah, I know. I'll, uh, see you soon?"

He came over after his Wednesday practice and spent the night, but I haven't seen him since. I was hyperaware of this trip looming, and maybe he was too.

"Yeah, text me when you're back. Night, Hayes."

"Bye."

We both linger on the line for a few seconds, leaving space where there are other words we could say. Where *I miss you* might fit, or even another three-word phrase. But we both hang up without saying anything else.

I drop my face into my hands, rubbing my temples. It's so strange being back here, where nothing has changed except me. Where I'm part of this tangible family that Conor's a ghost in.

I just spent hours—natural, comfortable hours—with his father and half-brother, and as far as I know he hasn't even talked to either of them in *years*. There's a huge blockade up ahead, one I'm pretending not to see because it's convenient.

Eventually, I'll have to acknowledge it. And the deeper I get with Conor—and I'm already approaching *Can't see the shore or touch the bottom* territory—the more it's going to hurt.

There's a soft knock on the door a few seconds later.

I clear my throat, then call "Come in."

The door opens and Allison peeks her head in. "Hey. Do you

need anything?"

I shake my head. "All good, thanks."

"I thought I heard some voices in here…"

"Oh, yeah. Mine. Eve called because she couldn't find some of her art stuff."

I'm getting better at lying, and I'm not proud of it.

Allison smiles. "I'm so glad you found a friend like her. Reminds me of me and your mom."

I smile back, nodding.

"I'm sorry if I was pushy at dinner, Harlow. I didn't mean to put you on the spot, and I know I can never replace your mom. I just want you to know you can talk to me about anything."

"I know that. Thanks."

"All right. Sweet dreams." She starts to close the door.

"Hey, Allison?"

"Yes?"

"Do you, uh, do you remember when my mom met my dad?"

"Of course."

"What did she say about him? How did she…know? That he was the one, I mean."

One of her eyebrows lifts. "So there *is* a guy, huh?"

"Yeah." I look down, playing with the thread again. "But it wasn't really dinner table talk. I'm sure Landon wouldn't approve of him. And it's more of a, um, physical thing. We're not actually dating, or anything."

Allison closes the door, then comes and sits at the end of my bed. "Why do you think Landon wouldn't approve?"

"He, uh, plays sports."

She smiles. "I think Landon might be a little unfairly biased there. He played football when he was younger, you know."

"He did?"

As far as I can remember, Landon's main interest has been

music.

Allison nods. "I think he felt pressure to play because Hugh did. Pressure when he did play, to live up to Hugh's legacy. It wasn't a natural fit for him, and that was hard. All I'm saying is, don't let Landon's biases become yours. What else is there to know about this guy, besides that he plays sports?"

I chew on the inside of my cheek, trying to decide how much else to share. She's not biologically related to Conor the way Hugh and Landon are, but he's technically her stepson.

"He's..." I shake my head. "I don't really know how to describe him. He's infuriating sometimes, but he can also be really sweet. Thoughtful. He listens and pays attention to me. If I mention a lab report to him, he'll remember to ask me about it when it's due a week later. I never told him I love ginger ale, but I guess he noticed at some point because now it's the first thing he offers me. He's considerate and he challenges me and I...I'm, um, rambling."

"He sounds wonderful, Harlow."

I nod, swallowing. "Yeah, he is. But it'll never work out between us. We're too different, and he's not interested in a relationship anyway. So I keep waiting for it to end, to fizzle out naturally, but it hasn't. I just keep getting in deeper and deeper."

"I think that's why they call it *falling* in love, sweetheart. Once you start, it's hard to stop."

"Well, I need it to."

"Tell him, Harlow. Tell this guy how you feel about him. And if he's everything you say he is, hopefully he'll surprise you. Sometimes we need people to show us a different way to look at things, when we can't see it ourselves. Were you expecting to have these feelings for this guy when you first met him?"

I shake my head. "Absolutely not."

"See? You never know. Maybe he's feeling the same way.

And if he's not, then he's not the one for you and it's his loss. Okay, honey?"

I nod, not sure it's any solution at all. Even if Conor does have some feelings for me, they're massively overshadowed by his hatred of the other people in this house.

Unless I turn my back on the Garrisons and decide to never speak to them again, I don't see how any type of future includes us as a couple. And I'm not sure if I could live with myself. Whatever mistakes Hugh has made, whatever resentments Landon harbors...they took me in as family. They're the closest connection I have to my parents.

I want them to be included in my life. I always figured I'd ask Hugh to walk me down the aisle if I got married. Have conversations like this with Allison, except using a guy's name. That isn't possible for me and Conor.

But he's become an addiction. I couldn't even go more than a couple of days without talking to him. I don't know if I'm strong enough to walk away from him, even out of self-preservation.

Conor is going to have to be the one who ends things between us.

And he'll earn his stupid nickname, because it *will* break my heart.

Allison stands. "Get some sleep. I made a brunch reservation and nail appointments for us tomorrow. Thought we could have a girls' outing?"

I nod. "That sounds great."

"Everything will work out," she tells me.

I force a smile. "I know."

I don't, though.

"I'd love to meet him one day, Harlow," Allison tells me, before heading toward the door.

You already have, I think.

CHAPTER SIXTEEN

CONOR

It's sunny outside, for once, with no hint of moisture in the air. I breathe deeply, letting the crispness fill my lungs. Rather than climb into my car, I shove my hands into my pockets and start walking along the sidewalk toward campus. It snowed yesterday, a few inches that have stuck around so far. The small piles on either side of the road are already gray and splattered with mud, but the rest is pristine.

It takes me ten minutes to reach the football stadium.

I spot Harlow's red hair after nine. She's by the gate that leads onto the running track, doing one of the stretching exercises I showed her.

"Did you already do your butt kicks?"

Harlow spins to face me, a smile spreading across her lips that I automatically match.

"Hey," she breathes.

"Hey."

We grin at each other like two fools.

"Congrats," Harlow tells me. "I saw you won again."

"Yeah, thanks. Every game, it starts to feel more unlikely."

All streaks come to an end. Most things do.

Like Harlow's smile. It slips off her face slowly, the longer we stare at each other.

"So…did you do your butt kicks?" I ask again.

"Why?"

I smirk. "Because I wanted to watch."

She rolls her eyes, then steps closer. Tugs my jacket to the side and then pulls my shirt up.

"Jesus, Hayes! We're in public!"

She ignores my mock outrage, studying the three-inch bruise spread across my ribs that's turned to an angry shade of purple. Her fingers trace it lightly, and I clench my jaw to keep from wincing.

"You played on Saturday with this?"

I nod. "We've got another game tomorrow. It'll be better by then."

Harlow drops my shirt, but she doesn't step away. "Even superheroes don't heal that fast, Hart."

"Aw, are you calling me a superhero?"

"What are your superpowers?"

"Well, you've told me I have a magical dick."

She blushes. "I have never, *ever* said that."

I shrug. "It's been strongly implied."

Harlow breathes a laugh, shaking her head. "Has Robby seen that?" she asks, nodding toward my bruise.

"It's a rough sport, even when we're practicing."

"It shouldn't be *that* rough, *when* you're practicing." She purses her lips, like she's considering telling Sampson off herself. It's adorable.

Robby has apologized to me a half-dozen times since it happened. He got tripped up, knocked me into the boards when I wasn't expecting it.

Jamison knocked out one of Collins's teeth last week.

Shit happens.

"I'm fine, Hayes. You weren't here to snuggle with, so I made do with a bag of peas."

Her eyes widen, and I wonder if maybe I'm not supposed to mention the way we always spoon after sex now. Hell if I know what the rules of this arrangement are. We *don't* have rules, and that's probably part of the problem.

"Is snuggling code for something else?"

"Would I have turned down a blowjob as a distraction? No. Bad timing you were gone this weekend."

"You could have still gotten one."

I stiffen as soon as she says the words. In addition to not having rules, I have no idea if we're exclusive.

I haven't been with anyone else since we started hooking up, and I don't think that Harlow has either. But again, *I don't know*. She's never asked me and I've never asked her. It's one of several things that floats ambiguous between us, like how she just spent a happy family weekend at my father's house.

"Well, I didn't." I stuff my hands into my pockets. "How was your weekend?"

She looks away. "It was, um, good."

Rather than accept that non-answer, I press. "What did you do?"

"Landon's gig was on Friday night. We went to that, then came home for dinner. A few of Landon's friends came over to watch a movie. Then Allison and I went to brunch and to get our nails done."

Harlow flashes her pink fingers at me, and since they're hers and I haven't had sex in almost a week, I immediately picture them wrapped around my cock.

"Hugh, uh, barbecued and we played Monopoly. Then on Saturday, we just lounged around. I left around lunchtime."

It's bizarre, hearing her use their names so casually. Imagining the happy, wholesome scene she's describing of playing boardgames and eating dinner together.

Strange that takes place without me, when I should be a part of it. I've had years to come to terms with that, though.

The weirdest aspect now is that Harlow—*my* Harlow—is a part of it.

"Sounds fun."

It's a struggle, keeping the sarcasm out of my voice. But I manage to.

"How was your weekend? Aside from the game, I mean."

"It was fine." I ate leftover pizza for breakfast, caught up on homework, and iced my bruise. More like super boring. "We should start running. I've got practice soon."

"Yeah. Sure."

She follows me onto the running track, which has been cleared of snow.

We start jogging in silence.

"What are you doing for Thanksgiving?" Harlow asks.

"Why? Do you want to carpool?"

She's silent.

I exhale. "Sorry. My mom has to work in the afternoon, so we're planning on brunch before she has to go into the hospital."

"What does she do, at the hospital?"

"She started as a nurse, then put herself through med school. She's an ER doctor now."

"Wow. Good for her."

I nod, then add, "She's coming to my game tomorrow."

"Has she been to one this season?"

I shake my head. "Not yet. She's busy."

"I wasn't judging, Conor," she says softly.

We run in silence for a couple of laps. I try to focus on rhythmic steps, instead of the redhead next to me. I'm happy she's back. But part of me is on edge. Waiting. Wondering if a weekend away changed her feelings about…whatever this is. Changed her feelings toward me.

"What do you think the odds are of me making it to the finish line next summer?" Harlow asks. She's breathing more heavily, I notice, so I slow my pace a little. "I was planning to go for a run this weekend, but then I…didn't."

"Why didn't you go? Do the Garrisons not know about the marathon?"

"They know. I was just being lazy." There's a pause, then, "They're running it."

"All of them? The whole thing?"

"Uh-huh. They're raising money by the mile."

I absorb that for a few seconds. "Have you been back home? Since…"

"I've been back to Canada. Not to the same town where I grew up. But the plan has always been to go back there after graduation, so…I'll have to face it sometime, right?"

"I mean, no. You could never go back." Some selfish part of me is fully on board with her remaining here, even if I have no idea where I'll be after graduation.

She laughs. "Yeah. True. I think…I've always been worried to make new memories in the same places, if that makes any sense? Being back there…going to the same spots and doing the same things, except without them, it feels like it could override what I remember. But I also want to do those things *to* remember my parents. Does that make any sense?"

"It makes a lot of sense. But I don't think you'll forget

anything. And if I had to guess, I don't think your parents would want you to stay away forever."

She nods. "It's the same reason I haven't gone back to Ireland. We used to visit there a lot to see my dad's family. My grandparents are gone, but I still have two aunts who live just outside of Dublin. They keep inviting me, and I always make excuses."

"What's it like there? I've never been out of the country."

Harlow looks surprised. "Never?"

I shake my head.

"It's beautiful. Green grass as far as you can see. Big cliffs overlooking the water. Villages with pie shops and apothecaries. Cobblestone streets." She smiles. "I used to pretend to talk with an Irish accent after every visit. Drove my parents crazy."

"You should go back, Harlow."

"Yeah." She nods. "I'm considering it, this summer. The, uh, Garrisons would always come stay with my family for a week in the summer. They've rented a place about an hour away from where I grew up, the last several years. Kept the tradition going, in a slightly different way. They've only missed one year since Landon was born, and it was a while ago. I don't want to be the one to miss it, so once those dates are finalized, I'll make other plans."

She's becoming more and more comfortable mentioning them to me, I've noticed.

"They didn't go that year because Allison found out Hugh had screwed my mom again, Harlow."

I don't look at her. I keep my gaze forward.

There's a long pause. Finally, "I…I didn't know."

"I know you didn't."

I'm well aware of how Harlow sees my father. In her eyes, he's the hero who opened up his home to his wife's best friend's orphaned daughter. He's been a part of her support system, and I don't resent her for it. I'm glad she had him—them.

But in my life, he's the villain. He's the asshole who blew up my mom's life, then my life, then my mom's again. My feelings for him have always been clear cut. Black and white.

And selfishly, I want Harlow to see that. Who knows what Landon has told her about me. If my father even mentions me.

I blurted out that ugly truth because I want her to see my side of things.

I've never felt the need to justify my behavior regarding Hugh to anyone. But I want Harlow to get why I *can't* forgive him.

"How old were you?" she asks.

"Seven."

"How did you find out?"

"Eavesdropped on my mom talking to a friend."

"And Hugh told Allison?"

I shrug. "No idea. He told my mom he was having problems with Allison. That he regretted not standing by her. Not choosing us. Then, he changed his mind again. Once a cheater and liar, always a cheater and liar, right? My mom never really got over it. Either time."

"Conor…" Harlow has no idea what to say. I don't blame her.

"You don't have to say anything, Harlow. It was a long time ago. Just not as long as most people think. I have my reasons, okay? I'm not a jerk about them—him—for no reason."

"I know that," she says softly.

We run in silence for a lap.

"I don't think Landon knows."

"I won't say anything," she tells me.

"You lie to your bestie?" The question comes out more mocking than I mean it to.

"You can be friends with someone and not agree with everything they do."

"True. Aidan only does laundry once a month."

Harlow laughs, lightening the heavy moment. The sound has a similar effect to the sun beaming down. "That's disgusting."

"I know. He and Hunter got into a whole argument about it."

She laughs again.

Harlow doesn't complain when I push the pace and add an extra mile to what we ran last time, but she does bend over as soon as we reach the finish line for the final time.

"Hold your arms up," I instruct. "It opens up your lungs."

She keeps heaving with her hands on her knees, so I step forward and do it for her. Surprised green eyes meet mine. She wasn't expecting me to touch her. Unless we're on a bed, or some other flat surface, I usually don't.

"I don't want there to be sides, Conor. But...don't assume I'm on theirs."

I nod. "You can mention him—them—to me all you want, Harlow. I get they're a part of your life. I'm not going to walk away when you do. But I'm never going to forgive him. If you think that'll change...it won't."

She nods, and I let her hands drop. Check the time on my phone.

"I gotta get to practice."

"Will I see you later?"

My dick twitches at the invitation. "Probably not. I've got five hours of film to watch tonight."

Harlow nods. "Okay."

Before I can talk myself out of it, I step forward and kiss her. She reacts instantly, pushing her hands in my hair and scraping her nails against my scalp.

I don't pull back until my phone starts buzzing in my pocket. I pull it out, see it's Aidan calling, and then answer.

"What?"

"Where are you?" he asks.

"I'm heading to practice."

"Can you pick me up? The truck won't start."

"The fire engine slash eyesore, you mean?"

Aidan sighs, no trace of his usual good humor in the sound. "I'll call Hunter."

"Jesus, Phillips. I'll be there, okay? Is everything all right?"

"Yeah. Just having a shitty day. I'll see you soon."

I hang up, then glance at Harlow. "I've gotta go."

"Okay." She's scuffing her sneaker against the track, hugging her middle.

I kiss her one last time, then head for my car.

CHAPTER SEVENTEEN

HARLOW

Eve and I are walking across campus when I spot him. Them. My grip tightens on the coffee cup I'm holding, the whole reason we stopped by campus before leaving for Thanksgiving break, which starts tomorrow. I'm dropping Eve off at the airport before driving to Claremont.

"Harlow, earth to Harlow!"

"What?" I ask Eve.

"What are you looking at?" She follows my gaze, then smirks. "Oh, look, it's our third roommate. Let's go say hi!"

"Eve, no—"

It's too late. I'm already being tugged in Conor's direction. He's standing with a woman I'm certain must be his mom, pointing at the main humanities building.

I'm about to meet Anna Hart.

I don't know very much about her. I know she and Hugh dated for a long time before she got pregnant. I know Hugh moved on quickly with Allison, who didn't know Anna existed. Thanks to Conor's little bombshell at the track yesterday, I know the history isn't as ancient as I thought.

215

And I'm guessing she views me as guilty by association the same way Conor did...or does. I'm not really sure how he views me.

I watch the two of them talk.

It's obvious they're close. There's no awkwardness or unfamiliarity as they chat and smile. I assumed they must be, but it's different to witness it in person. I can't picture Hugh Garrison as part of the scene in front of me, and it's strange to think he could have been. And even weirder to realize that, if he was, I would have never met Conor. He would have gone to Brighton or some other school with an amazing hockey program.

"Conor!" Eve calls out.

His eyes snap to her, then slide over to me as we approach.

Up close, Anna Hart is stunning. Shoulder-length hair the same dark shade as Conor's frames a heart-shaped face. And she has his eyes, the shifting shade of bluish gray. They're *his eyes* in my head, even if he inherited hers. She's dressed casually, wearing jeans and an oversize sweater.

"Harlow and I are leaving for break," Eve is saying. "I just saw you and wanted to say hi."

I appreciate she's making it clear coming over here was her idea, because Conor is giving no indication how he feels about me meeting his mom. He easily could have orchestrated this introduction himself. But he didn't, and that feels purposeful.

Anna looks to me as soon as Eve says my name. There's no malice in her expression, only interest.

I shift under her scrutiny. The deck is stacked against me, but for some reason I don't allow myself to dwell on, I really want her to like me.

"Hi, Ms.—uh, Dr. Hart. I'm Harlow."

I hold out a hand for her to shake. Her grip is firm.

"Anna is fine," she tells me.

"It's very nice to meet you."

"You, too." Anna is still studying me, her expression more curious than anything.

I wonder if Conor has ever mentioned me to her, or if she's relying on town gossip the same way I am. Allison and Hugh are very involved in the Claremont community. I'm sure them taking in an orphan was the gossip equivalent of local headlines.

Based on my eavesdropping over the years, my understanding is that things fell apart between Anna and Hugh before she learned she was pregnant, and Allison entered the picture soon after.

Maybe a moral gray area.

Maybe just terrible timing.

But it resulted in Anna raising a son alone. I kind of want to tell her that she did an amazing job.

"I'm Eve," Eve says.

Anna smiles. "Nice to meet you, Eve."

I shove my hands into my pockets, avoiding Conor's gaze.

"Well, we should get going. Good luck tonight, Conor."

I start walking before anyone can say anything, praying Eve will follow.

She does.

"Sheesh. Slow down a little, will you?"

"You don't meet a fuck buddy's parents, Eve," I hiss. "I *can't believe* you pulled me over there!"

"His mom seemed perfectly nice. And I hate to break it to you, Harlow, but you and Conor Hart are not *fuck buddies*. You are full-on dating, which is obvious to everyone who's been around you two recently. Except you. And maybe him."

"You're wrong," I tell her, but I'm not positive she is.

"Hayes!" is shouted behind me.

I turn to see Conor jogging toward me.

Eve gives me a *look*, then keeps walking. "I'll meet you at the car."

"I'm *so* sorry," I blurt, when he reaches me. "Eve saw you and pulled me over before I could—"

"It's fine, Harlow. I just, uh, realized I won't see you until after break. Wanted to say Happy Thanksgiving."

I raise one eyebrow. "You do know I'm Canadian, right? We celebrated weeks ago."

He snorts. "Yeah, I know you're Canadian. But we go to an American school and live in America and you're celebrating on Thursday, right?"

"Right."

"Yeah, so, Happy Thanksgiving." He glances over one shoulder at his mom, who's reading a plaque next to the giant elm in front of the library. "I should go. See you."

Our gazes connect, neither of us moving. For one wild moment, I think he's going to step forward and kiss me, the way he did at the track on Monday.

But he doesn't. He takes one step back, then two.

"Happy Thanksgiving, Conor."

He grins. "Thanks."

Then he turns and jogs back toward his mom. I spin and continue walking toward the parking lot and a waiting Eve.

We'll be in the same town for Thanksgiving. But he made no mention of us seeing each other or hanging out.

And I know that means no matter what *has* changed between us, some things haven't.

Some things *won't*.

CHAPTER EIGHTEEN

CONOR

There aren't many things about Claremont, Washington that I like. It's a fine town, I guess. Small and stereotypical. It's the type of place where people are overly friendly and gossip is scarce. A large percentage of the town's occupants are employed at Brighton University, which is located only twenty minutes away.

The quiet, simple pace makes scandal and controversy rare. It also means the most salacious gossip is dated by two decades. Both my mom and Hugh Garrison grew up here. Raised children here. And since we're not the type to forgive and forget—well, half of us, anyway—the state of my parents' relationship with each other and my relationship with the Garrisons is a town topic that's always of interest.

I'm reminded of that as I walk into Evan Sanford's house. He was my best friend growing up, and we're still close. Not as tight as we were in high school, but we've kept in close touch.

And I was well-known in high school for a lot more than my parents' fucked-up dynamic. That's probably why I did half the shit I did, to draw attention away from it. To carve out my own notoriety. I probably would have gone totally off the rails if not for the fact I didn't want to make my mom's life harder than it already was, and I wanted to get a hockey scholarship.

Being back in Claremont and among former classmates, it's easy to revert to a more reckless version of myself. Thanksgiving is tomorrow and I don't have practice for the next three days. Tonight, I'm loosening my no-drinking rule for the first time since my senior season started.

I head toward the kitchen first, progress slow as I get stopped repeatedly.

Evan's holding court by the island. My former winger gives me a broad grin. "Hart! About fucking time, man!"

"You said nine. It's only nine thirty," I point out.

"Details." Evan waves his hand. "Want a beer?"

"Hell yeah."

He hands me a bottle so cold I can see the condensation sneaking down the sides of the dark brown glass. I grab the opener off the counter, pop the top, and take a long sip. Chilled, brewed hops hit my tongue and I grin. Hits the damn spot.

"Still not drinking during the season?"

"Nope. Going pretty well for me, though."

Evan grins. "Yeah, I'd say so. Undefeated?" He shakes his head. "I knew you were good, man. But the way you've been playing?" He whistles. "Your whole team has been tight. I can't get half my guys to show up at morning practice."

I snort. Evan went on to play Division III, just like me. Unlike me, he didn't do it with any higher aspirations. "The whole leadership thing is less effective if you're the one handing them shots."

"Nah, that doesn't sound like me."

I laugh before taking another sip of brewed bliss. I forgot how good a cold beer tastes, especially after a grueling workout. I only got to Claremont a couple of hours ago, deciding to work out this morning despite our game yesterday.

"You're Conor Hart, right?" a female voice asks.

Evan smirks at me, then takes off.

I turn to see a blonde smiling at me. She's pretty. Purposefully so. Each strand of light hair falls in a perfect ringlet and her lips are painted an artificial shade of crimson.

"Right," I confirm, taking another sip of beer.

The final sip, it turns out. I set the empty bottle on the island counter and it clinks against the marble.

This is when I should flirt with her. My first night to really let loose in over a month. And, based on the look the blonde's giving me, she'd be up for anything I wanted.

But there's...nothing. No interest at all.

"I go to Brighton," the blonde tells me. She looks me up and down. "None of the guys on our hockey team are as good as you. You should have played for us instead."

I tense at the reminder. There was plenty of speculation as to why I'd turn down a full ride to play at a Division I school in favor of Holt. Some people correctly guessed it had something to do with Hugh. But the only person I've ever outright admitted that to is Harlow.

"I like being the underdog," I say.

The blonde laughs. "You call setting an all-time leading scorer record being an underdog?"

My intuition flickers. I don't have any problem with girls who want to be so-called puck bunnies. Whose sole interest in me is the fact I play hockey. But it's strange this girl knew my name, mentioned not playing at Brighton, and knows my stats.

I decide it's a good time to go to the bathroom.

"I need to take a piss." I purposefully put it in crude terms, hoping it'll scare her off toward a guy with a less foul mouth. "It was nice meeting you…"

Did she say her name? If she did, I have no clue what it is.

"Kelly," she supplies. Still looking plenty interested.

"Nice meeting you, Kelly."

I force a smile and leave the kitchen, heading for the bathroom connected to the guest suite. There's a line of at least a dozen people waiting to use the other half bath downstairs. I spent a lot of time here growing up, and it doesn't take me long to locate the right room. I pee, wash my hands, and then head out into the attached bedroom.

It's no longer empty. Rather than a horny couple, I'm confronted by the same blonde from before. Kelly.

Surprise slows my steps.

She followed me in here? What the fuck?

"Landon wasn't lying," she says, crossing her arms. "You really don't know *anything* about him, huh? Not even the name of the girl he's spent the last two and a half years dating."

I just stare at her. My brother's girlfriend, apparently. Not who I pictured him with, but I haven't even seen the guy in person since graduating high school.

"He's not going to be happy you're here talking to me."

Kelly laughs. "Duh. Why do you think I'm here?"

Well…that backfired.

"I'm the one who ended it. He was cute when we were fresh-men. But…" She shrugs. "You're hotter."

I just stare at her. Coming back here always includes reminders of Landon and my dad. But this? This has not happened before.

All of a sudden Kelly's shirt is off, her boobs spilling out of her hot pink bra.

And still…nothing.

"Come on, Conor. What do you say?"

"That Landon has terrible taste in women," I reply honestly.

Who breaks up with a guy after dating him for over two years and then turns around and tries to screw his *brother*? Half, but still.

Kelly smiles, not looking the least bit offended. She steps closer, and I step back.

"I'm not interested."

"What?" Kelly looks stunned by my response.

"I'm not interested. Whatever this is—" I wave toward her. "It's pathetic. I want no part in it."

If this was high school, maybe this is a mistake I would make. Imagining the look on my half-brother's face when he found out I screwed his ex-girlfriend. That she'd all but begged me to fuck her.

But not only am I not attracted to Kelly, I know why.

If Landon hears I slept with her, Harlow will too. And we might not be dating—I don't know what the hell we're doing, honestly—but I do know having sex with someone else would feel like cheating. Hell, I'm uneasy just being alone in a room that has a bed with a girl who's not her. And that was before Kelly took her shirt off.

Ever since I was old enough to fully comprehend my family's messy dynamic, two things have been my primary motivators to make some questionable choices: the desire for my father to recognize how badly he messed up my life, and the need to be nothing like the son he chose over me.

For the first time, there's a third, less sabotaging influence.

I care about what Harlow thinks.

I don't know how to feel about it. How I should feel about it. The two devils on my shoulder have been joined by an angel. And all three of them are probably playing Monopoly right now, or some other equally wholesome family bullshit.

I leave the guest room before Kelly can say another word. Or take off any more clothing. Maybe I could have phrased my rejection better, but she's the one who made a move on her ex-boyfriend's estranged half-brother.

Evan shoves off the wall when I emerge back in the living room, shaking off the brunette he was talking to and returning to my side.

"Saw the blonde follow you five minutes ago. Little quick on the trigger these days, Hart?"

I roll my eyes, grabbing an unopened can of beer off a side table and cracking it open. "Wasn't feeling it. She just wanted to fuck with Garrison."

"You mean, your favorite hobby?"

I shrug, not denying it. Except...I'm not sure it still is. "I'm gonna bounce. Mom wants to go tree-killing tomorrow, if you want to come with. We'll probably go around eleven, before her shift."

Evan grins. "Hell yeah, I do. Those pines won't know what hit 'em."

"Great. See ya, man."

"Don't forget about Zeke's on Friday night."

"I didn't. I'll be there."

I bump Evan's fist and weave through the crowd toward the front door. A few people call out to me as I pass, but I ignore them. Easy to do in the loud house.

Cold air smacks me in the face as I step outside. I chug the rest of the beer I'm holding, then toss it in the Sanfords' trash bin as soon as I reach the street.

I bury both hands in the pouch of my sweatshirt. It can't be hovering all that far above freezing, but I've spent most of my life in an ice rink. This is nothing.

Rather than climb in my car and drive home, I keep walking. My mom is working, so all that's waiting for me is an empty house.

I pass the occasional adult out walking the family dog. A group of girls who look like they're in middle school who are clearly heading to or leaving a sleepover. They all giggle as they pass me, clutching fluffy blankets and sleeping bags.

Four blocks later, I reach the brick house.

I wasn't sure I could find it, after fifteen years. But I recognize the columns on either side of the black front door. The neatly trimmed hedges. The pristine path leading to the porch.

I huff a laugh as I stare at it, watching my breath hover in the cold night air for a moment. Below freezing, then.

In another life, I could have lived here. If I was a more forgiving person, I might be coming over here to eat turkey tomorrow.

My fingernails are pressed so tightly into my palms I'm worried they'll draw blood.

Ever since I graduated high school, I've been able to cut the Garrisons out of my life completely. No more seeing Landon in the halls or watching him drive an expensive, European car into the school lot. My mom never used any of the money Hugh sent as child support. It's all sitting in an account somewhere, and I hope I'll never have to touch it. My father has never *bought* me anything. He's just sent checks.

Harlow's car is parked next to Landon's in the driveway, which is bizarre. It's one thing knowing she stays here. Another to see solid proof of it.

I plan to turn around and walk away. But instead, my feet keep walking forward. Some compulsion to stop pretending like my father doesn't live in the same town mixing with the urge to see Harlow.

I don't have anything to be ashamed of; he does. Me steering clear just allows him to forget that. And this visit has nothing to do with my father, honestly. I'm here to see Harlow, because it's an impulse I'm choosing not to fight.

I blow out another breath as I continue walking forward. This is a bad idea. I know it with each step, and yet I can't shake the propulsion to do it anyway. The same reckless energy as when I drop gloves on the ice pinballs through me. I'm reacting—to Kelly reminding me I'll never be able to escape the Garrisons in this town and to knowing exactly where Harlow is right now.

I reach the front porch and scuff my feet against the welcome mat. It's bright and cheery, covered with sunflowers and loopy writing spelling out *Welcome*. Two pumpkins sit next to the mat.

The cookie-cutter condo I live in when I'm not at college serves its purpose. It's all we can afford, since my mom took out hefty loans for medical school. I know she's done the best she could, and I don't resent her for it. The exact opposite.

Hugh Garrison? I resent *him* plenty.

I hit the doorbell. Hear it echo through the massive house.

The condo could probably fit into one room of this place.

"Coming!" a woman's voice calls.

It's not Harlow's, so that means…

"*Conor!*" Surprise makes Allison Garrison's voice come out higher pitched than sounds natural. Like the call of one of the whales Harlow loves.

Allison looks exactly the same as the last time I saw her, wearing an ironed blouse and a cardigan. Like a stereotypical housewife, not a homewrecker.

My hands form fists in the pouch of my sweatshirt.

"Is Harlow here?" I ask abruptly.

"Harlow? Uh...I can—I think..." Whatever immediate conclusion Allison came to about why I'm on her doorstep, it didn't involve her adopted daughter. She's completely thrown by the question. "Yes, she's here. Hang on." She turns, then spins back around. "Did you want to come in...?"

"No, I'm good here."

Allison nods, then heads deeper into the house, leaving the door wide open. I study their entryway for a minute. It's just as stately as the exterior of the house. The wide bannister is part of faded—shoved out of my brain—memories. The wall art and rugs are new, though. They've redecorated in the fifteen years since I've stepped foot inside.

Appraisal over, I turn back around to face the street, leaning against the railing to survey the road I might have grown up on, once upon a time.

It's easy to ignore the past when I'm at school. Where I'm Conor Hart, the cocky captain who doesn't appear to have anything to worry about besides the next hockey game and which girl to choose for the night.

It's a lot harder to do that on this front porch.

CHAPTER NINETEEN

HARLOW

Landon misses the piece of popcorn—again—and I laugh. We're in the middle of a board game that got paused when the doorbell rang. Allison went to get the door, and Landon has entertained himself by trying to catch pieces of popcorn in his mouth ever since. So far, he hasn't caught a single one.

"Your turn, Mom," Landon says as soon as Allison reappears in the den.

"Oh, okay." She replies right away, but her voice sounds distracted.

Allison looks at me, her forehead creased.

"Who was at the door?" Hugh asks.

"It's for you, Harlow," Allison tells me, rather than responding to her husband.

"For me?"

I'm surprised. I don't have much of a social circle here. Or *any* social circle here. The few people I see when I'm in Clare-mont on breaks are mostly Landon's friends, who I've gotten to know over the years.

"Who is it?" Landon questions, abandoning his popcorn attempts.

The only people I'm close to who live in Claremont are in this room.

Except…

My stomach somersaults. *He* wouldn't come *here*, right? Wouldn't choose—want—whatever we are exposed to the estranged half of his family.

I didn't think so, but I don't know. The last adjective I'd use to describe Conor Hart is predictable, which Allison confirms with her next words.

"It's Conor."

"*Conor*? Here?" Hugh sounds stunned.

"*What?*" At the same time, Landon sounds incredulous.

Fuck. I only think the word, but I'm tempted to say it aloud.

"I'll be right back." I stand from my spot on the couch, brushing my salty fingers off on my leggings.

"You're…what? I'll come with you." Landon stands too. "I can't believe he thinks he can just show up—"

"I'll handle it, Landon." My voice comes out sharper than I mean it to, because whatever reason Conor is here, I'm sure Landon getting involved won't help.

My best friend opens his mouth to protest, but Allison's soft "Landon" causes him to close it again.

I glance at Allison. She's looking down at her wineglass, swirling the red liquid around.

I'm guessing she's realized which guy I was talking about the last time I was here.

Conor has burned a lot of bridges in this family.

Whether or not he was justified in lighting those fires is a matter of opinion. Of perspective.

I don't say anything else before leaving the room. There's a draft through the front hall that I follow to the open door. A lone figure is leaning against the railing that surrounds the front porch. One I would recognize, even if *Hart* and *15* weren't emblazoned on the back of his sweatshirt.

I grab my jacket off the hook, slip it on, and then step outside, closing the door behind me.

Conor turns at the quiet *click*, his eyes skimming up and down my body. Despite my annoyance that he didn't give me a head's up he was coming over and my confusion about *why* he's here, excitement is the primary emotion I'm experiencing. I'm *always* excited to see him, and I didn't think it would be until Monday at the earliest.

"You lost?" I ask.

"No, I just happened to be walking by."

I roll my eyes at what I assume is sarcasm. But then I realize there's no car on the street and his cheeks are red from the cold. "Wait, you actually walked here?"

"A high school buddy of mine lives a few blocks over. I was there for a party…and ended up here." He sucks his bottom lip into his mouth, then glances at the house we're standing in front of. "Haven't been since I was seven, you know."

"I…figured it'd been a while." I step closer, so there's about a foot of space between us. Lean against the railing, mirroring his casual pose. "Streak didn't end."

One corner of his mouth—the side I can see—curls up. "Look at you, checking scores. I thought you had better things to do with your time than follow hockey, Hayes?"

"I didn't just check the score. I watched the game."

He glances at me, surprise sketched into the lines of his face.

"They, um, livestream them."

"Yeah, I know." Conor pauses. "I just didn't know *you* knew that."

"I'm glad your mom was there."

He looks down at the wooden boards of the porch. "Me too."

I'm out of small talk. He showed up here—after fifteen years —and I want that to mean something. But I'm not sure if it does, or how to ask him that. And it's a conversation I'd rather have at Holt, when I'm not about to have to go answer a bunch of questions about us.

"What are you doing here, Conor?" I ask softly.

"I just wanted to see you." He shoves away from the railing. "I'll let you get back to your board game."

"How did you know we were playing a board game?"

He rolls his eyes. "Lucky guess."

"What am I supposed to say to the Garrisons about you coming here?"

"Whatever you want."

"I didn't think you'd want them…knowing about this." I wave a hand between our bodies.

"I don't care what they know," he tells me. "You're the one who has the relationship with them."

"He's your dad, Conor! You want me to waltz in there and tell Hugh we've been sleeping together for weeks and *that's* why you showed up here?"

"I'm sorry, okay? I shouldn't have come." He runs a hand through his hair, tugging at the strands roughly. "I'm just…I'm back here and it feels different. You're here, and that's different. I want to see you and not see them, and I *can't*."

"What do you want me to do? Go sleep at a hotel?"

He exhales. "No, of course not."

I step into him, so we're only inches apart. The hoppy smell of beer mixes with his usual pine and salt scent. "You were drinking?"

One of his hands tangles in the ends of my hair, tugging

231

gently at the strands. "I had a couple. This and Christmas are the only vacation I'll get before we hopefully make it to the finals."

"Before you *definitely* make it to the finals, you mean."

He smiles. "Yeah."

I rise up on my tiptoes and kiss him, moaning when his grip tightens in my hair. His other hand sneaks under my jacket and the sweatshirt I'm wearing underneath, exploring my stomach and then moving up to my breasts. I put on a sports bra after showering earlier, the stretchy material moving out of his way easily as he cups my breast and rubs my nipple until it's an aching point.

Conor groans into my mouth as I tug his bottom lip between my teeth. He tastes like beer and mint and desire. I slide my hands under his sweatshirt. Hot, firm skin tenses under my touch. I can feel him hardening against my stomach.

"Worth the walk right there," he whispers, when our lips finally separate. He drops his hands, and reluctantly, I do too.

"Were you not having fun at the party?" I ask.

"Not really." He studies me for a second. "Did you ever meet Landon's ex? The blonde?"

"Kelly? Yeah, why?"

"She was at the party earlier."

"Okay…"

He looks away.

"She hit on you?" I sound annoyed, and it's not on Landon's behalf.

"Little more than that."

"What did she do?"

"Uh, followed me into a bedroom and then took her shirt off?"

"That's…descriptive," I say.

"You asked, Hayes."

"And…"

"And I told her I wasn't interested and left."

I want to fling more questions at him. Ask why he was in a bedroom. If he was tempted to take what she was offering. Whether other girls at this party hit on him.

But I swallow them all.

"I should get going," he tells me.

"You're good to drive?" I hear the naked fear in my voice, and he does too.

"I promise."

I nod. "Okay."

Conor shoves his hands into his pockets and nods back. "I'm going to a party on Friday night. Another high school thing, but much bigger. Half the town usually shows up. If you're around and want to go…let me know."

He leaves it as an open invitation, but I don't have to think about it. I've never been to a party in Claremont. And, more significantly, I'm curious to see what Conor's life here is like.

"Yeah, sounds great."

"Yeah?"

He sounds surprised I want to go, which surprises me.

"Will all your high school exes be there?"

Conor looks amused by the question. "I don't have any exes, Hayes."

"High school's where the heartbreaker nickname originated, huh?"

Rather than smirk, he turns serious. "You're the one who broke Williams's heart."

It's the first time he's mentioned Jack to me in weeks. Maybe he thinks I'm judging him?

"You worried?" I ask, feigning disinterest in his answer.

"I don't have a heart to break." He flashes me a cocky smirk —the one I hate. The arrogant *I don't give a shit* expression. "I'll text you about Friday."

He turns and walks away, leaving me standing on the Garrisons' front porch.

———

The house is silent when I walk back inside. There's no sign of Hugh or Allison, but Landon is slouched in the same spot as he was when I left the den.

"Long chat." Landon speaks first. "Lot longer than it takes to tell a guy to fuck off."

I sigh. He's not going to take this well, no matter what. "Landon, I'm sorr—"

He cuts me off. "What was he doing here, Harlow?"

"He wanted to talk."

"About what?"

"Just…stuff. We're…friendly."

"You said you *never see him*." Landon's voice is accusing.

I swallow. "That was true, when I said it. Things…changed, and I didn't know how to tell you."

"Are you dating him?"

I shake my head. "No."

"Have you slept with him?"

"That's none of your business."

Landon snorts, both of us knowing that's the same as a yes.

I study my hands, clasping them together so tightly I can see the bones beneath the skin. "I didn't mean for it to happen."

"He's a mistake, Harlow."

"I can make my own choices. I never liked Kelly, but I didn't tell *you* she was a mistake."

"Kelly didn't make it her mission in life to make my family miserable."

"She wasn't very welcoming toward me," I point out.

Landon looks away, at the roaring flames licking the logs in the fireplace.

"What could you *possibly* like about him?"

I sigh. "A lot."

"I can't believe this." Landon rubs his eyes with his palms like he's trying to erase the sight of me. "I really can't believe this is happening. After all the shit Conor's pulled? He used to mail back the birthday cards my parents sent him, did you know that? He locked himself in a bathroom here once, and they almost had to call the fire department because his mom was at work and they couldn't reach her and he refused to come out. In high school, he would make out with one girl in the parking lot before school, and a different one at lunch. But, yeah, there's *a lot to like*."

"What would you have done, in his position?" I ask.

"None of *that*."

"Your dad left you and your mom, you would have been fine with it?"

"That is *not* what happened, Harlow. He's feeding you bull-shit. For *years*, my dad tried to make amends—"

"I know he's tried, Landon. But…you don't try to make amends unless there's something to be forgiven *for*."

"I can't listen to this."

Landon stands, then stomps out of the room.

I exhale, slumping back against the cushions. I should probably be mad at Conor for putting me in this position—for showing up here and making me have to answer Landon's questions. But a big part of me is relieved. I've hated keeping this secret, not only from Landon but from Allison and Hugh as well.

A door slams upstairs, suggesting Landon made it up there. I should probably go to bed too. Tomorrow is Thanksgiving, and after tonight it'll probably be an awkward day. Being exhausted won't help.

"That turned into quite the evening."

I glance over at Hugh, who's appeared in the den's doorway, watching as he takes Landon's empty seat. Exhale. "Yeah."

"Conor hasn't been here in a long time."

"Yeah. He mentioned that."

"You two are…involved?"

I almost smile at Hugh's tactful language. "We're friends, I think. Maybe I should have mentioned it sooner, but…Landon reacted about how I expected him to. I was never sure how to bring it up."

Hugh sighs. "He and Conor—well, that's my main regret. Aside from my own relationship with him. I hate that my boys became enemies, not brothers." He looks at the fireplace. "I've made a lot of mistakes, Harlow. A lot of mistakes that hurt a lot of people. No one is perfect, but I'm a damn ways away, that's for sure."

"Conor mentioned some…more recent history."

"Allison knows everything that's happened. Landon doesn't."

I nod, having assumed as much. "Landon resents Conor for how he's treated you. Treats you."

"I know."

"I'm not saying Conor handled things the right way. But…he had some good reasons to lash out. Landon doesn't know that."

"You're right," Hugh says quietly.

A log cracks in the fireplace.

"What's he like?"

"Conor?"

Hugh nods.

I know Landon is hoping my connection to Conor is temporary. But Hugh? His face is lit up with the feverish light of forbidden knowledge. He doesn't have anyone else to ask about

Conor, I realize. Their lives are totally disconnected, with the one exception of me.

"He's…incredible." Softly, I add, "You missed out."

Hugh's smile is sad. "I know I did. I always hoped…pushing for a relationship didn't seem to help. I thought if I backed off for a while, he'd reach out on his own one day. Never happened."

"I wish things had worked out differently," I say.

I'm not going to offer Hugh any false hope. I know Conor has absolutely no interest in a relationship with his father, and it seems cruel to suggest otherwise, knowing he'll be shot down.

And…I'm angry at Hugh, for how he handled things. Maybe that's not fair, in a situation that has nothing to do with me directly. Everyone makes mistakes, and it's obvious he regrets the past. But that past is affecting my present. My future.

Maybe Conor would have no interest in a relationship with me regardless of my connection to the Garrisons. Maybe I'm using the history as an excuse for a *happily never after* that would have happened anyway.

But I'll never know for sure, because Hugh's actions drove Conor away to the point he won't even come inside this house. Can't even stomach being civil to his father. Ignored me for three years, because I accepted their offered kindness.

And maybe Hugh hears that, because he tells me, "I would make different choices if I could, Harlow. And not just for my own sake."

I nod, then stand. "I should get to bed."

"Good night."

I leave Hugh alone in the den. With his thoughts…and with his regrets.

CHAPTER TWENTY

CONOR

My mom's dancing around the kitchen listening to Christmas carols when I walk in.

"Really letting Thanksgiving have its moment, huh?" I ask, pouring a generous helping of coffee into a mug.

"Tell me a Thanksgiving song to listen to, and I'll put in on," she tells me.

I take a seat at the counter, studying the reddish mixture in the bowl next to the stove. "Um, what's that?"

"I'm making cranberry French toast."

"Interesting." I sip. "I thought we were just having a normal breakfast?"

"I decided to get creative. Here, grate the potatoes." She hands me three peeled potatoes and a grater.

"Where are the potatoes supposed to go?"

She rolls her eyes, then pulls a tray out from one of the bottom cabinets. Passes it to me.

"How was Evan's last night?" she asks.

"Uh, fine. I invited him to come with us later, to get the tree."

"Great. How's he doing?"

"Good, I think. You can ask him yourself."

She nods, then grabs a baguette and starts slicing it. For the maroon mixture, I guess.

"I took a look at my schedule for the next few weeks. I think I can make it to another one of your games the second week of December."

"You don't need to do that, Mom. I know how busy you are."

"I want to, honey. I would go to every single one, if I could."

And there might not be that many more. She doesn't say it, but we both know it's a strong possibility.

"Okay, well, if you can make it, I'd love to see you."

"Does a certain redhead attend these games?"

I glance up, almost grating my finger in the process. "What are you talking about?"

"It seemed like there was something going on there, when we ran into Harlow on campus."

My focus returns to the potatoes.

"We don't have to talk about, if you don't want to."

"She's like his daughter. She's Landon's best friend." I spit the two sentences out, making my distaste clear. Not that my mom doesn't already know I feel about the Garrisons. She understands it better than anyone else could comprehend.

"Most of life is messy, Conor."

"It would never work out between us."

"How do you know?" my mom asks.

"I just...do. And I can't believe you're *encouraging* it."

She raises one eyebrow at me. "How is any of what happened her fault?"

"It's not. But she's this...connection to them. A constant reminder. I'm not going to ask her to choose, and she probably wouldn't pick me even if I did. It's better to just keep things the way they are."

"And how's that?"

"Just, uh, casual."

"You've never taken her on a date?"

I shift awkwardly on my stool. My mom and I are close. I share most of my life with her. But aside from her giving me a safe sex talk, we've never really discussed girls. There's never been a girl to discuss.

"We went bowling once. With friends."

"How romantic."

"*Mom.*"

She laughs, then turns serious. "Do you want more than casual?"

"I...don't know. It wasn't supposed to—I wasn't expecting it to become anything. I should be totally focused on hockey."

"There's more to life than hockey, honey. And neither you nor I can predict the future. But if this is your final season, if things don't end up the way you're hoping? You might wish you'd spent your senior year a little differently."

It's basically the exact opposite of the advice Hunter gave me: focus on hockey and the girls will be there later.

I fall somewhere in the middle of my mom and Hunter, I guess. There are still things under my control. We're not even halfway through the season. I have chances left, and nothing has been decided for certain. This isn't the time to back off and get distracted, to shift my attention elsewhere. But what my mom seems to get and Hunter doesn't is that Harlow isn't just another girl to me. She won't be easily replaceable, if I prioritize hockey and lose her.

"I went over there last night," I admit.

"To the Garrisons'?" My mom's voice is high and surprised. She knows exactly how long it's been since my last visit—she was the one who picked me up.

"Yeah. I…I wanted to see her. I didn't talk to anyone else. Well, Allison opened the door. But that was it."

"How was it?"

"Weird. Not only being back there, but seeing her there. Knowing she's staying in that house…" I shake my head, finishing the final potato and then going over to the sink to wash the sticky starch off my hands.

My mom sighs as I sit back down.

"I'll say this once, and then we can go back to not talking about it, unless you decide otherwise."

I nod.

"Your father has a lot of regrets, Conor. But I have some too. I was young and scared when I found out I was pregnant with you. Your dad and I were in a bad place, I found out about Allison, and I…I was hurt. But I was an adult. I was supposed to be one, at least. And it's the most selfish thing I've ever done, letting my pride get in the way of you knowing your father. Letting my feelings toward him impact yours. Hugh chose Allison over me. He didn't choose Landon over you. He tried—for years—to be a part of your life. He invited you on trips and tried to buy gifts for you and…he just wanted to spend time around you. But for a long time that meant I had to spend time around him. Or coordinate plans with your school or your daycare that made my life more difficult. Then you got old enough to have a say and I was… relieved. A petty part of me was so relieved that you chose me over him. That you wanted nothing to do with him. But I should have been devastated by that, not celebrating. Hugh made mistakes, but he's not a bad man. He's your father, and he wanted to be your father. If you want no relationship with him, that's your decision to make. To keep making. But if that changes, if you decide that is something you want, that's a choice I'd support. Okay?"

"Okay."

"Good. Can you turn the music up?"

I shake my head but get up to adjust the speaker. It feels way too early to be listening to carols chiming, but watching my mom sing and dance around is worth it.

And way more enjoyable than talking about my non-existent relationship with my father.

CHAPTER TWENTY-ONE

HARLOW

I'm sitting on the back porch with a blanket wrapped around my shoulders when Allison appears in the doorway, holding two glasses of wine.

She exhales, taking a seat in the rocking chair next to me. "I love hosting, and I hate it."

I smile. Allison's parents and sister came over for Thanksgiving dinner yesterday. Her sister—and three kids—ended up spending the night. They only left a couple of hours ago, and one of those hours was spent scrubbing marker off the wall in the den.

"All the food was delicious," I say.

"Thank you. It was a nice holiday."

I nod, studying the fogged glass. The back porch is usable year-round, with screened sides that get covered with glass panes during the winter months. There's an electric unit tucked away in the corner that works as both a heater and an air conditioner.

"Here." Allison holds one of the wineglasses out to me.

"Thanks."

"So...do you want to talk about it or pretend it never happened?"

I sip. "There's not much to talk about."

"I very much doubt that."

"I had no idea he was going to show up here. If I had…I wouldn't have ever mentioned him to you."

"Why not?"

"It's…weird, Allison. You guys have this whole history with him. And I always knew it was there. I just…never thought about it much. And then things changed and…I thought about it a whole lot."

"Has Conor made it an issue?"

"It's…come up. We fought about it, at first. Then he got… resigned, I guess." I drink more wine. "He ignored me for three years, Allison. He'll never forgive what happened. Never forget. I knew that when this started."

"He came here, Harlow. That was a step."

"Here, as in the front yard. He wouldn't come inside."

Allison exhales. "I wish I had answers for you, Harlow. And I wish you didn't have to think about this. Wish everything was different."

I nod. "Me too."

My phone buzzes with a text.

CONOR: Be there in ten.

"Shit." I sit up, wine almost sloshing past the rim of the glass.

Allison looks alarmed. "What is it?"

"I, uh, Conor invited me to a party tonight. I totally lost track of time." I stand, nearly tripping over the blanket as it falls off my shoulders. Grab my phone and quickly text him back.

HARLOW: Twenty? I lost track of time and still need to get ready.

CONOR: Wow. I'm flattered.

I shake my head and laugh.

HARLOW: You should be *flattered* I'm dressing up for you. I could wear sweatpants.

CONOR: Wear whatever you want, Hayes. You look good in anything.

"That," Allison says softly.

I glance up at her, staring at me with a warm smile on her face.

"You asked me how your mom knew your dad was the one? I can't speak for her, but I saw her look at him the same way you're smiling at that screen." She takes a sip of wine. "I know Hugh made his mistakes. But Conor made choices too. Don't let him act like those decisions were all made by someone else. And…don't accept they're all final. If you see his side of things, he should see yours as well."

I nod. "Thanks, Allison."

"Anytime, honey. Have fun tonight."

I walk back inside, headed toward the stairs. Landon is paused on the landing, pulling on a jacket. I swallow, then start to climb them. We meet halfway.

"You headed out?"

He nods. "I was coming to see if you wanted to join. Going over to Steve's for a bit, and then we'll probably go to this party he got invited to."

I close my eyes for a second. In a town as small as Claremont, I'm guessing the party Landon is headed to and the party I'm headed to are probably the same. This is the most we've spoken since our argument on Wednesday night, and I'm anticipating this will lead to another one.

"I'll, uh, probably see you there."

It takes him three seconds to jump to the correct conclusion. "You're going with Conor."

"Yes."

"He invited you to mess with me, Harlow. Everyone in town knows who you are. You showing up with *him*? They'll all talk."

I say nothing. What Landon believes Conor's intentions are and I what I know they are…they're so separate it seems pointless to reconcile them.

"At least I'll be there to hang out with when he tries to hook up with someone else," he tells me.

"*That's* what you think of me, Landon? Forget Conor. You think I'd spent time with a guy who treated me that way?"

"I don't know what the hell to think anymore, Harlow. I never thought you'd *fuck my half-brother*, and here we are." He looks away, shaking his head. "I get you think you know this other side of him, but you don't. It's an *act*. He took Kelly into a bedroom on Wednesday night, then came here to see you. He's a player and an asshole, and I hope you see that sooner rather than later."

"Nothing happened with him and Kelly."

"How do you know?"

"Because he told me."

Landon shakes his head. "And you *believe* him?" He pulls his phone out of his pocket, scrolls for a few seconds, and then flashes me the screen. "Look at this."

I squint at the photo of Conor standing in a kitchen, smiling at a blonde.

It bothers me, but I don't let it show. That's the exact fuel Landon is looking for.

"That's not them having sex in a bedroom."

He pockets his phone. "Whatever. I probably *could* show you that, and you'd say it was edited. Believe whatever you want."

Landon continues down the stairs without saying another word to me. I watch him depart with what feels like a heavy weight sitting on my chest.

Conor thinks I'm on Landon's side.

Landon thinks I'm on Conor's side.

And me...I don't know what the hell to think anymore.

———

I don't run into anyone on my way out of the house. Landon is gone, but I'm not sure where Hugh and Allison are. No sign of them makes it easier to shove all the unpleasant thoughts away and resolve to just have fun tonight.

As soon as I step onto the front porch, I hear a dulled staccato. I head down the steps and turn the corner of the house, watching Conor shoot at the basketball hoop next to the garage. It goes in.

"Is there a sport you're bad at?" I ask him.

"Nope." Conor retrieves the basketball, goes in for a layup, and then turns toward me. Whistles once, long and low. "Damn, Hayes. Not bad for a rush job."

I roll my eyes. "Are you ready to go? It's freezing out."

"Not so cold if you're moving." He passes me the basketball. By some miracle, I manage to grab it. "Come on. Take a shot. I won't laugh if you suck."

"Wow. That's *really* nice of you."

Conor grins.

I spin the ball in my hands, trying to recall the last time I held a basketball. I can't come up with it, which means that despite what Conor says, he's probably going to be laughing really soon. I squint at the net, trying to visualize the ball sinking right through the metal circle and through the hanging strings. Then I shoot, the ball bouncing off the rim before dropping back down on the asphalt.

Not great, but not embarrassing either.

Conor snags the basketball before it rolls off into the bushes.

"Try again." He bounces it back to me.

I grab it and gesture to myself. "Do you have any idea how long this took me?"

"Yeah, twenty minutes."

I laugh. "I don't want to show up looking like a sweaty mess."

"Why not? *I* already saw it all." The devastating smirk I wish I was immune to makes an appearance.

"Cocky is not sexy," I inform him.

Conor laughs, and the husky tone of it warms me more than the jacket I'm wearing. "Just make one basket and then we can go."

I shoot the ball. This time, it bounces off the backboard. I huff a sigh. At this rate, we could be out here all night.

Conor retrieves the ball again. Rather than pass it to me, he walks over while still holding it. He hands the basketball to me, then moves behind my body, positioning my hips to face the basket.

"Hayes?" he murmurs.

"Yeah?" I whisper.

"You look gorgeous. Always."

It's his earlier text all over again, except in the more potent form of his hard body against my back and his deep voice next to my ear.

"If you keep distracting me, I'm never going to make a basket."

"Just try one more time," he says.

I propel the basketball out of my hands again. This time, it makes a satisfying *swish* as it drops through the basket.

"Yes! It went in!" I tell Conor. In case he missed what just happened ten feet in front of him.

"I saw, Harlow."

He sounds amused. Looks even more so when I sling my arms around his neck as part of my celebration.

"Is that what it feels like to score a goal?" I ask him.

"Dunno. Try scoring one, and then you can tell me."

"You will *never* catch me playing hockey, after seeing what your ribs look like from *practice*. I'm a wimp and I'm fine with it."

"I'm not suggesting you face off against a two-hundred-pound defenseman. Just that you skate around and send the puck into an open goal."

"I doubt I could stay up on skates long enough to *shoot* at a goal, much less make one."

"I'll teach you, if you want."

"You're definitely overqualified for the position. I probably just need one of those orange cones little kids push around."

He laughs, a genuine one that makes me smile automatically. "Overqualified or not, I'm applying for the position. If you want to learn to skate, I'm your guy."

"Okay," I say. "Let's do it sometime."

We head toward Conor's SUV, parked on the street. As we pass by one of the living room windows, I think I see a curtain move. But I can't be certain. Maybe it's just a trick of the streetlight.

"Whose party is this?" I ask as I climb into the car.

"Zeke Ledger. We went to high school together. He was in my year."

"Did he play hockey?"

Conor shakes his head. "No. We weren't close. He has rich parents who don't care if he hosts huge parties. He had most of the ragers in high school, and the tradition continued after he graduated when people were back on breaks."

"You went last year?"

"Yeah."

That's weird to think, that he and I were in the same place doing the same things—but as strangers.

"Landon is going to be there."

"Makes sense. You won't be home to play board games with."

"*Conor.*"

"I won't start shit, okay? As long as he doesn't."

"He heard about Kelly. There's some photo going around of you two talking in a kitchen that he showed me."

"He thinks we hooked up?" Conor asks.

"Yes."

"Is that what you think?"

"*No.* You told me what happened, and I believe you. I just… between finding out about us and what he thinks happened with Kelly, you're not Landon's favorite person right now."

"I've never been his favorite person, Hayes."

"I know."

It's part of why I'm in this mess. Trapped between two guys I care about, who can't stand each other.

We pull up outside a massive mansion a few minutes later.

"Wow," I say, studying the exterior of the modern-looking house. It's mostly dark siding and gray stones, the front door surrounded by huge panes of glass and flanked by twin columns that take up two stories.

"Yeah. Rumor is his folks dropped four million on this place."

"Seriously?"

"Uh-huh. Come on."

Conor climbs out of the car, and I do the same. Nerves ricochet around in my stomach as we approach the front door. Not just because of what Landon's reaction to seeing me and Conor together might be, but because Conor's high school friends will all be here. And…I want them to like me, the same way I felt around Anna Hart.

The entryway we step into is soaring, a fancy-looking chandelier hanging from the high ceiling. Just past it are clear stairs that lead to the second level. The walls are painted a light gray, the same wood and stone from the exterior scattered in random spots.

"I hate it," I whisper to Conor.

He laughs as we walk into the living room. "Me too."

"Hart!" A guy with dirty blond hair bounds over to us, holding out a fist that Conor taps.

Then he wraps an arm around my waist, pulling me closer and forward. "Harlow, this is Evan. Evan, Harlow."

I smile at him. "Hey. Nice to meet you."

"You too. What a day, huh?"

I glance at Conor, confused. "Uh, Black Friday?"

Evan laughs. "Nah, Hart bringing a date. Never seen it happen before."

I wait for Conor to correct his friend, to tell him we're just friends or drop his hand and make it clear we're not together. But all he says is, "You left your gloves in my car."

"Oh, yeah. I was looking for those." Evan looks to me. "Hart tell you we went Christmas tree hunting yesterday? Poor guy was worried he couldn't carry the Douglas fir by himself."

"Fuck off, Sanford."

Evan laughs. The guys start talking hockey, and I shrug out of my coat. It's not that warm in here—the minimalist interior doesn't just look chilly—but it's warmer than it was outside.

"I'm going to head to the bathroom," I tell Conor.

He nods, holding a hand out for my jacket. "It's past the kitchen, to the right."

I nod, pass him my coat, and smile at Evan. Then head toward what I think must be the kitchen. It gets progressively more crowded the deeper I walk into the house.

The kitchen isn't to my taste either, brown marble countertops and a backsplash of more gray stone. I push through the crowd, spotting a closed door about halfway down the connecting hallway that I'm guessing must be the bathroom.

There's a line, of course, but it's only two girls. One's scrolling on her phone, the other tapping her fingernails against the plastic cup she's holding. Neither pay me any attention as I join the end of the line, leaning my head back against the wall and shoving my hands into the back pockets of my jeans. I haven't seen any sign of Landon yet, and part of me is hoping he decided not to come.

"I can't believe how many people are talking about Conor Hart and that blonde girl," the girl on her phone says. "Who is she again?"

"I don't know," the bored girl replies. "But Megan told me she used to date Landon Garrison."

"Wow. So she was trying to upgrade?"

"Seems like it."

Landon doesn't like to talk about high school. I've always had a good idea why. It can't be easy watching other people fawn over someone you have such a complicated connection to. And I also figured Conor enjoyed the same popularity in high school he does at Holt. But there's a fresh twinge of guilt, realizing Landon thinks I'm just one more person who chose Conor over him. That if I was a loyal best friend, I never would have exchanged enough words with Conor to appreciate there was more to him than I originally thought.

"Is Conor here? I haven't seen him."

"Dunno. He usually shows."

The bathroom door opens, and a blonde girl comes out. The girl with the cup goes in next. Rather than wait around, the girl next to me shoves her phone away and heads for the kitchen, leaving me standing in the hallway alone.

Cup Girl takes a good ten minutes in the bathroom, giving me a discerning look when she leaves.

The bathroom is huge, larger than my bedroom at Holt. Both the floor and the walls are a smooth, cream-colored marble, interrupted by thick gray veins. There are twin sinks with a massive mirror hanging above them, and a glass-enclosed shower that takes up most of the wall next to the toilet.

I look around for a good minute, taking it in, before going pee and washing my hands. My makeup and hair fared better than I thought they would following basketball earlier. I fingercomb one section of my hair, then head for the door.

Five girls are now waiting in the hallway, making me glad I went when I did.

Rather than head into the kitchen, the same way I came, I go left, continuing down the hallway and into a formal dining room. People are playing Flip Cup on the long table that looks like it could seat twenty.

Once I'm through the dining room, I'm back in the front entryway. I walk in at the same time as Landon, who's following Steve Essex in through the front door.

"Hey, guys!" My tone is too cheery. High and false.

"Hi, Harlow." Steve smiles, but then casts a nervous look at Landon that causes the unease I'm already experiencing to spike.

"Where are the rest of the guys?" I ask.

"Not their thing," Landon answers.

I didn't think this was his thing, either. According to Conor, this party has taken place for the past three years. Landon has never once attended. He prefers smaller groups, unless it's a crowd he's performing in front of.

"Crazy place, huh?" I say, striving for something neutral to discuss.

Steve laughs, looking around. "Yeah. It's something."

He seems on board with acting like everything's fine, which I appreciate. Landon is just scowling.

I follow his gaze to Conor, who's standing with Evan in the living room. They're both talking to a brunette girl, and I'm sure it's another mark against Conor in Landon's mind. But from my perspective—which might just be wishful thinking—Conor doesn't look interested in her. He's nodding politely, with plenty of space between them. And he's still holding my coat, the pink lining visible, and I realize that might have been a purposeful move, not just thoughtful.

From this angle, I can see all the scrutiny he's receiving. It grows more noticeable when Evan nudges Conor and then nods this way. I'm not expecting them to both head this direction, but they do.

People are shouting at Conor. Grabbing him. Desperate for some small scrap of attention.

His is on me.

My stomach somersaults as Conor approaches, having no clue how this will play out.

"Was worried you fell in."

I roll my eyes, painfully aware of Landon's eyes on me. Watching me talk to his brother. "There was just a line. Like usual. And you think this is strange—" I wave a hand around at the entryway. "Check out the bathroom."

Conor grins. "Yeah, I've been in there before."

Steve and Evan are chatting easily, which is nice. I'd forgotten Steve mentioned they played soccer together. It bridges a little of the awkwardness, makes it so I'm not the only link between the two groups.

Then Conor shocks me by taking a deep breath and acknowledging his half-brother. "Landon."

There's a flash of surprise on Landon's face, before it shutters back to neutral. "Conor."

Conor glances back at me. "I was just going to grab a drink. You want anything?"

"I'll come with you."

He made a tiny effort just now, one I appreciate. I'm getting the strong impression Landon doesn't want to talk to me right now, and I'm not thrilled with him either.

"See you guys later," I say, then follow Conor into the dining room.

Calls of "Hart!" and "Hey, man!" echo around us. It feels exactly like walking into the hockey party with him did. That same spotlight, just moved to a different location.

Conor stops to talk to a few people, introducing me every time. The reaction is always different. Interested... surprised...jealous.

When we finally reach the kitchen, Conor heads straight for the fridge. Opens it, and then huffs a laugh. "All beer. You want one? I'm not drinking tonight."

Immediately, I feel guilty, knowing why he was fine having a drink before driving the other night but is choosing not to now. "This is your last night of freedom."

He's headed back to Somerville tomorrow for a Saturday afternoon practice. All of the sports teams have slightly different schedules than the rest of the student body—fall sports return to campus early, winter sports have shortened Thanksgiving and winter breaks, spring sports don't have a spring break at all—but the hockey team seems to take its training to a whole other level.

"So?" Conor asks.

"So, I don't want you to—"

"I'm not drinking, Hayes. End of the story. But you—you should drink as much as you want." He grins.

I arch an eyebrow. "You trying to get me drunk, Hart?"

"No. But it was fun, last time."

I blush, remembering what happened after the same party I was recalling earlier.

"Fine. I'll have a beer."

Conor grabs a can out of the fridge and hands it to me. I crack it open and then hold it toward him. "Take a sip."

"Hayes…"

"Don't make me drink alone. One sip, Hart."

He rolls his eyes but takes the can and swigs from it. "Happy?"

"Uh-huh." I take a sip, right where his lips just were.

His eyes darken, like maybe he's thinking the same thing. He hasn't kissed me yet tonight, and I keep wishing that he would. I wasn't sure how this party would play out, if he would be so busy catching up with old friends we'd hardly get to talk.

But his focus stays on me, even when a girl jostles into him and lets out a fake—in my opinion—laugh. "Oh, I'm so sorry, Conor."

"No problem," he tells her.

"How have you been?"

"Fine."

I hide my smile behind the can of beer as I take another sip.

After a couple more questions that receive monosyllabic replies, she moves on.

"Wanna go outside?" I ask him.

It's cold and dark out, but it sounds better than standing in the crowded, loud kitchen. The edge of the ugly countertop is digging into my hip, growing increasingly annoying. And Conor is still holding my coat, so I won't freeze like last time.

He nods immediately, grabbing my hand and pulling me out of the kitchen. We head the opposite direction from the bathroom, through a study and then out a back door. There's a stone patio that's empty except for a fire pit built into the very center and a wooden swing suspended from a pergola that covers half the patio. Tiny lights are scattered through flowerbeds that are filled with stumps at the moment, casting just enough light to see where we're stepping. I take my jacket from Conor, slipping it on for added warmth.

"I like Evan," I say as we sit on the swing.

"Yeah. He's a good guy. Stuck with me through some shit."

I don't ask what that *shit* was, or if it involved the Garrisons. If he would change anything that happened in the past. Hugh has some culpability. But Landon was innocent in everything that happened, the same way Conor was. They never got to know each other, both pretending they were only children.

"I'm sorry for what I said about Williams," Conor suddenly says. "You and him? None of my business."

"No, you were right. I messed up there. Honestly, I only dated him as long as I did because of you."

"What do you mean, because of me?"

"Because I'd avoided you and decided I wasn't going to make it that easy for you anymore."

"How's that working out for you?"

I laugh and drink more of my beer. "You're hard to ignore, Hart."

"So are you, Hayes. You have to notice someone, to avoid them."

"You're saying you *noticed* me?" I tease.

"That's *exactly* what I'm saying. I'm so attracted to you, it's insane."

I look over at him, chewing on my bottom lip.

"Come here," Conor murmurs.

I comply, sliding toward him at the same time he moves toward me. The wooden swing we're on creaks as we meet in the middle. I'm pressed up against him, but it's not close enough. I swing one of my legs over both of his so I'm straddling strong thighs. Conor's hands slide up my thighs, splaying on my ass. I stare into those blue depths, the color darker than usual in the limited light of the night. His pupils dilate with lust.

Slowly, I lean forward, hovering so close I can't see his whole face. I tease his lips like a whisper, feeling his breath leave his mouth in warm gusts.

"This party is really fun," I whisper.

His lips curve upward as they touch mine. "I'm glad you're enjoying yourself."

Conor traces my bottom lip with his tongue. I moan, and it ignites the moment like a flame touching gasoline.

Our mouths go from barely brushing to desperate. There's nothing but sensation. Urgency and need and heat. Desire dulls my reflexes, barely registering a slamming door.

The "Shit" rings through loud and clear.

I pull back from Conor and look toward the house, straight at Steve Essex's surprised face. Landon is right behind him, wearing a horrified expression I would find funny in any other scenario.

"Uh...bad timing," Steve says. "We came out here to get some air."

To escape, I'm guessing. Landon looked uncomfortable earlier, and I don't think it was entirely because of Conor.

"Oh," is all I can think to say.

Landon is doing a spot-on imitation of a statue, staring at me straddling Conor. Not moving. Not speaking. I can't even tell if he's breathing.

Suddenly, he turns and heads back inside. Steve smiles apologetically, then follows.

I sigh. "One sec," I tell Conor, climbing off his lap and jogging toward the door. Landon and Steve are standing next to the desk in the study, talking.

Steve takes one look at me, mutters something about the bathroom, and then leaves.

"What, your boyfriend didn't want to keep making out after rubbing my face in it?"

Landon asks the question in the same sharp, biting tone I've heard him use to discuss Conor before. It's never been aimed at me, though.

"Neither of us knew you were coming out there, Landon. We're not trying to rub your face in anything."

"Maybe *you're* not."

"*Of course* I'm not. Landon, I'm your best friend. I would never do anything to hurt your—"

"You're doing it, Harlow! This! You and him *hurts*! You've never acted like this over a guy. Anyone could have walked out there just now and seen you on his lap, looking like a—"

I still. "Looking like a *what*, Landon? A *slut*? Is that what you were going to say?"

"I didn't say that."

"But you were going to."

"I'm trying to protect you, because you don't seem interested in protecting yourself. This is all a game to him. You get that, right? Conor doesn't give a shit about you."

I sigh, sick of talking in circles. Maybe coming after him was a mistake. "You don't know him."

"I know all the guy cares about is playing hockey and getting laid. You're just another girl to him, with the added bonus of hurting me."

"He isn't—"

"Don't act like he didn't know exactly who you were whenever this thing between you two started. Like he didn't show up *at my house* to feel you up on the front porch."

"You were watching us?"

"I looked out to make sure you were okay," Landon snaps. "Sorry for caring."

"And you think Conor somehow orchestrated that too?"

"Nothing's a coincidence here, Harlow! You've been my best friend since we could talk. You've known Conor for how long? I'm probably the only reason he was even interested in you."

I suck in a deep breath, guilt mixing with anger. "I'm going to leave now, before one of us says something that ends this friendship forever."

For the first time, there's a flash of uncertainty on Landon's face. Like he's ranted through his fury and is finally registering everything he's said.

"Harlow—"

The back door opens and Conor steps into the study, carrying a gust of cold air with him. Conor glances between me and Landon, his expression smooth enough I don't think he overheard any of our argument. He hands me the beer I left outside.

"I'll be in the kitchen."

I nod. "Thanks."

"You're drinking?" Landon asks, shaking his head. "Wow, he's been a *great* influence."

It's like he's unable to help himself, lashing out every time Conor comes up. I used to think it was anger on Hugh's behalf. But now? Now I think there are a lot of feelings that are Landon's alone. Jealousy, seeing Conor's popularity. Resentment, maybe, that Conor never wanted to have a relationship with him.

"Watch your fucking tone when you talk to her, Garrison."

Landon laughs. "Wow, you're really committing to the hero act. Worried Harlow is going to see through it soon?"

Conor takes a step toward Landon, and I grab the back of his jacket. "Don't," I tell him. "Please."

Landon is in no state of mind to deescalate things. He's bitter and hurt and who knows what else. As far as I know, he's never been in a physical fight. But I wouldn't be shocked if he was the one to swing first.

Landon's stare is defiant. But thankfully, he doesn't say anything else.

"I'm ready to go, if you are," I say. "I'll meet you at the car."

Conor hesitates, but finally nods. I let go of his coat, watching him walk down the hall toward the kitchen. I know when he reaches it, because there's a fresh wave of noise.

"Hasn't he been drinking?" Landon asks. "You're seriously going to—"

"No, he hasn't been drinking," I snap. "He refused to, actually. But I'm done defending Conor to you. Done discussing him at all. I'm trying to be patient, and I'm trying to be understanding, Landon. But I'm getting none of that back. And until I do, I don't want to talk to you."

I spin and walk away.

CHAPTER TWENTY-TWO

CONOR

"Fun party, huh?" I say as I start driving.

Harlow huffs a laugh. "The end of it kinda sucked."

"I wish you'd let me hit him."

"Would have only made things worse."

She doesn't defend Landon, I notice.

It should make me happy, but I feel guilty instead. I've been mostly absorbed by how my feelings toward the Garrison affect us. Not giving enough consideration of how it might affect Harlow's relationship with them.

"I'm sorry, for just showing up on Wednesday night. I should have talked to you before, at least. Discussed it before dropping that bomb and leaving you to deal with it."

"I'm relieved, actually," she tells me. "I've felt guilty, keeping it from them. Lying to them. And I knew Landon would take it... about how he's taking it. So I'm not sure how, or when, I would have said something myself."

"How did...Hugh react?"

I feel Harlow's eyes on me. Mine stay fixed on the road.

"He was surprised. And...excited, I guess."

"Excited?"

"He's never had anyone to ask about you. Doesn't know that you love Mexican food or that you snore sometimes. And…" Her voice trails, like she's treading lightly. "I got the sense he really wants to know those things about you."

I'm silent, absorbing that. It lines up with everything my mom said yesterday morning.

"I don't snore, Hayes."

She laughs, sounding relieved. "I'll record you one night."

I like the way that sounds too much, the easy implication that there will be more nights we'll spend together.

"You in any rush to get home?" I ask.

She scoffs. "No."

More guilt. But also excitement, because I want to spend more time with her.

"Okay."

I keep driving. After about fifteen minutes, she glances over at me.

"Where are we going?"

"You'll see."

When I park outside our destination, Harlow glances at me with raised eyebrows. "A bar?"

"You'll like this place," I promise her.

"You've been here before?" she asks as we near the front door.

I hand the bouncer my ID, and she does the same before we get let inside.

"In high school," I tell her, once we're past the door and handing off our jackets at the coat check.

She shakes her head. "Of course you did."

"Don't act like you never rebelled, Hayes. I saw you play beer pong."

We keep walking, skirting around the small groups standing and talking. I grab Harlow's hand automatically, tugging her into my body protectively and guiding her toward the metal bar top that runs the full length of one side of the space.

"Do you want a drink?" I ask her.

She smiles. "Yeah."

We find an open spot near the end. Harlow orders a Moscow Mule, then leans back against the bar to survey the crowd. She spots the stage toward the back, where a guy with a full beard is plugging in wires and setting up microphones.

"They have live music here?"

"Uh-huh. And I know you like supporting local musicians."

Harlow narrows her eyes as she takes her drink from the bartender. "Subtle, Hart."

There's more I could say about the Garrisons. They're this huge cloud we can't escape the shadow of. That has become harder and harder to ignore, correlating with my feelings for Harlow becoming stronger and stronger. But for tonight, I want to revert to pretending they don't exist.

"Come on." I grab her hand again and pull her away from the bar, toward the small crowd that's gathered to watch two girls and a guy climb onto the stage that's been set up.

We blend in with the group that's mostly other college students and a few young professionals. This bar is located a town over from Claremont, even closer to Brighton University.

When I came here in high school, I never paid much attention to the musicians. So I'm not sure what to expect, and maybe that's why I'm pleasantly surprised by the acoustic sound drifting out of the speakers. But I'm pretty sure it has more to do with the redhead by my side.

The lead singer has a raspy, worn voice that fits well with the darkened, no-frills atmosphere of the bar. But I have no idea what she's wearing. No clue what she looks like.

My attention is all on Harlow. It's like I have a new, sixth sense that's only attuned to her. I kept scanning the room for her earlier. Kept checking to make sure she was still behind me.

I wasn't sure how much to touch her at the party. What amount of public affection she was comfortable with, off campus, especially once Landon showed up.

I'm not worried about that here. I position her in front of my body, and Harlow leans back against me naturally. She lifts the hand not holding the copper cup, sliding it into my hair as she relaxes even more. Then Harlow tilts her head back to look up at me, her green eyes sparkling and her cheeks flushed pink. Winks at me, before glancing back at the stage to focus on the music.

And all I'm thinking about is how good it feels to have her look at me like that.

———

"What's wrong?" I ask as Harlow walks toward me.

I'm waiting by the coat check. She had to go to the bathroom before we headed out and she wasn't wearing this glum expression when she left.

"I wanted to buy some merch from the band, but they're cash only."

"We can look for an ATM? I don't have any cash either."

"No, it's fine. Let's just go."

We retrieve our jackets and then head back outside. Halfway to the car, Harlow grabs my arm. I glance along the street, worried something is wrong.

"There's a doughnut place!"

I relax. "Jesus, Hayes. Have you never seen Holey Moley before?"

She stares at me. Laughs. "Never seen it? Hart, I'm their most loyal customer. Eve and I go there every weekend. Sometimes *multiple* times a weekend."

"Okay, okay. You love doughnuts. Got it."

"Can we go?"

I'm sure she could ask me to do absolutely anything right now, and I would. Just to keep that excited look on her face.

"Yeah, sure."

We pass my parked car and then head into the small doughnut place. It's popular, mostly filled with people who look like they came from the same bar we did. Neon signs decorate the space, and a few plastic booths line the walls. My stomach grumbles as soon as we enter, warm air saturated with the scent of sugar and fried dough surrounding us. There's a huge chalkboard above the metal bins that the doughnuts are stored in listing off all the possible flavors.

I order a maple bacon doughnut, and Harlow decides on a chocolate sprinkled one. We snag one of the open booths. I finish my doughnut in approximately two bites. Harlow is tearing off tiny pieces and eating them methodically, occasionally licking her fingers.

"So good," she moans, and just like that—I'm getting hard.

I grab a napkin off the table to wipe my fingers, then ball it up in my fist as I deliberate on how to say this.

"There's the, uh, winter sports banquet next Friday."

"What does that mean?" She's focused on her doughnut, pressing a piece of it into the sprinkles that have fallen on the plate.

"It's just a thing the athletics department does every year.

There's food and they hand out awards and stuff. No alcohol and we have to dress up, so half the guys hate it."

"Doesn't sound that bad. I'm sure you'll survive it."

I smile. "Yeah, I'm sure I will. But what I'm trying to ask, Hayes, is if you'll go with me."

Now I have her full attention. Harlow freezes, a bite of doughnut halfway to her mouth. "Go with you?"

"Yeah, we're allowed to bring guests. Family members, former coaches, whoever we want."

"And you're inviting me as your…"

"Date."

"Right."

She looks a little dazed. Stunned, actually.

I start to get nervous, worried I misread this whole thing. Maybe I'm the only one who's feeling this way.

"If you're busy or you don't want to, it's—"

"Ask me."

"What?"

"You said you were *trying* to ask me. Follow through, Hart."

I smirk. "Fine. Will you go with me, Harlow?"

She smiles back, her cheeks flushing as she picks up the last bite of her doughnut. "Yes."

CHAPTER TWENTY-THREE

CONOR

A sharp whistle cuts through the cold air.

I lean left, carving a tight circle into the ice before I hustle back up toward the bench. Come to an abrupt stop, sending a spray of shavings Hunter's way. He pulls off his glove and pretends to rub his nose, subtly flipping me off. I laugh under my breath.

Coach Keller starts running through his usual laundry list of improvements, ending with a reminder about the sports banquet tomorrow night.

Guys start to file off the ice, headed toward the locker room.

"A word, Hart?"

I hang back, leaning against the boards and waiting for Coach to come over.

"Heard of the Caddell-Spade Award, Hart?"

"Um, no?"

His grunt is disapproving. "It's an award, given to a senior student athlete who demonstrates outstanding leadership. Entire committee votes on the recipient. This year, that's you."

I blink at him, stunned. I was one of those guys I described to

Harlow, bored and impatient, at past banquets. Thought it was time that could be better spent elsewhere. I'm more excited for this year, simply because she's going with me, but the possibility of me receiving an award did not cross my mind.

Coach Keller is staring at me, waiting for a response. "I—wow. Thanks."

He nods. "Just wanted to give you a heads up. Recipients usually give a speech."

"A speech?"

"Yep."

"Um, okay."

He claps me on the back. "Get out of here."

I step off the ice and walk along the rubber mats that lead into the locker room.

Jack Williams is standing at the water fountain, filling his bottle.

I've debated all week whether to say something to Williams about who I'm bringing to the banquet tomorrow night. It's been two years since they dated, and according to Harlow it was never that serious. He's seen her with other guys, knows she's moved on. But I'm being honored with a *leadership* award, and he's been a teammate since freshman year.

I pause. "Hey, Williams. Can I talk to you for a minute?"

Jack glances up. "Yeah, sure."

"So...I'm, uh, bringing a date to the banquet."

He nods. "That's great, Hart. Glad a girl on campus is finally giving you the time of day."

I snort. I've never talked to Jack much, outside of practice. Maybe I misjudged him.

"Yeah. The thing is, *this* girl...you dated her."

He realizes who I'm referring to instantly. "You're bringing Harlow?"

I nod.

"Are you guys together?"

"I'm not sure." I haven't asked her to be my girlfriend. But that feels inevitable now, more of a *when* than an *if.* "I like her though. I like her a lot."

"I'm, uh, thanks for telling me."

I nod. "See you later."

Aidan is yawning at his locker when I sit down and start unlacing my skates. "Wanna go grab Mexican?" he asks. "Been a while."

I focus on loosening the laces, debating how to respond. I'm behind on watching film for Saturday's game against Edgewood, and they're not the team I can slack off before facing. Their captain, Jordan Driscoll, is arguable one of the best players in the entire division. We lost to them in playoffs last season, so there's plenty of bad blood on my end. And preferably, I was going to be watching that film in bed with Harlow.

But Aidan is right, we haven't hung out much. And he's been acting weird lately, like the day he called me for a ride to practice. Wouldn't tell me what his "shit mood" was about, just grumbled around the rest of the day. The next morning, it was like nothing had ever happened.

"Yeah, sure," I say, yanking off my practice jersey.

"Morgan? You in for burritos?" Aidan asks.

"Can't," he says. "My dad just got in. We're getting dinner."

"Your dad's here?" Aidan sounds surprised, and I am too.

Hunter never mentioned anything about a visit. I met his dad once; he came to a game of ours sophomore year. He was just as quiet and serious as his son. And Hunter has never once mentioned his mom, so I'm assuming she's not in the picture.

"Yeah." That's all Hunter says.

Aidan and I exchange a look. "You still in?" he asks me.

"Sure. Just give me ten minutes."

I finish getting changed, take a quick shower, and then Aidan and I head out into the parking lot.

"I'll drive."

I groan. "Phillips."

"My truck is way nicer than your SUV, Hart. And if the color bothers you *that much*, you can't even see it from the inside."

I roll my eyes but stash my bag into the back of my car and then climb into the passenger side of Aidan's eyesore. He is right about the interior. Everything is plush and it still has that new car smell.

While Aidan drives toward Loughton, I pull my phone out and text Harlow.

> CONOR: Grabbing dinner with Aidan and then I have to watch film. Probably won't see you until tomorrow night.

She likes the message right away, but doesn't respond.

It makes me nervous, and I'm not sure if that's the right instinct or not. I haven't asked where things stand between her and Landon after Thanksgiving, and Harlow hasn't brought him up. I know she likes the sex, because her appetite is almost as insatiable as mine. We've been sleeping together for weeks and still can't keep our hands off each other. I want her to know that I care, that she's not the *just sex* agreement we made to me anymore. That she hasn't been that for a long time. But I'm not sure how to, what she wants from me or what I can give her. We're on a tightrope right now, it feels like, and have to fall to one side or the other at one point.

"We're here, Hart." Aidan nudges my arm.

I startle, then climb out of his truck and stretch. Practice this week has been extra rough after our break last week. My entire body is sore.

Aidan and I head inside. It's crowded for a Thursday night, about six people in line in front of us and half the tables filled. The two girls in line in front of us glance back and smile.

Aidan winks at them. "Hey, ladies. What's good here? I've never been."

It's hard to suppress the eye roll. He's a proud playboy, and as far as I can tell he's always up front with girls about that, so I've never had an issue with it. But it's weird to think how, just a couple months ago, I would probably be chatting these girls up too, pretending not to know the menu for a place I've been to dozens of times before. One that, frankly, is basically identical to every Mexican restaurant I've ever been to before.

But just like with Kelly—just like with every girl who's been around me lately—there's no interest. I ignore Aidan and his flirting and act like this place is new to me too, studying the menu and then glancing around the tiny restaurant.

I order a beef burrito, my usual order, and then head for one of the open tables. Aidan joins me a few minutes later.

"Way to slack on the wingman duties, Hart. You totally left me flying solo."

"So you struck out?"

"Nah." He tosses a napkin on the table in front of me. Two numbers are scribbled on it.

I shake my head, smiling. Aidan's a good-looking guy, but it's his charm that seems to lure in chicks the most. His whole vibe is *I'm a good time*. Which makes some of his recent behavior even weirder.

"Everything good with you, man?"

"Yeah, why?"

I shrug, trying to act nonchalant. "You just seemed…off a few times lately. I wanted to make sure nothing was going on."

"I'm good."

"Okay." I start eating, groaning as I bite into the chewy, tender meat.

"My folks have a place in Vail," Aidan tells me suddenly.

I chew and swallow, surprised. I've always gotten the sense Aidan comes from money, but he never mentions his family. "That's cool."

"I'm headed there for winter break. If you're interested."

"You're inviting me to Colorado?"

"Yeah. We could ski, snowboard, whatever. There's a hot tub. Whole house is pretty sweet, actually."

"Will your…folks be there?"

Aidan shakes his head. "My brother could come by, but that's it."

"It sounds awesome," I tell him. "Can I get back to you, though? I haven't talked to my mom about the holidays yet, not sure what she's planning on."

We have a shortened break, thanks to hockey. Unlike most students, we have to be back on campus right after New Year's.

"Yeah, of course." He takes a bite of his taco. "You ready for Saturday?"

"I hope so."

"You'll lead us to victory, Captain. Like always." He mock-salutes me.

"Coach told me I'm getting an award tomorrow night."

"No shit?"

I snort. "Don't look so surprised."

"I forgot they gave out awards at this thing, is all."

"You forgot—that's the whole point of the banquet, Phillips."

"I thought it was to eat and hang out with all the other athletes. Like a sports-only party, without any alcohol or fun."

"You never noticed people get awards at this thing?"

"Nope." He pops the P. "Last year I was trying to hook up with Macie Crawford."

I shake my head. "If someone finds you having sex during my speech, I'm gonna be pissed."

"You're giving a speech?"

"Apparently. And…I'm bringing Harlow. As my date."

Aidan's eyebrows fly upward.

"Don't make it a thing," I warn him.

"It seems like you telling me not to make it a thing, makes it a thing." He takes a sip of water. "Are you officially dating her, then?"

"We haven't had the conversation, but that's basically what we've been doing for a while now."

I think. I've never really dated a girl in the past, so there's nothing to compare it to.

"Yeah, I know. You've just been saying you weren't, so I was letting you keep saying that."

I sigh, the usual combination of amusement and exasperation I experience around Aidan appearing. "You ready to head out? I've got Edgewood film to watch tonight."

"Yeah. Let's go."

CHAPTER TWENTY-FOUR

HARLOW

The burning smell is concerning me.

"Eve..."

"Almost done," she assures me. "Just two more sections."

"This has to be worse for my hair than chlorine. I can literally *hear it* frying."

"I put protective spray in. Just stay still or else I'm going to burn your neck."

I sigh but stay motionless. When I told Eve Conor invited me to go to his sports banquet—as his date—the first thing she asked was if she could do my hair.

She's amazing at it, thanks to all the tips and tricks she's learned from her mom. It's just always been a lengthy process the few other times she's styled it for me, and tonight is no exception. It feels like I've been sitting here for an hour.

And it gives me too much time to think. To focus on the nerves mixing with excitement.

"Conor is going to lose it when he sees you."

Eve's voice is giddy with excitement.

For her, this is my happy ending. She thinks Conor finally

decided he wants more from our no-strings arrangement and is thrilled for me. She doesn't know any of the other, more complicated details, like how I haven't spoken to my best friend for a week.

Landon and I didn't exchange a single word, between arriving back at the Garrisons' on Friday night and leaving on Sunday. And I haven't heard from him since.

Allison has texted me every day this week, checking in and asking how I'm doing. My response has always been *Fine*. It's one thing to discuss Conor with her, but I'm not sure how I can ask for her opinion—her advice—when it comes to Landon's behavior. Part of me is hoping he'll magically get over his issues. The rest of me knows that it won't happen, and that me having a relationship with Conor will cause permanent damage to my friendship with my oldest and closest friend.

I miss my mom. Wish she were here to share her opinion on all this.

"Okay. All done."

Eve unclips the pile of curls on top of my head, runs a brush through them, sprays something that smells fruity, and then nudges my arm.

"Go look."

I walk over to the mirror. My normally wavy hair has been transformed into perfect ringlets that fall effortlessly. It's a style I never would have had the patience or skill to pull off myself. I'm scared to touch it and mess something up.

"Oh my God, Eve. It's amazing."

She smiles at me, satisfied. Then the doorbell rings.

"Crap."

My hair is done and I finished my makeup before Eve pulled out her curling iron, but I'm still in sweatpants.

"I'll get the door," Eve tells me. "Just put on your dress."

"Okay, thanks."

My only insight to the dress code was Conor's comment that the guys "dressed up." Eve and I spent several hours searching for the dress I'm stepping into now. It's silky, long, and dark green. It dips low in the front and even lower in the back, straps criss-crossing my shoulders.

Even if I'm overdressed, I feel confident in it. The nude heels I've worn for every fancy occasion over the past four years make the dress the perfect length, keeping the hem from dragging on the ground. I grab my dress coat, phone, and keys, then head into the hallway that leads to the living room.

Conor's leaning against the opening that separates the entryway from the living room, talking with Eve.

He straightens as soon as he sees me, rubbing a hand along his clean-shaven jawline.

"Holy fuck, Harlow."

I smirk. "You clean up well too."

Conor's wearing a navy suit with a white button-down, and it's the most dressed up I've ever seen him. It fits him perfectly, showing off the muscular frame I'm intimately familiar with.

As soon as I reach him, Conor wraps an arm around my waist and pulls me straight into him. "Hey, Hayes."

"Hi, Hart."

He kisses me before I can say anything else, tasting like mint and smelling like pine. It's just a peck, probably so we don't scandalize Eve, but it's still enough to get my heart racing. Or maybe that was seeing him in this suit.

"How long did this take?"

"Longer than twenty minutes."

He chuckles. "You ready?"

"Uh-huh." I pull on my coat, now that he's gotten the full effect, sliding my phone into my pocket and then glancing at Eve.

She's beaming at us like a proud mother sending her daughter off to prom. "Bye, Eve."

"Bye. Have fun, guys."

Conor steps outside first. I've barely closed the door behind us when he spins me around, presses me against the siding, and kisses me again. Deeper and longer and harder, with an urgency that seems unfair considering we'll be at a public event for the next few hours.

"This fucking dress, Hayes." He groans the words like they're physically painful to say. "How the hell am I supposed to focus on anything else when you're wearing this fucking dress?"

I smirk at him. "If you like the dress, wait till you see what I'm wearing under it."

I slip out of his grip and keep walking, headed toward his car. Smiling when I hear a low curse before his footsteps follow me.

———

The sports banquet is being held inside the basketball gym, which is not exactly the most glamorous venue. At least the smells of old popcorn, sweat, and chemical cleaner are mostly covered by the aroma coming from the buffet table set up along one wall. A local Italian restaurant is catering tonight, oregano and garlic the strongest scents.

Like Conor mentioned, there's no alcohol being served, since at least half the students in attendance are underage. But there's a station set up that has an assortment of coffee, tea, soda, and water.

It's already crowded when we arrive, chatter echoing off the high ceilings and cinderblock walls.

"Look for Morgan," Conor tells me. "He's supposed to be saving us a table."

I scan the round tables that have been set up around the center of the court, in front of a stage with a microphone, finally spotting Hunter seated at one close to the bleachers. There's a middle-aged man next to him, and they look so much alike I'm certain they must be related.

"Back left," I say. "By the bleachers."

Conor sees him too, and we head in that direction.

"That's Hunter's dad?"

"Yeah."

"Is his mom here too?" I ask.

"No, I don't think she's around."

"What about Aidan? Is his family here?"

"Not that he mentioned. I don't think he's that close to his folks."

We reach the table and introductions get made all around. Robby Sampson is seated at the same table, with his parents, and then Aidan strolls over a few minutes later.

He smirks when he sees me sitting next to Conor.

The guys start talking hockey, while I glance around at the other students here. I recognize Clayton Thomas and a few other guys on the basketball team, but that's pretty much it.

A middle-aged man with an impressive mustache approaches our table a few seconds later.

"A word, Hart?" he barks.

I'd know this was the hockey coach based on how all the players at the table immediately sit straighter, even if I didn't recognize him from the game I went to.

"Sure," Conor says.

His coach is already walking off.

Hunter snorts. "Wish Coach would take his job a little more seriously."

"Have we recorded a smile yet, Sampson?" Aidan asks.

I'm distracted by their conversation by Conor leaning over and kissing me. "I'll be right back," he tells me.

"I—okay."

My brain is surprised mush at the moment. We've kissed before, obviously. But never this publicly, this openly. In front of his best friends and teammates and everyone else packed in here.

Conor smirks, then stands and follows his coach.

"Hard launch," Aidan coughs.

I roll my eyes, but I'm smiling.

When Conor still hasn't returned after ten minutes, I stand and head toward the drink table. I'm filling a glass with sparkling water when I hear "Hey, Harlow."

I turn to see Jack has appeared beside me. He grabs a teabag from the display of them and drops it in a mug, then pours hot water over it.

"Hi, Jack. How are you?"

We've run into each other a handful of times over the past couple of years, but this feels different. And I know it's because of Conor. Because I didn't use to understand why I couldn't recip-rocate the way Jack—a nice, good-looking guy—felt about me. On paper, everything worked. But now, I've experienced those feelings. I know exactly what I was missing, and it pales the past.

"Not bad," he tells me. "Season is going well, so that's great."

"Yeah. I heard something about that."

"You made it to a game yet?" The question is teasing, not annoyed.

"I did," I admit.

Back when we dated, I told him hockey wasn't my thing. And Jack easily accepted that, because hockey never held the starring role it does in Conor's life.

"That's great."

"Are you still planning to move back to LA after graduation?"

"Yep, that's still the plan. My dad can't wait for me to graduate. Has more work than he can handle."

Jack's family owns an accounting firm that's very high-profile. They handle taxes and other money matters for a bunch of A-list celebrities.

"That's great."

"Yeah, it is." He picks up his mug. "Take care, Harlow."

"You too, Jack."

"I'm happy for you, by the way. Hart's a lucky guy."

I smile. "Thanks."

By the time I finish my water, there's still no sign of Conor. People are starting to line up for the buffet to grab dinner.

I walk out of the gym and glance left, then right. Realize this is the same door I left the basketball game from. The same hallway I deliberated direction in then. I go right again, my heels tapping softly against the linoleum as I round the corner.

He's standing in the center of the weight room, staring off into space.

I step in the open doorway. "Hey."

Conor turns, hands in his pockets. "Hey."

"I got worried you were ditching me when you didn't come back to the table. Everything okay?"

"Yeah…" Conor exhales, glancing at the ground and then back to me. "I'm getting an award tonight."

"You are?"

"Yeah. Coach told me about it yesterday." His smile is wry. "Wanted to give me time to prepare my speech."

"Do you want to practice it on me or something?"

He snorts, then shakes his head. "I didn't write anything. I'm just gonna wing it."

"Bold."

"I try."

"Is that what he had to talk to you about tonight?"

"No, that was about the game tomorrow."

I walk closer toward him, Conor's eyes tracking each step. It's much dimmer in here than the fluorescent lights of the gymnasium, most of the hazy illumination from the moonlight spilling in from the high windows. My eyes take a few seconds to adjust before I can make out anything more than his basic silhouette. He's standing next to the same weight bench he was using to work out when I stumbled on him during the basketball game.

"What were you thinking?" I ask, nodding toward it. "When you saw me in the doorway."

"Probably how hot you were."

I know he's attracted to me. It's still fantastic for my ego, hearing him say it. There's something extra special about knowing the way you feel about someone is reciprocated, like two puzzle pieces fitting together perfectly.

"I *was* checking you out," I admit.

He laughs. "I know." Then something shifts in his expression. Turns serious. "You want to know what I was really thinking?"

I swallow, reacting to his intensity. "I don't know. Do I?"

Does it have to do with the Garrisons? is what I'm asking. If it's some version of the animosity that used to exist between us, I'd rather not know. At least for tonight, I'm trying to pretend it doesn't exist. That we're just a guy and a girl who started as casual sex and ended up becoming more. Tale as old as time.

"I thought, *I have absolutely no game when this girl is involved.* Because you were standing there, just looking at me, and I couldn't think of a single fucking thing to say. And it had nothing to do with anything except *you*, Harlow."

I smile, then close the remaining distance between our bodies.

Conor groans when I kiss him, his hands finding the exposed

skin of my back. It's not like there's a shortage of it. I suck on his tongue, and he growls.

"Hayes, it's gonna be really awkward for me to give a speech with a hard-on."

"I can fix that."

"Actually, you're making it worse...*fuck*."

His eyes flash with understanding as I get down on my knees and unbuckle his belt. The zipper parts easily, like it's relieved to no longer be straining to hold in his huge cock. Conor's dick bobs up straight toward his stomach as soon as I tug his pants and boxer briefs down.

"Someone could come in," he tells me, his voice hoarse.

"Then come fast." I lean forward, licking the raised vein that runs the length of his shaft before sucking the fat tip of his penis into my mouth. Conor grunts, his expression slack with pleasure as he watches me take more of him.

I've never liked giving blowjobs.

I love sucking Conor.

Love his taste, the way the thick shape of him feels in my mouth. Love teasing him with the tells I've learned, like how he groans extra loud every time my tongue swipes the leaking slit at the end. Love how his thighs tense and his abs tighten, trying to keep from thrusting so I can control the pace. Love knowing I have this power, that the awed, overwhelmed look on his face is all for me.

I reach up and massage his balls. There's one spot behind them he always reacts to. His hips jerk, and I know I found it.

Usually, his hands would be in my hair. But they're fisted at his sides, and I know it's because he's trying to preserve my appearance. When we walk back into the banquet, he doesn't want everyone here to know I was just on my knees for him. And that consideration, while not the traditional definition of a gentleman, drives my own arousal even higher. Makes me want to please him even more.

I hollow my cheeks, fighting the urge to gag as the tip brushes the back of my throat, and grip the inches I know there's no chance I'll be able to take with my hand.

"I'm close," he chokes out.

Another attractive thing about Conor—he's warned me every time. He's never acted like I had to swallow or he expected it of me. And it has the same arousing effect as him not touching my hair.

This time, the throb is harder to ignore. I slide my left hand between my thighs, moaning with relief when I reach my aching clit.

Conor realizes exactly what I'm doing underneath my dress, his cock thickening in my mouth. And then he's swearing and praising me, filling my mouth with warm, salty cum. I swallow as fast as I can, and some still spills out of my mouth. I lick it away with my tongue, and Conor shakes his head like he's in some sort of daze.

I haven't come yet, but I'm close. I can feel the tingling beneath my skin and the tightening low in my pelvis. And Conor's cock is still out, directly at eye level. It's so easy to imagine it sliding into me, stretching me, making me see stars. He's already hardening again, watching me get myself off to the sight of him. I don't know if it's an elite athlete thing or a Conor thing, but his stamina is insane.

And I decide I'd rather have his dick than my fingers.

"Sit on the bench," I tell him.

Conor raises an eyebrow but complies, taking a seat on the weight bench where he was working out shirtless the last time I was here. He's still fully dressed except for his unbuckled pants, his cock fully erect as he watches me approach.

I tug my dress up to my knees and straddle his lap, the same way I did on the porch swing in Claremont. Unlike then, the only barrier between our bodies is my tiniest thong, the one I wear when I'm worried about panty lines.

"Fuck, Harlow." My fingers already pulled the crotch to the side, so I'm basically rubbing against him bare. I can feel the scratch of his pubic hair. The hot skin of his erection, still wet from my mouth. "Fuck," Conor says again, except this time, it's frustrated. "I don't have a condom."

I pull in a deep breath, then ask him the question I promised myself I'd never voice. The question you don't ask the guy who's *just sex*. "Are you sleeping with other girls?"

Rather than a simple—useful—yes or no, his response is, "Are you serious?"

Hesitantly, I nod.

"This whole time, you think I've been *fucking other girls*?"

He sounds incredulous. Mad.

"*I don't know*, Conor," I hiss. "That's why I asked!"

"Have you been with other guys?" he demands.

"I asked you first. We're not in a relationship. We've never been in a relationship. Or been exclusive. It's a valid question."

And of the many times I've considered bringing this up and asking for answers, this situation—straddling his bare erection on a weight bench with a couple hundred people a short hallway away—was definitely the least ideal.

There's a long pause, and I only catch a few of the emotions that flash across Conor's face in the dim light. Anger, annoyance, indecision, uncertainty.

"Is that something you want?" he finally says, his voice low. "Do you want this to be a relationship?"

"You said you don't do girlfriends."

Was I hoping he'd changed his mind, that tonight was a step

in that direction? Absolutely. But he's never explicitly said so, and I know it's not because he has an issue being blunt. He's never suggested I should rely upon him for anything except regular sex.

"I know what I said."

I rock my hips against his, reminding him of the position we're in. That this isn't the time or place for a lengthy conversation. "I only asked because you said you don't have a condom. I haven't been with anyone else. And I'm on birth control, if you want to…"

His thumb runs along my jawline as he tilts my chin up, forcing me to look at him.

"I haven't been with anyone else, Hayes."

A different answer would have surprised me. But it's still a relief to hear.

I reach between our bodies to find his cock, gripping it and then guiding the tip to where I want it. We both groan as he slips inside, deeper and deeper until I'm taking all of him.

Everything about this moment—our fancy clothes and the shadowed room and the lingering tension in the air and the distant chatter that's a reminder someone could walk in here at any time —imprints itself in my memory.

Conor's hands find my hips beneath my dress, his hot skin a contrast to the cool silk. His grip is tight and restrained as he guides my movements. There's nothing sweet or tender about it. It's like he's using himself to pleasure me, and his cock is just a toy to get me off.

If it didn't feel so incredible, I'd hate it. He's fucking me like he *owes* it to me, like this is repayment for sucking him off. Like this *is* a mutually beneficial arrangement instead of a relationship.

I slide my hands under his suit jacket and spread them across his chest, feeling the steady thump of his heartbeat beneath the warm fabric. Maybe he's mad I didn't answer his relationship question. Maybe he's as uncertain and confused about us as I am.

It's something we need to discuss.

But right now, all I want is for him to acknowledge what's happening here. I've never let a guy inside me bare, and I'm incredibly aware of it as he moves inside of me.

"Does it feel different for you?" I whisper.

His Adam's apple bobs as he swallows. "Yeah."

"I'm going to walk around for the rest of the night with your cum dripping out of me."

"*Hayes.*" His voice is hoarse, on the edge of restraint.

I lean close so our faces are only a couple of inches apart. "I'm really glad you haven't fucked anyone else."

"I don't want anyone else, Harlow." One of his hands glides up my side, finding the swell of my breast and rubbing it softly. Knowing it'll make me arch against him and press me tighter against his pelvis. I'm not the only one who's learned tells, I guess. "You know what's going to happen now, right?"

"Uh, you'll make a mess?"

He grins. "No. Well, yeah. But this is going on my list."

"What list?"

"Of pregame rituals. If I play well tomorrow, I'm going to have to fuck you like this the night before every game."

He hits that perfect spot, and my eyes flutter closed. "I'm totally on board with that."

"Good." His lips move to my neck, pressing a kiss right to my pulse. "You're getting tighter, Hayes. I can feel you clenching my cock. Do you want me to fill this tight pussy, the same way I filled your mouth?"

"Yes," I gasp.

He thrusts up and I grind down, trying to take him deeper than I ever have before. And then there's relief, my entire body contracting the same way I'm squeezing his cock as vicious waves of heat wash through me. I'm still trembling when I feel him swell inside of me, then the unfamiliar warmth as he comes without wearing a condom.

We're both breathing heavily, enjoying the euphoria, when a door slams down the hall.

I climb off his lap hurriedly, grabbing a paper towel from the dispenser off the wall and wiping away the white liquid that's dripped down the inside of my thigh. Conor watches me do it as he fixes his pants, his gaze so intense and possessive it sends a shiver through me. I toss the paper towel, then readjust my underwear and dress.

"Do I look okay?" *Not like I just had sex in a weight room?*

"You look beautiful, Hayes."

Conor leans forward and kisses me, not seeming to care my mouth tastes like him. When he pulls back, he searches my expression. "Will you go out with me, tomorrow night after the game? We can talk."

I nod, smiling. "Okay."

Tomorrow's my birthday, but I don't mention that. It's been a weird occasion for me, ever since my parents died. I don't want him to do anything special for it, and being around him is how I want to spend it, anyway.

He grabs my hand, squeezes it, and then we head back into the gym.

CHAPTER TWENTY-FIVE

HARLOW

R ain pelts the window. I stare at the streaks running down the glass, make a face, and then turn back toward the mirror so I can finish my makeup. I haven't washed my hair since last night, the spray Eve put in my hair keeping the curls intact. They're pulled up in a high ponytail so my hair isn't covering the back of Conor's away jersey.

It was the first thing I grabbed to put on this morning, and Conor told me I should keep it on to wear to the game tonight. I think he was teasing me, but I surprised us both by telling him I was going to. And then we had sex again, because apparently the three seconds it takes to roll on a condom were slowing Conor down before.

The doorbell rings.

"Harlow!" Eve calls. "I'm not expecting anyone."

"I'm not either!" I shout back.

"Well, it's definitely your turn to get the door."

I sigh, twist the mascara tube shut, and then head down the hallway. Eve is at the kitchen table drawing. "Probably your boyfriend," she tells me.

I don't deny the title this time. After last night, it feels like he might be. Will be. But Conor should already be at the rink, getting ready for his game.

I swing the front door open. I was right.

It's not Conor.

It's three people I wasn't expecting to see in Somerville until graduation in May.

"Wh—what are you guys doing here?" I ask Hugh, Allison, and Landon.

"Happy Birthday, honey," Allison says. "We wanted to come celebrate with you."

I was expecting a phone call. A card from them arrived in the mail Thursday. But the Garrisons have never just shown up here. And this year—the way Landon is avoiding looking at me and Hugh is focused on the *Holt Hockey* jersey I'm wearing—seems like suspicious timing. I'm certain Allison is using today as an attempt to address what happened over Thanksgiving.

The smile slips off Allison's face, the longer I stand here silent.

"I'm sorry. I should have called first. We were just hoping we could walk around campus a little, grab a late lunch with you?"

Landon still won't look at me. Hugh is smiling, and it doesn't look forced.

"Um…"

They drove all this way. But I told Conor I would go to his game. I *want* to go to his game.

Once again, I'm caught in the middle.

I decide to be honest. "I'm supposed to go to the hockey game. It starts in an hour."

"Who are they playing?" The question bursts out of Hugh like he's been dying to ask it.

"Edgewood." The team they lost to in the playoffs last year. According to Conor, this will be their toughest opponent yet.

"We could all go to the game, get some food after?" Hugh suggests.

It feels…strange, going to Conor's game with the Garrisons. But it's not like the basketball games' empty, conspicuous stands. I'm sure the game today will be just as packed as the Friday night one I went to. Possibly even more crowded, since it's in the middle of the day. I can go with the Garrisons, spend a couple of hours with them after, and then go to dinner with Conor.

"Sure," I say. "That sounds good. Let me just go grab my stuff. We can walk around campus before the game."

Allison smiles. "Perfect."

"Come on in." I leave the door open, then head into the living room.

Eve is standing by the couch.

It's your birthday? she mouths to me.

Later, I mouth back.

Allison has always attempted to make today a happy occasion for me. Finding out I didn't tell Eve because I've never wanted to celebrate at school will only make her feel bad.

"Eve!" Allison says, giving my best friend a hug. "How are you?"

"I'm good, thanks. Nice to see you guys."

She waves at Hugh and smiles at Landon. They've all met multiple times before.

"I'll be right back," I say, then head down the hallway to my room. Finish dabbing on some concealer and then grab my phone and keys.

There's a knock on my door.

"Yeah?"

I'm expecting it to be Eve, but Landon's voice is the one that asks, "Can I come in?"

My chest contracts. The first words he's spoken to me in over a week. "Sure."

The door opens and Landon steps into my room. He glances around the space quickly before his gaze settles on me. He came to help me move in August, but this is the first time he's been to Holt since.

"Hey," he says.

"Hi." I play with my keys nervously.

Landon blows out a long breath. "I'm sorry, Harlow. I'm really sorry. I...there's a lot there, for me, when it comes to Conor. Years of anger and resentment, and I haven't had to deal with it. I could shove it all away and act like he doesn't exist. And then you...you were my friend first. I had to share a school with him and a town and my dad—even though Conor pretends that's not the case—but I never thought I'd have to share you. Not with *him*. It messed with my head, and I didn't handle it well. Some of the shit I said to you—inexcusable. I mean it, I'm really sorry."

I nod. "Thank you for apologizing."

"You're my best friend, and I want you to be happy. I know you've had to deal with a lot. But as your friend... I *don't* think he'll make you happy. This isn't me giving my blessing. I think you're too good for him and I think he'll hurt you. I still hate him, and I don't see that ever changing. But...it's not worth our friendship. So I'll shut my mouth where he's concerned. Your life, your decision."

It's about the best-case scenario I could have hoped for. But it still leaves me right smack dab in the middle. "I might be dating him, Landon."

His arms cross. "Yeah. I noticed the jersey."

"And I'm just supposed to…what? Disconnect a huge part of my life like that?"

"You've never talked to me about guys much before."

"Yeah, because they weren't…" *Because they didn't matter to me. Because they weren't huge parts of my life.*

"Look, Conor made his choices. He decided he didn't want a dad, and he wasn't very nice about it, I might add. That's not on me. That's not on my dad. Are you asking Conor to mend fences? Inviting him to family dinners, on the trip to Vancouver with us this summer?"

"No."

He wouldn't go, if I did.

Landon nods, knowing the answer already. "Don't ask me to accept him if you're not asking him to accept me. I'm saying you can keep us separate, that I won't hold your shitty taste in guys against you. Don't ask me for more than that."

I sigh. "Okay."

"Great. Mom wants to take photos of us all over campus so she can relive her wild college days. Hurry up."

He grins at me, then leaves my room.

———

It's raining out as we approach the main entrance to the hockey rink. No surprise there.

The misty, wet weather matches my mood.

Walking around campus with the Garrisons wasn't as awkward as I was worried about. Landon is back to acting like his normal, upbeat self, laughing and joking with me. The relief was obvious on Allison's face, watching us.

Hugh spent the walk studying the campus curiously. Unlike Allison, who was here for four years, he's only visited a couple of times. He seemed lost in his own head, and I'm guessing he was thinking about Conor.

Allison was in her element. Just like Landon said, she took photos of us all over campus. In another life, I could easily picture my mom beside her, both of them giddy over seeing the changes on campus since they went to school here themselves.

My nerves ramp up to a new degree as we follow the crowd headed into the arena. I was right about the turnout being even larger than usual. We have to literally fight our way into the lobby. Part of the issue is that the lobby wall with the sad trophy display is cordoned off. All the plaques from last night's banquet are being added to the wall.

My gaze snags on the Caddell-Spade Award that's already hanging back up, and Hugh notices it too as we pass by. It's the largest one, which I guess is some indication of its prestige.

"Conor won that?" he asks me.

"Yeah. Last night."

We pass through the lobby and walk along the rubber mats that lead to the boards surrounding the ice. The bleachers are already packed, and more people keep streaming in.

"Wow. This is really something," Allison states, looking around at the crowd.

"Should we meet you after the game?" Hugh asks.

"No, it's fine. Let's try to get seats together," I say.

They came all this way. And part of me is curious to see what Hugh's reaction will be to watching his son play hockey for the first time.

After some pushing and shoving, we finally find a section in the bleachers wide enough for the four of us to squeeze into. They're not great seats, at an awkward angle and partially obscured by the net hanging behind the goal, but they're better than nothing.

Loud pop music is playing, and it continues blaring as players start appearing on the ice. Holt's blue jerseys are at the opposite end, Edgewood's maroon nearer to us.

I lean over Allison and hand Hugh the program I picked up on the way in. "Fifteen," I tell him.

He mouths me a *Thank you*, then alternates between studying the roster and glancing at the ice.

"How have you been? Really?" Allison asks me.

"Okay. *Really*," I tell her. "School has been crazy lately, with the end of the semester coming up soon."

"And everything else?"

"He's taking me out tonight. On a date."

Allison smiles. "Have you told him? How you're feeling?"

"Not yet."

I almost did, last night when we were lying in bed after the banquet. It seems like the way I feel about him must be obvious, the way Conor appeared stunned I thought he might be hooking up with anyone else. My feelings for him are so consuming, it's hard not to get swept up in them.

But I hadn't spoken to him before October. My experience with relationships is minimal, and I'm not sure there's any long-term future possible for us between the complication of the Garrisons and our individual dreams.

I've never asked Conor what his back-up plan is if hockey doesn't work out, because I don't want to imply he needs one. If he plays professionally, he could end up anywhere in the country next year. If he doesn't get signed, I have no idea what he'll do.

When I'm with him, it's easy to think emotionally instead of rationally. Sitting in a cold arena next to the closest thing I have to a mother figure is more confusing.

Allison squeezes my thigh, right as the loudspeaker crackles to life. The announcer runs through the same welcome and emergency evacuation information as before, then the national anthem is played. And then the starting line-ups are announced.

I glance down at Hugh the moment before I know "And your captain and leading scorer...CONOR HART!" will be announced. His expression is awed and proud as he looks around at the packed bleachers of spectators screaming for his son, and I wish I could snap a photo and show it to Conor. Wish he could see past his resentment and anger to acknowledge he has more of a father than he thinks.

The puck drops a minute later, and the clock starts ticking down. Edgewood is aggressive from the start, and Holt matches their intensity. For most of the first period, players keep zipping up and down the ice repeatedly, each team fighting for possession while only managing a few shots on goal.

The second period starts out the same. Then, five minutes in, Edgewood scores. There's a collective groan among the crowd.

Thirty seconds later, Edgewood gets called on a high-sticking penalty. Fresh excitement ripples through the crowd, watching the maroon jersey step into the penalty box and giving Holt a prime opportunity to even the score.

Conor's line gets sent out. Hunter is the one who carries it down toward Edgewood's goalie, passing to Robby Sampson, who then passes it to Conor. They set up a circular formation, their familiarity with each other obvious as the puck ricochets between their sticks, none of Edgewood's defensemen able to stop its trajectory.

Hunter is the one who takes the shot. The net bulges from the velocity, the siren sounds, and the arena erupts as the score gets tied.

I glance down at Hugh, who's beaming. Allison, who is not normally much of a sport spectator, is paying close attention. Even Landon looks intrigued, I notice. He's not even pretending to act disinterested, leaning forward on his elbows like he's trying get as close to the ice as possible.

Hockey's an easy sport to get wrapped up in. The energy humming in the air is electric, punctuated by the rattle of boards and the scrape of blades against ice.

Play resumes again, Edgewood clearly pissed about giving up a goal. They press harder and the game grows more physical. I wince, watching Conor take a hit that I know will be another bruise on his ribs. Conor manages to keep possession of the puck, skating behind the goal and then passing to a waiting Robby. Robby shoots, and the siren sounds again.

I relax a little once Holt is officially winning.

Four minutes later, Edgewood scores. The second period ends, tied 2-2.

I make small talk with Allison during the second intermission, my knee bouncing wildly the entire time.

I wasn't this invested the last game I watched, and I know it wasn't just because that score wasn't this close. It's because I *care more*, about Conor. I want this win for him, more than anything else.

The third period is a battle, both teams desperate to score. Edgewood earns two penalties and Aidan takes one for Holt. No one gets another power play goal.

And then, with just over three minutes left, Edgewood scores, pulling ahead. My hands curl into fists, my fingernails biting into my palm, the flash of each second expiring all I can focus on. Only one hundred and eighty-three of them left.

It's chaos on the ice, lines changing and boards clanging as Edgewood struggles to maintain its lead and Holt fights to protect its undefeated season. Time keeps ticking down. If they can get just one goal, they could win in overtime.

There's a whistle on the ice, then a congregation of jerseys near the center. A blue jersey is waving at the ref with his hand raised, while two other blue jerseys try to pull him back.

I have a bad feeling, even before the player turns and I see the number on the back.

"Holt penalty on number fifteen, Conor Hart. Two minutes for tripping."

Instead of heading into the penalty box, Conor steps off the ice at Holt's bench. He passes the row of his teammates. I watch his coach call out something that has Conor shaking his head, then continuing under the opening beneath the bleachers. He stops, a few steps later, swinging his stick against the cinderblock wall. The wood splinters, falling to the ground in a cracked heap. Conor keeps walking until I can't see him anymore.

"He left the game early?" I hear Landon ask Hugh.

"There's less time left in the game than his penalty," Hugh replies. "He wouldn't have been able to go back out on the ice."

Under other circumstances, I would take Landon's interest in Conor and hockey as a positive sign.

But I'm focused on the slumped shoulders beneath the blue jerseys on the ice. The cracked stick no one has moved yet. The quiet, somber crowd.

Fifty-three seconds later, Holt's winning streak ends.

CHAPTER TWENTY-SIX

CONOR

We lost.

We fucking lost.

I prepared for this possibility, or at least I thought I had.

There are never any guarantees in sports. I know that better than anyone. Ever since we started the season, I've known that losing a game could happen. At first, I thought it was inevitable. But at some point, the longer it didn't happen, the more I felt invincible. The more I thought it could *not* happen.

And I wanted that undefeated season. Wanted it so badly I could taste it.

And it's gone. Just like a professional career probably is.

I drop my head in my hands, staring down at my skates and waiting for the rest of the guys to come into the locker room. The insulation in here is terrible. I heard the final buzzer a few minutes ago. They're probably shaking hands right now.

I should be out there. I won a fucking leadership award last night, and I can't put on a brave face and take one loss without hiding away.

I just...couldn't. Couldn't stare at the red numbers displaying that final, losing score, knowing it would be burned into my brain forever. If I don't get signed, if this season is my last one, I know I'll trace it back to this moment. To the beginning of the end.

Maybe I would have never made it anyway. But I'll never *know*. This will always haunt me as a *what if*. Captain of an undefeated team sounds a hell of a lot better than captain of a team with thirty-four wins and one loss does.

If Edgewood was better, it would have been one thing. If they'd deserved the victory, I could have stomached this loss better.

But they didn't deserve it. We *could've* beaten them. *Should've* beaten them.

And it's my fucking fault.

I didn't prepare this week, the way I should have. I didn't get more than a few hours of sleep last night, because every time I got a glimpse of my cum leaking out of Harlow, I'd get hard all over again. And after she left to go out on Sam's boat this morning, I lay awake, trying to decide what to say to her at dinner tonight.

I was sluggish and distracted, and now I have to face the team of guys who I just let down.

The sound of skates trampling rubber reaches me. I lift my head and square my shoulders.

The team files in slowly.

I got used to celebrating in here. It's been almost a year since we were last in here as *losers*. The two freshmen on the team have never lost a game in their entire college careers. Every dejected face I see makes me feel worse.

Aidan squeezes my shoulder before taking a seat on the bench beside me, and it's worse than anything he could have said. There's no smile. No joke about how I'm too serious.

"That was a shit call," Hunter tells me. "Driscoll played it up."

I nod, acknowledging his attempt to cheer me up. But all I can hear in my head is the echo of what he said when he found out about me and Harlow.

We're all busting our asses, trying to get you your shot. You wanna tell the guys you were too busy getting laid to focus on winning?

That's exactly what I have to tell them. Or imply, at least.

Hockey is a team sport. And as long as I've been playing, I've had coaches tell me, *There's no I in team.*

It's true, and not just literally. Every guy in this locker room contributed to us getting this far in the season without taking a L. But there is an *I* in *winning*. And on every team I've ever played on, I've always been the star.

Football was more popular than hockey in Claremont, and Holt's program hasn't won a championship in forty years. Me scoring goals matters, and my only point tonight was an assist. Not only that, I took a sloppy penalty and left us short-handed when we should have been able to pull Willis and gain a man advantage.

I clear my throat. "My fault today, boys."

Murmurs fill the locker room, of "You played well" and "We'll get them next time" and a "Fucking Edgewood" from Aidan.

They're all trying to make me feel better, and it makes me feel like shit for all the times I wished I was playing at a more competitive school with more talented teammates.

I don't deserve to play with *these* guys, who relied on me to do my part while they did theirs. I wanted to win for them, not just for me. Wanted to be the one who put Holt Hockey on the map. Wanted people to hear the school's name and say *That's where Conor Hart went.* Maybe I'm being dramatic as fuck, but it feels like that all just slipped away.

Coach Keller steps into the locker room last, his clipboard tucked under one arm. He scans the room.

Usually, he comes in here and has to tell us all to settle down. Remind us of an early practice tomorrow and tell us not to get too rowdy celebrating tonight. Say there's a long time until playoffs begin and throw in some adage about a cart not going before the horse. Stay gruff and unsmiling and act like we're a bunch of immature idiots who never won a hockey game before.

Today? You could hear a pin drop on the rubber mats.

We're all totally silent as the door slams shut behind Coach Keller.

"Tough loss. No way to sugarcoat that. We knew Edgewood would be a tough team, and they were. Get showered, get some food, and get some sleep. Tomorrow's a new day, and it's one we'll start with an eight a.m. practice. Wanting has never been enough to earn anything, boys. And losing is a good incentive to work harder. I'm proud of you all. We win as a team, we lose as one too."

Guessing that last sentence is aimed at me.

Coach Keller heads into his office, and the guys start to move and undress. Most of them have already showered by the time I start pulling off my equipment. I'm moving slowly on purpose, wanting the time alone. By the time I leave the showers, the locker room is empty. I get dressed in sweats and am zipping up my bag when the office door opens again.

"It's not over yet, Conor."

I nod, acknowledging the words even though they bounce off me like I'm wearing Kevlar. This was an ending.

Three years of coaching me, and Coach Keller has never used my first name before. He knows I'm beating myself up. Knows whatever criticisms he might make tomorrow are better than what I'm telling myself right now.

"See you tomorrow, Coach."

He nods, his usual serious expression looking less severe.

Aidan and Hunter are waiting for me in the hallway, leaning against the wall. They each drove here separately, and my throat thickens at the silent show of support.

I'm sure they both heard me and Harlow last night, but there are no accusations. No *told you so*'s. Just quiet camaraderie as we head for the lobby. Neither of them says anything at all, which I appreciate. I'm not in the mood to talk. I need to sulk for a while, and then I'll probably come back here after the arena's been fully cleared out. Skate in circles until some of this weight on my chest lifts.

Our next game is Thursday. Almost a week for me to shake this funk and double down. Shoot harder. Skate faster.

"Are those Harlow's folks?" Hunter's question causes me to look up.

Harlow's standing near the rope that's been set up by the trophy case. She's wearing my away jersey, just like she said she would, and my body automatically reacts to the sight.

But then I see who she's standing next to, and everything around me tunnels.

The Garrisons are here. Landon is standing next to Harlow, saying something to her. Allison is talking to a couple of other women in the lobby. Based on their ages and her level of enthusiasm, I'd bet they're people she knows from going to school here herself. If I'd had more options, I would have chosen a school with no connection to the Garrisons at all, but it was better than attending Brighton.

And my father?

Hugh is looking right at me, a sympathetic smile on his face that tells me he saw the game. That my dad watched me play for the first time, and this was the game that he witnessed.

There's a hot creep of shame across my skin. Followed by disgust, that I even give a shit what he thinks. Anger that he came *here*, to *my school*, and is forcing me look at him for the first time in years.

Harlow spots me too. Steps forward, a smile forming on her face.

I keep walking.

CHAPTER TWENTY-SEVEN

HARLOW

It's raining even harder when we leave the restaurant. The Garrisons offered to take me out for a late lunch slash early dinner after the game. Since the alternative was going home and staring at my phone, waiting for Conor to reply to any of my messages, I accepted.

Unease joins the spaghetti in my stomach when I check my phone for the hundredth time and still have no messages from him.

"How's your marathon training going?" Landon asks me as Hugh drives back toward my house to drop me off. "Because that meal definitely set mine back a bit."

I force a smile. "Could be going better."

Conor has been too busy to run with me lately, and I'm not very motivated to train by myself.

"We should do some family runs while you're both back for winter break," Hugh says. "All get in the groove together."

"That sounds very lame," Landon says. "Next you'll be suggesting matching T-shirts."

"Oooh, that could be fun," Allison says.

Landon snorts.

I don't say what I'm thinking, that I'm considering finally accepting my aunts' invitation and returning to Ireland for the first time without my parents. My original plan was this summer, but I don't have any plans for winter break. And I'm hoping to graduate with a job lined up, so my time will be more limited.

I wanted to talk to Conor about it first, because at some point he became that person for me. The one I run everything by, the one whose opinion matters most.

The one who walked away, after telling me he wouldn't.

Hugh pulls up alongside the curb outside my house. I unbuckle my seatbelt. "Don't worry about getting out," I tell them. It's still raining steadily.

"Tell him he played well," Allison says softly.

I glance out the window, spotting the figure she already saw.

Well, at least I know he's not lying in a ditch somewhere. I figured he was ignoring me on purpose.

I swallow. "I will. Thanks for coming."

I climb out of the car, not bothering to pull up my hood as I approach the front door. Eve's car isn't in the driveway, and there's no sign of his either.

Conor glances up, watching me walk toward him. Stands, shoving his hands into his pockets. He's been here for a while, his blue jacket soaked black and his dark hair shedding water.

"I'm sorry about earlier. Walking off." His voice is hoarse. "I was having a shit day, obviously. I wasn't in the mood to talk."

"It's okay. I'm sorry about the game."

Rain has saturated my hair too, starting to slide down my face. Ruining Eve's curls.

"No. It's not okay." He exhales. "I can't do this, Harlow."

"This?"

"Us."

The pavement I'm standing on feels like it's shifting. Like the ground just got pulled out from under me. And all I can think to say is, "Oh."

"I thought I could. I never meant to…We lost today. And it wasn't because Edgewood was the better team. It was because I was distracted—because I've *been* distracted. We kept winning, and so I told myself it didn't matter. But I just let down every guy on the team, let down my coach, let down myself. And I'm not blaming you at all. I made my own choices, and I have to live with them."

The only sound is the patter of raindrops around us.

"You've got to be fucking kidding me."

Conor flinches, and I realize that came from me.

"*Weeks* of sex and snuggling and sharing, last night you took me to the banquet as your date and asked me if I wanted a relationship, and *this* is how you end things? You lose one game and remember all you care about is hockey? That's *bullshit*, Conor."

"I don't just care about hockey. I care about you too, Harlow. That's not the issue here. The problem is, whenever I'm around you, I get sucked in. Nothing was supposed to happen between us at all. Then it was only going to be once. Then once turned into a hundred times! I can't focus on anything else when you're around, and *I need to*."

"You can't play hockey twenty-four seven, Conor. It's not physically possible. No other player on the team is—"

"I'm not another player on the team, Harlow! In the league, in this division! I need to be the *best*. If I want any shot, I have to be the best. I have to work twice as hard, and I need to focus."

"If you'd won today, would we be having this conversation?"

He shakes his head. "I don't know. But we didn't. An undefeated season is gone. One fewer game for this season, maybe forever. I wish it were all different. That I didn't get that concussion and miss the combine and draft. That I wanted it a little less. But I want it, more than anything."

"More than me." I'm not sure if it's a question or a statement. If there's anything I can say to change his mind, or if I even should.

He kicks at a stray pebble, not answering. Although that is an answer, I guess.

Finally, he says, "How were we going to work, Harlow? Were you going to cut them out of your life, or was I supposed to accept they're in yours?"

"I didn't know the Garrisons were coming today," I tell him. "I didn't *ask* them to come. I know how you feel about them, and I've tried to respect that. To keep it separate from us."

"And you think it's a coincidence they showed up right after they found out about us? Hugh's using you to get to me, and I can't deal with that. Can't have him showing up here. At least in Claremont, it's on my own terms. This is my school. My team. *My place*. Three of my teammates asked me who the people you were standing with were."

Eve's car pulls into the driveway. I watch her climb out with a box clutched to her chest. "Got a doughnut cake for you, birthday girl," she calls out.

I want to hug Eve, because after this conversation all I want is to drink vodka and eat doughnuts all night.

And then I want to clap a hand over her mouth, when I see the look on Conor's face.

"Why are you guys out here?" There's a pause, where Eve must notice my expression. "I'll be inside," she says, then rushes into the house.

"It's your birthday?" His voice sounds choked. "Fuck, Harlow. I didn't…that's why the Garrisons were here?"

"You should go, Conor." My tone is sharp, because it hurts. This whole moment…hurts.

"I'm sorry, Hayes."

I want to snap at him not to call me that, but I'm striving for indifference at this point. Struggling to stay upright.

"We're done, okay? You got your priorities straightened out. Don't text me. Don't talk to me. And don't expect me to wait for you."

Conor nods once, his expression not even shifting. No reaction at all. Just apathy staring back at me, like he didn't hold me after every time we had sex last night. Like we're back to being strangers. "Happy Birthday, Harlow."

Then he turns and starts walking away, down the sidewalk headed toward his street a few blocks over.

I stay standing, inhaling the perfume of fresh rain. Watching the water fall around me and feeling the salty streams roll down my cheeks.

I told myself I'd never, ever fall in love with Conor Hart.

Famous last words.

CHAPTER TWENTY-EIGHT

HARLOW

I hit submit on my final assignment, and I'm *done*. Winter break starts tomorrow. When I come back to campus, it will be for my final semester of college.

"Yay! She's *finally* done!" Eve cheers.

She insisted on coming to the library with me, just like she's hovered ever since she watched me cry over the guy I always thought I'd be indifferent toward.

"So crazy we're almost finished with college, huh?" Mary says.

I nod, not sure how I feel about it. Part of me is dreading graduation, leaving Eve and Somerville and everything that's become familiar. The rest of me wishes it was tomorrow.

I haven't seen Conor since my birthday, but he's *everywhere*. The sweatshirt he left in my room. The way my bed still smells like pine and salt. The excited conversation two guys in my aquatic resources class had about how the hockey team won their game last night and how amazing Hart was.

Partly, I'm glad. Happy for him.

Mostly, I'm bitter. I wish he'd played the worst hockey game of his life. Not only because he was missing me, but as proof I wasn't the problem. That he could be *focused* and lose.

But no. According to the guys in my class, Conor scored his first hat trick of the season. Three goals in one game. For the first time since freshman year, I didn't read the game recap. I'm in the market for a new sport to follow.

"Ready to celebrate at Gaffney's?" Eve asks.

I nod, hiding how apprehensive I am about it. I'm sure it's where most people will end up tonight. Finals are over and winter break officially starts tomorrow. It's the last chance to party and celebrate.

I haven't gone out once since Conor ended things. Not just to avoid seeing him, but because I haven't been in the mood. I used studying for finals as an excuse, one I no longer have.

Mary asks me about my upcoming trip to Ireland as Eve drives to Gaffney's from the library parking lot. I booked my plane ticket a week ago.

Somerville isn't the only place that has memories of Conor. I'll stay in Claremont for Christmas, celebrate the holiday with the Garrisons, and then I'm eager to get away. To do something just for me, to push myself outside of my comfort zone.

Gaffney's is packed, just like I expected it to be. But there's no sign of Conor or any hockey players, which is a small relief. Maybe they have practice. Maybe he already left for break.

We manage to grab one of the hightop tables. A few of Eve and Mary's other friends approach, and I spend a few minutes talking to Eric about our aquatic resources final. I'm relieved Eric doesn't seem to have held our failed date against me.

A waitress comes to take our drink order. I ask for a hard seltzer, since Eve is driving. She promised me she was happy not drinking tonight. Even if she wanted to, we could walk home from here.

Our drinks get delivered right as the hockey team arrives. Fifteen guys, at least, and Conor is one of them. He's talking with Aidan, running a hand through his hair and ignoring all the heads turned his way. Including mine.

I'm staring, and I don't want to be. I don't want him noticing he has my attention. I want to be *fine*, the way he looks. No dark circles, no ratty sweats. He's smiling now, punching Aidan's arm in response to whatever he just said.

All the sound around me gets muffled, like I'm suddenly underwater.

It takes Eve tapping my arm to get me to look away.

"Are you okay? You looked…" Her voice trails, and I know she's seen what I was paying attention to.

They take one of the long tables near the bar, which remained empty even in the crowded space, like people were waiting for them to arrive. They might have lost one game, but they're still the most dominant sports team on campus—by far. Even students who don't follow hockey know exactly who they are.

The blonde waitress is over there now, right by Conor. I look away quickly. Right at Eve. Instead of sympathetic, she has her scheming face on.

I take a long drink and finally answer her question. "I'm fine."

She leans forward. "Two can play that game, you know."

"What game?"

"She's drooling on him, and he's letting her."

"He can do whatever he wants."

"So can you," Eve tells me.

"You want me to flirt with a guy?"

"Or more than flirt with him."

"Hook up with someone else? I don't think I can do that." The thought of having sex with a guy who isn't Conor makes me feel nauseous.

"Don't *actually* hook up with him. Just sell it. Show that dick what he's missing."

I edited out the Garrisons when I told Eve about Conor breaking up with me, and I'm worried she landed a little too firmly on Team Harlow as a result. In her mind, Conor dumped me for hockey because he changed his mind about a relationship. And now he's here getting *drooled over* like he never gave a shit at all.

I pretend to stretch and discover Eve's right. The blonde could be sitting in Conor's lap, she's so close to him, and he's talking to her.

"With who?" I scan the bar.

"Clayton Thomas is here."

I glance at Mary, who's talking to a friend a few seats down the table. "What about Mary?"

"Oh, she's over him. She's been out on a few dates with David, actually. They seemed to really hit it off."

I nod, glancing over at where Clayton is standing with a few teammates. Eve's right; he's my best option. *If* I do this, which I haven't decided I will, he'll draw the most attention. Affect Conor the most.

He ended things, I remind myself. *He chose to walk away.*

Clayton straightens from his spot at the bar, then heads toward the doorway that leads to the bathrooms. This is my window, if I want it.

I slide off the stool and hurry after him, catching him in the hallway right before he heads into the men's room.

"Clayton."

He pauses, then glances back at me. "Hey, Harlow. How are you?"

I glance over one shoulder, making sure no one else has walked in here. Still empty.

"What did you say to Conor about me?" I ask.

Clayton grimaces. "For context, I was drunk. And I know it was dumb and disrespectful, and I'm sorry."

If he's trying to make me *less* curious about what was said, he isn't succeeding.

"Okay…"

"I bet a few guys I'd get you in bed by graduation."

His expression is tentative as he watches me carefully. The bet is news to me, but the rest is about what I expected.

I step closer, lowering my voice. "Want to make it up to me?"

One eyebrow lifts. "Uh, sure?"

"Win the bet."

Clayton looks shocked. "What?"

"I'm not actually going to have sex with you. But I want you to come over to my table and flirt with me and ask me to leave with you. And then I want you to walk me home. Tell the guys that you won the bet and to pay up, then donate the money to charity or something."

He studies me. "What are the odds Hart hits me over this?"

I'm not surprised he made the leap so quickly. Conor kissed me at the banquet in front of everyone, then walked past me without a word just now.

"Zero," I tell him.

"You sure about that?"

"Certain."

"Can I kiss you?"

I want this to look believable. And this is probably not the healthiest way to get over a guy, but I need for Conor to think I moved on.

He distracts me too. I never expected—wanted—to fall for him, and it happened anyway. I'm trying to protect myself, to

314

make sure I won't do something desperate like show up at his house and tell him I love him.

"Once. No tongue."

Clayton grins. "You've got a deal."

"Great." I duck into the bathroom, pee, wash my hands, and then head back toward my table.

The whole hockey team is still here, which is a relief. The plan with Clayton would be way less effective if they weren't. Although it seems like most of the senior class is present, so there's a good chance he'd hear about it anyway.

"How did it go?" Eve whispers when I sit back down on my stool.

I flash her a subtle thumbs up.

She leans forward. "Forget your phone on the table when you leave with him. I'll call you back over loudly, make sure everyone is looking."

My best friend is a mastermind.

I nod, watching Clayton walk over this way. He stops at the end of the table, flashing a dimpled grin around.

"Evening, ladies."

I smile back at him, resisting the urge to glance at Conor. There's no ideal reaction. Either he's paying attention to the blonde, not even realizing I'm here. Or he's looking this way and will notice me paying attention to him.

Clayton leans closer to me. "You wanna get out of here?"

"Wow. You don't put much effort into picking up girls, huh?"

I keep my voice low, so no one except possibly Eve could hear.

He chuckles. "Oh, I've got game, Harlow. Lemme pull a stool up."

I have absolutely no game when this girl is involved.

I push all thoughts—and memories—of Conor far away. I

need to get out of here. Winter break is over a month long. Hopefully my heart will be healed by then, and returning to campus in January won't hurt this much.

I stand, grabbing my coat from the hook off the table and pulling it on. "No, let's go."

I wave goodbye to the other girls at the table. Eve winks at me. And then Clayton is grabbing my hand and pulling me close. I'd forgotten about this part. The scientist in me sees it as an experiment. I haven't kissed anyone except Conor in months.

Clayton's warm lips brush against mine. No tongue, like I asked. It's a soft, gentle press that lasts fifteen seconds. I know, because I count them. Because there's no thrill, no pulse between my thighs. No reaction and nothing to do, except count.

Conor Hart ruined the number fifteen for me too.

Clayton grins at me. "That was worth getting decked for," he murmurs to me. Then pulls me toward the door.

"Harlow, wait!" I turn back at Eve's call. She's waving my phone around in the air, but she doesn't bring it to me. I actually forgot to grab it, not just pretended to.

Clayton and I walk back over. I take my phone from Eve, ignoring the eyes I can feel on us. Avoiding looking toward the bar, toward that long table.

Once we're outside, I exhale. It's cold out but not raining.

Clayton talks the whole walk back to my house. He has a shortened break because of basketball, but he and some friends are going to Mexico. I nod along as he talks about the resort they're headed to, glad he's not asking me questions or flirting with me.

When we reach my house, he offers a wry smile. "I'm guessing that was a one-time kiss?"

I nod.

"I am sorry, Harlow. It was a dumb bet."

"Donate the money, Clayton. I mean it."

He laughs. "Yeah. I will. Promise."

"Have a good break."

I start up the walk, not expecting him to call my name.

"Yeah?" I turn back around.

"Hart has never suddenly hated me over any other girl. Just sayin'."

Clayton turns and heads back the way we came before I can respond. Which is good, because I have no clue how to.

The chill starts to creep under my coat, so I continue walking toward the house. I still have some packing to do before leaving tomorrow. I have a final fishing trip with Sam, and then I'm planning to head to Claremont right after.

I check the mailbox out of habit, since we rarely get anything. But there's an envelope addressed to me sitting inside. I stare at the return address, my stomach twisting into knots.

I forgot I ordered these. And it's a sick joke, them showing up tonight when I did my best to make him hate me.

I open the envelope and look at the two tickets, my heart crumbling in my chest. I slip them back into the envelope and then head inside. When I check my phone there's a new message, sent ten minutes ago.

EVE: He definitely saw.

"Have a great break, Harlow. And an amazing time in Ireland."

I smile at Sam, waving goodbye to the rest of the crew.

"And wish that hockey player of yours good luck."

The smile gets harder to keep on my face, but I manage. "I will."

I leave Sam's boat's slip and head toward the gangway, the envelope in my pocket feeling like it weighs fifteen pounds.

I bought the two tickets for a professional hockey game in Seattle a few weeks ago. They were supposed to be Conor's Christmas present, and now I don't know what the hell to do with them. I'm tempted to burn them. I'll be in Ireland when the game takes place, so I can't go with someone else. And I don't want to. It would be a form of torture, sitting there and thinking about him the entire time.

Not using them is a waste of money. But I don't even care about that.

I want Conor to go to a pro game, even if it's not with me. Or have the chance to, if he wants.

I drive to his house on autopilot, the steering wheel slick from my sweaty palms. Park along the curb and release a deep breath when I see his SUV in the driveway. A large part of me hoped I could hand these off to Aidan or Hunter.

My steps are rushed up the front walk. Now that I'm here, I'd love to get this over with as fast as possible. I hit the doorbell, watching my breath hover in the morning air.

Aidan opens the door.

"Hi." I shift awkwardly, keeping my cold hands in the pockets of my parka. "Is, uh, Conor here?"

He nods, and I curse in my head.

My stupid pride won't let me slink off. I don't want Conor to think I'm embarrassed to face him, especially after what happened last night. I'm sure Aidan isn't going to tell him he found the tickets in the mailbox or something. Conor will know I dumped these and ran.

"Can I come in?" I ask.

Aidan's typical grin is totally absent.

I'm not sure how much Conor has shared with his friends

about us. They saw us together at the banquet, our first and final appearance as a couple. Since then, we've reverted to our former behavior of acting like we have restraining orders out on each other. They all saw him avoid me at Gaffney's last night. Saw me leave with Clayton.

In answer, Aidan opens the door wider.

I walk into the front hall, glancing at the pile of bags by the bottom of the stairs. I have no idea what Conor is doing for winter break. If he's going anywhere. The hockey team has a much shorter break than the rest of the student body, but they still have a week off.

"HART!" Aidan shouts.

A few seconds later, there's a muffled "What?" from upstairs.

I rub a finger along the edge of the envelope in my pocket, deliberating if I should just screw my pride, hand it to Aidan, and leave.

He ended it, I remind myself for the thousandth time.

If it were up to me, I would have given him these under very different circumstances.

"Harlow is here!"

I exhale, both relieved and concerned that my escape door just closed. Now that Conor knows I'm here, I really can't leave.

Hunter leaves the kitchen a minute later, holding a plate with a sandwich on it and eyeing me curiously. "Hey, Harlow."

"Hi."

An awkward pause follows. "You guys doing anything fun for break?" I ask.

The guys exchange looks, like they're not sure if they should be talking to me, which is in no way reassuring.

Hunter replies first. "Just headed home to see family."

"My folks have a place in Vail," Aidan tells me. "Headed

there to carve up some powder." He hesitates, then adds, "Hart is coming too."

"Oh," is all I can think to say.

Pounding steps announce Conor's arrival.

"Have a good break," Aidan says, then walks quickly into the kitchen. Hunter heads upstairs with his sandwich.

My heart's trying to climb out of my chest, it's beating so fast.

Seeing him here is way worse than it was at Gaffney's. We're alone, instead of in a crowded bar with lots of other people. We're in his house, standing somewhere he's stripped me because we were too impatient to get upstairs. And he's shirtless, wearing only a pair of gray sweatpants that show off all my favorite parts of his body.

Suddenly, I'm sweltering.

Conor's expression is completely smooth as he stops a couple of feet away. Purposefully blank.

"Hey, Hart." I'm the one who showed up here, so it seems fair I talk first.

"Something wrong?" No pleasantry, cutting right to the chase. It's what I expected. What I *asked* for. And still, it burns.

"I'm not pregnant, or anything like that."

There's a twitch in his expression, and that's the only reaction. God, do I wish I could shove those words back in my mouth.

I'm nervous. I'm so, *so* nervous, knowing what he must think of me after last night. Knowing we're over, and this might be the last time we ever talk. Knowing I love him, and he doesn't love me back.

I clear my throat. "Sorry. Bad joke. I just stopped by to give you these."

I pull the envelope out of my pocket and hold it out to him.

Conor studies the address, then glances at me. "Am I supposed to open it?"

"Um…Yeah, sure." I shove my hands back into my pockets, twisting my fingers together nervously behind the barrier of the fabric as he opens the envelope. "I checked your schedule, and you guys don't have a game that night. So hopefully you can go with…someone else. And if you can't, or you don't want them, you can just sell them or give them away or whatever…whatever you want."

Conor is staring at the two tickets, his expression still unreadable stone. Then, he holds them out to me. "You use them."

"I, uh, can't. I'm going to Ireland for a couple of weeks. I won't be here. And…I got them for you. So, Merry Christmas, I guess."

I turn toward the door, intent on getting out of here as quickly as possible.

"Wait."

My spin back is slow.

"Stay here. I'll be right back."

I chew on the inside of my cheek, watching Conor jog back upstairs holding the envelope. A minute later he's back, minus the envelope, holding a paper grocery bag.

"Here." He holds the bag out to me. The knuckles on his right hand are red, one of them split.

"What is it?"

"Your Christmas present. Presents, actually."

The fist around my heart squeezes tighter. "You didn't have to do that."

"I know." He holds my gaze, like maybe he's silently recalling the last time I said that to him as well.

"Should I, um, open them?"

Conor shrugs. "I didn't wrap anything."

I pull a shirt out first, the green material soft against my fingers.

"It's the band we—"

"Yeah, I remember."

It's a shirt for the band we saw together, the one I wanted to get merch from but didn't have any cash on me.

"How'd you get this?" I ask.

"They have a website."

He took the time to look it up and order me this, and I'm dangerously close to crying. Because I'm so *mad* at him, for being this perfect and this wrong. For making me love him and then not letting me.

The box in the bag is a pair of ice skates. They're my exact size, and I know they're for the lessons he promised me.

"Guess I'll have to make do with an orange cone after all." The thought in my head slips out.

Conor's jaw clenches, like the memory of us in his dad's driveway is as uncomfortable for him as it is for me.

It's funny, how you appreciate the good times with someone so much more once you're on bad terms with them. Rather than forget them altogether, like you want to, your brain taunts you with what you should have appreciated more at the time.

"Thank you," I tell him.

"Have fun in Ireland."

"I heard you're going skiing."

"Oh. Uh, yeah." He rubs the back of his neck, glancing toward the kitchen. I'm worried I got Aidan in trouble.

"Okay. Well, bye."

I turn toward the door again. This time, Conor says nothing to stop me. He watches me fumble with the knob, then hurry out of his house. I rush toward my car, holding my bag of gifts, trying to figure out how that brief encounter was both so meaningful and so empty.

CHAPTER TWENTY-NINE

CONOR

Aidan's satisfied sigh as he leans back against the side of the hot tub is irritating. So is the owl hooting nearby. And the twinge in my hamstring from falling funny on the mountain earlier.

Lately, everything annoys me.

"This is the life." Aidan groans before chugging some beer.

Again, irritating.

"So I was thinking we could head down to the lodge tonight, grab a pint," Aidan says. "I've seen tons of hot snow bunnies around..."

"I was thinking an early night."

Aidan mutters something under his breath that sounds a lot like *what a surprise.*

"If I knew you'd be this much of a wet blanket, I would have thrown you in the dryer before we left Somerville, Hart."

I say nothing, just swish my fingers through the hot water.

Stare at the smooth surface. Ridiculously, it reminds me of *her*. Harlow Hayes ruined *water* for me.

"Do you think Coach would be up for installing one of these

in the locker room?" Aidan asks. "Can you imagine? Stepping off the ice into a hot tub with a cold beer?"

"I think that this hot tub probably cost Coach's annual salary, Phillips."

His family's ski house, chalet, whatever it's called, is even nicer than I was expecting. Nestled in the mountains, private access to their own ski lift, comes with membership at an exclusive lodge in town? Aidan is loaded, not just rich.

"Did you call her?"

I grab my bottle of beer and take a long swig. Aidan's right, about the combination being incredible. The jets are massaging my back with hot water, and the beer is ice cold against my palm. I'm in Colorado with my best friend, snowboarding all day and then coming back to what is the nicest house I've ever been to.

And Aidan's right, I've been a total wet blanket. I'm like Coach, not cracking so much as a smile.

"Text her?"

He's not dropping the subject, the way I hoped. Aidan and Hunter have tiptoed around the topic, which is not like either of them, ever since Aidan asked why Harlow hadn't been over and I responded with a curt "I ended it."

"I'm worried about you, Hart."

I sip more beer. "I'm fine."

I'm not, though. I keep waiting for this feeling to go away, and it hasn't. Each morning, I wake up expecting for it to hurt a little less. Hasn't happened, and it's been *weeks*.

We've won every single game we've played since losing to Edgewood. Hockey, the one thing that's always, unequivocally, mattered, is going as well as it possibly could again.

And I'm miserable.

I'm terrified I fucked up, worse than I ever have before.

I think I'm *in love* with her.

The real, scary thing.

Not lust or fascination or obsession or any diluted form of it.

I think I truly *love* her, to the point that I hate what my life looks like without her in it.

To the point that, if I miraculously make it to the pros, I'll look up in the stands at the tens of thousands of people packed in to see me play, and it won't matter very much if hers isn't one of the faces in the crowd.

To the point that I'm worried I'll spend the rest of my life wondering where she is and what she's doing and who she's doing it with, the same way I've spent these past weeks.

"Bullshit."

I refocus on Aidan. This whole time I've been spiraling, he's been staring at me.

"I'll get over it," I mutter, then drink more beer.

I thought the self-loathing after losing a game was bad. Turns out it's nothing in comparison to letting the girl you love slip through your fingers.

She was *right there*, asking if I cared about hockey more than her. And I walked away.

"Then bring a girl back here tonight."

I wince.

I haven't touched a girl since Harlow. Just like when we were sleeping together, I have absolutely no desire to. Aidan has brought back three girls in the three nights we've been here, and I lay in bed on the other side of the wall—alone and awake with a pillow pressed against each ear.

Aidan has the gall to remind me, "She hooked up with Thomas."

Something I'm furious about. Something he *knows* I'm furious about. He and Hunter have both seen the cracked plaster.

And I have no right to be mad.

She warned me she'd move on, and that's exactly what she did.

I couldn't react—couldn't punch Thomas, instead of my bedroom wall—because I never told her how much I cared. Because I was the one who ended things and let Clayton swoop in.

I ran into her on two dates last semester, and it bothered me both times. Now, I don't even know how I would react. Don't know if I could keep *from* reacting.

Seeing her talk to another guy? Laugh with another guy? Touch another guy?

I might commit murder, trapped in a hell of my own making.

Aidan sighs, long and exasperated.

And then we continue sitting in silence, drinking our beers.

CHAPTER THIRTY

HARLOW

My phone rings, interrupting the music that's playing through my headphones. It's the band I saw play with Conor, which I'm listening to while wearing the shirt that he gave me.

Most masochists have nothing on me.

I pull my phone out of my jacket pocket, my steps slowing when I see Landon's name. I'm almost to the stone cathedral that's my destination anyway. My finger taps the green button as I stop jogging altogether.

"Hey, Landon." I force as much cheer into my voice as I can, but it sounds flat even to my own ears.

"Happy New Year!"

"Yeah, thanks. You too." Even flatter.

"How's it going over there?"

"It's great." I glance around at the green grass and the gravel path. At the huge church that looks like it was plucked out of medieval times up ahead. "I'll send some more photos soon."

I texted the Garrisons when I landed in Dublin, but we've barely spoken since. I know they're worried about me. Caught the concerned looks when they saw the circles under my eyes and noticed I was wearing nothing but sweatpants.

I'm sad and depressed.

Being in Ireland has helped a little. I've seen family I haven't in years, gone to museums and markets and done lots of running. My aunts arranged for us to take a day trip to the Cliffs of Moher, which is one of the most stunning sights I've ever witnessed.

But no matter what I do, where I go, there's still this gaping hole in my chest.

I'm running out of time away. In two days, I'll be back in Washington. In a few weeks, I'll be back on campus. And whoever said time heals wounds was wrong, because my heart is still broken. It's looking more and more likely I'll have to face Conor while still being very much in love with him.

"We booked another gig," Landon tells me. "Not until early March, but still something."

"That's great, Landon. Congrats."

"Yeah, thanks."

"I've been doing a lot of running here," I tell him. "Out on a run right now, actually. We should go together, once I'm back."

"Sounds good."

There's a long pause, where it seems like Landon is searching for something to say and I can't come up with anything to contribute. Lately, I've been at a loss. Like a void, absorbing but not giving.

"Well, I should—"

"I went to Zeke Ledger's New Year's Eve party."

I'm silent.

"You were right about the bathroom, by the way. Weird space."

Still, I say nothing.

"He looked like shit. Left alone, before midnight."

My inhale is sharp and surprised. Not only by the update, but that he's bothering to tell me.

"See you when you get back, Harlow."

"Bye, Landon."

I hang up, shove my phone in my pocket, and then decide I can make it farther than the cathedral.

CHAPTER THIRTY-ONE

CONOR

The puck leaves the ref's hand, and my stick is already motion. Northpoint's center is slower than me, swiping across the ice a split second too late. I'm already charging toward their zone, the roar of the crowd fading as I focus on nothing except the red pipes in front of me and the goalie between me and the netting. Between me and him, there's nothing but a stretch of smooth white.

I fly across the blue line after the puck, debating on whether I circle and pass or try to capitalize on this breakaway. We're up by two goals with five minutes left in the third period, which is a pretty comfortable lead.

Three goals sound better.

I shoot, the satisfying sound of the siren blaring through the arena as soon as the puck finds the back of the net.

"Hell yeah, Hart!" Hunter pounds the top of my helmet, his voice jubilant and excited.

The fans packing the bleachers are excited. My teammates are excited. I even catch a glimmer of a smile beneath Coach's bushy mustache as I skate along the bench, tapping gloves to celebrate my goal.

I think the one person in this rink—aside from those affiliated with Northpoint—who's *not* excited is…me.

Sure, I see the excitement. Hear it. Understand it.

But I don't *feel* it.

It's like checking a task you have to complete off a list.

Score goal, *check*.

Four minutes and fifty-four seconds later; win game, *check*.

I shake hands with Northpoint on autopilot. Walk into the locker room on autopilot. Listen to Coach's gruff congratulations on autopilot. Shower and change on autopilot.

Aidan and Hunter are bickering about where to get dinner as we walk down the hallway and into the lobby. I don't care what kind of food we get, so I stay silent.

I'm trying to revel in how it's January and we've only lost one game this entire season. That doesn't sound as impressive as undefeated, but it's a whole lot better of a record than anyone expected us to still have. And it means I might actually get that championship.

The last item on my list.

Win championship, *no check yet*.

"You gonna chime in, Hart, or keep up with the zombie impression?"

"I…" My voice trails as soon as I spot him.

The lobby is close to cleared out by now. The game ended at least thirty minutes ago, so the only people remaining are purposefully staying behind.

Hugh Garrison is standing in almost the exact same spot as the last time he was here, right by the spot on the wall where my plaque for the Caddell-Spade Award hangs.

His expression shifts to apprehensive as soon as he recognizes I've spotted him, possibly waiting for me to walk away again.

"One sec," I mutter to Aidan and Hunter. We drove here together, so they have no choice but to stick around, or else walk.

My father's face is chaotic with emotion as I approach. He's never chosen to hide any of his feelings around me. Back when I had a schedule of going over to his house, anytime I made an excuse not to he would tell me, "Conor, I'm disappointed." But he would look it too, have that disappointment written across his face. It would make me feel guilty. And then I'd be angry about feeling guilty. His obvious emotions encouraged me to hide my own, to shut down rather than react. Something I still do.

But, for the first time, I don't resent Hugh's openness. I can read the pride and excitement in his expression, and it's a relief, almost, that the Edgewood game wasn't the only time my father saw me play hockey.

"Hi, Conor."

"Hey." My grip tightens on the strap of the bag that's slung across my shoulder, but I don't otherwise react.

"That was an incredible game. You're…" He shakes his head. "You're one hell of a hockey player."

There was a time when I would have snapped *And you had nothing to do with it* in response. But I'm tired of lashing out. Tired of being angry and bitter.

"Is Harlow okay?" I blurt, instead of a more appropriate response, like *thanks*.

He's a link to *her*. If Harlow was in a plane crash, they would call the Garrisons, not me. I'm desperate for any connection—for any information—at this point. I don't even care that Hugh's the source.

"She's fine."

I exhale, relieved. I've written dozens of texts to her, then deleted them without sending.

There's so much I want to tell her.

Random shit, like how I watched an orca documentary the other night because I was thinking about her. How I gave Aidan and Hunter the tickets she got me for Christmas because I couldn't stomach going knowing it was something she'd planned for us together. How I drove down to the Sound on Saturday morning to watch Sam's boat head out without her, too much of a coward to go say hi to the guy because he told me to take care of her and I didn't.

Important shit, like how I love her.

I have no clue how to say any of it.

"Fine might not be the right word, actually," Hugh continues. He's studying me closely, and I shift under his scrutiny. "She's clearly...down about something."

I break eye contact. For the first time, I feel ashamed, standing in front of my father. I've been uncertain and uncomfortable, but never ashamed. That was always his role in my mind.

"I'm impressed—proud—Conor. Everything you've accomplished with hockey, with so many things."

"Thanks."

Hugh nods. "I knew it would impact your life, Conor—the poor decisions I made. Knew you'd have hard questions, that they'd maybe lead to some uncomfortable conversations. Worried how to ensure you and Landon both felt like you were priorities to me. But I never...I never thought *this* is where we'd end up. Not talking for years. All I know about you is that you're a terrific hockey player. And that you light up the woman I love like a daughter in a way I've never witnessed. I glanced out my living room window and saw Harlow playing basketball in the driveway, looking happier than I'd seen her in years. Maybe ever. I've known that girl her entire life. Allison threw her mother's baby shower. She's sweet and polite and considerate. And do you want to know what she told me, when I asked what you were like?"

I stay silent. Because, yeah, I want to know.

"She told me 'You missed out.' And she was right. I know she was right. I'll tell you I'm sorry a thousand times, Conor. Sorry about what happened with your mother, sorry how it resulted in us not having a relationship. I never thought my mistakes would affect your life this way, would impact the relationships you have with other people. I don't know what happened between you and Harlow. She wouldn't talk about it. But if it had anything to do with her living with us, I feel like I owe you another apology for that."

"I fucked it up on my own," I tell him.

Nothing in Hugh's expression lightens.

"The worst thing you can experience as a parent is seeing your child repeat your mistakes. Realize they'll carry your regrets. And Conor, if there's one thing I say to you that you take the time to listen to—other than that I love you—it's to fix things before it's too late. Before something happens that you can't take back. Make different choices than me, Conor. I pushed the woman I loved away. Tried to forget her by meeting someone else. I was lucky that woman was Allison. That we grew to love each other. But there will always be a part of me living an alternate life. That wonders if your mom still plays Christmas carols at Thanksgiving and wishes that I'd been the one to buy you your first pair of skates."

I swallow, trying to clear the lump in my throat.

He holds out a piece of paper.

"Here's Harlow's flight information for tomorrow. If you decide not to pick her up, my number is at the bottom. And if there's ever anything else you need, I'll always answer."

He turns to leave.

"I'm not sure if I'll ever get over it. What happened with you and Mom. What happened with you and me."

Hugh looks back. "You'll always be my son, Conor. Whether or not you let me be your father is your choice. And I realized I stopped asking you to make it. So I'll be here, every home game for the rest of your season. Whether you want to talk when I'm here? Your choice. I can be another face in the crowd, cheering you on. Cheering for my son."

He stares at me, and I stare back.

"Okay."

"Okay," he repeats, then walks out of the lobby.

I stand, watching the door swing shut behind him. Then head back toward where Aidan and Hunter are waiting by the side exit that leads straight into the parking lot.

"Was that Harlow's dad?" Hunter asks.

I never answered his question, last time. I just stormed off.

"No. That was mine."

CHAPTER THIRTY-TWO

HARLOW

The wheels hit the tarmac with a jolt that bounces the entire plane. I exhale, loosening my grip on the armrest.

I'm home, I guess.

I don't know quite what home is anymore. If it's Ireland or Somerville or the town where I grew up. They're all some different version of it, none exactly right.

The plane parks at the gate, and everyone starts standing and moving around like they'll be able to disembark anytime soon. I look out the oval window, down at the orange vests waving lights and the luggage carts driving around. It's dark out, but the bustling airport casts so much light it's hard to tell.

I pull my phone out of my pocket and text Hugh and Allison.

> HARLOW: Landed! Not even off the plane yet though.

> ALLISON GARRISON: See you soon!

No response from Hugh, which isn't all that surprising. He's not a big texter.

Fifteen minutes later, they open the door and passengers start exiting.

The man seated beside me, wearing a tweed jacket that smells like tobacco, helpfully grabs my carry-on out of the overhead compartment when he gets his own. I thank him and then head down the aisle, my steps uneven as my cramped muscles readjust to movement. I pass the flight crew and then head up the enclosed walkway that leads into the main section of the airport, breathing in non-recycled air for the first time in ten plus hours.

I had an amazing trip to Ireland, but it will be a long time before I can talk myself into taking that long of a flight again.

I stop at the first restroom I see so I can use a bathroom bigger than a postage stamp, then continue on to Customs. There's a long line to wait in, then a series of questions about why I'm a Canadian coming from Ireland planning to remain in the US for the next six months.

Once I'm past Customs I head to baggage claim, down a long corridor with several security guards lining it. I leave the secure section of the airport, stopping to buy a bottle of water at one of the convenience stores. I'm tempted to get a coffee as well, but I should go to sleep as soon as I get to the Garrisons'.

It takes fifteen minutes to find the right, empty carousel assigned to my flight. I text Allison and Hugh another update on my progress through the airport, then cover a yawn. It's just past six p.m. here, and my tired brain can't even do the math for what time that is in Ireland. I don't even know what day it is.

The carousel shudders into movement, bags dropping onto the sheets of silver metal. The tired passengers around me perk up as we all scan the suitcases. Mine is black and generic, and I wish I'd remembered to tie a ribbon to the handle as lots of black, generic suitcases shuffle by.

Finally, I spot the familiar pink whale tag. Step forward and reach for it, only for another hand to get there first.

"I got it."

I'm frozen, all of a sudden. Because I recognize that arm, the body attached to it. That voice, right next to me.

Conor's amused by my surprise. He studies me gaping at him, carefully setting my suitcase down between us.

"What are you doing here?" I choke out.

I can't believe he's *right here*. It seems like I should pinch myself or poke him or do something to confirm this isn't my brain losing it after a long day of travel and little sleep.

"Hadn't been to Seattle in a while. Decided to take a quick trip."

"There are nicer places to visit than the *airport*."

"You weren't at any of those places, though." He's holding a colorful bouquet of flowers, which I don't realize until he's offering them to me. "These are for you. I tried to get shamrocks. Weirdly, they didn't have any."

I snort. "Thanks."

"See any leprechauns?"

I shake my head. "Conor…the Garrisons will be here any minute to pick me up and—"

"They're not coming."

"What do you mean, they're not coming?" I dig my phone out of my pocket. "They were supposed to—"

"Come here, Harlow."

Conor grabs my hand and pulls me toward the wall covered with safety posters, away from the crowd clustered around the carousel. Thanks to a mixture of shock and exhaustion, I let him.

"They're not coming because I told them I was picking you up."

I stare at him. "You *talked* to—"

"That's not important." For a third time, he cuts me off. "Just let me say this, and then we can go. We don't have to talk on the way home, if you don't want to. I'll just drop you off at their place and that will be…that."

"What will be that?" I'm not sure if he's making no sense because my head is foggy or because he's making no sense. I never considered he'd be the one waiting for me at the airport, and I haven't fully processed it yet.

Conor sucks in a deep breath. "You asked me if I'd play hockey, if Hugh had. Remember?"

My nod is slow.

"Do you remember what my answer was?"

"That you'd have to decide if you love hockey more than you hate him."

"Yeah. And I decided I do."

"Okay…" I'm not sure what else to say. Not sure what it has to do with him being here. I already know he loves hockey.

Conor smiles, noticing my confusion. "Ask me if I love something—someone—more than I love hockey."

I stare at him.

He rolls his eyes. "Follow through, Hayes."

God, I missed hearing him call me that. Missed everything about him, actually. And I don't know what Landon was talking about, because Conor does not look like shit. He looks gorgeous, and there's a flare of lust low in my stomach as I *really* look at him for the first time.

"Do you love something more than you love hockey?" I ask.

"Someone. I love *you*, Harlow."

The ground is shifting again, no longer solid. "No, you don't."

Conor nods his head, like he was waiting for that response. "Do you know what I've done, since we broke up? Moped around. Ask Aidan and Hunter, they'll happily bitch about what a moody asshole I've been. We keep winning games, and it's like white noise around me. When we were in Colorado, Aidan brought back a different girl every night. I didn't touch anyone. All I've done is sit around and think about how badly I fucked it up with you. How much I wish I could go back and ask you on a date the first time I saw you, freshman year, instead of pretending you didn't exist."

"We didn't *break up*, Conor. That implies there was something to break."

"There was. There *is*. For me, at least."

"What about next week, if you lose against Driscoll?"

"You memorized my hockey schedule?"

"Not the point, Conor!" Although, yeah, I didn't mean to tell him that. So far, I've been unsuccessful at finding another sport to follow.

He blows out a long breath. "I freaked out, okay? Things were getting really serious between us—which I was good with. Which I wanted. But it happened right at the same time that hockey stopped going well. I knew you were distracting me. Knew how much I thought about you, how easy it was to get wrapped up in us. But as long as I was winning…it felt like having it all. Then we lost."

"And you still had me, but it felt like nothing."

"*No*. That's not what I'm saying at all. I just—a lot of shit was coming at me at once. The Garrisons were there, and the guys were all disappointed in me, and whenever that's happened— whenever I've been stressed and overwhelmed and upset, about anything—I've focused on hockey. I've pushed away everything else, because it's simple when I'm on the ice. Because it's my happy place."

He glances down, shoving his hands into his pockets.

"I panicked, and I should have told you I needed time. We

were supposed to go out that night, and I wasn't in the right head-space for it. I felt like I needed to watch every hour of film on our next opponents. Add in extra weight sessions, more ice time."

"I get why you ended things, Conor. What I don't get is why you're here, explaining it all over again."

"Because I had plans, Harlow Hayes, and you messed them all up. Because I didn't think that I could turn those plans into reality and also be with you. But then, I realized..." Conor focuses on me, his gaze blue, unwavering steel. "Mess up all my plans, Harlow. Because I don't want to be part of any plans unless they include you. I need you in my life, for anything to mean some-thing. *When* I play in my first pro game, I want you to be behind the bench wearing my jersey. If you're not, it'll just be another hockey game."

I can feel the prickling in my eyes. But I don't realize I'm actually *crying* until Conor reaches out and wipes the tears away with his thumbs. There's no rain to hide them this time.

"What about the Garrisons?" I whisper. "You were right, I don't know how—"

"We'll figure it out. My whole life, I've tried to be different from Hugh. But I've carried his mistakes around, instead of letting anything go. I let it impact my life, let it affect things with you. I won't do that anymore, I promise."

"I love you, Conor."

It comes out like a scratchy whisper, and I sort of want to uncap my water bottle and take a sip. But that doesn't seem very romantic, and I forget about hydrating after catching the look on his face. I can see it—how much he loves me. How much he meant every word of what he just told me.

"I love you so much that I memorized your hockey schedule even though I was supposed to stop caring about the sport. So much that I've probably run a marathon in the past few weeks, trying to escape thinking about you. So much that—" I glance away, not sure how he'll take this one. Again, it's borderline on romanticism. "So much that I talked Clayton Thomas into pretending to hook up with me so that you'd hate me and I couldn't beg you to change your mind."

"You didn't have sex with Thomas?"

I shake my head. "I haven't been with anyone...since you."

His exhale is long and relieved.

"You didn't seem that...bothered."

Conor raises one eyebrow. "I punched a hole in my bedroom wall, Hayes."

"Oh. Uh, sorry."

He laughs, then rubs a palm across his face. "You ready to go home?"

I nod. "Yeah."

He grabs my suitcase and my hand, and we head toward the automatic doors that lead outside.

Home.

With him next to me, it feels like it might be.

CHAPTER THIRTY-THREE

HARLOW

I stare at the ice, willing my foot to step forward. It *really* wants to stay on solid ground.

"Hayes, I can't teach you to skate on *ice* while you're standing on the *mats*."

I place one blade on the ice, sliding it forward a tentative inch. It glides about a foot, leaving me half on the ice and half off it as I quickly grab the door to stay upright.

Conor sighs, then skates closer.

"Don't you trust me?"

He's using his soft, cajoling voice, the one I'm a complete sucker for.

"I trust *you*. Not my own feet."

"The faster you move, the easier it is to stay upright."

"Yeah, that logic just does not track. I'd rather just stand —*shit!*"

Conor ran out of patience, I guess. He grabs my hand and pulls me into his body, away from the safety of the bench. And then we're moving, flying across the ice at a *much* faster pace than I anticipated working up to.

"Keep the blades straight," he tells me.

He's doing all the work, pulling me along and keeping me upright. I'm clinging to him like a barnacle, glad the rink is empty and no one is around to witness this.

"Bye, Coach Conor!"

"Bye!" Conor calls back.

Never mind. People are witnessing this.

I forgot about the kids in the locker room. The PeeWee practice Conor helps coach only ended a little while ago, so I'm surprised they're already changed. Or maybe that means Conor wasn't *that* impatient and it took me longer to get one skate on the ice than I realized.

"Okay, now you try."

Conor spins so he's skating backward, still holding both of my hands with his.

"Show-off," I grumble. I knew his skating was impressive, but I've gained a new appreciation for it since being out here myself. He makes it look easier than walking, while I would argue it's like walking blindfolded while juggling.

"Don't look down. Lean forward. Separate your skates. Little to the left, little to the right. Get a rhythm going."

"I'd like to stay upright, actually, not do a split. Just keep pulling me."

"C'mon, Hayes. Do a *little* of the work instead of relying on me." He smirks. "Feel like I've said that to you before…"

"That must have been your *other* girlfriend giving you a blowjob this morning, then."

Conor's grin widens. "Is that the incentive you need? The locker room will be empty pretty soon. We'll go in there, and I'll pull these"—he pinches at the black leggings I'm wearing —"down. And then I'll yank off whatever little thong you have

344

on and have you sit on the bench in front of my locker and spread your legs to show me how wet you are. And then—"

"Hart!"

I blink at Conor, dazed. He's smirking as he looks to the left. I follow his attention to where Hunter and Aidan are standing by the home team's bench, right next to the open door where I stepped onto the ice.

Hunter is attempting to hide his amusement about how Conor is pulling me around like I'm a small child.

Aidan's grin is huge.

And I really wish Conor had finished what he was saying. Wish we could skip past the rest of my skating lesson and straight to *that*.

"Wonderful." I sigh. "More witnesses to my humiliation."

Conor chuckles, carefully turning us so we're headed toward the bench instead.

"Hey, Harlow."

Hunter greets me first. I feel like he's warmed significantly toward me since Conor and I officially started dating. Maybe I just didn't spend enough time around him before. Or maybe he— along with every other guy on the hockey team—is glad Conor has been in a great mood lately.

I'm not projecting that. Robby Sampson flat-out thanked me for "fixing Hart." I guess Conor wasn't exaggerating when he called himself a moody asshole.

"Hey, guys," I greet.

"What are you guys doing here?" Conor asks.

"I'm meeting with Coach. I mentioned it earlier, remember?" Aidan rolls his eyes when Conor shakes his head no. "I asked you for a ride. You were 'busy' later."

"I *am* busy."

"Yeah, yeah, looks like you've got Boyfriend of the Year in

the bag. But Hunter's my new favorite best friend, because he actually drove me here."

"I left my favorite sweatshirt in my locker, actually," Hunter says.

"Eyesore broke down?" Conor asks.

Aidan sighs. "Yeah. I don't know what's wrong with it. I need to call a garage and get them to take a look at it."

"I'll text you the name of the place I used," Conor says. "They did a good job."

"Great, thanks. See you guys later."

Hunter and Aidan continue walking toward the locker room.

"If I'd taken you up on your *incentive*, Aidan and Hunter would have walked in on us."

Conor scoffs. "I would have locked the door, Harlow. No one gets to see you like that except me."

I experience an erotic thrill at the possessiveness in his voice. Turn into him, pressing my lips against the hollow of his throat and then slowly working my way higher.

"This isn't going to work, Hayes. I'm not—" My mouth moves to his jaw. He hasn't shaved for a couple of days, so there's a light layer of stubble rubbing roughly against my lips. I imagine that rasp elsewhere and have to clench my thighs together.

"Not what?" I whisper, then kiss his mouth.

"Damnit, Hayes." But he doesn't sound mad. Not really.

His hands move to my hips, and he lifts me like I weigh nothing, setting me on the wall that separates the bench from the ice.

"Not getting distracted?" I tease.

He kisses me, greedy and hot and possessive. I twine my fingers into his hair, tugging at the short strands. I can't wrap my legs around his waist with the clunky skates on, so I settle for squeezing my thighs.

We're acting like this is the first and last time we'll ever get to touch each other.

I keep waiting for the draw toward Conor to fade. It always has, with every other guy I've been attracted to. There's an initial spark of interest, some intrigue, and then the novelty disappears.

That hasn't happened. I don't think it will happen.

He's like the ocean for me. No matter how many times I see it —it's never enough. I never want to look away. I never think *Okay, I've seen it.*

I never want to stop kissing him, even if his stubble is scratching my chin.

We're both breathing heavily when we separate. Conor's fingers brush along my lower lip. I'm not expecting the regret that flares in his eyes. "I'll shave tonight," he tells me.

"I liked it."

He shakes his head, then presses one final, soft kiss to my lips, careful not to brush the irritated skin. "Make it a lap around the rink, and then we can spend the rest of the night however you want."

Clearly, Conor figured out the incentive he mentioned earlier was responsible for this moment.

"You promise?"

"Have I ever not followed through on fucking you, Hayes?"

Giggling, I shake my head. He's as insatiable as I am.

Conor helps me down from the wall, then moves out of my reach. I pull in a deep breath, staring at the scuffed surface in front of me. Holt's team practiced before the PeeWee practice, so there's barely an inch of ice not marred with a scrape from a skate.

I force myself to focus, because I know sharing this means something to Conor, just like it meant something to me when I took him out on Sam's boat. And as much as I love touching him, it would be nice to be able to get around the rink on my own.

"Hey, Conor?"

"Yeah?" His tone is resigned, like he's waiting for me to step off the ice or ask him to pull me around again.

"I love you, Hart."

His expression softens, the same way it's done every one of the fifteen times I've told him. Then he tells me "I love you, Hayes," and I'm sure I'm looking at him the exact same way.

I take another deep breath, then push away from the boards and start skating as fast as I can.

It feels like I'm flying.

In more ways than one.

EPILOGUE

CONOR

"It's raining," I state flatly as we walk toward the automatic doors that lead outside the airport. They glide open silently as we approach.

Harlow laughs. "Why do you sound surprised?"

"I'm not surprised," I reply, studying the water dripping off the overhang built for precisely this purpose. "Just underwhelmed."

"The weather isn't supposed to be sunny *every single day*. It's not natural."

My water-loving girl. All of Harlow's favorite places—Somerville, Ireland, the town near Vancouver where she grew up—have damp, wet climates. One of many reasons I thought me getting signed to Tampa Bay's team would complicate our relationship. Harlow shocked me by making it a non-issue. She applied for a research position studying and rehabilitating manatees and started lining up apartments to tour.

I've adjusted to living in Florida more easily than Harlow has. Not just because I don't have to slather myself with sunscreen every day. Because it's me achieving the dream I've been chasing for as long as I can remember. Would Tampa have been my first choice of location? Probably not. But beggars can't be choosers, and I was *begging* for a team to take a chance on me. Plus, I was used to wearing blue.

And Harlow chased my dream with me, setting all the other opportunities she could have pursued aside. I'm not sure if she understands how much that meant to me—her choosing me so thoroughly and resolutely. Rearranging her whole plan to accommodate me.

So I booked this trip back to Washington for Thanksgiving, so that Harlow could wear her yellow raincoat and see the Garrisons. Thankfully, I play for a professional sports league that allows its players to have the holiday off.

"There she is!" Harlow waves to my mom, who's pulled up alongside the curb. She heads for the silver SUV, and I'm right behind her.

My mom's wearing her usual scrubs. I wouldn't be shocked if she came here straight from the hospital. She hugs Harlow first, then turns to me, beaming. "Hi, honey."

"Hey, Mom." I hug her tightly.

She came to Florida for my first pro game, but that's the only time I've seen her since I moved. She smells the same as always, like the mint lotion she uses to moisturize her hands between frequent washings at the hospital.

I load our bags into the trunk while Harlow gets into the backseat.

"How was the flight?" my mom asks as we join the long queue of cars leaving the airport.

"Not bad," Harlow replies. "Just long. Conor already misses the sun."

"I didn't say that," I protest.

"Honey, it's almost always raining here," my mom says.

"Yep," I say. "It's so…peaceful."

Harlow snorts in the backseat.

My mom parks outside the condo where I grew up fifty minutes later. It looks the same as when I was last here in May, right after graduation to pack up my stuff. This is the first time Harlow has ever been here.

I give her a quick tour of the downstairs: kitchen, living room, and the dining room that doubles as my mom's office. Then I carry our luggage up to my old bedroom so we can both change out of our travel clothes. Try to talk Harlow into fooling around, which she more than considers until my mom starts banging pans around downstairs.

When we get back downstairs, my mom has warmed up some soup and bread. Christmas carols play in the background as we sit and catch up. Eventually, my mom asks what time we need to leave for the Garrisons'.

"Probably pretty soon," Harlow says, glancing at me.

I know she's nervous about how dinner will go. She talks to the Garrisons regularly, but my relationship with them hasn't thawed much. Hugh followed through on attending all of my games, but those were, at most, followed by small talk. Aside from graduation, I haven't seen him since I got the offer from Tampa at the end of March.

Just like I told him, I'm not sure I'll ever get over it. I don't know how to have a relationship with my father, a man who's basically a stranger to me.

But, for Harlow, I'll eat a meal with the guy. And my half-brother. And the woman he picked over my mom.

"You should take the flowers," my mom suggests, nodding to the colorful centerpiece. "A neighbor brought them, and they'll just go to waste sitting here. There's a pie in the fridge for you to take, too."

"You don't need to do that, Mom."

I feel guilty that I'm going over to the Garrisons'. Like I'm letting Hugh off the hook. I know my mom understands why. Know she gets it's tied up with Harlow's happiness now, that I'm doing this for her. But still, it's strange.

"I know, Conor," she replies, her tone a little sharp. "Moving forward is important. Logan said—"

My mom stops talking abruptly.

"Who the hell is Logan?"

Pink tinges my mother's cheeks, and I'm pretty sure she's blushing. "A friend from work. He made the pie."

"A friend? Are you *dating* this guy?"

As far as I know, my mother hasn't gone out with anyone since her relationship with my father ended. She focused on her job, and on me.

"We've…spent some time together outside of work."

"How long have you known him?"

"Nine years."

"Have you been *spending time* with him for nine years?"

I've never asked her about guys, because I assumed she would tell me if there was someone. Now, I'm wondering if that was a mistake.

My mom looks affronted. "You think I would be in a relationship with someone for that long and not tell you?"

And *now*, it's a relationship.

"I don't know, Mom! You've never mentioned him before. It didn't even seem like you meant to just now. You stopped talking as soon as you said his name."

"Well, I wasn't sure how you'd react." She sniffs, like my response has been subpar.

"What does he do?"

"I told you, he works at the hospital."

"Yeah, but what specifically does he do *at* the hospital?" I ask.

"He's a trauma surgeon."

"Oh." I can't come up with any criticism of that career path.

And I'm not trying to interrogate my mom. I just worry about her, living alone in a town that knows her whole past. I like the sunshine, but I'd much prefer to be closer to my mom. If anything happened, I'm halfway across the country.

"He sounds wonderful, Anna," Harlow says. "I hope we'll get a chance to meet him soon."

"I hope so, too," my mom replies.

"How old is he?" I ask, reaching for my water glass.

"Eighty-two."

I choke. "What?"

My mom laughs. "He's a year *younger* than I am, Conor. Age appropriate."

I exhale, relieved. "As long as he makes you happy, Mom."

"He does. He's a hockey fan too. I think you'll like him."

"You guys should come visit. I can get you both tickets to a game. And Harlow redecorated our whole place since you were last there. Rain paintings everywhere. You'll feel right at home."

"There's *one* rain painting," Harlow says.

I glance at the clock on the wall. "We should get going. It's almost four."

My mom nods. "Don't forget the pie in the fridge. Or the flowers. I'll see you two tonight." She stands and starts clearing the dishes.

"Let me help with those," Harlow says, standing too,

"No, no," my mom replies, shooing her hands away. "You two get going. Really."

"Okay," Harlow answers, glancing at me.

We slip on our jackets and head for my mom's car. Harlow climbs into the passenger side, holding the flowers and pie, while

I readjust the seat so I can drive without my knees knocking my chin.

"My mom has a boyfriend. How weird is that?"

"It's exciting for her, Conor. She seems happy."

"Yeah, she does," I admit. "He's a surgeon. Do you think that means he's a total tool, like the guys on the medical drama you like to watch?"

"The medical drama *I* like to watch that you're just pretending to not know the name of and the same one that you got mad at me for watching without you *one time*?"

"Yeah."

She laughs. "I think your mom is a good judge of character."

"That's debatable," I reply pointedly.

"*Conor.*"

"What? I'm getting it out of my system now."

Harlow mutters something under her breath.

The drive from my mom's condo to the Garrisons' takes less than ten minutes. Claremont is filled with winding, quiet streets that are empty at the moment. Most people have reached their Thanksgiving destinations by now, multiple cars parked in many of the driveways we pass.

I stop in front of the Garrisons', my stomach clenching uncomfortably as I turn off the car and glance toward it. For a place that houses a lot of negative memories, it's beautiful. Against the backdrop of orange and red leaves, the brick home stands tall and proud.

Harlow passes me the pie, keeping the flowers herself. My mom tied a plastic bag around the bottom and then wrapped them in brown paper with a ribbon holding everything together. Way more effort than I would have put in, but I can admit they look nice.

Hand-in-hand, we approach the front porch. The doormat has

changed from the last time I was here. Rather than sunflowers, there's a scattering of multi-colored leaves illustrated on the stiff brown fibers. And no pumpkins.

"You ready?" Harlow asks.

"Sure," I reply.

The door swings open before she can hit the doorbell.

"Oh. Hey." Landon is standing in the doorway, still holding the door handle.

"Hi, Landon," Harlow says cheerfully. She drops my hand to step forward and hug him, carefully keeping the flowers from getting crushed. He returns it, holding my gaze the whole time.

I've exchanged a few words with Hugh. Landon? We haven't spoken for exactly three hundred and sixty-four days, since I almost punched him at Zeke Ledger's party.

"Conor," he acknowledges.

"Landon."

At least I have the satisfaction of knowing Landon knows he was wrong about me and Harlow.

"You're heading out?" Harlow asks.

"Uh, yeah. Mom forgot to get cranberries earlier. Mel isn't here yet, so I'm trying to be fast. You guys are early."

"We had to leave for the airport at four a.m. It already feels like midnight to me."

"Don't fall asleep at the table. You're referee tonight. I'll grab you a whistle while I'm at the store."

"*Landon*," Harlow hisses.

"What? I thought Mr. Athletic would appreciate the sports metaphor."

My younger brother has a sense of humor. Who knew.

"Landon! Why haven't you left yet—*oh*. Hi, Harlow." Allison Garrison appears in the open doorway behind Landon.

"I'm leaving now, Mom," he tells her, then continues past us and down the stairs.

"Hi, Allison," Harlow says, leaning forward and giving her a hug as well.

I swallow, shoving my hands into the pockets of my slacks. My stepmother has never been anything but kind toward me. I don't feel the same animosity toward her as I do toward Landon or Hugh. And I know Harlow thinks highly of her, especially because of Allison's connection to her mom. But I've never felt comfortable around Allison. In my head, she's the woman who ruined my parents' relationship.

"These are from Anna." Harlow hands Allison the flowers. "So's the pie."

"Oh. How lovely. Please thank her for me."

"I will."

"Hello, Conor."

I nod at her. "Hi, Allison."

"Come on in, please."

She beckons us inside, and I walk into my father's house for the first time in sixteen years. Allison takes our coats, then ushers us into the kitchen. Unlike the entryway, this room hasn't changed from my memories. It sends a ripple of unease through me, recalling all the uncomfortable moments I spent in here. I set the pie down on the counter.

"Hugh is in the den, making a fire. Or setting the house on fire. One of the two." Allison chuckles. "Can I get you guys anything to drink? Wine? Beer? Water?"

"I'm good with water," I say.

Allison nods, then rushes to fill a glass.

"Have a drink, Conor," Harlow whispers to me.

"No."

"I promise you, I'm a thousand percent comfortable with it.

And I know *you're* uncomfortable here, so it would make *me* feel better if you had a beer."

"No."

Her sigh is exasperated. "You're so fucking stubborn."

"I told you I'd never have a drink before driving you, and I meant it. And I am 'fucking stubborn,' as you so sweetly put it, so you're wasting your time trying to change my mind."

"I love you," Harlow mutters, sounding irritated about it.

I laugh, then plant a kiss on her cheek.

When I look up from our whispered conversation, Allison is staring at us and smiling. As soon as she notices me looking she turns away, busying herself with something inside one of the four pots on the counter.

"I know you had your doubts, Allison, but—" My father stops speaking when he realizes his wife is no longer the only person in the kitchen. "—the fire is going," he finishes.

"Nice work, honey," Allison replies. "Harlow and Conor are here."

"I see that." My father aims a nervous smile this way. "Welcome."

"Thanks, Hugh," Harlow replies.

She doesn't hug him the way she did Landon and Allison, and I wonder if she usually does.

We're inside my father's house, but I'm the outsider. She's the one with all the familiarity and insight, the one who's celebrated Thanksgiving here before.

"How was—" The sound of the doorbell cuts off whatever else Hugh was going to say.

"Landon wouldn't..." Harlow starts.

Allison's eyes widen. "That must be Melanie!"

Harlow grins. "Landon's going to be pissed we had the chance to embarrass him."

"Yup," Allison agrees. "Do you want to go, or should I?"

"I'll go," Harlow replies, then darts out into the hallway.

"Melanie and Landon just started dating at the start of the fall semester. We haven't had the chance to meet her yet," Hugh tells me.

"Uh, yeah. Harlow mentioned," I reply.

"Ah, right."

The sound of voices drift in from the hallway, and Harlow reappears in the kitchen a few seconds later. A petite girl with light brown hair is following her.

Harlow is talking about cranberries, so I assume she's filling Melanie in on where Landon is. Hugh and Allison introduce themselves, and then I step forward.

"Hi, I'm Conor. Harlow's boyfriend."

There's a pause where I debate if I should add anything else, deciding not to. I assume Landon mentioned to his girlfriend that I also happen to be his half-brother. And if he didn't, I don't really want to be the one to mention it.

"Nice to meet you." Melanie smiles at me, and it's much more genuine than I recall Kelly's being.

Already a massive improvement from the last girlfriend of Landon's that I met.

The front door's slam echoes through house.

"I had to go to three different—Mel! You're here!"

"Yeah. Traffic wasn't bad," Melanie replies, smiling at Landon as he walks into the kitchen holding a grocery bag. He sets it on the counter, and we all watch as they attempt an awkward hug. Harlow smirks at me and I wink back.

"Is everyone ready to eat?" Allison asks. "The food is all set, but I can keep it warm if we want to wait."

"I'm hungry," Harlow says. I nod my agreement, and so do Landon, Melanie, and Hugh.

Ten minutes later, we're sitting around the large dining room table with full plates. There's no attempt to go around and list all the things we're grateful for, or anything like that, which *I'm* grateful for.

The food is all delicious, and I shovel it into my mouth as I listen to Allison and Hugh pepper Melanie with questions about her family, her interests, and her time at Brighton so far. She handles it better than I would have, which I suppose is the one upside of being Hugh's estranged son. He's too nervous around me to give me the third degree about dating Harlow.

"Landon mentioned you play professional hockey, Conor?" Melanie asks me when Hugh and Allison run out of questions to ask. Her attempt to shift the attention away from herself, I'm guessing.

"Yeah," I reply. "I do."

"That's so cool!"

"Yeah, thanks." I smile at her.

"Landon said you're really good."

"He did, huh?" I look at my half-brother. He doesn't meet my gaze, which doesn't surprise me. The fact that he complimented me about anything does.

Melanie seems oblivious to the fact she said anything out of the ordinary, which makes me think Landon didn't tell her how dysfunctional this family dinner is. That she thinks I'm just her boyfriend's best friend's boyfriend, which is fine with me.

Dinner ends. Allison serves the apple pie we brought, along with a pumpkin one.

"This looks delicious," she says as she drops crust and cinnamon coated apples on a plate. "Homemade?"

"Yes," Harlow replies, then looks to me. She's wondering how much she should share about the baker.

"My mom's boyfriend made it," I say.

"It looks delicious," Allison says.

I don't check Hugh's reaction.

The apple pie *is* really good, I admit. It elevates my opinion of Logan the trauma surgeon.

We all help clear the dishes and then stand around the kitchen, unsure of what to do next. Despite a conflict-free meal, uncertainty and awkwardness still hover in the air.

Before I lose my nerve—or someone suggests playing a board game—I grab the basketball out of one of the cubbies by the back door that leads out onto the deck.

I spin it on my finger. "What do you say, old man?"

Harlow beams at me, and I roll my eyes. But her expression makes the offer worthwhile. I haven't changed my opinion of my father or half-brother much. I don't know if I ever will. I've harbored resentment toward them both for my entire life. It will take a lot more than the small number of hours we've spent around each other to chip away at any of my resolution. But we're not quite the total strangers we once were.

All thanks to Harlow Hayes. Because she was nothing like I expected her to be and everything I didn't know I needed. Because there isn't much—anything—I wouldn't do to put a smile on her face.

"Old man who ran a marathon a few months ago," Hugh responds. He's trying to hide them, but I can see both the excitement and eagerness in his hazel eyes.

That was the only downside of getting signed as an undrafted free agent—I couldn't run in the marathon with Harlow like I'd planned to. But Landon, Allison, and Hugh were all there to support her, and a bonus of working for an employer that clears tens of millions of dollars in revenue a year is that you can make suggestions on where they donate fat checks.

"Landon?" I ask.

My brother—half-brother, rather—looks shocked.

"Uh…"

"Why don't we all head outside?" Allison asks with a gentle smile.

During the little time I've spent in her presence, I've learned that's her preferred role: peacekeeper. It makes me wonder if maybe she was better suited to Hugh all along. There are a lot of ways I'd describe my mother. Headstrong and obstinate are two of the first adjectives that come to mind.

It makes me wonder things I've never considered before. Like whether things work out the way they should. Like whether my parents were always doomed to be a failed relationship, even before Allison entered the picture.

The six of us head outside. The November air is brisk, but nothing too terrible. I begin bouncing the basketball against the hard asphalt of the driveway.

"H-O-R-S-E?" I suggest.

Harlow snorts. "First to ten, Hart."

"I'm not sure you know what you're getting into, Hayes," I tease.

"Please." Harlow scoffs. "I've seen you play."

"Yeah, exactly."

"I wasn't in top form last time."

I smirk. "Oh, yeah? You've been practicing?"

She nods, but I know she's full of shit. Since the marathon passed, the only form of exercise Harlow engages in is swimming. "Make it, take it."

I nod. "So do you wanna go first or never touch the ball?"

Harlow reaches for the ball. I pivot so it's out of her reach, wrapping an arm around her waist to keep her to the side and then shooting one-handed.

It goes in.

Harlow shoves me. "Illegal shot."

"I was warming up."

She pulls the elastic off her wrist and ties her hair back in a ponytail.

"Taking this pretty seriously, huh?"

"I want to *see*, when I beat you." She nods toward my sweater. "Take that off."

"What? Why?"

"Because it has to be hand-washed, and we both know you won't be the one doing that."

I roll my eyes before shrugging out of the sweater. "I did the load of laundry last night of all the stuff you said you weren't going to pack but then decided to bring anyway. And I carted your *overweight* suitcase through two airports this morning."

"Are you guys done arguing yet?" Landon asks.

I turn to see he and Hugh are hovering at the edge of the driveway. Allison and Melanie decided to stay on the deck.

Harlow snorts. "That was not us arguing."

I nod in agreement.

"Landon, you play with Conor," Harlow says.

Landon looks doubtful, but he does swap spots with Harlow so that I'm next to him and she's next to Hugh. We start playing. Harlow is decent, and so is Hugh. I could beat them both single-handedly if I tried. Landon is terrible, but I keep passing to him anyway.

Hugh's face is lit up like a Christmas tree. For once, I feel like a kid hanging out with his dad. Carefree. I'm not thinking about the past. Analyzing what I need to say or do to ensure the interaction with my father is as quick and awkward as possible.

It feels like a snapshot in time of a different life. Anyone driving by would think we're a happy, normal family.

The game ends a few minutes later.

"Jeez," Landon huffs. He winces as he stretches his arm. "I'm going to feel that tomorrow."

"Imagine how you'd feel if you hadn't gotten paired with the professional athlete on the court," Hugh comments. The pride when he says "professional athlete" is unmistakable in his voice, and it affects me more than I expect it to. Strained, barely existent relationship or not, it feels really good to hear my father sound proud of me.

"No offense, Harlow," Hugh adds quickly.

"None taken," she replies. "I know my limits when it comes to sports."

Hugh and Landon walk over toward where Allison and Melanie are sitting on the deck, watching.

Harlow and I stay in place on the court. She nudges my arm, nodding toward the garage. "That's Hugh's car," she tells me.

The coupe in question has a new blue bumper sticker with a lightning bolt on it.

I nod, letting her know I saw it. Then I lean down and give her a quick kiss, before we start walking toward the back door. Everyone else has already headed inside.

"Thank you," she tells me.

I know she's not talking about the kiss.

"I told you we'd figure it out, Hayes."

We walk toward the big, brick house, and I know the next time I'm here—however soon or far into the future it is—it won't just be bad memories that come to mind.

All because of her.

THE END

ALSO BY C.W. FARNSWORTH

Standalones

Four Months, Three Words

Come Break My Heart Again

Winning Mr. Wrong

Back Where We Began

Like I Never Said

Fly Bye

Serve

Heartbreak for Two

Pretty Ugly Promises

Six Summers to Fall

King of Country

Rival Love

Kiss Now, Lie Later

For Now, Not Forever

The Kensingtons

Fake Empire

Real Regrets

Truth and Lies

Friday Night Lies

Tuesday Night Truths

Kluvberg

First Flight, Final Fall

All The Wrong Plays

Holt Hockey

Famous Last Words

ACKNOWLEDGMENTS

I loved Harlow and Conor's story when I released it two years ago. But working on this version, I felt like I lived it right alongside them. Some of the changes were necessary to accommodate the timeline for Aidan and Hunter's books. Others were scenes that I cut from the previous version for various reasons. I loved writing (and rewriting this book) and I hope you loved reading it as well.

Mary Scarlett, this is the perfect cover. I love every detail, from Harlow's rain coat to Conor's hair color. Thank you for being such a delightful person to collaborate with and I am endlessly in awe of your immense talent! I can't wait to work on the covers for the rest of this series.

Britt, I am so, so grateful for your enthusiasm and energy on this special project. You went above and far beyond on helping me improve this story into exactly what I wanted it to be, and I always adore working with you. Truly, I can't thank you enough!

ABOUT THE AUTHOR

C.W. Farnsworth is the author of numerous adult and young adult romance novels featuring sports, strong female leads, and happy endings.

Charlotte lives in Rhode Island and when she isn't writing spends her free time reading, at the beach, or snuggling with her Australian Shepherd.

Find her on Facebook (@cwfarnsworth), TikTok (@authorcwfarnsworth), Instagram (@authorcwfarnsworth) and check out her website www.authorcwfarnsworth.com for news about upcoming releases!

Made in United States
Orlando, FL
02 February 2024

43186930R00226